The Court Singer

A Year and a Day: Part One

Lisa Courtney

Cover design by Sally A. Sloley of daisyprincess.com (Guitar photo: Sally A. Sloley; Bokeh background image: Matt Higby: https://www.facebook.com/matthigbyphotos); Illuminated "O" by LeAnne Constantine: https://www.facebook.com/leanne.constantine.16

First published in 2015
ISBN 978-0-9861837-3-7

A Dedication

Child of the pure, unclouded brow
And dreaming eyes of wonder!
Though time be fleet and I and thou
Are half a life asunder,
Thy loving smile will surely hail
The love-gift of a fairy tale.
          —Lewis Carroll, *Through the Looking Glass*

A small but important matter...

Once upon a time, two women sat at a dining room table, drinking tea and talking about magic and things.

One woman told the other a tale that deliciously haunted her sleep and fed her dreams; some of the characters had lived in her imagination for as long as she could remember. She was animated and breathless as she talked about the story. The telling took a couple of hours, but they had a lot of tea on hand.

She was consumed by the story, and believed she needed to write it, but was afraid to face the work it would take to do it right. She did not know where she would find the time.

Most of all, she worried about what she was going to learn about life (and about herself) while she wrote it.

The other woman, the long-cherished sister-friend who knew magic when she felt it, listened carefully to the tale, and to her friend's fears about the creation of it. She asked few questions, simply allowing the layers of the story and the back-story to wash over her; she recognized that this tale, sparkling in the telling, could be radiant in the reading.

They talked for a very long time. "Should I write it, then?"

"Yes. It's going to be so good."

"What if no one ever wants to read it?"

"We'll read it, and we'll love it."

In my entire creative life, I have never loved writing anything as much as I loved writing this story and living with its characters.

So this is for you, Jane. I think it always was, and now it always will be.

Table of Contents

prologue

HE LAY MOTIONLESS in the crisp white sheets of the hospital bed, stared up at the dull white ceiling and wondered how, after all the roads he'd traveled, he could possibly have ended up here.

Things were bad; he knew it, even though the doctors and nurses who moved in and out of his room seemed cheerful enough. His friends pressed smiles onto their lined and tired faces when they came to see him, but he knew they were working those smiles much too hard. The artificial laughter they brought with them was strained and uneasy. Despite her best efforts, the unspoken pain in his wife's troubled eyes spoke volumes of despair. She held his hand and told him softly that things were looking up and that he was getting better; this made it clear to him that things in fact were going incredibly badly.

He had tried for days, without success, to philosophically accept the possibility of his own death. He wasn't entirely sure he was afraid of dying, but that could have been due in part to the intravenous drugs dripping into his left hand from the stand above his bed. It was hard to be afraid of anything when he was high on whatever they were giving him; it didn't bother him that he didn't care which drugs were in his system. It was no secret that a significant part of his early life (and okay, part of his mid-life too) had been spent in varying degrees of chemical highs, so the awareness that he was not feeling the pain while his mind flew into very familiar territory was actually comforting to him.

How had this happened? Why had it happened? And why was it happening now? He sighed. The drugs blurred the edges of his thoughts, but he could still trace some of the threads between where he'd been and where he was now, and this private exercise kept sleep away tonight.

He was a Rock Star. Hell, he was more than that, he was an icon, had been an icon for the better part of three decades. He smiled a little at the immodest but true admission: he was considered a national treasure to an entire generation, maybe two generations now that he was in his late sixties. (How in the hell was he in his sixties? When had that happened? The sheer shock of the numbers and what they meant was cruel and somehow harder to grasp than the possibility of imminent death.)

He'd started off slow and small and uncertain, knowing only in his early twenties that he had to write songs and sing them to anyone who would listen. When there was no one to listen, he sang them anyway, to the ocean, to the night, to anything and to nothing at all, just to get the words and music out of his soul and into the air, and so fill needs in himself that he could not easily explain to anyone else. Sometimes he thought he'd strangle on the process of writing the songs in the first place, the pain of it and the joy of it so intense and real and unreal and...

...and he could never get enough of it. He had spent his life detailing pieces of his dreams and his feelings through the near-magical act of writing poetry and then writing music for his poems. Because he'd been honest in the telling, his songs were as true for those who heard them as they were for him, and so his popularity had grown steadily throughout his career. The money came in, and so did the women.

Oh, there were lots of women; too many women, some would say. He'd had hundreds of women. Maybe thousands. So many women that he couldn't remember them all, nor ever felt the need to remember. Women gave themselves to him gladly, and he took them all, in hotel rooms, limousines, backstage dressing rooms...

He thought of his beautiful wife, Susannah, then, and smiled at how happy they were together.

Still, something deep in him stirred at the memories of the taking of women. He was aware that there was too much pharmacological chemistry dripping into his body for a healthy erection, but he felt the shadow of delicious pressure in his groin fleetingly, and he smiled.

"Not dead yet," he said wistfully into the darkened room.

After ten long years of writing songs, singing them in bars and clubs and at county fairs and weddings, he was the proverbial overnight success. Suddenly, there were concerts all over the country. His albums (and as technology changed over the decades that followed, his cassettes and his CDs) sold throughout the world and he was famous. And rich. And often drunk, or high, or both.

He'd been married twice, was still happily married. And of course there had been the pre-Susannah love affairs, some serious, most of them not. Still, nearly all of them had been public. Generally, it was more than fair to say that he was loved by everyone who knew him, everyone who wanted to know him, and everyone who loved his music.

It was, in particular, his love songs that the world seemed to want most of all, and despite the love affairs and the marriages and the fact that he had, in the beginning, lived a mostly loose and happy life, and much later settled down into a faithful married relationship, he had always secretly ached for a lover to fill the dark and light places in him like nothing else had. Although he'd looked for her continuously throughout the years, he hadn't found her, except in his dreams. She had never been in any of the beds he'd jumped into for temporary refuge. She hadn't looked back at him from behind the eyes of any of the women he had so effortlessly played with. This lover was not his wife, although he loved Susannah deeply. It had taken him years to realize that if he wanted the perfect love, he'd most likely have to write her for himself, and then live with her in the only place that kind of love could ever truly exist: in his songs. And so he did; he wrote the love and the lady the way he needed them to be, and then the world fell in love with love, and with the songs, and by extension, the world fell in love with him.

Especially in the years before Susannah, he had lived with his private longing for the woman he yearned for and the love he needed but couldn't find, wrote songs about it often but not exclusively, drank to relax and get numb, took drugs to get happy, and got himself through his days and his nights as self-indulgently as he could.

Then, about twenty-five years ago, with almost no warning, he'd crashed hard and burned down. He'd had no choice then but to clean up his act. The details were as public as his feelings stayed private. He had disappeared for a while, and when he came back, he stopped the drinking, entirely gave up the drugs, sped up his writing, and slowed down the concert schedule. A few years after that, he had married Susannah. He was happy enough, he supposed. Or, if not exactly happy, he was content with the way his life with her had played out. At the very least, like everyone else in the world, he was content most of the time.

Perhaps his age was showing now, that was it. His previous lifestyle, which he had worn so well for so long, had begun to tell on him. Perhaps this nasty medical adventure wasn't fatal; it might be just another loud warning signal to slow down, focus on what was important. He was a good person, a good husband, a good friend and, through the years of speaking and writing the truth about himself, he had come to know and understand his true self, the genuine Thomas Lear, better than he had ever expected to. His music was still popular (especially the now-classic songs from his wild-living days as he'd tried to chase down that one elusive love), but his fans were growing older along with him. Instead of the romantic hell-raiser he'd always been, he was now seen as something of an elder statesman of folk music and rock and roll. He could never admit that the thought utterly galled him.

It dawned on him, though, just as the sun quietly rose outside his window, that somehow he'd begun to see himself in much the same way.

He sighed, too tired to acknowledge the tears welling in his eyes.

What the hell had happened to him? What was going to happen now? What about the music still in him, the poetry, the love songs? Was it possible he hadn't written his best songs yet? If he died now, and that seemed to be a serious possibility, what would happen to all the truths he had left to tell? And, Oh God, what about the searing, ecstatic, passionate, soul-crushing love he still secretly held his breath for—was it that unreal after all, and would he actually die before he had a chance to taste it?

Damn, he thought, a tired but wry smile playing on his dry, cracked lips. *I'm tying myself in knots. As usual.*

As he finally felt himself drifting toward a numbing sleep, a sudden, unbidden and nearly explosive impulse hit him hard and poured itself into him.

Wide awake now, he fell heart-first into a vibrant river of long-forgotten memory; its sweetness and intensity made him want to laugh and cry at the same time. In the same moment, he felt mentally and emotionally refreshed in ways he didn't have energy enough to contemplate.

He smiled as he imagined himself contacting an old friend. He understood at last that he needed to get himself sorted out. He needed to find his balance, and soon.

Once he finally slept, he dreamt of a beautiful mahogany guitar.

When he opened his eyes, she was sitting in the chair beside his bed, smiling at him. All the sleep and the drugs had made him fuzzy; it took him a few long moments to come fully awake. He looked at her, taking in every remembered detail and savoring it before he could find words.

He hadn't seen her for more than twenty-five years, except perhaps in vague, unfulfilling dreams where—he realized in a spark of recall—she'd remained unknown to him. He couldn't think of a single thing to say; all he could do was stare, and drink her in. He wondered distractedly if she was really in the room with him, or if she was a delicious by-product of his friends the drugs.

When she finally spoke, he knew in a fast heartbeat that she wasn't a dream, not this time. She was here, and he knew her well.

"Hello, Thomas," she said.

Her voice hadn't changed at all. His throat caught at the instantly familiar music and cadence of her voice. He could have wept, but instead steadied himself with a deep breath as he flashed her the best smile he could manage.

"I'd ask you how you're feeling, but it's obvious you've been feeling like hell," she said.

He slightly lifted the bruised hand that had the IVs in it. "It's not so bad, at least, not with the help."

"You look like shite, Thomas," she pointed out.

"Doesn't surprise me," he shrugged. "This hasn't been much fun." He looked around the room. "Where is everyone? This room is usually crawling with people."

"Let's see...a nurse came in and took your pulse and temperature about fifteen minutes ago. Your wife, who is at home, will be here sometime this afternoon, and your band mates will be here around dinnertime. At least, that's the plan, or what I heard of it when I came past the nurse's station on the way in. Oh, and everyone is singing the praises of the press, who are marking your progress regularly but not bothering your family or the hospital very much. Although I think the security guard out there deserves the credit for that."

"Oh," he said, dismissing everything but the sight of her. She was as lovely as ever. "What day is it?" he asked.

"Thursday," she told him.

"I started calling for you in my mind on Monday. Or, I *think* it was Monday. It took you three days to get here?"

"I don't travel as often or as easily as I used to," she admitted. "But as soon as I knew that you wanted to see me..." She smiled expansively at him. "And so here I am, Thomas. Tell me what I can do to help you."

Her deep brown eyes were alive and beautiful. The golden flecks in them danced, and he could feel the strength and power in them. Almost as dark as her eyes, her hair was a deep shade of brown, a tumble of chestnut streaked with sparkling amber. She wore it now much like she had when he had known her, falling in loose curls nearly to her waist. He noticed that there was no gray shining in with the long chestnut strands, and he marveled at that. He knew that his own subtly-dyed golden-brown curls and beard were shot through with much gray, especially since this illness had begun.

She hadn't aged at all, but then again, that was to be expected, he supposed. If there were in fact any small wrinkles around her enchanting brown eyes, he knew that laughter would have been the cause, and that only added to her loveliness. She had always been both timeless and ageless.

She was, without a doubt, the most beautiful woman he had ever known.

He patted the bed beside him with the hand without the IV needle in it. "Come and sit here, Callie, will you? I'd like you close."

She nodded, rose gracefully from the chair, and moved to sit beside him on the bed. With the ease of shared intimacy and history, she took his unencumbered hand into both of her own, and held it. At her touch, he trembled faintly with remembered pleasure.

"I'm here," she said lightly. "Tell me what you need."

It occurred to him now that he was very tired although, as usual, it was his sense of utter frustration that rankled him the most. He frowned, forehead creasing as he tried to think. "I don't think I know *what* I need, but I need to work some things out. I'm..." he groped for a word. "I'm *hungry* for something, and I'm drawn to it. My life's good, it really is. But I'm twisted up. Does that make any sense?" He sincerely hoped he wasn't whining.

Laughter sparkled in her eyes, but her voice was both serious and serene. "So you've once again come full-circle?"

He wasn't sure she wasn't laughing at him. "I don't understand."

"Thomas, you said almost exactly the same things to me during one of our very first serious conversations. I have followed your progress from time to time; this 'unsettled' energy has been a prevailing theme throughout your entire creative life, despite the good things that have filled your days. It explains the *why* of you, so very clearly. It's why you needed me in the first place, don't you remember?"

He did; and remembering, felt himself fully infused with the warmth of her, the scent of her, and his aching need for her. "Have you come to stay?" he asked her in a hopeful whisper.

She squeezed his hand in between both of her own. "Let's see what happens, all right?"

"All right," he murmured, and slipped contentedly into sleep, his hand still held safely between hers.

He slept through the doctor's and the nurses' multiple rounds, although he was thoroughly examined and notes were copiously taken. He didn't rouse when Susannah sat for two hours in the uncomfortable chair beside the bed and knitted, chatting to him quietly as he slept. He had only a vague recollection of his band mates and other close friends coming nervously into the room, hanging around for a few uneasy minutes, and then leaving him in silence.

He didn't wake again until nearly midnight, and when he opened and focused his eyes, she was sitting on the bed beside him, holding his hand.

"Callie," he said.

"You slept a long time."

"Did I?"

She nodded. "They're all glad. Are you feeling better than you were?"

He squeezed her hand, and tried not to mind that the action itself seemed feeble to him. "I suppose so. I don't know. I'm not in pain. That should count for something, right?"

She smiled approvingly at him.

He tried and failed to smile back at her. There was too much on his mind, and she'd come such a long way to talk with him. He decided to forgo the preamble, and just get on with it:

"Am I dying, or not, Callie?"

"I don't know. I would imagine that's largely up to you, isn't it?"

He frowned at her. "Don't play games. I need to know."

She touched his cheek with a soft hand. "You don't need me for that. That's what your doctors are for."

"They're not telling me much. They say this thing is serious but treatable, that the surgery saved my life, just in time. They tell me that my progress has been slower than expected, but that it is still progress."

She tilted her head, and he got a small whiff of the earthy fragrance of her hair. "What does all their talk tell you, Thomas?"

He sighed, as much from the familiarity of the scent of her hair as from the inexplicable talk of doctors. "It wouldn't surprise me much to know that there's a good chance I'm not going to walk away from this."

"And...?"

"And I need to come to terms with it. Probably soon." He steeled himself, with effort, and tried once again to smile at her. "Are you going to help me work some of this through?"

"Yes," she said kindly. Without letting go of the hand she already held, she leaned over him, and kissed him softly on the mouth. The kiss was sweet and tart and earthy, and lingered between them even after she sat up to look at him again. Despite the drugs flowing through the IV drip, he felt his body begin to respond, fully and immediately.

Maybe things were going to be all right after all.

"I think," Callie said with only a touch of sarcasm, pretending not to see the self-congratulatory grin growing on his face, "that since you're clearly coming back to yourself in so many ways," she chuckled, "perhaps that's the key. You may need only to look at the circle of your life, meet again and test the things that are still at the heart of your questions and your desires, take what you need from them, and then move forward in peace, in whichever direction you choose."

He was surprised at the note of calm blandness in his voice. "A direction I choose?" he echoed. "Like, life or death?"

"Like life or death," she agreed.

"Can I do that? Look everything over, and actually make the decision about what happens next?" This had not occurred to him before.

She laughed at him then, merrily, a sound not unlike bells chiming in a sunny spring wind. "Thomas, it's *your* life, filled with your dreams, your music, your passions, your memories. You can do with it anything you wish, whenever you wish."

He smiled at her, almost faint with the aching, and whispered: "Oh, then, Callie, I wish...I wish..."

And he fell asleep.

one

WAKING SLOWLY FROM the gentle embrace of a nearly-remembered dream, Thomas Lear cracked one eye open to confirm his surroundings. He immediately slammed the eye shut, wishing he'd stayed asleep. There was a long arm stretched across his belly, and it did not belong to him.

He took a deep, slow breath, and inhaled the musky scent of the previous night's feverish playtime. Exhaling as quietly as he could, he felt the arm fall heavily against his diaphragm. Closing his eyes more tightly, he stifled a sudden urge to yawn.

He had no clue to whom the arm belonged. He was almost afraid to look.

But look he did, after a few minutes of calmly organizing his thoughts and planning his standard escape.

This morning's companion was a woman. That was not a surprise—although admittedly he had been surprised on occasion, back in some of the murkier moments of his past. With a mental shrug, he let his mind wander for a moment, and then vaguely remembered this bed-mate's pretty face, despite the fact that it was currently hidden under long and luxurious black hair. He wondered if he remembered her name, or if he had even asked it.

Sally? Or Sarah? Sandra? Something with an S. His satisfaction at remembering the name, or something close to it, disintegrated when he recalled that the S-name he was groping for had been the blonde from a couple of nights ago. He had no idea whatsoever about the name of the woman in whose bed he found himself this morning.

A muffled groan beside him indicated that, whatever her name was, the woman was waking. He hated this part, and wondered belatedly why he hadn't left her here last night, afterward, and just gone home.

He knew his car was parked outside, and he started thinking about the day ahead. All he had to do was get up, dress as quickly as he could, force himself to be as charming this morning as he had been last night, and then get the hell out of here. It was a routine he had perfected over the years. It was all but expected of him, thanks to his carefully-cultivated reputation.

In his darker moments, he considered his unquenchable need for sex even more consuming than his need to write and sing his songs. This observation sometimes upset him to the point of augmenting the intensity of his sexual behavior with ever-increasing journeys into other, more private, vices. These, in their turn, lured him further still from the poetry and music he ached to write but often could not reach for weeks and sometimes months at a time.

That it was becoming difficult for him to write at all these days made him feel slightly sick. At times he thought he would drown in the unspoken grief he only barely contained. He constantly worried about the loss of what was magic and true in him. What the hell was he doing to himself? And why couldn't he stop?

The arm still stretched across his belly was wide awake now. It moved slowly, smoothly, sinuously downward.

His moment of silent, self-directed turmoil evaporated. It was apparent that he was not going to think about anything right now. There was no need.

A warm hand curled around him; he quivered in response.

Thomas Lear sighed, closed his eyes, and let another day begin.

Two hours later, he mused over his easy escape from Dark-Haired Pretty Face as, after a long and solitary shower, he stood in front of his own bathroom mirror and shaved as he thought about it. After an extra half-hour of wake-up sex, he'd simply looked down at all of that lovely dark hair and said without apology, "I've gotta go," and, amazingly, he did just that, without any difficulty. It occurred to him now that she may have, at first, thought he'd meant that he needed to use the bathroom, and would be right back to bed, but it didn't matter. She untangled from him with the all-too-familiar star-struck smile, and he stood up, grabbed his clothes, headed for the bathroom, and then was out of her house and into his car in less than five minutes.

He never did catch her name.

That's how it is, he now reminded himself cheerfully, *and that's how it works here in Los Angeles in 1975, Babe.* You had an itch, you scratched it; any port in a storm would do, at least most of the time. *And you, my friend, have an itch that doesn't stay scratched*, he told the guy in the mirror, regarding himself critically as he shaved. Brown curly hair, streaked with natural honey highlights. High cheekbones, a strong jaw and an easy smile complemented his dark brown eyes, which were deep but perhaps a bit too sensitive-looking; *soulful*, a female interviewer once wrote, *the kind of eyes that women love to get lost in.*

Distracted, he nearly cut himself with the razor. "Great, just great," he muttered, examining the potential nick on his throat. Not a good thing on a show day. "Forget the eyes, folks...what about the *music*? The music's what it's all about."

He was instantly side-swiped by a harsh, stray memory. In the hall outside the court room, just after his divorce five years ago, his newly-ex-wife told him coldly that his eyes were in fact the only good things about him...

"Yes, I'll remember your eyes, and the music we shared, you miserable, pathetic bastard," she had hissed at him, "But that's it. You killed the love because you never showed up for it. You figured I'd hold the place for you. You're too busy looking for something safe, and you haven't figured out that it isn't really out there. You sacrificed us—you sacrificed me—for a dream. I want to hate you, but I..." Her small hands had been clenched into trembling fists, arms held rigidly by her sides; it had been all she could do not to beat him with them. The sad truth was that he wouldn't have blamed her at all. Even now, he winced a little at the vibrant image of Maryann, the hollow look of burned pain in her eyes just before she turned away from him that last time. He'd really blown it there. He couldn't even pretend to himself that he had tried and failed with her; he had never tried at all.

He shook his head as he saw only himself again in the mirror. How had she managed to cross his mind? He hadn't thought about her for a year or more. One more solid fact of his life: the less he thought about Maryann, the better. He didn't need the guilt.

Dismissing her, he took a shaky breath and finished shaving. The soulful eyes in question looked back at him. He smirked and made a face at himself. His lips seemed too thin, unless he was talking or singing. No woman had complained about them, as far as he could recall. He shrugged, and wiped his face.

He still had the short, close-cropped beard he'd been sporting since the tour, which had ended three months ago. He kept threatening to shave it off but Jack Grandberg, his record producer, and Stan Williams, his business manager, who never agreed on much of anything that had to do with Thomas Lear, both told him that he looked better with it than without it, so the beard was staying. Good God, the things he did for business. He shook his head and smiled.

Thomas' stomach growled suddenly, protesting that he hadn't eaten since early last evening and now it was already past noon. He pulled his bathrobe off, pulled jeans up and a sweatshirt over his medium-framed, slightly damp body, and walked toward the kitchen to get something to eat.

He was in mid-shout to ask Myra to put something together for lunch, but he remembered that today was Saturday, so he was on his own.

He had not forgotten for a moment, however, that he had a show tonight. It would be fun, almost relaxing, to perform at one of his favorite small clubs in Hollywood, the first gig since the tour. There was a sound check at six. He had time to eat, make some phone calls, read a little, play a couple of his guitars, then rest and dress before he left for the night.

"I've gotta go," he said playfully as he swung open the refrigerator door and looked over its appetizing contents. When he realized what he'd said, and flashed back to the same phrase uttered almost exactly the same way only a little while ago, he chuckled and reached for some deli meat, a wedge of cheese, a Kaiser roll and some condiments.

He wondered if he should rethink the staff's working hours.

The staff always had the weekends off, unless Thomas needed something specific. The grandmotherly housekeeper/cook, Myra

Butler, kept his house running smoothly. Unless he actually walked into the kitchen, he rarely saw her. He never heard a vacuum cleaner or saw her in a hallway as she carried clean, folded laundry to his bedroom. He never saw bags of groceries sitting on the kitchen counters, but there was always good food in the house, and it always seemed to be ready when he wanted it. Sometimes he wondered if the place was cleaned by elves; he never saw Myra physically doing housework, but his home was always clean and neat and comfortable. Myra's husband, Ben, managed the property. He personally kept the lawns trimmed and the garden weeded, too, but Thomas never heard a mower or saw yard waste. The Butlers were good people; they'd been with him for almost seven years, and he trusted them. He could leave booze and drugs lying around, and Myra simply picked up after him, or stashed the drugs in the drawer under the coffee table. If she or Ben had opinions about Thomas' recreational habits, they kept their views to themselves.

In a way, they were simply part of his house. They took care of things, and left him alone unless they, or he, needed something. On the other hand, he had the sense that the Butlers genuinely liked him, and watched out for—and maybe watched over—their famous employer and his home as if he were a slow-witted yet precocious child.

The other member of the staff was Joel Toshino, his ambitious, hard-working (and slightly annoying) personal assistant. Joel had studied acting at Northwestern, but should have studied chemistry instead, a notion that was clear to everyone but Joel himself. He was handsome and smart but not gifted, understood the fundamentals of acting but could not act his way out of a small sandwich bag. A dramatic soul who could not see past the drama enough to make everyday conversation sound entirely natural, "Go-Joel" was present in the house most afternoons, and on call the rest of the time. Joel could be relied upon to do Thomas' bidding in most things (legal or otherwise)—the more theatrical the need, the better. He easily took direction from both Myra and Ben, ran errands, ordered wine, Scotch and other potables, booked appointments and meetings, answered the phone, screened messages, and generally ran primary interference for Thomas with his lawyer, his accountant, his producer, his business manager, and everyone else involved with the business side of Thomas Lear, Rock Star. Go-Joel was a pain in the ass, but he was an effective pain;

everyone knew that good personal assistants were hard to come by. Thomas had gone through two in the past eighteen months. He hoped Go-Joel, irritating as he was, was going to last for a while.

After the sound check and a lighting change, followed by a quick visit from the makeup lady, Thomas sat in an easy chair in the dressing room, hanging out with his lead guitarist, Chance Ekland, and his bass player, Rick Baines, who sat together on a couch opposite him in the smallish room. Chance and Rick had backed him in the recording studio and on stage for almost ten years. While it was true that Thomas was a good guitar player, Chance was an undeniably great one who had backed up most of the biggest names in the business at one time or another. Rick had been a member of several modestly-successful rock bands before hooking up with Thomas and Chance. The three men shared an easy camaraderie that made their working relationship a great deal of fun, despite the fact that it was always understood that Chance and Rick were the talented backup musicians for Thomas Lear, Rock Star. While Thomas never failed to introduce his band when he was performing onstage, and of course they were listed on the album jackets, they otherwise remained unacknowledged, generally staying out of the spotlight that fell radiantly on the man that everyone came to see and hear. Consummate professional musicians, his friends had no real issue with their apparent anonymity; rather, they accepted it as a matter of course. It was all about the music, and both Chance and Rick liked what they were doing. They had professional recognition and the respect of their peers. That, to say nothing of the healthy paychecks they earned when they worked with Thomas, was enough to make each of them quite happy with the world.

"Okay," Thomas was saying, looking at his watch. "We're on in ten minutes. Remember, the lighting's going to change; everything's going to turn blue and flash a little when we finish up with 'Dangerous Blue Eyes.' It's different from how we did it on the tour, so don't forget to close your eyes because if they don't do it right, it'll blind you for a second.

Chance laughed and drank his beer. "Don't worry. I'll wake Rick up right before it happens," he winked at Thomas, "so he won't forget to close his eyes in time."

The bass player flipped him a meaningful salute, and finished eating his sandwich.

"I don't know, Thomas...now I'm wondering if Rick'll wake up and scream or something," Chance continued playfully. "You know how bad he freaks out. It's the poor quality of the cheap-ass alcohol he consumes."

Rick chased the sandwich with a sip of beer and shrugged. "Nah, I'd only be freaked out if the song had been all about Thomas on tour...you know, we'd have had to call it 'Dangerous Red Eyes'. Too damned scary to contemplate!" He faked a shudder.

Chance laughed. Thomas did, too, then he grinned, informing them with playful pride: "I'll have you know, Gentlemen, that I am, at this moment, relatively sober, straight, showered, in a very good mood, and ready to do the thing."

Rick and Chance applauded appreciatively.

"Un*Lear*like, but worth noting nevertheless," Rick snickered.

"Hooray for momentary sobriety, for as long as it lasts, before it staggers all over the stage," Chance declared with a touch of mock reverence. Without looking down, he opened the small refrigerator beside the couch. He reached in and grabbed a can of beer and shook it in a swift, smooth movement. He nodded at Thomas, and threw the can at him. "Here—have a beer."

Rising from his chair, Thomas laughed again as he caught the can easily, opened it without getting sprayed, and took a long drink. "It's almost time. We should get out there. Let's go make some music."

SUSANNAH RICKERT HAD spent much of the afternoon telling herself that it was only business that explained her presence at the show tonight, but she knew she was lying.

She couldn't believe she was sitting here in the dim light of the club, anticipation rising and then reality falling with every breath she took. She didn't like the musician very much. He was an arrogant, self-absorbed bastard, and she was not impressed. She wouldn't have paid for a ticket to save her life...maybe. But this was another comp from the office, of course, and it was perfectly natural for her to be here. She was, after all, in The Business.

No, she did not like this musician at all. But she loved his music. She could have listened to him at home; she had all five of his albums. But to see him play, that was something wonderful. She could watch him lose himself in the words and the melodies and almost feel the ache in his guitar when he sang the love songs that had made him famous. When he was playing up there on the stage, she could almost forget what a bastard he was in real life. She absently wondered what it would be like to watch and hear him play away from the crowds, in a quieter, perhaps more intimate setting...

He'd still be a selfish, egocentric bastard, playing those songs, she guessed darkly, and tried to shrug it off.

He was handsome, though. And he was unbelievably talented. And he had a gorgeous voice. The problem was that he knew all of these things, far too well, and he used them to his best advantage. With women, mostly, although he also had a certain charming effect on most of the men he met. For various reasons, men wanted to be him; women merely wanted him.

She'd seen him do it, enchant everyone in sight, countless times. She worked at the record company as the assistant to the producer who handled all of Thomas Lear's work, and she'd sat in meetings where Thomas had been present. She'd even had to spend time, sometimes literal days, trying to track him down when her boss needed to find him. Thomas was very good at disappearing, whether it was with a woman for a week, or for an extended period when no one heard a peep out of him for months. With very little effort, Thomas Lear could be the worst headache in her job description.

"Oh, give him a break, Susie," Jack Grandberg told her constantly. "Thomas isn't a bad guy, he's just restless and stressed sometimes, and then he can't find his groove. We can be patient with him. He'll find it."

"It's '*Susannah*'," she grumbled under her breath, correcting him for the thousandth time. She disliked being called "Susie" but in the six years she'd worked for Jack, she hadn't been able to make him stop using any nickname that occurred to him in the moment. She cleared her throat. "Thomas Lear is a jerk, and you know it, Jack. I mean, really!"

Jack, chain-smoking while opening a can of juice and glancing through a trade paper, gestured noncommittally. "He's at his peak, he's talented as hell, he's rich, he's attractive, everybody loves the guy. Hell, *I* love the guy. He's entitled to flake out every once in a while and misbehave. His divorce was a rough one, you know. It really kicked his ass."

Susannah glared at her boss. "Yes, I know. I'm the one who had to try to keep it as much under wraps as possible, remember? The press wasn't bugging *you* about it, Jack, you were as cushioned as he was. Besides—" she was about to say something about how Thomas' reported infidelities and drug and drinking habits were what probably killed the marriage, but she closed her mouth. No one can really know what goes on in the private worlds of other people; despite the evidence of the obvious problems in the Lear relationship, she knew it wasn't her job to blame him, even if he had that blame coming in a big way.

"Just give him a break," Jack said again. "He's bringing in all that money, and keeps the label fat and happy in the black. As long as he stays on top of the pile, he can be as impossible to deal with as he wants to be, as far as I'm concerned, SusieGirl."

Susannah wished that she could think of something blistering and brutal to say to Jack. More than that, if she *had* thought of something scathingly clever, she wished with all of her might that she could be the kind of person who would have said such a thing.

She wasn't.

She was thirty-one years old, single, and, for the most part, happy. She was a natural (as opposed to a California) golden blonde, with large, expressive hazel eyes, and a nice enough figure. She was graceful and competent, and that offset her innate shyness and the unfair sense that she was a very good little girl in a nasty, grown-up world.

Unfortunately for Susannah, she was seen as a complete misfit among the professionals who worked in the recording industry in Los Angeles. She didn't take recreational drugs, she didn't drink much, rarely swore out loud, never stayed out all night partying, nor did she sleep around. She had never in her life flipped anyone The Finger. She was almost a classic Good Girl by contemporary standards, but couldn't find a reasonable way to do much about it. She wasn't comfortable indulging in too many of the behaviors that (as Jack cheerfully pointed out one day) could have saved her from herself and made her far more interesting.

On the plus side, however, she was smart, and she was extremely good at her job. Most of the time, she loved the work. It wasn't easy being the grossly-underpaid assistant to a busy record producer and dealing with his high-maintenance artists, but she handled both Jack and the musicians he shepherded with capable hands and a creative mind. She knew Jack would be lost without her; efficiently taking care of things for him gave Susannah her sense of professional (and sometimes personal) self-worth.

She encountered Thomas Lear practically every time he came in to see her boss, and often Jack dragged her over to watch Thomas when he was in the studio working. And in all the times she'd encountered him over the past two years, he had only spoken a dozen words to her directly. Not that he was tongue-tied; his attitude toward her indicated that he saw her as nothing more than semi-functional furniture. Most of the time, he ignored her.

For her part, she understood completely; he easily overlooked her because she didn't possess the kind of beauty that poets write about. She didn't positively crackle with unsubtle hints of untamed sexuality, and so, from her take on what must surely have been his viewpoint, she wasn't really a desirable woman, and therefore was of no genuine interest to him.

It drove her crazy that she spent so much time thinking about someone who annoyed her as much as he did. She did not want to consider why he was never far from her thoughts, especially since it was obvious that he didn't think about her even when she happened to be talking with him. Sometimes she wanted to smack him.

At other times, she wondered what it would be like to kiss him.

The bastard. The prick bastard, she thought, narrowing her eyes. She felt herself blush, her face suddenly hot and throbbing in the darkened club. She ducked her head and took a long, slow breath.

Susannah was not in denial of her feelings; she understood her own emotional make-up very well. She felt things deeply, with an intensity that often frightened her. The trouble was that she simply couldn't articulate whatever she was feeling, neither the good, happy, joyful emotions nor the frustrated, miserable, painful ones. Not at all, not to save her life. That was why she...

Maybe that was why she was here at the concert tonight: to spend anonymous time in the dark watching Thomas Lear accomplish something that Susannah Rickert could not. He would feel all of his feelings, share them with a heartbreaking clarity, and take everyone who heard him into the searing intimacy of his own wistful soul, giving the audience something that would touch them profoundly.

She nodded her head gently, acknowledging a truth about Thomas Lear: he was making magic, and sharing it both openly and secretly with anyone who knew how to listen.

It was an emotional intimacy that all but left her breathless and aching when she played his albums while alone at home. But to see him actually perform—to feel him make the music, and to follow the waves of energy as they came from him and flowed out into the audience, then poured back into him *from* the audience—to see him perform live was an intense experience she craved.

It was as close as she came to sheer, overpowering addiction.

Never mind if he was a pain in the ass when she had to deal with him at work, or when she had to know about or handle unpleasant things related to him (she thought fleetingly of the last paternity suit allegation). He was almost someone else when he sang and played in front of an audience. He was someone she could almost have feelings for.

In those moments when he was playing, he was tapped into something greater and truer than Thomas Lear himself, and he knew it. The audience knew it as well, felt it, and was wholly transfixed in his presence.

Susannah knew it, too. She sighed. In these moments, when she was surrounded by his music, she could let herself forget what a complete bastard Thomas Lear could be.

"LADIES AND GENTLEMEN...Thomas Lear!"

Flanked by his band, Thomas Lear walked onto the small stage and smiled as eager applause filled the room.

"It's good to see you guys, too," he told the audience wryly, and got a laugh. "I'll tell you what...let's fall in love tonight."

The audience applauded again, responding to the familiar opening line of all Lear concert performances. Thomas turned to look at Rick and Chance, who were positioned on either side of him and six feet behind, before he gave the set list taped to the floor one last look. *One, two, onetwothreefour...*

...and the concert began.

Susannah watched him play, heard every note and listened to every word. There was no other way to say it: he was *magnificent*. The songs—whether they were filled with longing and hurt, or happiness and satisfaction—moved her even as they entertained her. Listening to Thomas Lear made her want to wrap herself in love, the way he did through the sheer artistry of the stories he told and the secrets he whispered in the songs he sang.

She could not get enough of the enchantment he skillfully created. Looking around at the audience (because she knew Jack would ask her in the morning), it was clear that they could not get enough of Thomas Lear, either.

two

HE OPENED THE door, and nearly fell over a long, gold box that had been left on his front step. He hadn't heard the buzzer from the gate at the end of his long driveway, so he was startled as he looked around for an unheralded delivery person. Seeing no one, and sensing no danger, he sat down on the steps and opened the box.

Inside were a dozen white roses. Thomas smiled, mentally ticking off the faces of possible senders as he hunted for the card, which, strangely, was not there. At least, there was no small, identifying note in the conventional sense. There was, however, an LP cover taped to the box. The album was titled "No Fire Tonight" and the cover featured the face of a raven-haired beauty with sparkling azure eyes glowering venomously.

He knew those azure eyes, and the glower, too, very well. They belonged to the lead singer of the band Lady Luck: Julia Willingford, with whom Thomas had been intimately involved a year and a half ago. Like all of his relationships, his love affair with the talented, sexy singer/songwriter had started out with burning-out-of-control, wild sparks and delicious, all-consuming fire. And like the others, it ultimately burned out in especially ugly flames. He did not like to relive the final scorching; it was bad, and it still hurt him. When the ashes from this one had finally cooled down, he went out of his way to avoid any contact with Julia. She joined the ranks of the women from his past that he needed to stay as far away from as possible.

Thomas flipped the album cover over, tension building in his chest and stomach. Scrawled across the back of it, handwritten in black magic marker, over a photo of the band members and the titles of the tracks, was a message meant for him. His eyes widened in dismay as he read it aloud. "Lady Luck no longer smiles on you, fuck you very much. I hope you choke on this, you lying, cheating bastard!"

Thomas Lear, Rock Star and Cheating Lover, groaned and went back into his house, leaving the roses and the album cover on the steps. This was going to be a bad day.

STONED OR NOT, Jack knew better than to try to placate Thomas. They sat in his office, looking out over Los Angeles as they shared a joint.

Jack exhaled slowly, and shrugged at his friend. "Man, it is what it is. Sorry. She's been mad at you for a long time. And now she's smacking back. Nothing you can do about it."

"Except maybe move out of the country," Thomas whined.

Julia, Thomas remembered with miserable clarity, had been deeply in love with him. He loved her, too—or so he told himself. He was happy enough with her, liked going places with her, liked talking with her, and liked her cooking. The sex was good, and they had lived together for about six months. Julia gave him all kinds of space, because she needed space too. Things were good, at least most of the time.

Then she'd lost her mind and wrecked everything. Over breakfast one morning, she announced that she felt they were ready to talk about making a serious commitment. He had been unable to finish his coffee, and left the house sweating.

By lunchtime, he'd met up with the pretty journalist for the scheduled interview in the bar at the Beverly Hilton. He laughed through much of the hour-long talk, and easily charmed the socks off her. Not long after that, he charmed the jeans off her, too; up in one of his favorite suites at the Beverly, Thomas managed to get to know the lady quite thoroughly.

It had taken a while for Julia to discover that Thomas had been fooling around. He'd been through about ten other entirely meaningless encounters before she found out. He hadn't exactly been trying to hide the fact that he'd been unfaithful; he was half hoping she'd recognize that his forays into other women's beds was largely her fault, and that once she mellowed out and stopped insisting on a commitment, things would be okay between them again.

Not surprisingly, Julia didn't see it his way at all. The threats, the negotiating, the "what do you want from me?" discussions, and, ultimately, the shouting began in earnest.

In self-defense, Thomas treated himself to a much-needed, spontaneous (and oops, largely unannounced, even to his friends, his band mates and his management) month-long vacation in Brazil. When he'd finally partied himself out, and sobered up enough to remember where he was, he headed back to Los Angeles to work things out with Julia.

Julia Willingford had not liked being cheated on, and, while it was certainly debatable at the end of their final fight who had dumped whom, it was undeniably clear to Thomas today who had gotten the last word on the relationship and, unfortunately, on Thomas Lear as well. Lady Luck's new album had hit the stores and the air waves this morning. It was hitting him, too.

He hadn't seen Julia since the breakup, thank God. It was inevitable that he'd run into her somewhere, since they had so many people and places and the music business in common, but he fervently hoped that he wouldn't cross her path anytime soon. He dragged his fingers through his hair and groaned. "This is not good, Jack. I am so screwed."

Jack was treading carefully, glad that Thomas didn't know that he was currently dating Julia's lawyer. He rolled another joint and lit it, took a deep toke, then passed it. "Thomas, it could be worse. She could have had you shot on stage."

"Oh, I think she's done worse than that. This shit could do some damage to my image that we aren't going to be able to fix easily. Dammit!" He had a thought: "There should be enforceable non-disclosure agreements on relationships, I swear to God. She shouldn't be able to talk about it." He shook his head at the audacity of his remark; even with a decent buzz on, he couldn't let himself get away with that crap.

He was—at least for the time being—toast.

"Well, she's a helluva lyricist, you know that. Uh, oops. Sorry, man..." Jack shrugged again. "You fucked up. She's evened the score, more or less, but you're okay, you're not dead, just...um, hanging out there a little with your pants down. But you'll be all right. Give it time, it'll all blow over."

Thomas frowned. This was not going to blow over anytime soon.

It was bad enough that Julia hated him. He thought they could be friends after the chill was gone. Apparently not. She wasn't going to forgive him, any more than Maryann had, any more than any of the others who'd said they'd loved him ever had. And Julia was a force to be reckoned with; he might never live this down, would never get away with what he'd done to her, even if it was partly her fault. She'd never let him (or anyone else) forget any of it, not with song titles like "Love & Pain & Death," "Lonely With and Without You," "Not Worth Much," "(There's Gonna Be) No Fire Tonight," and the dubiously-named "Doubting Thomas (I'm Leery of the Man)."

The whole world would know intimately how Thomas had broken Julia's heart, and that he had severely pissed her off. "No Fire Tonight" was the very big machine gun she shot him with, would continue to shoot him with. He was in for a world of hurt, and there was no way to get around it.

What was even worse was that he was absolutely certain that Lady Luck's new album was going to be a huge success. Julia's great writing and fabulous voice aside, Thomas' involuntary presence behind the music would act as an additional boost for the publicity.

He wanted to scream. He also wanted a drink.

The next day was Saturday. He was glad he'd gone to bed alone on Friday night. He was not in the mood for companionship of any kind; The Monster In His Head was company enough.

After he'd jolted awake from another bad dream, he'd staggered through the house aimlessly trying to decide what the hell was wrong with him. He made a few valiant tries to throw off The Monster. He recognized that he needed to find something or someone to make him feel better. Over coffee and a few generally thoughtful moments, he found himself unable to accurately determine what was eating at him now, and this added to his distress. There were too many unhappy and frustrating things vying for his emotional attention.

He was shaken and lost, shattered this morning before he'd had a chance to fight back. But fight back at what?

"What's usually wrong at the bottom of the well?" he asked himself icily, smoothly adding self-hatred and disgust to the mix of emotions setting fire to his soul. The Monster had him now; he either had to face it and fight it, or run like hell from it.

He chose what he always chose. He ran.

Thomas fled to the one physical place in his life where he could most genuinely be himself: his music room. He knew that sitting in the music room would make him feel even worse than he already did this morning, and he *wanted* to feel worse. So he walked stiffly down the stairs, along the hallway, and then all but threw himself into the oversized leather recliner that sat in the middle of the sunny room.

He hadn't been in here a single time since he'd come home from the "Dangerous Blue Eyes" tour. Before that, as his pre-tour angst and frequent outbreaks of desperate hell-raising had grown, he'd only crossed the threshold long enough to grab a guitar, or find some paperwork. Drugs and drinking kept him cheerfully away from reading, composition, or serious practice. He told himself that he didn't mind at all, that it didn't matter a damn if he came down to work or not.

When things were good, he loved this space. He often spent consecutive days and nights in this big room, writing lyrics or music, thinking, listening to albums, reading, playing the piano or one of the seven or eight guitars that lived here. It was his private sanctuary; he bared his soul and wrote its passionate secrets in the safety and magic that this room provided for him.

When things were not good, he avoided the music room as religiously as he avoided the happier and healthier version of himself that thrived here. He may have believed that the resident creative force that sparked within the confines of these walls, free and wild with the power to feed him, would instead poison him or drive him over the edge to a danger-filled, self-induced hell that he could not face and would not survive. Better to not come here at all, now, except to use it to set a purging fire all over the Monster In His Head, the damned beast that cataloged, carried, and fed his indecipherable levels of pain already burning too far out of control.

With a growl of loathing for everything he was and everything he knew, Thomas hurled himself into the leather recliner, and glared at the far wall, which held four platinum albums and a fourteenth-century

French battle shield he'd bought at an auction in Paris on one of his "spontaneous getaway" vacations. Eventually his glare faded into a blank stare, and he saw nothing at all.

In ragged silence, he followed internal threads of frustration, doubt, loneliness, fear and contempt, willing himself to pinpoint the source of his current session of the increasingly frequent exercise he called *Lear: Crash and Burn*. Maddeningly, each emotional string he examined tied itself to other, more subtle, threads, weaving a coarse tapestry he could hardly bear to touch, the confused anger in the fabric cutting emotional blood vessels as sharply as razor blades. He saw but didn't care much that his tension was building, coming at him faster and more ravenously than he could manage. The Monster was, as usual lately, winning. For all the frantic, nearly-manic energy dancing feverishly behind his eyes, he sat rigid in the comfortable recliner, as still as death and twice as cold.

An hour later, exhausted and bitter, the Monster momentarily quieted, Thomas admitted to himself that the best way to deal with today's *Crash and Burn* was both astonishingly simple and mercilessly impossible: he needed to write. There was no avoiding it, not really. There was music in him today, aching to come out. There were words ready to wrap themselves around his pain, and heal him with images and notes, poetry and light.

He had written some of his best and most beautiful songs in this room. He knew how to do it, having done it a hundred times before. All he had to do now was take a deep breath, move away from the parts of himself that felt heavy, unsatisfied and silent, and open himself to the words and music.

He trembled, and swallowed hard to steady himself. Thomas stood slowly, resolution—and possible salvation—clear in his mind. He would write today, even if the words didn't come easily. He would work at it, all day if he had to, and he would be patient. He knew that if he sat there and picked up a pen, he'd eventually rebuild the connection that mattered most to him; he would find the words, and, in turn, the words would help him find himself again. He would come a little bit closer to being all right.

As if on cue, The Monster In His Head woke up, and took a swift and greedy bite out of Thomas' aching heart. The pain of it was searing, and the betrayal he felt for carrying the pathetic burden of vulnerability and the ridiculous need to save himself from himself flooded him with a rage that was impossible to contain. Fury stormed through him. He thought he might explode.

Instead, he closed his mind, and waited testily for the silence.

It came, and when it did, he surrendered himself to it. There would be no salvation today.

Bored now, Thomas stood, wrapped himself in a defiant swagger, and strode out of the music room, slamming the door behind him with a finality that was as cold as it was loud.

The worst week of his life began that day, commencing with his pathetic surrender to The Monster. By the time he reached the stairs that carried him more than just physically away from the music room, Thomas was already mentally dialing the number of his personal drug dealer.

After that, and for the next seven days, everything in his world went absolutely, conclusively, unconditionally, entirely, completely, thoroughly, unavoidably to hell.

three

THOMAS WOKE ON Sunday morning and was glad again that he had the day to himself. After last night's bitter loss to The Monster, he was not in the mood for company, even the invisible Butlers.

The Sunday Morning Hangover was not a big deal (made easy to manage with the help of some very nice pills he'd gotten from his doctor), and Thomas sat in his living room drinking coffee and reading *The Los Angeles Times*, front-to-back, as he did nearly every Sunday morning when he was at home. The process generally took him anywhere from half an hour to three hours, depending.

When he saw the cover of the Times' Sunday Entertainment supplement, he did a fast double-take.

The cover of the supplement heralded its feature article: "Rock Star Wives and Lovers—Past and Present." The various rockers pictured in collage on the cover (Jagger, all four Beatles, Taylor, Clapton, Cocker, Henley, Frey, Dylan, Diamond, Crosby) did not include Thomas' shining face, for which he was thankful. But a quick skim of the feature article inside made his jaw clench as he saw his name in bold type, followed by that of his ex-wife, and his currently-quite-popular former lover. The Thomas Lear paragraph (no photo) was only five sentences long, but it was more than enough to ruin his day:

Thomas Lear & Maryann Conlon; Thomas Lear & Julia Willingford

Lear, known for his beautiful and melodic ballads, has lived a couple of love songs of his own, first with songwriter Conlon, to whom he was married for two years, and then with former live-in love Willingford, lead singer/songwriter for the band Lady Luck. Conlon, who still writes songs – which are recorded by singers other than her famous ex and won Kenny Rogers another Grammy last year for her song "The Look in Your Eyes"— was wistful about her years with Lear. "It was magic for a while, when the words and the music, and we, too, went in the right direction," she said, "but once Thomas knew what it was he wanted, he quickly found his own road – and it was in the opposite direction of the one we'd chosen to walk together. Suddenly we were done, it was all over." Lady Luck's album, "No Fire Tonight," which premiered last week, was penned almost entirely by Willingford, who asserts that "the pain, sadness, and ultimate fury in the songs" were wholly inspired by her own breakup with Lear. It might be a good idea for our favorite hopelessly-romantic balladeer to sing his songs to ladies who don't know how to get even.

Infuriated, he hurled the Sunday supplement across the room, kicked the couch a few times with all his might, and filled the air with particularly colorful profanity.

Even then, he could not calm down. Still raging, Thomas paced his large living room furiously. His eyes settled on the telephone, which sat on a table beside his burgundy leather recliner and the large picture window that looked down over the city. The view usually calmed and relaxed him. Not today, though. Seething and storming, he called his lawyer at home.

Linda Elizandro had been Thomas' attorney for almost ten years. She knew exactly how to handle him. She listened carefully, and took notes while he raised hell about the feature article and very loudly told her all the things he wanted to do to everyone involved with it.

Undaunted, Linda counseled him with the frankness he liked best about her. "Don't let it get in your way, Thomas. Like everything else, it will blow over as soon as something else makes a little noise, which means that you—and everyone else in the world—will have forgotten all about it by tomorrow, in the next news-and-gossip cycle. There's no point in giving it any room to bother you; it doesn't mean shit. Ignore it. It's already in the process of going away, all by itself. Don't give it momentum, and it'll disappear."

Fifteen minutes later, he hung up the phone, more depressed now than pissed off. Linda, as usual, was right. There was nothing he could do about the article, or to the person who wrote it, or the newspaper that published it. The text was not even remotely slanderous; there was no photograph or drawing of him, so he couldn't accuse them of using his likeness without his express permission. The article simply existed; that was bad enough. The entire world could read it, and would have some unpleasant information about his private life that he wished had stayed private.

His interest in the still-unread sections of the newspaper was gone. He considered canceling his subscription altogether, but knew that was stupid and childish. Besides, he didn't want to have to look for the subscription phone number. He would have Go-Joel cancel the damned thing tomorrow.

No, of course he wouldn't. He groaned and dropped into his recliner, and looked out at the ruined morning.

It didn't feel good at all that he had seen Maryann's name. The intense guilt he denied that he carried washed over him.

"I don't need this shit!" he whined, at no one in particular. For a fraction of a second, he thought maybe he should own up to it all, and actually call Maryann, talk with her, and see what was on her mind. Then he could give her a small preview of what was going on in his own mind, to see how she liked it. But sanity slinked back into position; he couldn't, wouldn't, call Maryann. Not today, probably not ever. His guilt was too heavy for that. He knew that even after all this time, he did not have the courage to face her, in any sort of encounter. She wouldn't hurt him; Maryann was not that way. She would simply step back and allow him (and The Monster In His Head) to do all the damage he had coming. There was a lot of well-deserved pain waiting around in the dark, biding its time, with his name all over it.

It also occurred to him, perhaps a touch belatedly, that he no longer had any idea how to directly contact his ex-wife. He didn't know for sure what city she lived in now.

It was probably just as well, all things considered.

Irritated and sad, Thomas growled at the bright, warm Sunday morning, its cheerful appeal as dead now as his earlier good humor. He moved, without further comment, up the stairs and down the hall to his bedroom. Once there, he pulled a medium-sized vial of cocaine, a clean razor blade, a mirror and a tired-but-useful rolled-up fifty-dollar bill from the back of his underwear drawer, sat down heavily on the bed, and gave himself up to a much better mood.

The next day, Monday, started off well enough. Thomas was up, showered, dressed and out of the house early, a full hour before The Butlers' normal arrival time. He had a breakfast date in the Valley with Chance and Rick at Steiner's, Thomas' favorite upscale deli/restaurant.

They sat in one of the exclusive back rooms at Steiner's and toasted each other with cups of much-needed black coffee. While they waited for their breakfast orders to arrive, they fell into old business, and conducted yet another dry post-mortem of the tour.

"Thirty cities. We're getting too old for that shit," complained Rick. "My fingers work fine, but my back doesn't, any more. And my wrists were miserable that whole last month. Next time, let's take longer to hit thirty cities, you know, more time between concerts. I started hating weekends, and that can't be right."

"Jesus. We'll just roll you out in a wheelchair, GrandDad. It isn't like you don't mostly sit on your ass to play bass. And hell, you might want to remind your wussy-ass little wrists that you only have to play four fucking strings," Chance reminded Rick helpfully.

The band's bass player made a face, followed by a sincere but rude gesture. "Know where you can slide any one of your guitars, man?"

"Philistine," Chance grinned.

Rick laughed. "Damn straight."

"We shouldn't have pissed off the promoter in Vegas," Thomas said, bringing them all back to business. "That is going to cost us a headache down the road."

Rick shook his finger lazily at Thomas. "Correction: You shouldn't have pissed off the promoter in Vegas. You're the one who blew up at him and told him he'd fucked up."

"Well," Thomas grumbled in self-defense, "he did fuck up. He had the wrong posters printed and hung all over the city. The wrong one, and the bad photo—I told them all not to use that one!—it looked almost okay on the program cover, but blown up? That billboard on the Strip made me look like Keith Richards' grandfather." He shuddered.

Chance finished his second cup of coffee, and shrugged. "Very true. But you should have shut up, like I told you to, and let Grandberg's people handle it. That way, when the promoter was nailed for fucking up, Grandberg would be the bad guy, and not you."

"That promoter's got contracts for most of the tour concert business in Vegas. He could make it tough for us later. Likely he will," Rick pointed out.

"Okay, okay," Thomas admitted. "Guilty as charged. Next time the situation comes up, I'll close my mouth and walk away and leave it for Jack Grandberg. All right?"

Chance and Rick looked at each other across the table, and grinned as they said in singsong unison: "Oh, no he won't."

"Shut up." Thomas rolled his eyes and reached for more coffee.

Over a delicious oversized bagel weighted down with cream cheese, lox, red onion, thin-sliced tomatoes and capers, Thomas laughed as Rick regaled his bandmates with another tale of his failure to pick up a woman at a local club the night before.

"Your problem, Son," chuckled Chance conspiratorially, "is that you don't know how to talk to girls."

"My problem," Rick retorted, "is that I don't have Lear's little black book."

Thomas raised an eyebrow. "Hold on...there's nothing *little* about *my* black book, man." The three men dissolved into giggles worthy of seventh-grade boys in a locker room.

So how they ended up first sniping at each other, then arguing and finally shoving and shouting, completely confused and irritated Thomas as he thought about it on the drive home afterward. They were friends, and had been playing together forever, it seemed, at least since they'd met in the studio during the recording of Thomas' first album. Friends offstage as well as on, they had respect and deep (if unspoken) affection for each other.

Rick and Chance had not, of course, made the staggering amounts of money that Thomas had, but they had always cheerfully accepted their well-paying and fun positions as Thomas' backup band. They played well together, and loved the music.

And now they were not speaking to each other. It was unlikely that they would talk together anytime soon.

"So, Lear..." Chance had opened the conversation again after the breakfast plates had been removed by the waitperson, "when are you going to reconsider and record some of the songs I've written? You know they're good."

Thomas groaned to himself, took a breath, and met Chance's eyes. "They are good. But they're not my songs, they don't sound like me, and I don't do covers."

"Yes you do," Chance said. "You did a great cover of—"

Thomas' interruption was swift and to the point. "I know. But we've talked about this with Grandberg too. I don't do covers any more, won't do 'em, I write my songs, that's what I sing."

Frustrated, Chance was trying to hold on to his temper, with only limited success. "One of these nights, I'm going to start playing one of my tunes on stage, and you're going to have to deal with it, you'll have to start singing it."

"No, he won't," Rick interjected smoothly, in an attempt to cool things down. "You'll start playing something not on the sheet, and Thomas'll stop dead and say into the mike, 'Chance, man, what the fuck is that?' then the audience will laugh, and we'll get back to the playlist. Does he even know all the words to one of your songs, Chance? In the end you'll be standing there looking like someone just stepped on your puppy."

"Shut the hell up, Rick," Chance and Thomas said simultaneously. But neither of them smiled.

"So you aren't going to even think about taking my songs seriously?" Chance countered.

"I do take them seriously. Some of them are really good. Chance, you know that. But we've been over this ground before, and nothing's changed. I sing my stuff, not your stuff."

"Would you be willing to let me sing one?"

"During a show?" Thomas frowned, tilting his head in disbelief. "Are you kidding?"

Rick tried again to put out the smoldering fires he saw in the eyes of both of his friends. "Well, you know, Lear, other groups do it...remember when—"

Thomas' response was sudden and deadly: "Gentlemen, *we* are not a 'group.' I am not the lead singer, I am *it*. Your names and faces are not on the front of the album covers, nor are they on any of the music when it is published. On stage, you are beside but behind me." His brown eyes were tight with deep-burning rage. "They come to hear me sing my songs, they buy my records. I am Thomas Lear; you are Thomas Lear's back-up band."

Then they were all on their feet, standing too close together, and sarcasm, rage, hurt feelings and jealousy took over. The three of them stormed out of the restaurant in different directions, much to the relief of Mr. Steiner, who had run out of tactful excuses for the shouting and profanity pouring from one of the restaurant's back rooms.

No matter who'd said what, and how quickly it might or might not blow over, it didn't feel good, and Thomas didn't like it. But he liked that last look on Chance's face even less, so he growled at the lunchtime traffic as he made his way toward home.

He took a bottle of Scotch to his bedroom, locked the door, and as far as anyone knew (or cared), slept for most of the day.

Still painfully aware of the bad feelings he carried from Monday's breakfast, Thomas was careful about everything he said and did on Tuesday. He made a point of going into the kitchen in search of Myra, to tell her how much he liked the berry pie she'd baked the day before (she felt he'd needed cheering up, didn't know why). He walked around his back garden and chatted politely with Ben for half an hour. He curled up in the cozy red wing-backed chair in his library and read for most of the afternoon. He was back into The Canterbury Tales, which he read every couple of years. It was one of his favorite books, and had probably been one of the reasons he'd studied Medieval Literature at UC Berkeley and earned his Master's what seemed like forever ago. It struck him as strange now that he'd actually considered teaching as a career, back in the days before he started performing. Even though he had no room for it in his life any more, he still loved Things Medieval. Ah...Chaucer! He sighed contentedly and re-read "The Wife of Bath's Tale."

Later in the day, Thomas even managed to be relatively kind and attentive rather than dismissive to Go-Joel when the assistant pompously pushed some stupid suggestions for Thomas to change guitar manufacturers and supply vendors in favor of ones that Go-Joel had researched and cut tentative deals with on Thomas' behalf.

Thomas' mistake was taking a pretty actress to dinner at Chasen's in Beverly Hills at 8:30 on Tuesday night.

He walked into the restaurant knowing that it was likely he'd run into either someone he knew, or he'd be recognized instantly by people he didn't know. He was accustomed to this, and wore a benign but dazzling smile as he walked behind his date and the maître d' toward the table, which was in a quiet, candle-lit corner.

He was looking at the wine list (and wondering why his date's name had traitorously eluded him) when he was indeed noticed by someone nearby.

"Well, well," said a voice draped in icy sarcasm, "isn't that, wow, isn't that Thomas Lear? *The* Thomas Lear?" Her laugh carried a distinct chill as it pushed his stomach through a cheese grater.

Momentarily defenseless, Thomas super-glued his eyes to the wine list and wished desperately that he were having dinner tonight in Tibet. He groaned, but pulled himself together in record time, and slid a practiced, confident grin on his face as he moved into performance mode. He forced himself to wink at the woman who sat across the table from him (and abruptly remembered that her name was Arlene), then turned his head with a deliberate laziness to face Julia Willingford, and her three dinner companions, at the next table.

"I thought you might be hiding in a cave somewhere. Nice to see you out and about, Thomas," Julia observed, revving up for a skirmish. "You may have noticed that I sent you a small gift, which begs the question, my dear: Heard any great albums lately?"

Thomas shook his head at her with artificial woe. "Nope. Sorry, Jules...I listened to that thing of yours, too, but...no. Nothing worth remembering."

The three people at Julia's table, two men and a woman, gaped at Thomas, then looked nervously back at Julia, whose angry eyes were narrowing. People from other tables were beginning to notice the conversation.

"Pity. I didn't realize you'd gone deaf, dear," Julia returned with feigned lightness, although her volume was increasing. The waiters were growing uneasy.

Thomas' artificial smile deepened as he rested his eyes on his former lover. He spoke softly, knowing that he could be heard across the room. "Not deaf, just immune to pathetic high-school attempts to get even, over something that was as much your fault as mine." He paused. "Which reminds me, Jules...have you and your therapist been working on your frenzied need to own and smother people?"

"You bastard!" Julia spat in surprise.

"Just checking." Thomas turned his gaze from Julia to the wine list, and then to his date. "Arlene, what do you say to the '72 cabernet?"

"I am not finished with you, Thomas Lear," hissed Julia.

Thomas shot her a startled look. "My God, Jules...I was pretty sure that you were." He graced her with an ironic sigh. "My apologies if I misread the signs there."

It did not occur to him until a bit later that there were indeed some people who were not meant to play with fire, or even view it crackling at close range. Arlene whispered that she had a terrible headache and would like to be driven home. With infinite grace, Thomas nodded, then signaled to a nearby waiter, who gratefully nodded his understanding, signifying that it was clear that Go-Joel would take care of the Chasen's check the next day.

Thomas Lear, Rock Star, rose smoothly, his eyes fixed solicitously on his date.

Over the top now, Julia pointed at him and roared. "Yes, that's right, disappear, Thomas! Maybe you should disappear, run away again for a long time, at least until the world is ready to trust that you're really the guy who writes those love songs, and means them! You are such a bastard!" Her companions, and even a waiter or two, continued their useless attempts to shush her. "I know, I know, but he makes me crazy, he just pisses me off!"

With attentive elegance, Thomas escorted Arlene away from the table, through the sea of watchful eyes, and out into the night as if nothing had happened at all.

But later, as he wearily let himself in his front door, The Monster In His Head (who apparently had patiently waited up for him) punched him hard in the stomach with such dark and excruciating precision that he almost didn't make it up the stairs to the bedroom.

He had neither the will nor the energy to face the morning, so Thomas stayed in bed until nearly half-past two on Wednesday. He had remembered to shut his bedroom door before he'd fallen miserably across the bed the night before, so he was left alone and undisturbed, even though he knew Myra was somewhere in the house. Myra never allowed anything or anyone, not a phone call or the pesky Joel or even Myra herself, access to Thomas when he was in a room with a closed door.

There was a meeting scheduled with Jack Grandberg around 4pm, and, while he didn't feel like thinking about it, Thomas knew he should probably get his act together and be there close to on time.

His mistake came after he got up, showered, dressed and crept into the mercifully Myra-less kitchen to track down something to eat; this he carried down to the library, which was located downstairs at the opposite end of the hall from his long-vacant music room. The library had huge oak double doors, which he closed firmly behind him to avoid intrusion while he woke all the way up and considered the meeting he could no longer avoid.

To ward off The Monster In His Head, who already had spent several hours of this day insidiously reminding him about the anxiety he felt about the upcoming meeting with his producer, Thomas leveled the playing field (or so he told himself) by indulging in a little coke, and eventually smoking a much-needed joint or two just as Go-Joel brought the car, a sexy-red 1967 Mustang, to the front door.

SUSANNAH RICKERT LOOKED at her watch and sighed; it was nearly 4:20pm. She sat at her desk and tried not to listen to Jack yelling behind his closed office door. This was a pointless exercise, since Jack's big, sunny office opened directly into her smaller one. No one got to Jack's office without going through Susannah's. In the beginning, she had liked this idea; she could be part of everything. She had had ample time to reconsider her position on this notion, however. Exposure to some obnoxious artists, a handful of slimy business people, and the not-infrequent dreamy-eyed sycophants (whom Jack invariably said he'd met at parties, and whom, of course, had dreams of being rock stars) often made her wish that her office was safely down the hall from Jack's.

"Where the hell *is* he?" Jack Grandberg's frustrated roar was not muffled in the slightest.

Susannah sighed again, and glanced at her office door, which was always open— literally. A four-foot-tall, leafy potted plant that Susannah privately referred to as "Mildred" acted as a permanent doorstop, so that she could always see or hear what was coming down the hall toward the production offices. She could also tell who was not coming down the hall, and she waited for Jack to yell some more.

Thomas Lear was late, as usual. She could not remember a single meeting where he'd made it to Jack's office on time. The only part of the production process Lear seemed to be interested in was in actual studio time; for that, he was always on time, early, even. Jack had said more than once that Lear was almost as amazing in the recording studio as he was on stage, and Susannah, who had seen him both perform and record, was forced to agree.

Still, Lear didn't like meetings, or any of the other necessary evils of the music business. He was twenty minutes late for this meeting with Jack, a meeting that Lear had cancelled three times and Susannah had had to reschedule repeatedly.

"I don't have time for this! I swear to God if his records didn't bring in so damned much money..." Jack's voice rumbled on the other side of the wall. Suddenly there was a sound of the slamming of a couple of desk drawers, followed by silence.

Glancing at her watch again (4:22pm), Susannah did the math and figured that if Thomas was only another five minutes late, Jack would be mellow enough to thoroughly enjoy their meeting.

A SOMEWHAT DISTRACTED Thomas Lear walked into Susannah's office at 4:30, followed by his assistant, a handsome, young Asian man with too much attitude.

"Hello, Mr. Lear," Susannah said, covering the irritation he inspired in her with a professional courtesy she did not feel. "He's ready for you."

Thomas nodded vague acknowledgement in the direction of his producer's blonde secretary as he walked across to Jack's office. He knocked once, and strode in without ceremony.

"Thomas, man, there you are...great to see you," Jack's voice drawled lazily as he closed the door behind them.

Lear's assistant stood in front of Susannah's desk, making a show of the fact that he was checking her out for some disreputable purpose or other. The only thing that kept her from quivering in disgust was that Joel Toshino was wholly unnatural and handled his come-ons so very badly.

"Hey, Babe," Joel began, half-closing his eyes in what he believed was a bedroom-ish, come-hither gaze but was actually more of a too-much-sunlight-not-enough-sunglasses squint. "How long will they be in there, talking or whatever?"

She was not good at these games, never had been. Susannah made it a firm practice to stay off the court, the field, the game board, whatever, at all costs. "Hard to say. Probably an hour." She opened a file folder and started reading.

"Well, I need to get some stuff done while he's in there. He's got an interview with Rolling Stone on Friday, and I have to head over to Century City to pick up some paperwork from his business manager for that, and I think he might need something to, you know, aid in his relaxation, so I have to arrange that, quietly of course." Joel watched Susannah to check for a sign that she was properly impressed. He couldn't quite find one.

"Mmmmmm," Susannah mumbled, eyes glued to the paper in the folder.

"So I'll be back in an hour. If he needs me before then, page me, okay, Babe? I know," breathed Joel in a manner that was nowhere as sexy outside of his head as it was inside, "I *know* you have the number,

Susie, and we *both* know that it would be just fine if you decided to use it..."

Fortunately for Joel, he managed to slither all the way out of earshot before Susannah dissolved into giggles tinged with complete disbelief. How could a guy be absolutely no threat, but still exhaustively disgusting? She laughed some more, shaking her head, and closed the folder as the phone on her desk rang.

INSIDE JACK'S OFFICE, a tired, red lava lamp and the cannabis smoke soothed Thomas' discomfort over the topics they had discussed for the past half-hour: how much money the tour had brought in, what the current record sales were to date, and what the projections looked like. There was also an uncomfortable bit of conversation about his reported falling-out with his band mates.

To avoid Jack's eyes, Thomas stared out the windows that covered most of the outside wall. Los Angeles was treating itself to another gorgeous day; Thomas found himself wondering why he wasn't out experiencing it in person. He was not surprised that at the moment he wanted to be anyplace but here with Jack. He reached for, and lit, another doob.

Jack asked him something else, but Thomas wasn't paying attention.

"Come on, Thomas, it's not that hard a question. The 'Dangerous Blue Eyes' tour is history, and it was a great success, but it's done. We've talked it to death, we've rehashed the issues, we know what to do better next time to make the bosses happy and keep the big money coming in. We need to move to the next space, man, and get our heads around what your next project is.

"So what I'm asking is this: Where are the new songs we talked about before you guys headed out on tour? That was months ago. You said there'd be about a dozen, and that's all we need to get started on the next big thing for you." Here in his element, Jack looked hungry; Thomas couldn't tell if he had the munchies from the pot, or if Jack was mentally resetting the table to help himself to another overflowing plateful of Thomas' soul. "Did you bring a guitar, or should I send Susannah for one? I want to hear your new stuff, man, I can't wait."

Grimly, Thomas thought it was a good idea not to remind Jack that he rarely went anywhere without a guitar in the trunk of his car, even when he had no intention of playing it. This was a habit he'd started from almost the moment he'd first picked up a guitar at age sixteen. He was relieved that his producer didn't seem to remember it. There was a good reason for his growing discomfort; he had a small problem.

Or maybe it was a big problem.

There wasn't any new material. He hadn't written a note, nor had he strung five words of a lyric together, since two months before the tour started. He'd steadfastly lied to everyone, all but announced that he had new songs finished and ready to be heard.

It was one more layer of fiction he easily justified to himself; he hadn't been ready then to write them, but he knew he'd get around to it. His songs were always worth waiting for, weren't they? He had written "What I Need Tonight" in less than twenty minutes, and that had been a huge hit, hadn't it, goddammit? Did they want to check and see how much money that song had brought in for everybody concerned?

There should have been new songs, but there weren't any. He was dried out, tied up, and empty—and couldn't understand why. Apart from the club show, he hadn't seriously picked up a guitar since the tour ended. In his head, he carried a couple dozen ideas around—great ideas—but nothing would come together the way it was supposed to. He knew the music was in him; the words in his heart danced to it. How could he tell his producer, his companionably high, sometime friend, that these days he couldn't exactly hear the music, and he couldn't seem to find the words, no matter how hard he tried?

How would he ever be able to admit to Jack that the magic was gone—and that the knowledge of it was slowly destroying him?

As it turned out, Thomas didn't have to admit to anything at all, at least, not that afternoon.

Just as he was about to fumble toward an ugly but full confession, there was a spontaneous commotion in the outer office: shouting, shrieking, a huge crash and the violent slamming of Susannah's ever-open office door stopped the meeting dead in its tracks.

Startled, and noticeably unsteady on his feet, Thomas followed as Jack raced out of his office to see what was going on.

The big green ceramic pot where Mildred had lived for about a decade was in pieces on either side of the now-closed door to Susannah's office. Voices outside the door indicated that the crash, slam and general uproar had been heard throughout the entire department, and added to the confusion and tension before they were swiftly silenced and dispersed by a senior office manager.

A panicked Joel Toshino had slammed the office door shut without moving Mildred. The sound of shattering ceramic blended with Joel's desperate, rapid-fire cries to locate Thomas, and Susannah's shrieks of alarm.

"What the hell is going on?" Jack bellowed to be heard over the craziness. "Susannah? You okay?"

Susannah nodded lamely, her quiet voice all but drowned out by Joel's frantic one.

Thomas moved to stand directly in front of Go-Joel. "What are you yelling about? What happened?"

Meeting Thomas' eyes, Joel slid into silent panic, which scared Thomas. "What happened, dammit?" he snapped.

Joel stammered the words breathlessly. He'd gone to Century City to get the documents from Thomas' business manager, as requested. He'd gone on that other, special, side trip for Thomas, too, as requested—that one was in Culver City, remember?

Thomas nodded dully, and Joel continued, aware that Susannah and Jack were staring at him too. For once, Thomas Lear's personal assistant did not bask in the attention of others.

"And then I headed out to North Hollywood, I needed to take care of some, um, personal errands, and I didn't think you'd mind," he sputtered.

"Mind *what???*"

On the way back from North Hollywood, Joel had stopped at a drive-through burger place, ordered a huge cheeseburger, a double order of fries and a giant Coke. Somewhere on the Hollywood Freeway just before he returned to Beverly Hills, he dropped part of the burger on the passenger seat of the Mustang. He attempted to hurriedly clean it up as he drove, and managed to spill most of the giant Coke on the passenger seat and the floor, and on the dashboard as well. Still trying to mop up, he made a too-late left-hand turn onto Beverly Boulevard, and was rear-ended by a huge Chevy pickup. The Mustang's back end was smashed.

Thomas began to shake. Smashed?

"Smashed," Joel choked.

Jack stepped in deftly. "Where's the car now, Joel?"

"Half a block from here, down Beverly. I told the police the car belongs to Mr. Lear, and that he was here in a meeting, and that I'd bring him right away," Joel whined weakly.

"The police were there?" Susannah interjected.

Joel nodded. "Well yeah. There were two police cars on the other side of the road, coming from the other direction when I got hit."

"They let you leave the scene?" Jack was amazed.

"Not exactly," moaned Joel. "One of the officers drove me here, and another one's waiting in the lobby for Mr. Lear. He gave me ten minutes to find you."

Mr. Lear went pale; he still had a buzz on from the meeting. There was no way he could talk to the police yet; he was stoned. *Wait—the red Mustang had been hit? Rear-ended? How badly?* Thomas loved that car, and his lame-ass assistant had stupidly gotten it mangled. He felt pushed toward overload, and felt utterly helpless, which was making him angry. On top of it all, something else was attempting to occur to him, too, but he couldn't quite get his head around it.

Not surprisingly, despite the fact that he was a little high, Jack took over. "Susannah, take Mr. Lear to the executive washroom on the tenth floor, and keep him there. Get him some coffee, some cold water, too, and if anyone shows up to use the place, keep 'em locked out. Tell 'em I'm in there, sick as a drunk dog—that usually works. Stay there until I come get you myself. Joel, you and I will go down to the lobby and talk with the police officer, and get things straightened out. Do not tell anyone that you found him. Everyone clear?"

Susannah nodded. Joel nodded. Jack quickly yanked off his jacket, peeled out of his gray pullover sweater, and began to mumble about changing his jeans and finding another shirt in his office before he had to talk to the cops.

At that moment, Thomas found the elusive thought his fuzzy brain had been reaching for.

There had been a guitar, one of Thomas' favorite Martins, nestled in the trunk of the sexy red Mustang.

Thomas Lear, Rock Star, felt his pleasant, cotton-candy buzz melt away in a single breath. He glared with uncontrollable, fiery wrath at a thoroughly-miserable Joel Toshino. That the threat-filled vocalization of his rage was not in fact directly proportional to the serious nature of the incident did not concern him in the slightest. Even as Susannah all but dragged him out of her office to the elevators and up to the executive washroom, Thomas continued shouting and swearing at his wretched assistant, who was left in the dubious care of Jack Grandberg, and, ultimately, in the capable hands of the Los Angeles Police Department.

It was safe to assume that Go-Joel was fired. Although the words were never officially spoken, everyone involved seemed to be certain about that.

four

THE NEXT DAY, which was the Thursday of the worst week of Thomas' life, Linda Elizandro called him and told him as calmly as possible that there was yet another paternity complaint against him, filed that morning. Linda informed him of the name of the woman involved; not surprisingly, it rang no particular bell.

The punch line, however, was a bit of a surprise: the alleged "wronged" woman, it seemed, was allegedly pregnant with twins.

He could not believe this was happening. "Suggestions, Linda?" Thomas muttered unhappily.

"My professional opinion, as your attorney? Get a vasectomy," she advised. "In fact, get two."

Had his week not been so entirely horrific and unhappy, Thomas would have arranged for the *Rolling Stone* interview to be conducted at Trader Vic's at the Beverly Hilton. Trader Vic's was one of his favorite places for business meetings. He liked the food, he'd been going there for years, the maître d' doted on him, the wait staff knew him well enough to be able to meet his needs, and, of course, he had a comfortably intimate knowledge of the many private suites discreetly tucked away throughout the hotel.

The last seven days had been beyond brutal. Thomas was feeling the full weight of the personal and professional disasters that had all but flattened him. He had wanted to cancel the damned interview, or maybe reschedule it far enough out into the next month that he could regain some internal composure. But Stan had put his foot down and told

Thomas that the interview had to happen today, and Thomas was going to have to suck it up and get it right. More than that, Thomas was going to have to shine. The tour had proven to be one of the most critically-acclaimed (to say nothing of financially successful) worldwide concert events of the past five years. The album itself was selling very well, too; it had already gone platinum.

Everyone was talking about him; he was golden. He was, as his no-nonsense business manager reminded him, a constant—currently meteoric—commodity, shining bright and peerless in a city always brim-filled with a million other glowing, rising, or falling stars.

"You need to let them see you dance around on top of the pile," Stan insisted when Thomas called him about bailing on *Rolling Stone*. "You know how to do this, you can do it in your sleep. Be wonderful. Show off. They love you over there. Talk about the tour, talk about the album, tell 'em what's next. Leave them wanting more. You won't even have to breathe hard, and it'll only do you good." Stan urged.

"But..." Thomas interjected.

"You just have to decide to have fun with it."

In the end, they struck a compromise: Thomas would indeed talk with Rolling Stone that Friday, but he would do the two-hour interview from his home, in his library. The reporter would come to the house at two o'clock that afternoon with a photographer. Pictures of a relaxed and charming Thomas Lear At Home would be taken while they talked; the photographer would leave sometime in the first half-hour. Thomas would answer more questions, make nice with the reporter, and be the perfect image of the passion-driven, romantic troubadour that he was expected to be (thus getting the job done and keeping everyone off his back).

And then it would be over, and maybe he could breathe.

He was almost afraid to wish for more.

He spent a couple of hours in his bedroom, mentally positioning himself for any and all questions about the tour, the album, last Sunday's article in *The Times*. He drew polite but firm boundaries around his personal life, practicing a few light-hearted jokes about Julia and the new *Lady Luck* album, just in case. He promised himself he would not lose his temper, say anything unkind about anyone at all (including the *LA Times*), and he would charm his way around questions he did not feel like answering. He could talk about his music, of course, the songs that everybody knew and loved. He would even speak casually about the songs he was working on now, sliding an easy fiction safely in front of the cold, privately painful facts.

Four or five times, he considered rolling a couple of joints for a fast smoke, doing a few lines, popping a couple of pills or opening a bottle of Scotch. The Monster In His Head was itching for something soothing. Anyway, the behavior was expected of people in his business, wasn't it? Surely *Rolling Stone* would not have been surprised. It was tempting.

He was dismayed when he realized that, as much as he'd prefer to have a little chemical help to mellow things out so he could relax and do a good interview, he was also worried that if he used anything, he might make a stupid misstep, cross a line and not be able to keep it together. If he screwed up here, Monster or no Monster, it could get messy. Exhausted by stress, he wasn't convinced he could handle stupid mistakes or their dangerous aftermath today. Grudgingly, he chose to do the interview without the help.

Thomas Lear could not afford one more failure this week.

When Myra phoned him to tell him that the people from *Rolling Stone* had arrived, he was ready. He put on his most charming self-deprecating Rock Star smile, and went downstairs to meet them.

Casey Tourlin had written for *Rolling Stone* for three years. She'd built a solid reputation throughout the music industry as a smart, savvy and informed music lover, fascinated by and appreciative of the art and craft of contemporary music and performance. She'd made her mark early on with an insightful, creative and fun-to-read cover article about Mick Jagger that had turned out to be as good for Jagger as it had been for *Rolling Stone Magazine*. Casey's prose was engaging, her reporting was accurate, and her questions were provocative, revealing shades and color variations of her subjects that had not been seen before. She was friendly, easy to talk to, and gently but firmly professional in her dealings with musicians.

Mrs. Butler had shown them to the library. Casey looked around; it was a comfortable space, tastefully decorated in subtle tones of green and brown. The room was furnished in solid oak, and there were floor-to-ceiling bookcases on two walls. Another wall held four platinum albums and an impressive, ancient-looking warrior's shield. It occurred fleetingly to Casey that there were enough novels crammed into this room to last a reader a lifetime. Thomas Lear, it seemed, liked fiction. She made a mental note of this discovery as she continued looking around.

A long leather couch had two leather ottomans in front of it, and there was a big, red wing-backed chair by the windows, which gave the feeling of being often occupied. At the moment, a thick book with a worn cover sat in it, as if left there only temporarily. Personal photographs cluttered shelves and the tops of two end-tables. Several pieces of exquisite artwork, and a few books and magazines in a pile on the floor made the room feel both lived-in and private.

She was glad this pleasant, informal room had been chosen for the interview; her subject would be far more relaxed here than at the restaurant. The photographer, who had already organized his lighting setup, was peering into his camera lens and planning his shots. Casey turned to face him.

"You ready?"

The photographer nodded. "Yeah. I think he'll look great on that couch, with the Leighton painting behind him. Sets the subliminal for his ballads, don't you think?"

Pleased, Casey grinned, and shook her head to loosen the anticipatory pre-interview tension in her neck. Her reddish-blonde curls were still spinning when Thomas Lear, Rock Star, entered the room with an easy smile and a strong handshake.

Thomas had met Casey Tourlin a year or two earlier, at some media event. She was good; he'd read several of her articles, and had heard positive things about her. He took a breath, and hoped that she would not see past whatever fiction he ended up handing her.

"*Let the games begin*," Casey thought happily, her bright smile aimed at the singer-songwriter.

"*Let the games begin*," thought Thomas, tired and unsettled beneath his shiny, well-practiced veneer. He felt his very-public persona click into place, and, thus protected, he hit his stride; prepared but unregimented, he was free to take the interview anywhere he wanted it to go. Finding his balance in the familiar process, he could hardly wait to hear what he was going to say. It was going to be all right.

He smiled back at her, nodded at the photographer, too. "Hi. Welcome. I'm Thomas Lear."

The "Dangerous Blue Eyes" Tour has been hailed as one of the most successful tours in rock history. What was the highlight of the tour for you?

The photographer, quick and efficient, was most satisfied with the quality of the shots he got as Thomas and Casey talked; they would add much to what promised to be a great feature article. He loaded up his lights and his camera, thanked Thomas, told Casey he'd see her back at the office, and followed Mrs. Butler down the hallway.

What's the hardest thing for you about dealing with your fame?

Does your popularity affect your writing, in terms of how you think about the way you write your songs or what you might or might not be willing to say to stay commercial and marketable?

Is it the music that comes first, or the words? How do you wake up one morning and arrive at, for example, something as beautiful and painful and wistful and evocatively memorable as "I Never Meant to Love You"?

Seriously, why do you think we never get tired of hearing you sing your songs?

You write songs about all the aspects of love, the good times and the hard times—and we wrap ourselves up in them. Several of your classic songs have become anthems, in a way. Since love changes without our consent, and we can fall in and out of it so easily, do you ever feel cynical enough about love in general, or maybe blasé enough about love in general, that you feel like you need to take a break from the ballads and the wistful dreams you paint, and just, I don't know, go fishing?

If you weren't doing this now, what do you think you'd be doing instead?

Obviously Lady Luck's new album came out last week, and of course you've been pointed to as the "inspiration" for many of Julia

Willingford's passionate and sometimes ironically funny and sometimes unkind lyrics. It's no secret that she had an axe to grind. Have you heard the album? What do you think of it? How does it feel, really, to be perceived in a negative way through her lyrics, since it's so very different from the way you're generally perceived through your own lyrics?

Will there be a new album from you this year, taking Julia on, setting the record straight or at least telling your side of the story?

Okay, I had that coming. So what's next for Thomas Lear? What are you working on now? Are you still searching for that one illusive love that will ultimately fill your life and, as you've sung, "finally bring you home to stay"?

I've caught myself singing Lear ballads in the shower. I think we all do it. What do you sing in the shower?

Finally, will you sing something of yours for me before I go?

Thomas was, throughout the interview, everything he was supposed to be: a little modest, yet witty, wry, wistful, funny and sweet. He positively glittered as an intelligent, educated, and gifted musician and poet. He was also kind about Julia and complimentary about her brilliant-if-barbed lyrics, and only made one small but clever joke about their failed relationship.

It was clear to him, too, that, despite her full focus on him, and her experienced, intuitive gaze as she asked and he answered her questions and skillfully expanded on them, she had no idea that he was handing her a fascinating but entirely artificial portrait of a famous rock musician, one that never hinted at the troubled, miserable, frustrated and often frightened man who had begun to worry that he was never going to write or perform well, or even feel better, again.

Although Casey thanked him and indicated that she needed to get going, at Thomas' insistence they celebrated the end of a good interview with exquisite Scotch, a little Hawaiian cannabis and some small talk.

For a little more than two hours, he had taken Casey Tourlin's interview questions, and, by extension, the *Rolling Stone Magazine* audience, for a ride.

Then, mostly because The Monster In His Head snickered and pointed out that Thomas was wholly unworthy of love, and that he was unlikely to ever find the woman his soul and body ached for in his songs, it came as no real surprise that after the pot, Thomas took Casey for a ride, too.

Somehow, despite her specific end-of-interview request for it, he never got around to singing a song for her before she left.

HOURS LATER, WHEN the house was quiet, he poured more Scotch into his glass. Thomas heard The Monster applauding him, wildly stomping its feet and crowing with approval for the successful interview and the equally-successful sexual conquest of the lovely Casey Tourlin. He didn't know her well, of course, but he was pretty sure that right about now, despite the fact that his new favorite journalist had a good bit of exclusive Lear information to work with (the factual stuff as well as the undetectable personal fiction), she could be struggling with her professional objectivity, and would probably hide (at least from her editors) the fact that she and Thomas had had sex. The Monster reassured him with a wink and a shrug that Casey Tourlin's work ethic issues, and whether or not she kept her personal life secret from her bosses, were not his problem. And, really, since it was consensual, who cared anyway?

Thomas conceded that The Monster was right about all of that. The Monster was also right about this second bottle tasting as good as the first one had, and he found himself wishing that he had a few more bottles in the house tonight. He was not exactly in the mood to call Go-Joel to tell him to go get another case and bring it to the house, but he'd probably call him later anyway. Thomas was going to need all the booze he could get his hands on if he was going to get past all the nasty shit he'd been swimming in.

And then he remembered: he'd fired Go-Joel four days ago. By then, the week had been such a fucking freak show, a continuous bleak disaster, he hadn't had time to think about hiring a new assistant. He hadn't had time to do anything, he realized now, except maybe duck and cover as his world unfairly tumbled around him.

"I wonder how this week measures on the fucking Richter," he mumbled to The Monster, as he emptied his glass in one long, unsatisfying gulp.

How he ended up in the music room was anyone's guess. All he knew was that he was putting his empty glass down on the end table beside his favorite chair, rehashing the insanity of the past week. Then he shuffled The Monster into the mix, and added to it the deeply private anguish of his present inability to write. This was the worst part; there was too much going on inside him, but he could not process and release it if he couldn't hear the music or give words to his pain, frustration and fear. Songwriting and performance was not art for him, and he knew it well; it was emotional, intellectual and spiritual survival. It was what made him happy.

It also justified his existence in all the best ways. He needed it as much as he needed air.

The enormity of his wretchedness crushed him; he sank into the chair, staring at nothing, focusing on his unsteady breathing.

And gradually he looked around the room. His eyes rested on his favorite guitar.

The sight of it, sitting silent and solitary on its stand, hit him hard.

"What are you staring at?" he choked. When not in use, he always left his guitars in their cases, to protect them from temperature, moisture, dust and stray damage. In a flash he realized that Myra had left his guitar out today so that, if he wandered in here, he'd see it, and maybe pick it up. He scowled, annoyed that he was touched by the gesture.

Resigned now, he stood, and walked over to the guitar; with pain-filled defiance, he gently lifted it from the stand. Three tall bar stools were lined up against the far wall. He lifted one with his empty hand, and moved it toward the center of the room.

Thomas sat on it, exhaled a ragged breath, tuned two strings, and began to play.

He fought the music, or perhaps it fought him. His nimble, experienced fingers did not caress the strings with the ease and precision that marked his performances, or even his rehearsals. Only slightly daunted, he kept going, making small mistakes with touch and timing.

He chose not to mind it very much, and began to sing one of his most popular ballads (thankfully it only had six chords). His voice sounded hollow and forced, disconnected and shallow, making a lie of the famous lyric.

He stopped in his tracks, and slid into another song, one he'd played in concerts for years. It trickled out of him as dismally displaced as the first one had. This was not good. The guitar was in perfect tune; Thomas was not. The songs themselves were pure magic, yet somehow Thomas had not only lost it, but also his access to it. He could see it, all around him, but he could not touch it, could not wrap himself in the process or, it seemed in this moment, the expression of it.

In what may have been the most awful moment of the worst week of his life, Thomas Lear bent over in agony, wrapped his arms around the guitar he could not play, and wept as though his soul had shattered and died.

"YEAH, HE CALLED me at home this morning," Jack Grandberg told Stan Williams. "When did he call you?"

"There was a call on my service, from late last night,' Stan replied. "I called him back two hours ago. I thought he'd be wasted, or hung over, but he didn't sound that way. Something's definitely up with our boy." Thomas' business manager sighed like a trying-to-be-patient parent. "He said he needs a vacation, and he needs it now."

"Did you tell him this isn't a good time? He has talk shows to do, he has songs to write, and about a dozen other—"

"Yeah, I did."

There was a brief silence, then Jack groaned in despair. "Goddammit. He's going to pull another 'Lear Disappears', isn't he?"

"Grandberg," Stan said without a hint of a smile in his voice, "I bet he's already gone."

five

HE SAT AT a corner table in the dimly-lit bar at the Caledonian Hotel on Princes Street, in the heart of Edinburgh's New Town, moodily drinking single-malt Scotch. No matter how much of the companionable amber liquid he had consumed since he'd arrived, he was not sure he'd ever get around to calling it "whisky" or "malt" as the locals did. All that mattered was that when he mumbled "Scotch—The Macallan—neat," someone brought him more.

More was all he cared about.

It was relatively quiet tonight, and he was glad. He cringed as he recalled the wacked-out woman he'd spent last night with. He'd dubbed her "The Shrieking Woman" because she had gasped loudly with pleasure then immediately shrieked every single time he'd touched her, and possibly a few times when he hadn't. She had given him a headache that hadn't gone away yet.

He had spent most of the day sleeping off a nasty drug hangover, and now that he thought about it, he was fairly certain that the cocaine The Shrieking Woman brought with her had likely been cut with something else. She should have told him, and yeah, he should have asked. He found that he didn't care what the other thing was, but it might have been good to know, all the same. The backs of his eyes still ached. He shuddered at the thought of her. What had he been thinking? He was glad now that he had worn a condom, although that was not his habit. Downing his Scotch, he signaled to the bartender for another.

He knew he needed to straighten himself out, and stop playing with the drugs. But it was much easier in the thinking than in the doing, especially when he was this frustrated with himself. He'd only been in Scotland five days, and already he was bored and dissatisfied. What the hell was he doing here? Getting away from the shit in Los Angeles had made sense at the time. Now he wasn't so sure that this was what he wanted. The problem was that he didn't know what it was that he did want; this carried him immediately back to Square One, which of course did him no good at all. He didn't want to have to think about any of it.

A waiter brought the next glass of Scotch and moved discreetly away. Thomas sighed. Hell, he knew precisely what he was doing here, an ocean and a continent away from home. He'd come here to breathe new air, to spend time with himself and find the way back to his far-too-elusive Muse. So far, all he'd done was drink too much, use too much cocaine, play anonymous tourist on Edinburgh's Royal Mile, and fuck every woman who'd crossed his path and smiled at him the right way.

There was no love song in that.

He knew he needed a love song very badly. The realization, so clear in his mind despite his nasty headache, made him both bitter and sad. Maybe love songs, especially the best of his own classic "four-minute love affairs," were too costly for him, at least in his present frame of mind. He was tired.

He scowled at himself, finishing the Scotch in one toss. He decided to go back to his room, and lose himself in someone else's fiction. He needed an escape, a safe one that helped him keep away from recreational chemistry for a while. Yeah, he'd sprawl on the couch and dissolve into the pages of a book; he could let go and float for a while. Thomas closed his eyes and rubbed his temples with his thumbs to ease the dull throbbing.

A moment or a half-hour later, he opened his eyes, prompted by the pleasant sound of a woman's laughter.

She stood at the bar, talking with the bartender. She had a soft, even-toned voice, with a melodic cadence and a distinct Scottish accent, which his ear picked up without hearing what she actually said. Paying attention now, the gentle burr that lived in her words made him smile even before he could get a good look at her.

When he saw her, his breath caught in his throat.

She was beautiful. She wore her hair long, nearly to her waist; it was a deep shade of brown. As the lights in the room hit it, he could see gleaming strands of gold and auburn, too. She had a straight nose, and a very generous mouth. She was not reed-thin, in the way most of the women he played with were almost boyishly built. She wore a simple, tailored white blouse and black jeans, and he could see that her body curved in delicious places: full round breasts, a soft and curving waistline, inviting hips. His eyes rested on those hips for the space of several heartbeats.

She laughed again, at something the bartender said. Her laughter was easy, almost pure music in its pitch and tone. He found it sweetly intoxicating.

Thomas was instantly enchanted. He bit his lip and willed her to look across the room at him.

The bartender put a glass of red wine in front of her, and she lifted it to him in salute before she took a sip.

Thomas willed harder. Look at me, look at me...

The dark head turned; she looked at him. Her gaze was direct and faintly amused.

She watched him for a minute, smiled warmly and, with a quiet final word to the bartender, walked slowly over to Thomas' small corner table.

"Hello," she said simply.

He tried but failed to pull his well-practiced "Thomas Lear is immensely bored" expression across his face. Instead, he wisely settled for not tripping over his tongue. "Hi."

She beamed at him. "You're Thomas Lear, aren't you?" It did not seem to be a real question, the way she asked it, but he nodded anyway. "Are you on tour?"

"No," he said. "I'm kind of on vacation."

"Oh." Her brown eyes glittered merrily at him.

He realized that she had entirely disarmed him, with no apparent effort. Stunned, his voice came out almost hoarse, but he didn't care. "Would you like to sit down?"

She slid elegantly into the chair across from him, and sipped her wine. "How do you like Edinburgh, Thomas Lear?"

He cleared his throat, worked to remember that he was in fact Thomas Lear, Rock Star, and smiled back at her, all charm. "I've done some walking around. I've been to the Castle, and I've strolled the Royal

Mile all the way down to Holyrood Palace and back. There's definitely a touch of Things Magical around here."

Pleased, she nodded and grinned. "I find it so, too." Her eyes flashed rather prettily, he thought.

"Except for the Royal Mile, I'm afraid I haven't spent much time outside of the hotel. But I was thinking about taking a train through the Highlands. We don't have places like that in the States."

"Indeed." After a small silence, she chuckled. Too late, he realized that he had been staring at her. He might even have been drooling a little.

He blushed, and worked hard not to stammer in his embarrassment at being caught. It was worse that she'd been entertained by it. He was never awed by women; he must have been more hung over than he'd thought. "God, I'm...sorry. It's just that...you're very beautiful," he declared lamely.

She laughed again, easily and without malice. "Thank you."

"What's your name?"

Her smile never faltered. "I answer to many names," she told him cryptically. "We Scots don't give them up too easily, you know. You have to get to know us a bit before we get around to telling you our secrets."

"I see," he said, but he really didn't.

"So," she said, deftly changing the subject, "How long are you staying in Scotland, then?"

"I haven't decided. I needed to get away..." he began, then hurried to add "—to get some writing done," embellishing his current protective fiction. "I only finished touring three months ago, so I am taking some time off. I'd like to drink up some Celtic culture and write some new songs. That's me, in a nutshell."

She sipped her wine. "In a nutshell," she repeated, and then grinned provocatively. "Thomas, do you have any idea just how large a nutshell really is?"

"What?"

She didn't answer him, she only grinned wider, her brown eyes warming him far more than the Scotch had done.

He felt a pleasant tug in his groin, and effortlessly fell into familiar territory; he liked this game. He would charm this pretty local without even working up a sweat. He'd have her up to his suite in under five minutes. This was so easy that it was almost unfair. He graced her with his most disarming smile, and played one of his standard opening moves:

"I don't know your name, yet, Beautiful Lady, but I'd very much like to kiss you."

She actually laughed; not unkindly, but she did laugh. "Now *that* is a daring proposition. I find it's always wise to be fully aware of who it is that you're thinking about kissing, before you announce your intentions. Otherwise, the results could be...unpredictable."

Covering his surprise at her reaction, he laughed with her. "Is that a challenge?"

"Perhaps," she admitted, then added, almost to herself: "I'm a good deal less selfish than I used to be."

He leaned forward and touched her hand. It was both delicate and amazingly strong. He liked the fact that it was warm and steady. He studied it for a few seconds before he met her eyes again, offering her his next slick, well-practiced move. "Does that mean you're going to let me kiss you?"

"It's a possibility."

He raised an eyebrow. She was enchanting; there was no other word for it. This was a game he usually played with women, before he systematically took them to bed and then walked away. He was unaccustomed to the reversal of the process, but he thought that he might enjoy it this time. Something else was different about this encounter, too, and the realization surprised him: he was captivated by her, and they both knew it.

She regarded him carefully, then spoke. "There's a price for kissing me, Thomas. I can see that you'd like more than a kiss, and I find I am willing to give you that, as well. But it comes at a cost."

He was intrigued, now; he couldn't help himself. He was almost focused on someone other than himself, for the first time in a long while. He wanted to kiss her. "What's the going price in Edinburgh for kissing a beautiful woman?" he asked her slyly.

She took his hand in hers and gazed deeply into his eyes, her flashing brown ones searching the hungry dark brown depths of his own. Her voice was husky and low, and sent a shiver of delightful apprehension coursing through his body. "If you kiss me, and more, you must come with me, to my home, for the space of a year and a day. Your music and I will be the only life that you have from the first day until the last. After a year and a day have passed, I shall release you, and then you can continue on with your life as you left it, in the world as you know it now. But for the time you are with me, you will be mine. You must live by my rules. You will live only to give me pleasure, and music. In turn, I will give you pleasure, too—and freedom, and solace, and life."

Maybe it was the Scotch, the drug hangover, and the fact that she was so damned beautiful. Dazzled, he gave her some sarcasm in an attempt to restore his faltering balance. "Sounds like you're going to keep me pretty busy. Will you at least give me time to write some new songs?"

If she knew he was baiting her, she didn't acknowledge it. She beamed brightly at him instead. "Thomas, your songs are the reason I wanted to kiss you in the first place."

He was struck speechless by her directness and, at the same time, aroused down to his socks. He wanted her; he did not want to wait. He'd play any game she put in front of him, as long as he could kiss her, touch her, and take her.

"Are you listening to me? I'm serious, deadly serious," she told him carefully. "You will be with me, and will belong to me, for a year and a day."

A thought struck him. "A year and a day? Sounds like a line from a fairy tale."

"That's 'faerie' tale, Thomas. 'Faerie'."

If he looked at her, he couldn't think clearly. He sat back for a second, closed his eyes, and tried to remember the way the mythology worked. *A year and a day. Away from the world for a year and a day...*

He got it. He opened his eyes and gazed at her warily. "Wait a minute. A year and a day isn't right, it's seven years, isn't it? That's the way the story usually goes."

Delighted, she clapped her hands. "Clever man! You know the tales, then."

He grinned, and lowered his voice conspiratorially. "Not that I ever did anything serious with it, but I happen to hold a Master's Degree in Medieval Literature." She nodded her approval. He was immensely pleased with himself. "It's supposed to be seven years, Dear Lady. Seven years is the price a mortal man must pay for a kiss on the lips of the Fairy Queen."

"It's 'Faerie,' Thomas, not 'Fairy'."

His expression changed slowly. Calm as starlight, she waited while he tried to take it in. He looked at her, searching, lust still evident on his face. But his brain was working again. "So...you're the Faerie Queen?" He hoped he'd kept the smirk out of his voice.

She nodded, looking at him with such earnestness that he very nearly believed her for a second.

"And so if I kiss you, et cetera, according to the mythology, I'm really yours for the next seven years?"

"Not seven. Not anymore. The world moves so quickly now that a year and a day is sufficient for everyone."

"Everyone? Who's everyone?"

Her smile was mysterious. "Leave that, for now. Do you still want to kiss me? Will you stay with me for a year and a day?"

Sure, he'd play along. Why not? He'd been looking for something, and here was an adventure. What could go wrong? He needed a diversion, didn't he? Obviously she was as good at casual seduction as he was. Thomas was already planning all the wonderful things he was going to do with her when he got her into his bed. Under the present circumstances, he could certainly let himself be led into her delicious game; he'd be a fool to walk away from this.

There might even be a love song in it...

He smiled brightly. "Absolutely yes, Beautiful Lady. Tell me what you want me to do."

She looked pleased; not at all surprised, only pleased. "Very well. You will need to check out of the hotel. Remember, you're going to be gone for a year; you don't want it to look as though you've been kidnapped. Make arrangements so that no one will worry about you, no one will mistakenly believe that anything terrible has happened. That is unkind, and would ruin the game."

"That's easy," he told her. "I have a sorry reputation for disappearing when I'm in the mood." He shrugged; stepping away from the fiction wouldn't hurt him with her, since he was about to score. "I've just done it again, as a matter of fact. I'll call my business manager, my producer, and, oh, and probably my mother," he teased. He couldn't help it; the sarcasm was there as he continued: "There will be some impact on my career, if I'm away from the business for a year and all, but I'm pretty famous, so think I can handle it."

She knew he didn't believe her. Still, she wanted him. He'd have to come to terms with his bargain, one way or another, soon enough. Let him play, it was all the same to her. "Either have your clothes and your luggage stored here, or send them back to your people in the States. You will well and truly be gone for a year and a day. Believe it, Thomas."

"Got it," he said. "When can I kiss you?"

She trembled, then; he was absolutely sure that he saw her tremble. "Meet me at midnight, at Calton Hill, overlooking Princes Street. Take a cab; the driver will take you to the carpark at the top. After the cab is gone, you will see a path that begins in the grass. It will be easy to see in the dark. Follow it up the wee hill toward the city lights. I'll be waiting for you there."

"Can I bring anything with me?" he said, still teasing her.

"Bring your guitar, and some personal belongings, if you wish. I shall provide everything else."

She stood, and turned to go. "I will see you in three hours, Thomas. Be sure to arrive at midnight, or just after."

"Calton Hill. Midnight," he murmured, letting out a slow breath as he watched her walk away. She didn't look back at him, but nodded at the bartender on her way out.

Thomas Lear, Rock Star, was wildly aroused. He could barely breathe as he dropped a huge tip on the table and hurried out of the bar.

In the bedroom of his hotel suite, Thomas tossed clothes and toiletries into a small, brown leather suitcase that could pass as an overnight bag. He was close to electrified at the prospect of intimacy with the Scottish delight he'd just met. He chuckled as he remembered the details of their encounter. The fun had started, and he could hardly wait—

The Monster In His Head tapped him for attention.

"Not now," Thomas muttered, trying to decide how many pairs of briefs and socks he should take with him to his assignation. He was a master at pretending, so it was high time it paid off for him, wasn't it?

It was important she saw that he was willing to participate in her fantasy, at least until he was bored with it, or with her.

He would get bored with her, of course he would. It might take a while, but he always got bored with them.

The Monster temporarily forgotten, another part of his brain worked on his back-up plan. When he was done with the so-called Queen of Faerie, what then? What if he wasn't ready to head back to LA and (he groaned as the bad joke crossed his mind) face the music? What if he needed to lay low for a month or two?

He had friends from college living in Italy—Florence, he was pretty sure. He hadn't been to Greece yet; that could be fun. He liked Spain, and he liked France, too. If he felt like being fussed over, he'd hit Paris and make a little noise. If he didn't want to attract attention, if he could get back into the writing, he might check into that quiet little hotel in Madrid...

Then again, he could blow off Europe altogether, and head for Australia. Or Nepal.

He didn't have to make the decision tonight, he reminded himself.

"Drink?" The Monster countered, sensing his resolve.

"Nope," Thomas confirmed, closing the leather suitcase and dropping it on the floor neatly beside his guitar case.

He poured himself a glass of cool water and thought about the calls he would have to make to play this new game.

He placed a call to Stan first, knowing that his business manager could handle everything well enough even if Thomas didn't bother to talk with anyone else. Stan was generally okay with most everything Thomas did, as long as it wasn't too much of a surprise. Thomas was fairly certain that Stan had known that this particular vanishing act had been easy enough to read on the recent horizon, so he wasn't concerned that he'd broken the only tacit rule between them: *No left-field surprises*. The reverse was true as well; Stan didn't drop bombs on Thomas, either. This made for a good working relationship, and that was all they required from each other.

It was nearly 10pm in Edinburgh; that made it almost 2pm in Los Angeles.

"Stan Williams' office," answered a very young female voice after the tenth ring. Thomas knew this was not Stan's regular secretary, whose name might have been Carla.

"Hi. I need to speak with Stan," Thomas began. "It's kind of urgent."

It was clear by the way her sentences ended in interrogative pitches that the temp sitting at maybe-Carla's desk was not altogether bright. "I'm sorry, Mr. Williams is in meetings all afternoon? He said he would be available after six? I could take a message and have him call you back later?"

Thomas sighed. Grudgingly, he jettisoned his clever planned speech for Stan. Despite the temp's loud gasp of recognition and whisper of "Oh my God, oh my God" when he told her his name, he breezed through a spontaneous message, aware that most of what he was telling her might not travel all the way to Stan's desk.

"Okay," Thomas took a breath, then revved into gear. "What's your name, Darling?"

"Jessica?" the voice said tremulously.

"Okay, Jessica. I need you make sure that Stan gets this information. Can you see that he does?"

"Oh my God," Jessica repeated.

"Here goes, Jessica; I hope you have a pen handy. I'm not in LA. I'm on vacation." He considered this quickly. "I need to talk directly with Stan, and I will. He'd prefer to know what I'm up to. Mostly I'm planning to get some writing done. You getting this, Jessica?"

"You're on vacation, to do some writing?" Jessica choked.

"That's right. Tell him I'm fine, I'm going to be writing and chasing women, and will probably go dark for a while. He'll know it's no big deal. Tell him we'll figure it out when I get back." He waited a respectable ten seconds, with no response from poor Jessica. "Jessica?"

"Yes, Mr. Lear?"

"Tell him to call Myra and get some things sorted out. He'll know what I mean. Thanks for taking the message. See ya!"

Thomas hung up the phone, then lifted the receiver again, and called home.

Myra answered on the second ring, and listened carefully as Thomas gave her instructions.

"...so keep things running any way you feel like it, until I call you. Call Stan Williams tomorrow if he doesn't call you first, tell him I told you to do what you want about the house and property. If you need anything, anything at all, call him, and he'll handle it. There's plenty of money in the house accounts, so don't worry about that. Nothing has to change, except I'll be AWOL for a while. Don't worry if you don't hear from me; I could be away for two weeks, it could be a few months," he shrugged, "or it could be as long as a year, although I kind of doubt that." *How long could the game with the pretty brunette really last, after all?*

"Are you all right?" Myra asked him kindly. "Are you taking care of yourself? Are you keeping an eye on your...habits?"

If she had been there in the room with him, Thomas would have hugged her, hard. "I'm fine. I'm hooking up with a friend, and don't know yet how long I'm going to hang around and play. But as soon as I'm ready to head back to Los Angeles, I promise I'll call. Honestly, Myra."

A mildly skeptical "hmmmmm" sound came out of the phone. Thomas laughed. "Didn't I call you as soon as I checked into the hotel and tell you exactly where I am and mostly what I'm up to here?" he reminded her.

"You did," Myra admitted. "And you sound a lot better, too. That was a week ago, though. Are you staying at least a little bit out of trouble?"

"Yes ma'am," he teased. "There's a little bit of trouble that I'm staying all the way out of, Scout's honor.

"Seriously, Myra, don't worry, I'll be back, whenever I am. Remember, there's money in the house account—use it like you always do. Stan will take care of everything. You'll get paid, same as always. I want you guys to take care of yourselves. Are we clear on this?"

"We are. But take care of yourself, will you?" she asked a little sadly.

"I will. Be a good girl, Myra. Don't worry. I'll see you when I do."

He hung up the phone and sighed. He had only been away for a week, but he found that he missed her—and Ben, too—much in the way he'd missed them both when he'd been on tour. They were solid and steady fixtures in his erratic and often messy life. In a strange way, he supposed that they were *Home* to him. It was better not to think about it.

He sighed again and made one last call.

"Jack Grandberg's office," Susannah answered the phone.

"I need to talk with Jack. It's Thomas Lear," he said. "It's important, and I'm in kind of a hurry."

Susannah did not allow her surprise to show in her voice. "Hello, Mr. Lear. I'm sorry, but Jack's not in the office. He's on his way to New York for a meeting." A trace of parental disapproval crept into her voice, but Thomas ignored it. "He'll be very sorry he missed your call. He was, well, a little concerned when you, um...left."

Thomas Lear, Rock Star, grunted.

"He'd probably want me to ask you where you are, and when you're coming back," she continued.

"He probably would. And you'd probably like to be the bearer of the tidings, too," scoffed Thomas. "I'm away, I'll be back. That should be enough."

"Um..." Susannah replied as professionally as she could manage. "Mr. Lear? Can I do something to help you?"

He looked at his watch. He didn't have time to mess around.

"Mr. Lear?" she prompted him.

"Yeah, sorry. What's your name again?"

"Susannah."

"Yeah, thanks. Susannah, tell Jack I'm having myself an adventure, and I'll be back whenever I get back. I'll do my best to color inside the lines whenever possible, and I'll drink all my milk."

"Funny. So if you're six years old, everything's fine, right?"

He chuckled; he couldn't help it. "God, I guess I sounded like a jackass there. Sorry about that. Seriously, though," he added, "would you please tell Jack that I'm going to get some work done, and I'm going to play a little, so I can get my head around what I want to do next...I want to have ten or twenty new songs to show off next time I see him."

"I'll tell him," Susannah promised. "And, Mr. Lear?"

"Yeah?"

"I'll trade you intel for intel..."

"Oh?"

"Tell me where you are, and I'll only tell Jack, I promise. I'll trade your location for something that will make you laugh."

He considered this. "Really?"

"Yes. He gets to know you're all right and where you are, and you get a little entertainment."

Thomas considered this, and then conceded. "Okay, then, Susannah-in-Jack's-office. It's a deal. I'm in Scotland. Edinburgh. At the Caledonian Hotel. Now make me laugh."

Jack would be glad to get the information. "Thanks for telling me. Here's the funny: when Jack found out that you'd gone without talking with him about it, he got on the phone with Stan Williams, and they had a rather heated discussion about why you'd gone, and where. Stan got a little bossy, and roared that he could get your personal assistant to spill the beans on your whereabouts without too much effort. Jack said he was sure that Stan *couldn't* get Joel to tell him where to find you."

Thomas shook his head in confusion. "Joel is, as they say, 'no longer with us.' You and Jack were there when I fired his ass," he declared.

"True," Susannah agreed. "Only Stan didn't know that. He made a bet with Jack that he could get Joel to talk—a five hundred dollar bet!"

Wincing at Stan's bad move, Thomas laughed. "I'd imagine Stan is pissed."

"So I hear. But I think Jack wants to kiss you."

They laughed together. Feeling pressed for time, Thomas was ready to hang up. "Susannah, I'll be back when I finish what I'm doing. Could be up to a year, you never know. Tell Jack I may stay quiet for a while, but if it's been too long between albums by the time I show up in your office, penitent and ready to get back to work, I promise I'll listen attentively to his back-breaking plans for my creative comeback. Tell him I'll even take notes. Nice talking to you, Susannah," he finished.

"Can I tell him you'll stay in touch? You'll maybe send him a postcard?"

Maybe he'd send *everyone* postcards, Thomas mused with a snort as he hung up the phone. Postcards from Faerie.

Thomas had never liked explaining himself, so it was enough that everyone would loosely know that he was taking up to a year's vacation, and that he was safe and well and would resurface when he felt like it. Everyone who knew him was used to that, even if he hadn't been away for more than a couple of months at a time before. There was money enough, there was time enough, and he was absolutely up for the adventure. He repacked all of his suitcases, and cleared away all evidence of his presence. He filled the overnight bag with all the paperback books that would fit, along with his last two joints, a bottle of Scotch, some pens and paper, and his wallet.

Then he called the concierge, and asked that his luggage be held for him until he or one of his representatives called for it, and mentioned blithely that it might be a long while. He also provided the concierge with Stan's address and phone number in case the hotel wanted to speak with his business manager. It was clearly all part of the game, and he was going to play it straight for as long as he could, to please her.

He took a shower, shaved, and dressed in his favorite jeans and a brown cashmere sweater. He pulled on his sneakers, and slid into his black leather jacket. He grabbed his razor, his toothbrush, his sunglasses and a handful of condoms, and crammed them all into the now-overstuffed leather bag.

At eleven forty-five that night, guitar case in hand and the heavy overnight bag slung over his left shoulder, Thomas Lear, Rock Star, checked out of the Caledonian and got into a cab, and drove off into the starlit night.

six

THE CAB DRIVER took him to Calton Hill. If the man was a little star-struck and also puzzled by Thomas' late-night trip, he kept his admiration and his questions to himself. He simply stopped the cab in the rounded, paved area at the top of the Hill, and smiled easily as he collected the fare and a sizeable tip, knowing that he'd have a tale to tell at the pub the next night.

The chilly September night air was fresh and brisk. Alone now, Thomas looked around, trying to get his bearings in the moonlight-streaked darkness. Had she set him up, somehow, for something weird or even dangerous? Was he about to be harmed, or perhaps made to look foolish? It was possible, he conceded grimly.

But when he remembered the look in her eyes, the hunger and the power, the grace and humor that he saw in them, he let his flash of suspicion evaporate.

Here he was, standing in the dark on Calton Hill, talking to himself. What the hell was he supposed to do now? And where was she?

A breeze danced past him, teasingly reminding him of the scent of her. Cocking an eyebrow, he looked all around, and then up at the sky, and finally down at his feet. There he noticed a faint dusting of glittering light on a path in front of him that he was positive hadn't been there moments before. Intrigued, he bent down to touch it. Nothing stuck to his finger. Still, the glow seemed more tangible than mere reflected light. Probably a trick of the night. He looked up. The moon was full, or close to it. *Moon magic?* He wondered. Probably not. Anyway, he liked the effect.

For several minutes, Thomas followed the softly glowing path to the end of Calton Hill. On a comfortable bench that glowed and flickered like the path, a figure sat, looking down on the sparkling city. She was there, waiting for him. His heart skipped a beat; the game was on.

Thomas took a deep breath, cleared his throat, and moved the two dozen paces toward her.

She was wearing a dark, hooded wool cloak that covered everything but her face. When she turned, she smiled up at him. He realized with a start that there had been no doubt in her mind that he would come to her.

"Here I am," he announced, then laughed in spite of himself. "Obviously."

"I'm glad," she told him. She patted the bench beside her. "Come."

She did not have to tell him twice. He put his things down on the ground, and moved to the bench. Edinburgh's lights glimmered below them. Across the city, a little to their left, he could see the Castle, its night lights bathing it in a rich, golden glow.

He sat down beside her, and looked at her closely. She was even more beautiful in moonlight than she'd been in the bar. He was about to tell her so, when, without a word, she leaned into him and closed her eyes.

Thomas kissed her softly, then, almost tentatively. Her lips parted against his slowly, and he found himself falling into the incomparable sweetness of her mouth. He touched her cheek with his hand, and pulled her closer. A keen ache in his body blended with the earthy scent of her, and excited him more. His kiss deepened and he pulled her against him as his mouth took hers with increasing force. He groaned with the pleasure of it.

After a while she touched his face, and moved a little away with a smile. Her hand was trembling. The moonlight and the shine still softly glimmering from the path and the bench allowed him to see the unmistakable twinkle in her eyes. He knew then that she was as aroused as he was, her need as naked and raw as his own.

"That kiss was worth anything, Beautiful Lady," he whispered, his voice ragged with wanting.

She took his hand, and squeezed it. "I'm glad you think so, Thomas. It was expensive for you."

If it was, he didn't care. He held her hand and raised it to his lips. He kissed it softly, all the way around to her wrist, which he nipped with his teeth.

She bit her lip and sighed happily, then stood up, her hand still in his. He noticed with a silent intake of breath that she was wearing nothing under the cloak but moonlight, and she wore that moonlight gloriously. She caught his eye and grinned, and led him to a grassy spot behind and beyond the bench, which he had passed on his way to her. She took off her cloak, and dropped it wordlessly on the ground beside what looked to be a large blanket and a basket with two bottles of wine, two glasses, a loaf of bread and some fruit in it.

No preamble was necessary. She settled into his arms as if she'd always been held there, and kissed him deeply, possessively, learning the taste and the feel of him. They explored each other, eyes and fingers and flesh discovering warmth and rhythm as the stars danced above them. By the time they sat down together on the blanket, he was as moonlit as she was.

Only the shining inhabitants of the night sky watched as they moved together, paired, and joined.

Of course Thomas had previously known desire and its dazzling fulfillment, but he had never experienced this. The more he touched her, the more he needed to touch her; her answering caresses took him deeper into desire than he had ever been before. Their coupling was something more than sex. He was consumed by a near-maddening desire, one that suddenly tripled in intensity. He wanted her more than he had ever wanted anyone or anything in his life.

Thomas looked into her eyes, wanting to but unable to form the words: *What are you doing to me?* Her chocolate-brown gaze met his, mirroring his unspoken question, which triggered yet another layer of desire. He pulled her against him and dug his hands into her hair, kissing her as if he was drowning, and she was his fresh air.

After a time, the enchantment was complete.

They lay on their backs, tangled together, drowsily considering the flickering lights in the night sky.

He ran his thumb over the back of her hand, and kissed it. "The stars seem so close tonight."

Sated, her voice was quiet. "From my home, they're closer still."

All right, she was sticking to her story. He didn't mind. He felt better, on so many levels, than he'd felt in longer than he could remember. He thought of their long and multiple couplings, and smiled as he pulled her in closer to him, her back against his chest, their legs still intertwined. He had never met anyone like her. After having spent only hours with her, he thought she might be closer to what he imagined a soul-mate could be than any woman he'd encountered. The sharp suddenness of this notion choked him, frightened him, taunted him, seduced him and tore at him all at once; then it took his breath away. He held her tightly. He wondered if he could lose his mind from the near-shattering intensity of wanting her. "My God. Who are you? What are you? Are you really a Queen, or a midnight fantasy, or a witch, or a bright dream?"

In response, she rubbed her fetching backside slowly against his abdomen. "Yes," she answered, and then giggled.

The sound of her laughter eased him from the torment of thinking, and into the reality of touching. Chuckling, he allowed himself to relax again, running a finger from her throat to her navel, just to feel her squirm delicately against him. "You know, you have the makings of a fine Muse."

"It wouldn't be the first time," she said simply, with an honesty that tickled the back of his mind.

"Well, I've never fucked a Muse before, but after this, I'm thinking it could be one hell of an experience."

She wrapped his arm around her. "Just so, Thomas."

He tightened his hold on her as she snuggled her back deeply against him. "You know my name. I want to know yours." He ran his tongue over her ear lobe, and she sighed. "Tell me."

"I already told you that we don't easily give our names—" she gasped as his tongue played in her ear.

Thomas' tongue probed her ear more aggressively, and he was rewarded by the strong and delicious shudder that rippled through her. He hadn't gotten to her ears before now, his focus having earlier been on other interesting parts of her anatomy and his own. Encouraged by her immediate response to a flicking tongue, he teased her ear again.

"No earring, not even pierced," he mumbled, sucking on it. She groaned and arched against him. "Oh, you like that. Want some more?" She made a sound that could only be interpreted as a garbled but happy purring, and he began to trace her ear, lobe to tip, with his lips and tongue, at the same time caressing her breasts.

When he got to where he knew the tip of her ear should be, there was, somehow, more ear than he expected. Intrigued, he continued to kiss it, and rolled his tongue over it while she pressed herself against him.

It distantly occurred to him, in some currently non-active but still vaguely cooperative part of his brain, that the ear he was tickling was a great deal longer than a normal ear should be. As he explored its outer edge with his mouth, he noticed that it came to what felt very much like a point, tipping back into her hair, and that it had to be at least twice as long as his own. Curious now, he moved his hand slowly from her nipple to her cheek, nibbling on the lobe as he gently ran a warm finger all the way around the outside of the longest, most perfectly pointed ear he'd ever encountered.

She writhed against him, moaning hungrily, and then she gasped, climaxing hard and long, slamming against him in her pleasure. When her breathing quieted a little, he kissed the side of her neck, then experimentally rimmed the inside of her ear with his tongue, and held her close as she cried out in another shivering release of pleasure.

They held each other in the final hour before dawn. It was cold but not bitterly so; they kept each other warm enough. They had spent most of the night touching, resting and even sleeping briefly, and then starting, feeding and sating their hunger again.

He realized sometime later that he was completely happy in this moment; it had been a long time since this particular thought had crossed his mind. He marveled at that, and at the woman who was, as he watched, waking up in his arms.

"When the sun comes up, the first thing I'm going to do is get a good look at your ears," he teased as he kissed her eyebrow. "And then I'm going to kiss them until you pass out."

She ran a hand along the muscles in his back, and rubbed her face against his chest. "What a lovely thought, Thomas. But when the sun comes up, we have to go. I need to get back, and you're going with me."

If he had, by force of habit, planned to walk away from her after this night, he consciously dismissed the idea now. Why should he leave her so soon? If she wanted him to go wherever she was going, that was fine. He had the time.

He pulled his head back to look her in the eyes. "I still want to know your name. I have to call you something."

"Thomas, I cannot tell you my True Name."

"'True Name'?"

"Yes, my True Name. My name at home."

"Why?"

"You're the one with the Master's degree in Medieval Literature."

He groaned at her in mock agitation. "You've fucked the life out of me, and now you want me to think?" She laughed. "Oh, all right. Your True Name. You can't tell me your True Name. Why...why..." He wasn't expecting to really think about it, at least, not now (not without a gallon of hot coffee). But as she watched him expectantly, he found he was doing just that. Things he hadn't thought about for a couple of decades came back to him in a flash. "Wait...I've got it. If you're faerie folk..."

"...and I am," she said evenly.

"...if you're faerie," he continued, "then if any mortal hears and speaks your True Name, you're vulnerable to that mortal, and you can lose your soul, or your freedom...or something." He faltered, memory suddenly failing him.

"Close," she told him. "Well, not that close. True Names in Faerie have power, and light. We know each other by our True Names, and that's as it should be. If a mortal uses a faerie's True Name, power can be used against the Fair One, and all kinds of magic is set loose, wild and uncontrollable. At least that's what I've been told. I haven't ever seen it happen, myself, but that's no guarantee that it couldn't. And I have enough to do without worrying about the potential of that possibility." She sounded determined. "No, Thomas, there are risks I will not take, and exposing True Names is one of them." Her mind moved to a different place, one he could not see. She didn't frown, but he could almost feel it just the same.

He did not want the mood around them to change, so he relented at once. "Then you should tell me what I can call you."

She kissed him with a laugh. "I am the Queen. You are in fact subject to me..."

"—in so many ways, Lady..." Thomas smirked and sighed with a theatrical flair.

"So you are," she replied. "And as Queen, I say that you shall make that decision. Choose a name that pleases you, and I'll answer to it for a year and a day. Fair enough?"

He thought it over. "All right." Something else occurred to him. "But what if you don't like what I come up with?"

"That's easy. I won't answer you unless you name me something I like. That way, we will both be satisfied."

As the graying darkness faded into the first rose-colored streaks of morning light, he held her close, curled up on the blanket, under the cloak. He smiled slyly and ran feather-light fingers along her hip. "And since we're speaking of satisfaction...?"

"Yes?" she asked blithely, enjoying the game.

"Oh God, I want you again, my Lady Queen. Uh...*now*."

"So it would seem," she laughed, and slid her hand down to meet him.

In the stillness of the early morning, they walked along a paved path that led them down and away from Calton Hill. Thomas carried his guitar case, his leather overnight bag, and the basket, which held the blanket, two empty wine bottles, the wine glasses, and the bag that had held the bread and the fruit they had just eaten for breakfast. The Queen carried her cloak over one arm. She was wearing the same clothing she'd worn in the bar at the Caledonian the evening before.

At the end of the path, they reached cement stairs that took them down to the street. The Queen looked at Thomas, one eyebrow lifted. "Are you ready to go?"

Thomas shrugged. "Why not?"

Her eyes held a hard look that might have been alarming had it not been for the genuine smile on her lips. "This is serious, Thomas, and you may as well begin to see it as such." That said, she traced a small sign in the air, and blew it at him. His eyes widened, and he thought he heard the sound of tiny bells chiming. He looked around, but didn't see them. Instead, her voice flowed into him in a matter-of-fact tone: *Come with me, or stay here, it is one and the same. You will still be mine for a year and a day.*

"Are you ready to go?" she repeated, reading his eyes.

For some reason, he completely believed her now, believed everything she'd said to him, although he wasn't sure when that had happened. He was certain, however, that she had told him the truth; for once, the truth didn't bother Thomas at all.

"Thomas?" she asked again.

He looked at her, and was surprised at how easily he was accepting her story. "Yes, I'm ready to go."

"Good," she smiled.

A pearl-gray car, a 1975 four-door Fiat, pulled up to them, slowed and stopped by the curb. A gray-haired, medium-sized, barrel-chested man who looked to be in his late fifties turned the motor off, and got out of the driver's seat. He was dressed in dark slacks, a white wool sweater and a slate-gray raincoat. He looked at the Queen respectfully. "Good morning, Your Grace," he said.

Thomas' mouth dropped open a little as he noticed the man's subtle but serious bow.

She smiled at the newcomer, and touched his hand with the ease of familiarity. "Good morning. Is everything ready?"

"It is, Your Grace," he said. "All is well, and is as you commanded." He handed her a thermos cup, into which he poured hot coffee.

"Thank you," she said gratefully, drinking some of the steaming liquid. She passed the cup to Thomas, who drank it down as he listened to her speak to the man. "Is there anything that I should know about before I return home?"

The man thought for a moment, and then shook his head. "Nothing that cannot wait, Your Grace." He turned to Thomas, smiled pleasantly, and opened the back door of the car. At the man's smooth gesture, Thomas handed over the leather bag and the guitar case, which the older man placed carefully on the floor of the back seat along with the basket. The Queen handed him her cloak; this he folded in half and lay across the seat.

"When shall we expect you, Your Grace?" the man asked as he collected the empty cup from Thomas, attached it back on the thermos and, placing it gracefully in the basket within reach of the driver's seat, closed the car door.

"Sometime between midnight and dawn, I'd imagine," she told him. The man nodded.

The Queen slid into the driver's seat, then looked over at Thomas, her eyes dazzling with mirth. He hadn't moved from his original place at the curb; he stared at them, trying to understand what was happening here. "Are you coming, Thomas?" she asked.

"Oh...yes," he mumbled, tearing his focus from the older man, who smiled kindly back at him. Thomas stumbled behind and around the car, and got in on the passenger side.

The Queen started the car's engine; it purred and hummed like a living thing. As Thomas got comfortable in his seat, he noticed the tiny silver bells woven into a leather thong which was braided around the steering wheel. He absently counted fifty-nine of them. He watched as the Queen touched the steering wheel and its bells; he assumed that their tinny, metallic tinkling would drive him crazy in short order. But the bells were not tinny and metallic when she turned the steering wheel; rather, they were sweet and soft and clear, somehow soothing as they jingled in the briskness of the chilly morning.

Without a backward glance at the older man, the Queen pulled out onto the street, leaving him standing on the curb, watching them go.

Thomas, who had looked back over his shoulder, was confused. "We're leaving him there?" he asked.

She smiled at him. "Don't worry. He'll be home soon. Sooner, in fact, than we will be." She laughed out loud when she saw the perplexed look on his face. "Oh, Thomas, it's all right, truly. Everything is fine."

Frowning, he raised an eyebrow. "He called you 'Your Grace'," Thomas observed.

"Yes, he did," she said.

He closed his eyes in an effort to clear his head. "You're a Queen. You're the Queen of Faerie."

"Did I not tell you that?" she asked him, the grin unmistakable in her voice.

He smiled, opened his eyes and watched her with an almost overpowering interest as she navigated northeast through Edinburgh's early-morning traffic. He shook his head. "Hard to believe I haven't had drugs of any kind in almost twenty-four hours." Amused, she glanced at him, then looked back at the road. "I'd swear I was tripping," he added. "Such is the life today of Thomas Lear, Rock Star. But what the hell."

The woman beside him kept her eyes on the traffic, only partially stifling a chuckle.

She followed the M90 north toward the city of Perth. As she drove, she told Thomas about her home. Fascinated, he hung on her every word.

"Elvenhome is the name of the castle, but it's also the name of kingdom, the lake—that's *loch* to you—the forest and the village outside the castle walls," she began. "The castle has always been there, so far as anyone knows. It's very old, almost as old as the trees that surround it. It's lovely there.

"You'll have your own apartments. When you are not with me, you'll be free to write your songs, and you'll be free to do anything you like, with anyone you choose—within certain boundaries, which we'll discuss shortly. You'll meet everyone at the castle; you're officially our Court Singer. We Fair Folk love music. It would please me if you'd sing for us often. There will be a welcoming feast soon. That will be the perfect opportunity for the entire assembled Court to hear you play and sing."

Thomas thought about this for a moment. "I don't know any faerie tunes," he said.

The Queen nodded. "I wouldn't imagine that you do. At least not yet, although our musicians will teach you as many as you'd like to learn," she replied. "Play your own music, Thomas, or anyone else's that you would share with us; although it's your music that draws me to you. I am happy to say that I am well acquainted with several of your albums. I have loved your songs since the first time I heard them. Play and sing all of them for us, the ones you like, the ones you have written, and the songs you will write while you are with us."

He sat back, and decided that he could manage that. "A castle, you say. With faeries. So, it'll be like living in the Middle Ages?" he asked the Queen dubiously.

She laughed. "My world is no more locked into the Middle Ages than yours is. I admit that we often prefer certain customs and clothing that are medieval in style and taste, but we are very aware of your world."

Despite his growing sense of uneasy apprehension about this adventure, he was completely charmed by her. "So, do you have television?" he asked, only half in jest.

"No, we don't have television. We don't need to watch it to have access to your world's noise. Television and most all of its offspring are *mortal* drugs, for all their communication benefits. Those things are largely irrelevant to us."

Thomas considered this. "Do you have electricity? Respectable plumbing? Hot showers? Alcohol?" His voice felt sharp and tight, rising in a slow panic as he realized that he might really be literally heading to an imaginary place called Faerie with someone he was beginning to believe might be its Queen. Was he actually enchanted, or would he wake up soon in his bed at the Caledonian with some woman he didn't recognize? He wondered if he was dreaming now, or only losing his mind. He did not dare to ask her about cocaine, but he suddenly wanted to, very badly.

Her voice was soothing, and she put her left hand on his thigh to calm him. "Relax, Thomas. Everything is fine. Hmmm...let me try to answer your questions. We don't have electricity as you're accustomed to it, but you'll find that Elvenhome has a lot of light, most of the time, and there is a kind of energy in the air that will give you access to things you might normally associate with the use of electricity. You may or may not encounter them, as you choose. As to 'respectable plumbing'," she smirked at this, "again, we don't have what you're used to; we have well-kept garderobes throughout the castle."

"Garderobes?" he asked.

"Yes," she answered. "Privies. Think of a very simple, clean septic system, minus the actual plumbing, and you have it. You won't give it a second thought after the first day or so, I can promise you that. There's one in your rooms, rather than down some dark corridor, and I don't think you'll find it too unpleasant.

"We don't have hot showers, of course, because we don't have plumbing. But we do have tubs for bathing, and we do know how to heat water. There are also several beautiful—and private—waterfalls not too far from the castle. I'll make a point of taking you there." Smiling, she patted his thigh, her eyes on the road. "And as for the alcohol, Thomas, you're in Scotland. Of course there's alcohol! The best whisky has been made in Scotland for centuries. Whatever you desire, you have only to ask. I think that you will be able to find anything you want to find in Elvenhome. So relax."

He wondered fleetingly if he was at all capable of relaxing, without benefit of drugs or booze; he was fairly sure he wasn't. He tapped his fingers nervously on the inside of the car door and fervently wished the joints stashed in his leather bag had been within easy reach.

"Now," she continued, pulling his focus again as she moved her left hand from his thigh and returned it to the steering wheel, "when you arrive with me at Elvenhome, you'll have some very important things to do. The first is that you will have to name everyone with whom you may have interaction of any kind, so that we'll all know who you're talking to, or about."

"What?" he asked. He was still thinking about the joints.

"Remember what I told you about True Names? You will not know anyone's True Name; it is not right for me to withhold my own from you but give you access to the True Names of the Folk at the castle. So you will give each of them names, and everyone shall answer to those names until you leave us. Do you understand?"

Thomas pondered this. After a moment he nodded. "All right. I can do that." He found that he was getting nervous and agitated, and wondered if he might strangle on the tension in his chest, but he was not going to mention it. At least, not yet. He could hold out a little while longer. He hoped.

Eyes on the road, the Queen made a small gesture with her left hand. A glimmer of green light leaped from her fingertips and then flashed for a fast second, unnoticed, immediately above Thomas' head.

She is utterly enchanting, Thomas told himself as he felt an inexplicable, warm relaxation seep into him. He forgot about the joints, and his fingers were now still and calm in his lap. Had he been edgy a minute ago? If he had been, he felt no evidence of it now. He settled comfortably into his seat and smiled at her.

There was a seductive twinkle in her eye when she looked at him. "Have you given any thought to what you're going to call me?"

He shrugged. "I've been thinking about it, Your Grace," he told her. "It's going to take a little time, but I'm getting there."

"Good," she said. "It would not do to have you 'Your Gracing' me in some of the more intimate moments we are going to share." With no overt provocation, his groin began to throb pleasantly; she laughed then, as if she had sensed it. "We are going to spend a lot of time alone, Thomas. I am hungry for your music, for your company, and for your body. I hope you're up for it." She grinned at him wickedly, and he couldn't help but grin back.

They didn't speak for a while, each lost in thought.

She was thinking of Elvenhome. She'd only been away for two weeks, but she had missed her castle and its people desperately. She was happiest when she was at home in Faerie, surrounded by familiar things. She knew she would be facing some razzing from the Folk at court for bringing another mortal to her bed. But the teasing would be good-natured as always; everyone knew how much she needed music and love, and no one ever begrudged her the right to have her pleasures. Not even—no, she didn't want to think about that. With no real effort, she pushed a particular thought away, and, watching the narrow Highlands road and the occasional car coming from the other direction, she drove northwest, summoning delicious memories of last night's sexual encounter with the man sitting beside her.

Thomas was pondering what to call her. She was right; "Your Grace" wasn't going to work, and he had already decided that he could never call her that facetiously. It surprised him that he'd bought into it all so easily, but he had. He had the excuse of enchantment to cover his thoughts and behavior at the moment—and as a man who'd lived his life by the power of excuses, he was good with that.

But what was he going to call her? Exotic names flashed across his mind, but they didn't seem to stand up next to his growing perception of her. He sighed, his frustration increasing. He was trying too hard. If he couldn't give her a name easily, how in the hell was he going to name an entire castleful of people? He had no idea how many people—how many names—that might be. His favorite excuse, the one he used when he did not wish to participate in some process or other, filled his mind with familiar comfort: *this thing was stretching his overtired creativity much too far.*

Except he was pretty sure that his excuse was not going to work with The Queen. The rules seemed to have been set before he'd gotten here, and he didn't see a way around them. At least not yet.

So he tried not to think about it, and watched the soothing Scottish scenery for a while until he realized that, of course, he was thinking about it.

He did not like to have to admit, even to himself, that the successful and effective naming of things was a gift he did not personally possess. Some musicians named their guitars; he didn't. He only pretended to have named his favorites, and maintained the fiction that each guitar's name was an intimate secret he had shared with no one, for some vaguely romantic reason. The Press and the fans had picked up this appealing fabrication, and handsomely embellished it over the years. All he had to do was close his mouth and let his seemingly modest silence speak for him; his embarrassing deficiency was hidden safely from the world.

Throughout his life, Thomas had failed miserably in the naming of just about everything, so he avoided it as much as possible. He once had a young Border collie that he'd named "You," until his then-current girlfriend had taken over and renamed it "Chopin." In the end it hadn't mattered much, because when they broke up, she took the dog with her. It had to be that no one understood his sense of humor when he named his first Mercedes-Benz "Crash." God help him, sometimes he wasn't all that good at coming up with good titles for his own songs.

That he was a gifted poet and brilliant and clever lyricist was never in question; he knew his way around songwriting whether he composed the music or the words. That he himself had not come up with the perfect titles for some of his most beloved songs was a source of private frustration and no little fear. It taunted him and gave the lie (or so he believed) to the overall quality of his music, of his place in the industry, of his true ownership of the art, and of the validity of the public image of Thomas Lear.

He knew that many record producers helped in naming or renaming songs, usually to make them more commercially viable. He also knew that other creative teams had input that sometimes led to changes. It was all part of the normal business side of creativity. He knew that, and appeared to accept it on the surface, making sure his poetic dignity was potentially caught in the crossfire, so that everyone contributing to the process would always walk softly around his artistic ego.

He never let anyone see the relief he felt when he got brilliant assistance with some pretty lame working titles. Despite his stunning record sales and his sold-out concert tours, he did not need any help in feeling like a fraud.

He would never admit to anyone, not ever, that he had not been the one to name "Dangerous Blue Eyes," which was currently one of his favorite lyrics out of the hundred or so that he'd written so far. While he had composed the poetry, the "dangerous blue eyes" had been almost a throwaway; he'd very nearly lost it. That his last official girlfriend, Annie DiMeo, had been around that day, keeping him company in the music room, was all that had saved the thing, allowed him to capture the elusive magic and translate it into something that was pure Thomas Lear.

"I think you're missing it, Thomas," she'd commented, looking up from a piece of paper he'd wadded up and tossed into the wastepaper basket with dozens of others. "But this line, 'I lose myself in her dangerous blue eyes,' you've got a glimmer here...maybe you could pull the focus away from the narrator and put it on the woman with the blue eyes?"

Instantly he had looked at Annie with the beginnings of an affronted glower, but knew in less than a breath that she had found the right words, ones that he had missed this time. So instead he blew the breath out hard, put out his hand for the discarded page she still held in her own, and accepted it from her with a chagrined chuckle. "Thanks, Babe. Maybe there is something there. Not the direction I was aiming for, but what the hell, it's worth a shot."

Delighted to be of genuine help to him, Annie beamed. "Start by calling it 'Dangerous Blue Eyes,' Thomas, and thread that through the full lyric, and see where it gets you."

Lost now in the words on the once-crumpled page, Thomas had nodded absently, and Annie had gone off to get coffee or booze or something. By the time she'd returned to the music room, the rewrite of the lyric was finished, and he was already toying with a possible melody line.

The song had won a Grammy, as had the album of the same name. And the world tour that followed it later bore the title as well. Thomas had thanked her privately countless times (and countless more times he had privately hated her for it). He could not forget that Annie DiMeo, the talented poet and ex-girlfriend who had lasted all of eight hot and heavy months, had actually framed and named one of his best songs. More than that, he could never forget that he himself had not.

So what the hell was he going to name the beautiful woman who sat beside him, driving silently northwest along the Highland road? God, he had to think of something. And it had to be good. She wasn't going to want to hear that he was lousy at this, and that he didn't want to do it. What was he going to do?

Think, dammit, he whined to himself, stealing glances at her through lowered eyelids. *Think!*

He already loved the sound of her laughter, but he did not want that laughter to be directed at himself. He had to come up with a name that would fit her.

His mind was a complete blank.

Miserable now, Thomas forced himself to retrace his steps since he'd left Los Angeles. He thought of the stewardess he'd banged in one of the plane's downstairs crew lavatories; her name had been...but he was terrible with names, he always had been. This was not helping.

His tired mind wandered through the plane's landing in Amsterdam (where he'd picked up some good drugs), then the landing in Edinburgh, where the taxi took him to...

With no warning at all, his mind instantly slipped into a comfortable, familiar space as the element of his nature that wrote beautiful songs abruptly unlocked itself and flowed freely through his awareness. He gasped mentally. He hadn't felt this in months. The realization that his own magic was back made his heart ache a little, even as it soared. But the ache didn't last; it faded effortlessly into the flow as his creative energy took over.

There was no question in his mind (or in his body, for that matter) that she was going to be his Muse for a while, maybe for the next year of his life. A Scottish, no, a *Caledonian* Muse, he smiled to himself. He already had small snatches of melodies playing in his head. Distantly his fingers itched for his guitar, but he let the feeling pass. He knew he would remember them later.

He considered the Muses he'd known personally, and dismissed those women from his past with a determined shrug. He then bypassed the Muses he knew from literature; those women and goddesses had belonged to someone else. He wanted a beautiful name for his very own Caledonian Muse. But what could be beautiful enough for the Queen of Faerie?

His reverie was involuntarily interrupted by a sudden and strong urge to touch her; images and scents and feelings tied to the previous night's activity on Calton Hill brushed with infinite sweetness across his thoughts. He glanced at her furtively; she was calmly driving, her thoughts clearly elsewhere, a dreamy, distracted look on her face. He smiled to himself and, remembering the night, returned to the task at hand.

seven

AT A PETROL station in Perth, they each cleaned up a bit in the rest rooms after Thomas filled the tank. The Queen brought a small plastic jug of water and two paper cups back from the cashier when she paid for the gas.

They got on the A9 near Perth, and drove north.

"Thomas, there are some rules you must honor and learn and abide by for all of your time in Faerie. Breaking those rules would be disastrous for you."

"No pleasure without some pain?" he joked.

"This is not a matter to be taken lightly," she told him patiently. "You must listen, and remember what I tell you."

He sobered, because she had. "All right. I'm listening."

She let out a deep breath. "From the time we enter Elvenhome, until we leave, you may not speak to anyone except me, unless you are in your own rooms, or are in the gardens immediately behind your own rooms, or unless you are quite certain that we are completely alone, anywhere in Elvenhome. The only exception to this is when I specifically give you leave to speak, which would be when you are singing for the court, or if I grant you permission to participate in conversation outside of your rooms. And in the event that I tell you to be silent, even if you are speaking only with me, in private, you must be silent, at once. Do you understand this?"

Thomas considered her words carefully; this was going to be a challenge. "Yes," he said slowly.

"The other rule is that at no time are you to eat the food of Faerie. You may drink the water, which is sweeter and purer than anything you can get here in your world, and you may have as much water as you choose. But the food of Faerie is absolutely off-limits to you. You are not to taste it, or to touch it." He made a face of protest; she cut him off with a reassuring smile. "You aren't going to starve, Thomas. Food that is familiar to you will be available for you at any time you wish. The food will be brought from your world, and prepared in our kitchens. You will have meat and fowl and wine and fruit and cheeses and sweets and whatever else you may desire, prepared by faerie hands, but procured directly from your world. And as a token that the food has come from your world and is not of Faerie, whoever brings you food will be able to tell you precisely from where it has come so that no mistake is made, and therefore there will be no chance that you will eat Faerie food.

"It's very important that you understand this. Have I made it clear enough?"

He nodded, ticking the items off on his fingers. "Yes, Your Grace. I don't speak to anyone at all outside of my rooms, without your express permission. I speak only to you unless you tell me not to speak at all. I stay away from all Faerie food, but I can drink the water. I've got it."

She sighed happily. "I'm glad. Keep faith with these conditions, and your time with me shall grant you all the things you require, spoken or unspoken."

He gave her a startled look. "That's an interesting choice of words."

She was unperturbed. "Just so," she said, her eyes on the road.

He changed the subject. "What would happen if I broke the rules? By mistake, of course," he added hastily.

"If you break faith with the rules, you'd never be able to leave Faerie, Thomas, no matter how much you yearned for your life here." She turned her head and gave him a grim look. "Do not toy with it. You must trust me about the ways of enchantment; there are things more powerful than..." She let her voice trail off, reconsidering her words. "I've seen mortals who have been forced to stay in Faerie after breaking faith with the rules. You don't want to condemn yourself to permanent separation from the life that you've worked so hard for. Obey the rules completely, keep them ever in your mind, and all will be well."

"I will," he promised, nervously pushing the thought of bad consequences away, and suddenly wishing very much that he had a drink.

Just after eleven a.m., they were nearly five hours north and west of Edinburgh. The Queen finally stopped the Fiat in front of The Queensgate Inn, a large, beautiful building that seemed more accurately described as Tudor than Tudor-style. It fronted a vast, lush forestland. "This is it," she said.

"We're in Elvenhome?" he asked stupidly. He was tired, and hungry, and a more than little overwhelmed by the events and possibilities of this day.

"No," she said lightly. "We're going to eat, and rest, and spend the day here. You are tired, and we still have much to discuss. We'll go to Elvenhome tonight."

"Oh," he said.

She turned and reached for her cloak, which was still folded on the back seat, and got out of the car. "Thomas, is there anything in your leather bag that you need before we get to Elvenhome?"

Getting out of the car tiredly, he stretched. "No," he answered, without thinking.

"What about your guitar? Will you need it before midnight?"

"I don't think so," he said, coming around the back of the car toward her.

"Very well," she said. She stared hard at the contents of the back seat. "Go," she ordered casually. Basket, guitar case and overnight bag disappeared at once in a bright flash of sparkling green light.

Seeing this, Thomas stumbled and nearly fell against the Fiat. "What the hell—what just happened?" he gasped.

She blushed at his obvious distress. "Sorry. I'm usually more subtle than that, but I'm tired, too." She flashed him a quick smile, but it didn't make him feel any better.

He looked rattled and a little ill. "Where did they go?"

She took his hand. "They're in Elvenhome. Unless you want them back here now...?"

He shook his head. "No. Don't bring them back. Just leave them. Damn…" he muttered. She laughed as she took his hand, then led him up the steps and through the front doors of The Queensgate Inn.

The Inn's only identifying feature indicating it as a bed and breakfast establishment was the very small but recognizable B&B logo next to the door bell, and a weathered gold plaque that stood beside the front door:

By royal appointment of the High Queen. Come and go as ye will, and do no mischief, else recompense is due. Come and go as ye will, and merry meet!

The place seemed much larger on the inside than it had from the outside, Thomas thought as he checked out the elegant yet friendly-looking lobby. It was comfortable and spacious, white walls with a high ceiling and dark, exposed hardwood beams. A solid staircase led up two floors. The sofas and oversized easy chairs that tastefully filled the lobby area were inviting. A blazing log in the huge fireplace gave the room a cozy sense of home.

While Thomas had been looking around, the Queen had moved directly toward a tall, attractive light-haired woman seated at the small maple reception desk, which stood beside the staircase. The woman, who was probably in her late forties, looked up from her paperwork when they entered. She stood at once, and with a joyful smile welcomed the Queen with a hug. Thomas was startled to see recognition and affection shining from the woman's eyes, although he was beginning to think he shouldn't be surprised by anything that happened around his lovely, mysterious companion.

"It's wonderful to see you back, Your Grace," the woman said happily, in a broad Highland accent. "I trust you're well?"

"Very well, thank you, Sheila," the Queen replied with a grin. "How is Sean, and how are the children?"

"Oh, they're all very well, Your Grace," Sheila declared. "Your room is ready. We have no other guests at the moment, so your rest will be undisturbed."

"Excellent," said the Queen. "Did you get instructions from…?" The Queen didn't say a name, but Sheila knew who she meant.

"Yes, Your Grace. I understand you'll be with us until just before midnight?" The Queen nodded. "Is there anything that you'll need before then? What about luncheon? And dinner?"

Both the Queen and Thomas were hungry. The Queen thought for a moment. "Sheila, would you please send a light lunch to the room? And dinner, also sent to the room, at around seven?"

"Done, and done, Your Grace," Sheila replied. "And if you think of anything else you would like, just let me know." Sheila opened the drawer of the reception desk, and took out a key, which she handed to the Queen. "There you are. Rest, and you'll have luncheon in about fifteen minutes, will that do?"

"That will do quite nicely, and I thank you." The Queen placed her hand on Thomas' arm, and they walked up the stairs to the first floor.

The door opened on a room that was big and bright, cozy and warm. The peat fire gave the place a scented glow that was at once inviting and soothing. The room was decorated in warm tones of several shades of forest and herbal green. It had a king-sized bed with a nightstand positioned on either side, a small dresser, two comfortable navy blue easy chairs with green wool blankets across their backs. A round oak table with two chairs placed before it, and a bowl of apples on it, stood in the center of the room, across from the fireplace. A small but comfortable bathroom was located through a door on the far side of the bed.

Thomas sank gratefully into one of the easy chairs. "You've been here before," he pointed out to her with feeble consternation, stating the obvious and not caring at all.

The Queen dropped her cloak across one of the dining table chairs. "Yes," she answered. "Since it's so close to Elvenhome, relatively speaking, it has always made sense to come here when there is a need for travel."

Thomas eyed her warily. "She knows who you are."

The Queen grinned. "Of course she does, Thomas. Sheila and I have known each other for her entire life. I knew her mother very well." The Queen reached for an apple, and bit into it hungrily. "And her grandmother, and her great-grandmother, too. Jane was a wonderful woman," she added, remembering her first encounter with a very young Jane, forever ago.

As she stood beside the dining table, the Queen watched as Thomas rubbed his eyes and his neck. He had a headache. "Lunch will be here soon. Would you like to relax in the shower, and then you can rest after we eat? You look as though you're going to growl at me." He looked over at her, and slowly eased the frown from his face. "That's better," she observed. "There will be clean towels in the bathroom, and anything else you need."

He smiled a little tentatively, and stood up. "Actually, that's a good idea." He moved toward the table to head for the bathroom, and as he neared her, she put her arms around him and kissed him softly.

His smile was steadier when he closed the bathroom door behind him.

Thomas felt much better after his shower; his muscles had relaxed a bit under the streams of hot water, and he found he was much calmer. Right before lunch arrived, the Queen took a shower too, and now they both sat at the table in warm, white bathrobes, sporting damp hair and easy smiles as they ate ham sandwiches and drank ale.

He reached for her hand and kissed it. "I think I've come up with what I'm going to call you. Pending your royal approval, of course."

She looked at him expectantly.

"Well," he began, "I have a reason for it, and I'll tell you that first, so you will understand what I was thinking. The name itself doesn't come close to suiting you, of course, but it's kind of an abbreviation. I don't know you very well yet..." He looked at her and rolled his eyes. "I'm maundering. Sorry."

Her smile widened, but she said nothing.

He laughed then. "You're not going to help at all, are you?"

"Not until I have a name," she said tartly, and shook her head, making her hair sway.

"Fair enough." He covered her hand with both of his own. "I know you're going to inspire some new music, and new lyrical poetry. I like the idea of having my own Caledonian Muse and so I'd like to call you 'Callie'," he finished softly.

"Callie," she said, testing the sound and deciding she liked it. "Say it again, and look at me," she told him.

"Callie," he said.

"Done," she said, with a tone of command, accompanied by a brief, nearly imperceptible sound: tiny bells, dancing far away. "For the next year and a day, I am 'Callie.' It's a good name, Thomas, I thank you." She leaned over and kissed him on the cheek, and then chuckled.

"What's funny?" he asked, suspicious now.

She eyed him devilishly. "Aren't you going to tell me how you truly came up with the name?"

He looked at her in surprise. "What?"

"I'm not certain that you pulled 'Callie,' which I like very much, from 'Caledonian Muse,' so I'd like to know the Truth of it."

The Truth of it? Busted, yet still hoping he could pull it off, Thomas was beginning to think he'd rather die than have to tell her.

"I am waiting. And I think it unwise of you to keep the High Queen of Faerie waiting, Court Singer or not," she said, struggling to put a feigned imperious threat on her face.

He wondered if he could yank something passable out of the air and still get away with it. One look at her efforts to smother the growing amusement in her beautiful brown eyes made him groan as he gave up altogether.

"All right! All right! But you won't like it," he whined.

With a little effort, she composed her face, and watched him.

He fidgeted, then straightened himself, and faced the music. "All right. When I was walking into the bar at the hotel, I heard someone refer to the Caledonian as 'the Caly.' I didn't even know I'd remembered the name." Thomas felt himself blush in a flood of frustrated embarrassment. He knew it had sounded bad when he'd thought of it; it sounded worse now.

She was quiet until he finally met her gaze.

"I have been named for a hotel?"

"Uh, yeah," he admitted with a pathetic frown.

"I see," she told him, considering this. "You have named me for a hotel."

Exasperated, Thomas did then what Thomas did best under similar circumstances: he got angry. "Well, at least it's a *good* hotel, isn't it?"

The High Queen of Faerie did then what the High Queen of Faerie did best under similar circumstances: she laughed merrily, with delight and invitation dancing in her eyes.

He couldn't help it. His sudden anger dissipated at once. The tenderness in her laughter blew it away, candles snuffed by a swift and sweet autumn breeze. He found, to his amazement, that he had begun to laugh too.

She stood up, and pulled him with her. "Where are we going?" he asked.

"Don't you *want* to christen me?" she countered, with a wicked twinkle in her eyes as she led him in the direction of the bed.

"That was the nicest christening I've ever been to," Thomas murmured into Callie's long and delicately pointed ear much later. She snuggled closer to him, her head beneath his chin, as she lay curled in the circle of his arms. "That may well have been the nicest christening *anyone's* ever been to."

She sighed, happy and sated. "Yes, I could do with a year and a day of you," she whispered.

He smiled, brushing her hair out of her face. "Can we talk about this? I mean, there are things...I have questions I probably shouldn't ask, but I can't help thinking..." He winced good-naturedly at his lame attempt to frame a question.

"Thomas, I have no need to withhold information from you. What would you like to know?"

"Well, Sheila downstairs knows you, and you said you've known her mother, and her grandmother, and her great-grandmother. How often do you do this?"

"Do what?" she asked, not unkindly. "Share my body with a handsome and gifted mortal whose words and music move my head and heart? Or, come to this place? Or, take men into Faerie? What?"

"Yeah," he said, and they both laughed. "All of those things."

Callie propped herself up on one elbow, and faced him. "I use The Queensgate Inn as a stopping place between Elvenhome and your world. It's safe here, and it's convenient, of course.

"I love music, and am drawn to musicians and poets, and pursue them when I choose to, within what I consider to be 'reasonable limits.' But that is not what you're really thinking about, is it?"

"Do you see how strange this is, from my point of view, even setting all the surreal stuff aside? Obviously, it's not that alarming for you, and that's a good thing—"

"Quite so," she interrupted with something not unlike a lazy smirk.

"—but I know the tale of the Faerie Queen, Callie. And I'm trying to get my head around this."

Callie kissed his bares shoulder, then nipped it with her teeth. Thomas closed his eyes and breathed in sharply, smiling in spite of himself. "All right," she said. "Ask your questions. But do not be tedious. Ask me the real ones."

Thomas considered this for a moment, and then began. "Okay. One of the early literary appearances of the Faerie Queen mythology came in the story of Thomas the Rhymer, who, as I'm increasingly certain that you know, was a thirteenth-century Scottish folk hero of sorts." He studied her eyes for a reaction, but didn't find there what he thought he'd see: she was regarding him with keen interest. He continued. "Thomas the Rhymer, poet and singer of songs, runs into the Faerie Queen in the Highlands of Scotland, flirts with her, wants to kiss her, and does, for a price. Right?"

"That is the tale," she agreed, the corners of her mouth twitching upward despite her best efforts to keep her face impassive.

"We've already established that the time of service to the Faerie Queen, at least in the stories I know of, is seven years. I understand the levels of significance of the number seven, and the use of the seven years as a literary and religious device. But back to the story, there are rules that Thomas the Rhymer must abide by, or he cannot return home at the end of his seven years of service. Right?"

"Right."

Thomas pulled himself up and leaned on his elbow, looking at her. Their faces were six inches apart. "Am I Thomas the Rhymer for you now? How often do you do this? And why do you do this, Callie?"

She beamed at him. "Good questions, all. Here are your answers: No, you're not Thomas the Rhymer, you're Thomas *Lear*. What is somewhat curious, though, is that while I shall always think of him as "My Rhymer," I am certain you are aware that he was also known in life and in literature as 'Thomas of Ercildoune' and once he inherited some more property, he was called 'Thomas Learmont'. You are Thomas Lear.

I don't believe in coincidences, I never have, so perhaps there is some strange magic at work meant for me as well. Would that it were so," she added to herself, with a wry smile. Then she shrugged at Thomas and continued: "But you are not so like the Rhymer, in face, in voice, or in heart, that I could easily mistake one of you for the other. So no, Thomas, you are yourself. Thomas the Rhymer was My Rhymer, but his time is long past."

He wondered if he detected a small catch in her voice. He met her eyes kindly. "Did you love him?" he asked carefully, not wanting to hurt her.

"My Rhymer? Oh yes, in my way, I loved him. But that was forever and forever ago, and in truth isn't worthy of any more mention than it got in the old tales." Callie moved her hand down the side of Thomas' face. "As for how often I do this, I think the only true answer I can give you is 'not very often from my perspective, but perhaps rather often from a mortal point of view'."

He was puzzled by this. "Let me see if I can help you to understand," she said. "I go through times in my life when I am lonely, times when I crave music not just for my own soul but for the souls of all the Fair Folk living in Elvenhome. And when feasting and dancing and chess and hawking and singing and riding and playing and dreaming no longer fill all of my needs, I choose to spend some time with someone with whom I can share myself for a time. The man I select brings me his music or his poetry, shares his body and his soul and his mind with me. In turn, I share myself with him. The time is sweet, and when it is over, he returns to his life, and I return to mine."

"And then?" Thomas prompted.

"And then, I move through my days and my years until a loneliness consumes me again, and I look for someone else to help free me from it for a time. Does that seem decadent or wanton to you?

"No, and yes," he admitted truthfully. "However, it somehow seems like a very good idea." Something else occurred to him: "How many men have you encountered in the world and taken with you to Faerie?"

She stopped and thought about it. "Seventy? Perhaps as many as one hundred over the centuries. The numbers, and alas, sometimes the faces, blur. I rarely look backward, Thomas. Memories sometimes can come at much too high a price..." She trailed off into an inner place he could not go, but she caught herself, laughed gently, and added "but we could find out if you truly wish to know the exact number."

He looked at her in utter amazement; he was thinking about something entirely different. *Centuries?* Seventy or one hundred mortal men over the centuries??? The implications held him tightly by the throat, shook hard, and would not let go. He gaped at Callie, stammering.

She met his stare calmly. "Yes, Thomas?"

"You said '*centuries*', Callie," he sputtered. He realized that he sounded and probably looked a little crazed, but he couldn't help it. It was almost too much for him.

She smiled at him sweetly. "Perhaps you should not ask questions you are not prepared to own the answers to, Thomas." She patted his hand. "Maybe you should start with something a little more palatable?"

Taking a long, deep breath, he regrouped and asked a different question. "Okay, so who have you taken with you to Faerie?"

Callie sat up in the bed, and, thinking for a moment, furrowed her eyebrows together. "That you might recognize, you mean?" Thomas nodded, eyes wide. "Well, Edmund Spenser, but he turned out to be a fat, demanding, bellowing swine, so I gladly gave him to one of my Ladies instead for his seven years, yes it was seven years then," she said, catching his eye. "And it was a long seven years, too," she added with a roll of her dark brown eyes. "And The Bard was here..."

"Shakespeare???" Thomas' voice came out in an awed whisper. Satisfying images of "Titania" streaked through his mind, but he ignored them. He didn't want to miss what she was telling him.

"Oh, yes, he was here, too (by his real name, though, of course). But I was thinking of William Yeats just then. And my sweet Rabbie Burns, naturally. Dylan Thomas—a magnificent Court Singer, marvelous to have around when he stayed a little sober. And—" She stopped abruptly when she noticed that Thomas' eyes had gone glassy. "What is it?"

He was gawking now, and more than a little dazzled. He thought about the body of work these men had produced, and of its mystical, magical content. He felt a thrill growing steadily in his stomach; it moved tantalizingly toward his chest. "I can see it, Callie, it all makes sense. It makes sense that they knew you, it makes sense that they were in Faerie, and they wrote pure magic. Wow..."

She kissed him on top of his head. "I told you last night I'd been considered a Muse before."

He pulled her firmly against him, and kissed her soundly on the mouth. "So you did."

"Not all of my mortal lovers have been famous men," she said later. "Most of them were local, of course. Travel was not what it is today. In his own way, each man was greatly gifted, beautiful to look upon, and most often entirely unknown. No, I did not rattle the wide world when I charmed mortals; I touched only gently the smaller worlds within it."

They were lounging across the bed eating apples. "When's the last time you took a mortal to Faerie?" Thomas asked, keeping it casual.

"Thirty years ago. He was a singer and poet in Glasgow. He stayed with me a year and a day, and then went on to write some more wonderful music." She smiled at the private memory of her last Glaswegian lover.

"Do you fall deeply in love with all of your 'Court Singers'?" he questioned her, hoping he'd asked lightly enough.

She faced him squarely. "No. It doesn't always happen. Sometimes there is only the excitement of having someone new close by, of learning a new body or mind, of being around new poetry and music. I don't fall in love with all of them. Sometimes it has backfired on me, too," she added with a rueful grin.

"Backfired? How?"

She shrugged, and then laughed out loud, genuinely amused. "Well, once or twice, the poor mortal in question had no eyes for me at all, apart from the excitement of the initial encounter. I have had to relinquish a few to the loving arms of one of the men at court." She chuckled, and Thomas, stunned, stared at her, his eyes wide with surprise. "Some of them were only interested in the creation of their music or their words, some had eyes for other ladies at Court. A few regretted their initial demands of me, and pined sadly for mortal women they'd left behind, and tried to stay true. They were obligated to service me at my will, but I rarely force anyone into my bed." She eyed him speculatively. "There were some, though, that I loved from the very moment I heard or saw them. Does that answer some of your questions?"

"I think it does," he conceded. "Can I ask one more?" She nodded. "How did you find me? I wasn't even thinking about Scotland a month ago."

She got up to put more peat on the fire, then came back to lie across the bed. "I dreamed about you, dreamed that you were coming here to Scotland. So I left home, came Upworld, and waited for you. Once I knew that you were indeed in Edinburgh, the search wasn't that difficult. Despite your attempt to keep a low profile, your fame helped me locate you quickly enough." He gave her a questioning look. "I have many ways to get information. Comes with the territory, Thomas." He nodded, and she ran her fingers through her hair absently as she spoke. "I've been away from Faerie for only a little more than two weeks, as you measure time." The interrogation over, Callie stretched like a cat, slowly and sensuously.

"I'm beginning to get a small sense of your networking abilities," Thomas remarked. "Sheila downstairs, the man who brought the car—"

Callie smiled. "You'll see him again, later tonight. He's not mortal, like Sheila. He's Fey. I have a very strong sense that you and he will like each other."

Thomas rolled onto his back and stretched. "This is unreal, Callie. No one would ever believe me if I told them about this."

"That's part of the point, isn't it?" she replied, now making a not-too-subtle play for the knotted belt of his bathrobe. "Mortals seem to understand and enjoy the magic that their poets and singers make for them, but they never completely believe it, no matter how true the words are. In that way, we're all safe in the hands of the poets, are we not?"

He hadn't thought about this before: *Safe in the hands of the poets.* He did not think he'd ever kept anyone safe with his own fevered words, but maybe that was something worth pondering, some day...

Before he could fall into deeper introspection, he realized that the belt of his bathrobe was untied. With a swift movement of Callie's hand, his robe came fully open from his chest to his knees.

"You know," he teased her with a decidedly devilish grin, "I could be on the road to falling in love with you."

The delicious wickedness in her eyes challenged him at once. "Of course you are falling in love with me. After the first kiss, Thomas, you had no choice in the matter. That is the First Law of Enchantment."

Callie's robe hit the carpeted floor beside the bed as she reached for him.

Dinner arrived at seven. After they'd eaten, they settled comfortably in the two easy chairs in front of the fire with a bottle of whisky, and talked. This time Callie asked the questions, wanting to know more about Thomas Lear than just the songs and the music.

He did not hear disapproval in her tone, nor could he read censure on her face when they talked about his use of recreational chemistry. "But why do you play with the drugs and the alcohol, when you carry such immense creative energy inside you? Don't you worry that you'll lose the music?" she asked.

Thomas frowned. "I worry about it all the time. And sometimes the fear that I'll lose the music makes me drink more, and do more drugs. I can't explain it. I don't think I'm an addict." He laughed, but there was a hint of sadness in the sound. "Which makes me wonder if I probably am one. But I like the way the drugs make me feel, and the drinking calms me down. I have needed the help."

Thomas drank deeply from his glass. One thing was clear to him: he would not tell her about The Monster In His Head. There was no point; she could not possibly understand.

"Truly, though, Thomas," Callie continued, "Do you not feel as though you're putting your gifts at risk?"

The seriousness in her tone was close to sobering. In his own defense, he shrugged off the game and answered her as directly (if not as truthfully) as he dared: "I don't think the drugs or the booze are really that much of a problem, because I don't need them, not really. I just like them." He'd never said these words aloud before, and he hoped he'd delivered them off-handishly. His ability to stay glib in the face of any honest self-pronouncement had kept him steady for years.

"Oh," she said. "And what are you trying to hide from, that you would imperil your music and perhaps your sanity and your soul?"

Thomas—and The Monster In His Head—nearly jumped out of his skin. She had deftly cut to the heart of him but, remarkably, there was no blood, and no searing pain, as there often was when he dared to ask himself difficult questions. He was going to have to make sure he didn't underestimate the quickness of her wit, her apparent sensitivity, or her exceptional intelligence.

"You are stalling, Thomas Lear," she murmured with quiet kindness. "I have answered your questions, and now you must answer mine. From what are you hiding?"

He did not know how to answer Callie's question. And even if he had known what to say, he would not have wanted to speak the words. He had always been content to articulate his private pain, fears and frustration through his music; he had control of that. But to sit across from this staggeringly beautiful and bright woman, and show her the tattered flags planted in the fertile but shaky ground of his soul? How could he talk with her about the things he never, ever wanted to completely know about himself?

He opened his mouth to protest, to put her off, and then, feeling awkward and lost, he closed it again, his discomfort almost palpable in the air around him. The Monster made silent threats, and Thomas held his breath.

Callie gave him a small and steady smile of encouragement.

"Let me see if I can help you," she began. "I have known many musicians and poets; some were easy with themselves, others weren't. I learned long ago that some of the burdens that serve to make magnificent poets and songwriters are the same burdens that can cause them the most pain." Their eyes met, but he had nothing to say.

"Does your life hurt you so very much?" she asked in a low, sad voice.

The look in her eyes was so gentle and so infinitely comforting that he could have wept. *What could she possibly understand about your life?* hissed The Monster angrily. Agitated now, Thomas wanted to shout at her then, or howl like a wounded wolf, move away from her, or maybe hit something. He felt trapped by the profound kindness he saw in her face. With an almost tangible bitterness, he realized that not only could he not change the subject, but in this moment he also could not give her anything but his own truth, even if he had to dig too deeply to go after it.

His voice came out in something just below a whisper, but he forced it out as best as he could. Once the words started, he was powerless to stop them:

"It's about worthiness. I suppose it's about never being good enough, no matter how good the collective "they" say I am. It's about always being hungry, never being satisfied, not wanting to live tied up in knots over things I can't seem to change, but living tied in knots just the same. It's about needing, and reaching to touch something I can never seem to completely define, and trying to live with the knowledge that whatever it is, it's right there, scant inches beyond my grasp. It's about the compulsion to say true things in a way that no one else has before, but not being able to, because there doesn't seem to be much truth in me, no matter how hard I try. And it's about explaining me to myself, which seems to be the most impossible and frustrating and pointless thing of all." He took a deep breath; he had run out of air. He had also run out of words, and he moved back into the unerring safety of his glib humor. "And you want to spend a year and a day with that?" he smiled ruefully, in spite of himself.

She smiled back. "I won't say that I completely understand everything you said—and more importantly, everything you meant, Thomas—but, yes. I can and will spend a year and a day with you, the music and madness and the poetry and pain, all of it. And if I can give you ease, I will, in my way." She got up from her chair, took the two steps over to his, and leaned down and kissed him, as if sealing the bargain one last time.

Callie brushed his cheek with her own, until she could feel him smile. "It's difficult to be a romantic in a very practical world, isn't it?" she whispered in his ear. She didn't wait for a reply, and added, almost to herself, "It's not always easy to be a practical person in a very romantic world, either."

She sighed, straightened, and ruffled his hair. "It's nearly eleven. We must prepare to go."

Thomas did not hear the quiet words Callie and Sheila exchanged just inside the front doors of The Queensgate Inn at eleven-thirty that night. He stood on the steps and gazed at the stars above him as the women said their goodbyes in breathy giggles and low-pitched conversation. He saw them embrace. Callie laughed in that light, sparkling way she had in the bar at the Caledonian...was that only *last night?* So many things had happened to him in such a short span of time. No wonder everything felt so damned surreal.

While he waited for Callie, he gave himself a quick mental check-up, a useful habit left over from the early days of long touring and hard drinking that had helped him function over the past five years. He let his thoughts wash over him. Was he all right? He smiled in the moon-dappled darkness; he was fine. He admitted to himself that he felt a little raw and exposed after his talk with Callie, but he also knew he felt energized by her. Callie herself was an amazing paradox, unfathomably complicated, yet basic and genuine in her simplicity. She was grounded and centered in ways he didn't know how to understand, and yet she was still as ethereal as tonight's starry sky. The sex he'd had with her had been intense and earthy and freeing and ecstatic, and he was already learning to want her in subtle ways he couldn't remember having wanted a woman before. There was so much to her, and he was filled with the desire to discover all of it. He wasn't certain that what he was feeling for her would qualify as story-book enchantment, but he did find Callie undeniably enchanting nevertheless. He smiled at her moonlit silhouette in the doorway. She was beautiful, but he already knew that she was more than that. How *much* more was going to be an adventure he resolved to move through carefully, not just because he had seen how powerful and other-worldly she was, but because instinct told him that he didn't want to miss a single moment with her. His body was relaxed and comfortable. He hadn't had coke in more than thirty-six hours.

He was going to think more about how to get some cocaine, but Callie and Sheila finally parted then, and Callie walked out the front doors and down the steps toward him, slipping her arm around his.

"Ready to go?" she asked him, eyes bright with anticipation.

"I wouldn't miss this for the world," he told her, and he meant it.

They walked around the far side of the Inn, in the general direction of some outbuildings positioned behind it. Thomas assumed they were heading for the garage, and he moved toward it. "How far is the drive, from here?" Thomas asked.

"It's only a short ride. But we're not driving," she said, a smile lighting up her face as she pointed at the barn.

Cassane was an extraordinarily handsome white-gray stallion. He stood a full fifteen hands high, and watched with radiant, liquid brown eyes as Callie and Thomas approached. He nickered happily when Callie kissed him on the face and patted him with an affection indicative of a long and cherished friendship. Cassane shook his proud head; there were silver bells woven into his long, dark mane, and they chimed softly.

The horse was bridled but not saddled. He seemed anxious to move, although he waited with what could only be described as exaggerated patience. Murmuring to the horse in words that Thomas could barely hear and could not understand, Callie eased into her woolen cloak and fastened it at her throat. After one more kiss and pat to Cassane's long face, she smiled at Thomas. "Let's go," she said, and swung herself up and onto Cassane's back. Then she reached her arm down to Thomas.

Thomas was studying the unsaddled stallion. It had been twenty years or more since Thomas had ridden bareback. He knew he could handle it for a short distance, at least.

Something else occurred to him. "Why not a Unicorn, Callie? After all, you are the Queen of Faerie."

"Don't be silly," she chided.

He frowned up at her. He had given himself points for getting into the spirit of the thing, and now she wasn't playing. He was serious as he asked, "Why is that silly? You're not going to tell me that Unicorns don't exist, are you?"

"Of course Unicorns exist. It's just that a Lady has to be a virgin to ride one, and that kind of lets me out." She snickered in a most unladylike fashion that delighted him.

"Come," she said, her arm still extended. She held his arm and pulled easily as he swung up behind her. He did not have time to ponder her surprising physical strength, but he would be thinking about that later. At the touch of her hand on his thigh, he put his arms around her waist, and held on.

"Wow," he said, "Cassane is patient. He hasn't really moved since we walked into the barn."

Callie laughed. "Cassane can be very patient, when he chooses to be. It depends upon the day, I suppose. He waits around for as long as he can bear it, and when he can't stand still any longer, he just…goes! Don't you?" She clicked her tongue lovingly at the stallion. "And woe to anyone, Elf or Dwarf or Queen, who keeps the noble Cassane waiting!"

They left the barn in a slow walk, and then trotted for a couple of minutes, until they reached the edge of the forest. The Inn was behind them, somewhere close by in the darkness. Before they crossed into the forest, Callie stopped, and put a hand on Thomas' thigh, squeezing it. "Are you all right?"

"Fine. It's been several years since I've been on horseback, and longer still since I've ridden without a saddle, so I might be sore tomorrow, but this is great."

"Good," she said softly, satisfied.

He had a thought. "What about your car?"

"Car?" she said.

"Your car. The Fiat…" He was struck by a strange, alarming thought. "Was that…?"

Cassane shook his head and did a little dance. The fifty-nine bells woven into his mane winked and sparkled in the moonlight, pealing sweetly.

"Thomas," Callie's voice came from in front of him, and she spoke quickly, in a noble effort to suppress a merry giggle, "I was serious when I told you never to ask questions you do not want to own the answers to."

Thomas' mind tried to bend of its own accord. Images danced crazily through his head like wildfire: *Pearl-gray car. Bells. White-gray horse. Bells.* No, it couldn't—could it? No, he assured himself it couldn't be. No way. He refused to believe it.

And so it followed that she wasn't the Queen of Faerie, he hadn't seen the stuff in the back seat of the Fiat disappear into nothingness, and he wasn't on a horse with a woman he'd only met last night, headed out of his real life and into hers for a year and a day.

Oh, shit…what was he doing? If he thought too much about this…

He took a steadying breath, and then another, focusing fixedly on the strong and very pretty hand that was still squeezing his thigh, the strength in her touch an anchor of reality in what his mind told him now could not possibly be real.

Thank God I'm a heavy drinker and an experienced substance-abuser, or I'd never get past this, he groaned to The Monster In His Head. The Monster mumbled a few words of disapproval, then went immediately to sleep in self-defense.

Callie's laughter cascaded across Thomas' uneasy ruminations. "Last chance, Thomas. Are you all right back there?"

He tightened his arms around her. "Let's do it."

"Hold on," she said, and gave the stallion a light squeeze with her legs.

In that moment, thirty-nine-year-old Thomas Lear, Rock Star, Gifted Musician, Womanizer and Soulful Poet, turned his hungry heart and tired mind away from the world as he knew it, and went with his Queen toward Elvenhome, in the lands of Faerie, without so much as a backward glance.

Cassane leaped headlong into the woods. Trees glided past them in the peaceful darkness; Thomas knew without fear that the stallion would not falter. After a few minutes, Callie gave Cassane his head, and with a sound that might have been a deep and happy laugh, accompanied by the soft, clear chiming of tiny bells, the magnificent horse very nearly flew through the forest, bound for home.

eight

Once upon a time there was an old woman who lived in a quiet cottage near a still and beautiful lake in the Highlands of Scotland. She lived alone with her two cats, who were called Abbey and Tristan. The old woman spent much of her time working in her flower garden, talking to Abbey and Tristan, and writing faerie tales. She was content in her small and uncomplicated world, and her writing kept her happy. It kept her publisher even happier, for she was one of the few people on earth who was keeping the magic of the Fair Folk alive with her many stories, and her books sold well enough to maintain her quiet, comfortable life.

She had been a widow for many years. Since the death of her beloved husband, her world had become a modest and sometimes lonely one, and over the long, empty days of her solitude she learned to appreciate and even cultivate the blessings found only in silence, and to be at peace with the world inside her cottage.

One evening, just as the autumn sun began to fade into a somber and dusky September sky, the old woman walked along the path by the lake. She was pondering a new tale for her next book of stories as she strolled, taking the time to watch with some amusement as a noisy family of ducks played in the water. She walked past an elder tree; he was considering dropping some of his browning leaves and taking a long nap. The old woman touched the tree fondly as she passed him.

She ambled along for some time, when out of nowhere an unexpected sound snatched her attention. Alert to it now, she kept walking, her gait remaining slow and steady. Listening carefully, she thought she heard the soft but unmistakable tread of footsteps behind her. This was odd, because she didn't have neighbors; her cottage was isolated, with the next nearest house some miles away.

Strangely, the old woman was not afraid. She did not stop and turn to see if anyone was walking behind her. She slowed her steps even more and tried to listen.

After several more paces, she was certain that someone was indeed moving up behind her. She stopped then, and whirled around to confront whoever it was.

The sound of the footsteps silenced when she turned; there was no one there. Or, rather, she couldn't actually see anyone there. But she felt as though someone were standing several paces behind her, whether she could see him or not.

"I am sorry I have nothing to offer you," she said in a calm voice to the person who wasn't there. "You'd be far better off if you went on your way, and found someone else to walk with."

With that said, the old woman turned and walked serenely back to her cottage, where she cooked dinner for herself and for Abbey and Tristan.

That night, while she was in bed asleep, instead of dreaming of her beloved, long-dead husband (which she did on most nights), the old woman dreamed of a hundred faeries dancing wildly around a huge bonfire in a dense forest beside a lake. She dreamed of Elves singing sweet and lyrical songs into the night skies, of Dwarves drinking ale from silver tankards, and of Pixies gleefully picking the pockets of the

Goblins who were serving food to all the merry Folk gathered there.

And she dreamed of a Water Faerie. He was tall and lean and, like most Water Faeries, he was entirely beautiful. He came out of the lake almost as if he were walking up a broad flight of stairs; his movements were graceful and purposeful. He was dressed in nothing but starshine and moonlight; he was glorious in his skin. She saw shining rivulets of water run off of him; in the breathless moments as she watched, the moisture on his skin and hair evaporated entirely, and he was nearly dry as he stepped on to the solid ground of the forest floor. Greeting the Folk who approached him, he had a ready smile for everyone. A Dwarf handed him a silver goblet, and he drank deeply from it. He seemed to look around for a moment, intent on finding someone.

She wondered who it could be.

Then the Water Faerie turned and, to her surprise, he smiled directly at her from across the bonfire, nodding his head and beckoning her with a strong and graceful hand. The glowing moonlight shone on his straight, shoulder-length golden hair. She could see him clearly, and couldn't take her eyes from him. *Come and dance,* she heard his deep, melodious voice whisper in her mind. *Come and dance the night away with me.*

Before she could tell him that she was too old to dance, she woke up.

The dream had been so vivid that it took her quite some time to go back to sleep. And when she did fall asleep, there was a smile on her face.

The old woman was amazed that the glowing memory of the dream stayed with her all the next day, and the day after that, and the day after that one—which was the day of the storm.

She liked storms, especially the storms that blew through the Highlands in the autumn. She liked the noise and the way the trees and tall grasses shuddered, and how the wind moaned and roared through them in the swirling rain. She always left a window open when the skies thundered and the rain fell hard on and around the cottage. The fragrance of storms was one of her greatest pleasures. The most furious squalls, with howling gusts of wind that hammered heavy rain against the house at night, were her very favorite ones.

As she sat in her rocking chair before the fire, sipping hot tea after her dinner while watching Abbey and Tristan play with a couple of crumpled-up wads of paper, she listened to the sounds of crackling thunder. She savored the delicious scent of the storm outside as it wafted in through the open window.

The wind was howling and the rain was slapping torrents of angry water against the cottage when a sudden flash of lightning lit up the night. The old woman glanced at the open window, and in the lightning flash, she saw that someone was standing on the other side of the window frame in the cold and heavy rain, looking in at her.

In less than a heartbeat, she recognized him.

It was the golden-haired Water Faerie from her dream, the one who had invited her to dance.

The old woman stared at him for a long moment, surprise and disbelief crowding out any thought of danger or fear. When she met his gaze, he smiled brightly at her. She stood up and moved to the front door, which was beside the window through which the handsome Water Faerie continued to watch her.

She opened the door wide, and said quietly to him: "Come in, then, if that is your wish, and get yourself warm and dry."

Nodding, he moved gracefully into the room. And before she had a chance to close the door or to say anything to him about how wet and cold he was, or ask how long he had been standing at the window watching her, he gently reached for her hand, and kissed it – softly and lingeringly. Her lonely heart filled with amazement and wonder; it had been a very long time since she had been kissed. Although she was nervous, she did not pull her hand away.

She did not know what to say to him. She could only watch him as he continued to kiss her hand.

When their eyes met again, they understood that there was no need for words.

"THAT'S REALLY PRETTY, Maggie, but you didn't get to the part about *me* yet," whined the Spriggan, pacing impatiently at her feet. He was almost three feet tall, and covered with coarse, wispy brown hair that had probably never seen a brushing—or even much of a cleaning, for that matter. He had a head that looked like a confused and unlikely cross between a large, rabid cat and a small, worried fox; he was all hair, teeth and eyes. The eyes that looked up at Maggie were black and definitely feline; they were the most prominent feature on his face. He was long-eared, long-limbed, and had a small, strong and compact body. Apart from his eyes, which seemed to be always vigilant, almost wary in observational motion, his most arresting features were his hands, which were small but long-fingered and amazingly agile. These twitched constantly, even when he slept. His voice was high-pitched and insistent. "I was outside the window, too. What about me?"

Sitting in her rocking chair, rearranging the pages from which she'd been reading aloud, Maggie smiled down at the Spriggan, whom she called "Menace," because most of the time, he certainly was one. "I'm not finished with the story, Menace, I've just barely begun it. This is as far as I got with the writing today."

"Just don't forget that I was there too, getting all wet and waiting for my chance to—"

Pushing her dark hair behind her ear, Maggie interrupted him with a knowing smirk. "You were waiting for your chance to kiss my hand, too?"

"That's right!" barked the Spriggan, who did not like being laughed at.

"Spriggans don't generally kiss the hands of ladies, and you know it well," said the golden-haired man sitting on the couch by the fireplace. It was September, and there was enough of a moist nip in the Scottish Highland air to warrant the cozy peat fire that was burning there. He smiled as he dusted either cat hair or Spriggan hair from the knee of his jeans. "I'd be more likely to wager that you were planning to bite her on the ankle."

The Spriggan turned and looked up at the man with as much dignity as he could manage. "I would *not* have bitten Maggie on the ankle."

"Yeah, right," Maggie remarked, rolling her eyes.

The man, whose name was Arrendel, winked at Maggie. "He probably would have. He's done it before."

The Spriggan glowered at both of them, and stamped his foot before he strode across the room to the fireplace and sat down in a huff, his back to them. "She has nice ankles, though," Menace muttered under his breath.

"That she does," Arrendel agreed.

Arrendel watched Maggie as she finished the dinner dishes, his eyes following the delicate movements of her hands.

She felt his gaze on her, and looked at him from across the room. "What is it?" she asked.

He sighed happily, smiling at her. "Nothing. I simply enjoy watching you move."

She stuck her tongue out at him, and he laughed. "Ever the one to take a true and well-meant compliment, my sweet Maggie." He nodded toward the evening on the other side of the window. "Come; walk with me."

He would never have to ask her anything twice. She closed the cupboard door, dropped the dish towel neatly on the counter below it, and walked toward him.

A sleepy, raspy voice rose from a pile of fur on the floor in front of the fireplace. "Do you want me to come with you?" Menace asked, opening one eye and moving a long, orange-striped cat tail out of the way so he could see Arrendel and Maggie. The Spriggan was snuggled between Abbey and Tristan, the three of them enjoying their regular after-dinner nap.

Arrendel suppressed a laugh at the sight of them. "No, no, stay here and sleep. We're going to walk around the lake a couple of times."

Menace closed his eye. Abbey, who was awake now, licked her front paw and gave her face a quick wash, and then licked Menace's closest ear. "All right. But if you need me..." he sighed, drifting off back to sleep.

Maggie laughed. She still couldn't believe that her cats had taken so easily to the nasty little Spriggan. They had, in fact, accepted him long before she had, now that she thought about it. *I'll have to write that story someday*, she told herself.

Arrendel slipped a heavy blue sweater over her shoulders, zipped up his own jacket, then took her hand in his and led her out into the early evening's slowly fading light.

They walked to the lake, and began the circuit around it. They passed Maggie's favorite elder tree. "It's going to be a chilly winter," Arrendel observed. "Your tree here has dropped almost all of his leaves, and it's not even the end of the season."

"I like chilly winters, now," Maggie murmured, squeezing his hand.

"I know," he grinned.

They'd walked for a few minutes, watching the autumn evening fall around them, when he looked down at her and asked, "Why this tale? And why now?"

She looked at him, and shrugged. "A version of our story? Oh, I don't know. I've been thinking about it lately, and since that's what's in my head, that's what comes out on paper." She stopped walking and studied his face. "Is it something you don't want me to write about? Because if you don't, Arrendel, you know that I'll—"

He put his fingers lightly against her mouth to quiet her. "Oh no, Sweet One. Tell the tale, if the telling pleases you."

The pale blue eyes that looked up at him seemed unsure. He put his arm around her and they started to walk again. "Tell the tale. I know a certain Spriggan who will love it, and who will also drive you mad every step of the way until it's finished."

She laughed then, and he felt her relax. "I wasn't ready to tell any version of the tale before now," she told him, her voice so low that she might have been speaking only to herself. "These last two years with you have been among the best of my life." She slid an arm around him now, and they walked holding each other. "I had forgotten what it was like to be this happy."

Arrendel gave her an affectionate squeeze. "I always believed that I was completely satisfied with my life as it was, until I saw you. You changed everything for me, too, you know. Finding you, and loving you, has been one of the greatest gifts of my life."

"You only wanted someone else around to deal with The Menace." she teased.

"Oh aye, there was that, too." He slid his hand under her the back of her sweater and tickled her waist. "He is such an awful burden," Arrendel laughed.

"There are days I'd prefer to drop-kick him out of the cottage." Maggie tried for firmness, but giggled instead. "Can't you see him flying through the air, ears-first, out the front door?"

He stopped walking, and bent down to kiss her. "You are not nice, Maggie." The kiss was sweet and long; he took his time. "And then again, you're also *very* nice, too," he mumbled against her mouth.

"Tell me why," Arrendel said as they finished their walk around the lake in the dusk, "in this new tale, you refer to the woman the Water Faerie comes to as 'The Old Woman'."

She looked away from the water, slammed her hands into her sweater pockets, and glanced at him. "Why?"

"Yes. Why?"

"It was probably a reflex; I'm not sure I really thought about it very much." They both knew she was fudging a little, since Maggie had a tendency to overthink just about everything that crossed her mind, but Arrendel chose not to point this out. Busted, Maggie continued: "The women in Faerie tales are either beautiful and young or not-so-beautiful and old, aren't they? They're goddesses and queens, or else they're hags and black-magic witches. Literature is filled with one or the other, and most readers don't like to be pulled away from the archetypes that often make the stories 'faerie tales' in the first place." He didn't comment, so she continued. "Arrendel, you can't begin a faerie tale with *Once upon a time, there was a middle-aged, average-looking woman who lived in a small and quiet cottage...*—it just doesn't work. Middle-aged women are not all that interesting in the scheme of things related to faerie tales." She hoped she sounded convincing; she had answered him more flippantly than she'd intended.

"All right, then," he said. "I suppose I'm wondering why you would specifically cast yourself as The Old Woman instead of The Young Woman."

Maggie grunted, as if that was the best answer she had.

"You're young, Maggie," he pressed.

"I am forty-five years old. That's not young, it's decidedly middle-aged."

"You're a lot younger than I am," Arrendel suggested.

"You're roughly eight hundred years old," she declared, with a hint of asperity. "*Everyone's* younger than you are, Arrendel. Countries are younger than you are. Land masses are younger than you are..."

He chuckled; he couldn't help it. He loved her when she was like this, moderately cantankerous, a little moody, and largely unwilling to easily give him the key to the heart of whatever was bothering her. Yes, something *was* bothering her, he could feel it. He knew her too well and loved her too much to push her before she was ready to tell him what was on her mind. He already had a good idea of what that might be. He wanted to spare her some emotional frustration, so he nudged her to try to get her to talk to him about it. He sensed that she wanted him to know, but that she wasn't happy about the telling.

"...Literature is younger than you are. It's alarmingly possible that *fire* is younger than you are," she continued her litany until he laughed long and hard. She gave him a dismayed smile but did not laugh with him.

He took her hand. "My dear, I assure you, I am not older than fire. Nor, just to set your mind at ease, Sweetheart, am I older than the wheel. Both were in use some months before I was born, or so I've been told."

She gave him a look of mock gratitude. "Well, that's a relief."

They were back at the cottage. He led her through her garden, and over to the bench swing that hung from the eaves on the side of the house. After flipping the switch that turned on a small light mounted above, he sat down on the swing, and when she did not, he gave her hand a small tug, his eyes sparkling. "Come. Sit."

She could never resist him when he had that look on his face. She sat beside him, and looked out at the garden as the last flicker of true daylight glided into night. She was calm and quiet on the outside, but, as he held her hand, he could still feel her tension.

"Talk to me, Maggie." She tried to wriggle her hand out of his, but he held on to it. "Tell me."

She didn't look at him. "It's nothing."

"I know," he said, and waited.

"It's really stupid," she told him.

"All right," he said.

"It doesn't matter," she added.

"Apparently it does matter," he countered.

She turned and looked at him, suddenly glad he was holding her hand and wasn't letting go. "Do we have to do this right now?" She was uncomfortable and self-conscious, and she was irritated about that, too.

His voice was tender, comforting. "No. We can do it anytime you wish to. I don't like to see you unsettled and frustrated, if talking will soothe it for you."

She strangled the urge to move into his arms and cry until she felt better. Things were as they were; mostly she accepted that. How could she not? And yet...

"Maggie?" he said into the silence.

She sighed, resignedly. "It's really stupid, Sweetheart," she repeated. When she saw that he would wait quietly all night if need be, she gave up and simply told him.

"My birthday is next week," she explained. He nodded but didn't speak. "My birthday, Arrendel. I'll be forty-six."

"I know that," he said gently.

"In the years after Sam died, I didn't much care that I was getting older. It didn't matter. Aging was aging, we all do it, life happens, life ends, we move on. I was fine with that. I didn't ask for anything more." She searched his face, willing him to understand without having to hear her tell him anything else. She shook her head and continued. "And then I met you. Oh, not the way we meet in the tale I'm working on, of course, since that belongs just to us—but we met, and you are so beautiful. And I was already past forty when we met, and before I met you it was okay with me that I looked it. But now..." her voice trailed off, and he put his arm around her to ease her with closeness.

"...But now," Maggie went on, "there are more and more gray hairs coming in, my skin is getting crêpey, my body is changing...and for all your years, you're faerie, my Sweetheart, you're practically immortal— and timeless and beautiful and strong, and will stay that way even as I continue to age. I don't delude myself that I'm going to age any more gracefully than any other mortal. God, I can't bear it, the thought of you having to live with some scary, ancient version of me."

Arrendel pulled Maggie closer, and held her against his chest. To her utter mortification, she began to cry. They both knew that she had gone as far as she could in the telling.

He brushed her dark curls with his lips, and whispered into her ear, "And you believe that it's possible that I'll stop coming to you."

She held on to him tightly. "Oh, God, Arrendel...I wouldn't blame you; I couldn't. I understand, I do! But I'm so very selfish, and I love you, and..." Maggie cried harder; she couldn't help it.

As he held her, making reassuring sounds to calm her, he felt another wave of love wash over him for the woman he held beside his heart. He disagreed with the idea that she wasn't aging well. He found her beautiful to look at, brilliant and witty to talk with, mostly a pleasure and sometimes a challenge to be around, and magnificent to make love with. But she didn't need to hear these things now; at the best of times, she would shrug them off. In this moment, she would flatly deny that he could truly feel this way, then she would beat herself with her own denials.

She was not always easy to deal with, but he loved her with every breath in his body. His soul needed her in much the same way that his body needed water.

She was composing herself now, her sobs collecting themselves into scattered hiccups. He found her adorable but did not smile yet; there was more to be said. The heart of the matter was at hand.

"This is really about the fact that I have to go back soon, isn't it?" Hearing this, she held her breath, and was grateful for the darkness around them. He held his breath, too, for a moment, and then expelled it. "It's only a little about getting older, isn't it?" She said nothing, couldn't make the words come. "Breathe, Lady Margaret," he said lightly, and she let go of the breath with a strangled chuckle. "This is about my going back to Elvenhome for a time. I don't want to leave any more than you want me to leave, but it has to be this way no matter how we feel about it, aye?"

She nodded but still couldn't speak. He noticed that since the truth was all the way out, she had released the tight grip she had on his jacket, and was relaxing a little. He hoped that she could face it more easily now.

"We knew, from the beginning," he said, as lightly as he could, "that we wouldn't be able to be together all the time. Because I'm Faerie, I can't stay away from my home too long—I have to go back, be around the Folk and the food and the light and the music and the air and the water that is Faerie if I am to survive."

Miserable, Maggie drew back, took his beautiful face into her hands, and met his eyes. "I know that," she sniffled. "I understand. I would never put you at risk."

He wiped her tears away with his thumbs, and left his hands on her face. "I know it well. The parting is never easy, Sweetheart, but it must be done. It's the only way we can continue."

"I know," she agreed, trying not to sound as wretched as she felt. "It's never been easy letting you go, Arrendel, but it seems that the longer we're together, the harder it is to accept. In the beginning, you were with me for a few weeks, and then left for a month or so."

"And I always came back, did I not?"

"Yes, you always came back," she conceded with a ghost of a smile. "As time's gone on, you've been here a month or more at a stretch, and then return to me after an even longer period away."

He looked deeply, searchingly into her eyes. "I always come back. I miss you terribly when I'm at Home, I long to be with you, and when I can leave there again, I always, always come back."

He kissed her then, hard, trying to erase her fears and sadness with his mouth. "I love you, Maggie," Arrendel said against her cheek. "I love you with my life, whether you're beside me or not."

"I love you," replied Maggie. "Whether you are here with me, or safe at Home."

"I will always come back to you, no matter what!" the Water Faerie exclaimed, his voice growing husky. He pulled away from her only so he could look into her face. "Say it!"

"You will always come back to me, no matter what," she repeated. "You will."

"I will. I swear it." He pulled her onto his lap and, taking her pressing his lips against hers again, he sealed the promise.

nine

OVER THE NEXT few days, neither Maggie nor Arrendel spoke directly of the coming separation. Talking wouldn't change it. Not talking about it made it seem as though the parting wasn't immediately in front of them, and that made both of them feel a little better somehow. She was not certain he had chosen the day, yet, but she did not ask him about it because she did not want to know.

They focused instead on her birthday, which was in a few days' time. He teased her about what he was going to give her to mark the occasion.

"I could," he said, mirth sparkling like sunshine in the blue oceans of his eyes, "see if I can't find you a Spriggan of your very own. I just have to figure out how to gift-wrap one without getting hurt."

Maggie scowled and made a most indelicate gesture. Caught off-guard by the ferocity of her movement and its translation, Arrendel burst into laughter. "Does that mean you'd rather *not* have a Spriggan of your very own?"

She couldn't glare at him for long, even in fun, especially when he was laughing. "Have you already forgotten what he did to my linen closet this morning?" she grumbled. "He tore it to shreds, Arrendel! He pulled the door off and tore out the shelves and—"

"I was trying to make it into a room of my own!" interrupted a loud, high-pitched voice from the outdoors side of an open window.

"—he rolled around on every single piece of the clean linen—"

"I was trying to get comfortable!" Menace barked.

"—and there was mud absolutely everywhere because the little parasite had been covered in it while he was playing in the dirt in the rain!"

Arrendel was still laughing, now slapping his hand against the top of the dinner table, trying to breathe.

"I said I was sorry," whined the Spriggan, who had been banished from the house. "And I've had a bath, Maggie..."

Maggie glared at Menace, who had just attempted a subtle move with one long and hairy toe slinking barely an inch inside the doorway, but stopped at once as Maggie's eyes narrowed into very threatening slits.

Arrendel, finally catching his breath, shook his head at the small faerie, unsuccessfully hiding a grin. "You'd have done a lot better, you know, if you'd at least offered to help her clean up."

Menace frowned, and confessed in all seriousness: "I was afraid she was going to stomp on me."

Maggie's eyes widened; her eyebrows shot up. She was both deeply offended and a little sick at the idea. "Stomp on you? *Stomp* on you?? That's the most hideous—" She looked at Menace, then at Arrendel, and then back at Menace again in horror. "How could you think a thing like that?"

Duly rebuked, the Spriggan swallowed hard, making a sorrowful noise. "I'm sorry, Maggie. I should have realized you'd never stomp on me."

"Damn right, I wouldn't. I'd never get the squashed Spriggan mess off my shoes," she told him, glowering with evil intention. Arrendel was laughing helplessly again. "Besides," Maggie continued, by way of explanation, "I'm not the stomping type. I'm the drop-kicking type. And if you *ever* make that kind of a mess again, Menace, I'll—"

"If I promise to be good, can I come back inside?" Menace whined.

Maggie rolled her eyes, but she nodded. "I'm not sure I believe you can be good, but yes, you can come back inside. Just stay out of my way, okay? And beware of my shoes."

Instantly happy again, the Spriggan leaped into the room and ran under the couch, looking for Abbey and Tristan.

"So," continued Arrendel smoothly, "That would be a *no* on the Spriggan for your birthday?"

She chuckled then, cherishing the laughter still shining in his eyes. "Yeah. That's a no. A *big* no."

They had just finished eating dinner when the telephone rang. Maggie rose and went to the table by her favorite cozy chair by the fireplace. She lifted the receiver. "Hello? Oh, hi, Nigel..."

Nigel was Maggie's editor at the publishing company in Glasgow. She'd been expecting his call. She sat down in her chair, and took her calendar out of the drawer in the table. "Yes," she said, "I'm fine. How are you? How's Ellen? Good." She dug around in the drawer for a pen, uncapped it, and made some notes on the calendar. "Yes, all right. Friday the fourteenth of November?"

Smiling, Arrendel caught her eye, and gestured that he was going outside while she talked. He opened the front door and stepped out into the crisp evening.

The Spriggan was waiting for him, sitting at the top of the stacked firewood just outside the door. "When are we going back? We should already be there," he fretted. "We're very late."

"I know."

"Too long," Menace explained. "I've been home three times. You've been here far too long."

"I *know*," Arrendel said again.

"It's not good for you to be away this long. We need to go soon."

"We will."

Menace's eyes mirrored the unhappiness in Arrendel's as he looked up at him. "Do you want me to—?" he began.

"Do nothing. I'll manage. It will be all right."

Menace hung his head, and vanished into the air.

A moment later, Maggie opened the door, wearing her heavy blue wool sweater. She handed Arrendel his jacket. "Nigel wants me to go down to Glasgow to proof the galleys with him. I told him early next month because by then you'll...be...you know. And the work will keep me busy until you get back."

"It'll be good for you to go to the city," Arrendel replied.

She looked at him critically for a moment. "Put your jacket on. Aren't we going to walk around the loch?"

He didn't meet her eyes, at least not right away. "Would it be all right if we didn't, tonight?"

She felt a little anxious, but didn't let it show. "Is anything wrong?"

"I'm only tired," he said. "We'll walk tomorrow."

She shrugged, and flashed him a smile. "Good idea. I'm tired, too. We should probably make an early night of it, what do you think?"

He nodded, kissed her on the forehead, and they went back into the house arm in arm.

She watched him sleep that night. She wasn't certain that she knew what she was expecting to see, other than his face relaxed in slumber. The moonshine streaming through the window over the bed streaked silver light into the long strands of his golden hair. He was sound asleep, and she had to admit that maybe he really was more tired than usual. She tried to remember if she'd noticed it before tonight.

He'd been here with her for very close to three months this time; usually he left after the second full moon they shared. She knew a good deal of Faerie lore, but she didn't know what, if anything, would happen if he stayed too long. How long was too long?

They had talked two years ago about the fact that he needed to return to Faerie regularly, but she had never pressed him so she didn't know whether it was that he needed certain kinds of food only found in Faerie, or if the air or water was really different and necessary, or if he had some kind of obligation that needed his attention. He wasn't committed to anyone else. She knew without a single nagging doubt that he loved her, and that he hated the thought of leaving her.

She touched his hair where the moonlight caressed it. She was tempted to touch his skin, to waken him, but she didn't have the heart to disturb him, so she settled for snuggling close, and breathed in the lovely scent of him. In his sleep, he turned toward her and she moved gratefully into his arms. He murmured her name, and she stroked his back until he fell again into deeper sleep.

Maggie spent the rest of the night memorizing Arrendel for the hundredth time.

The next day was Maggie's forty-sixth birthday.

Arrendel's gift to her was a delicate silver bell, no bigger than the first joint of her index finger. The bell hung from a purple velvet cord, and fell to just above Maggie's breastbone when he placed it around her neck. The bell was intricately carved; on its front was a lifelike quill pen, and on its back, a masculine, protective letter "A" wrapped around an elegant, feminine "M". The bell was beautiful, and Maggie's eyes were wide with wonder and delight.

"It is gorgeous! So delicate!" she gasped. "Thank you, Arrendel! I've never seen anything like it!"

"Very few people, mortal or Fey, have," Arrendel told her. He was sitting beside her on the couch, holding her hand. "I had it made especially for you. I brought it with me from Elvenhome."

"This is from *Faerie*?"

He nodded. "It seemed only fair," he reasoned with a wink, "since you've been keeping the place on the map for us."

"Is it...um...all right...that I have it, then? I can wear it?"

He laughed. "Of course it is, and aye, you can. It was made specifically for you, for us, actually. I have a friend whose family has crafted these bells from the silver in their own mines for generations. He was very pleased to do this for you; Rallien told me he has only had the opportunity to make five or six in the last forty years."

Surprised and thrilled, she put a hand on his arm. "Your friend. He's a Dwarf?"

"Not tall, but gifted in the art of fine silvercraft," Arrendel chuckled.

"This is simply gorgeous." She clasped the tiny bell between two fingers, and made it chime; the sound was sweet and comforting. "I love this! Thank you!" she said, then kissed Arrendel. "It is wonderful. And so are you."

She turned the bell over in her hand, studying it. She tested the soft, insistent sound as she gently shook it back and forth. She had never seen silver or art from Faerie before, and she was fascinated by it.

"There's more," he said.

"More?"

"More," he beamed at her pleasure in his gift. "This is called a 'Dunnor's Bell,' and it's a very rare thing, even in Faerie. And being from Faerie, there's—"

She interrupted him with a happy laugh. "There's a tale with it!"

Arrendel put his hand over hers and laughed too. "Yes, there's a tale with it...which I will tell you in a little while." His voice took on a rich, warm tone, the way she imagined he always sounded when he was in Elvenhome. She loved the way it surrounded her like a comforting caress. "But first, I need to give you, show you, something else."

Maggie nodded, and watched him.

He murmured, "Would you say that together we have found a true love?"

She had never doubted this fact, not once, from their beginning. "Yes. Without question," she assured him.

"I believe so, too." He opened her hand, and touched the bell that rested on her palm. "A Dunnor's Bell is a bond between true lovers. Once awakened, it sings and chimes and dances on its own when the lovers are near to each other. You can ring it and make it sing when you choose to, but once it's bound to us, it will also ring when we are near each other. That is the nature of the Bell. I have heard the tale, of course, but I had never seen any before this one, nor have I ever been bonded to one. But it is unique, Maggie, and it was made for you...and thus, for me, too." He sighed contentedly, and kissed her face.

Maggie understood the making and telling of faerie tales better than anyone Arrendel had ever known. "And is this the part where you awaken the Bell?"

"With your permission and blessing, of course."

She nodded, her eyes shining. "Do it."

Arrendel smiled. "As my lady commands," he murmured.

He moved her hand so that the Bell in it lay firmly against her heart, then pressed his hand over hers, so that they each touched the Bell. With his other hand, he took her empty hand, and placed it over his own heart, and held it there.

He closed his eyes, and said three or perhaps four sentences in what she knew was Old Elvish, beautifully-spoken words that Maggie could not understand, but could feel. His voice was resonant and strong, his words delivered in a cadence that was both powerful and reverent.

And then it happened.

The Bell in Maggie's hand felt moist, and began to move and pulse on its own. She drew in a surprised breath as a bright blue light flickered through the spaces between her fingers, and Arrendel's, around the Bell.

"It's all right," he told her. "It's going to move now. Just feel it."

The blue light was warm and inviting, and made her think of the very first time she'd ever seen Arrendel. Then she found herself remembering the first moment she knew she loved him. She felt the warmth from the Bell flowing through her hand into Arrendel's, and slowly into her chest.

She looked into Arrendel's face and knew that he felt it, too.

The now-sparkling blue warmth moved through Arrendel's other hand, which still held her empty hand against his heart, and moved into his chest.

He was radiant. "It is done," he breathed, then released her hands as he kissed her. "Happy Birthday, my Maggie."

Her Dunnor's Bell jingled merrily, all by itself, chiming softly as she kissed him back.

During dinner, he told her the ancient tale of Dunnor's Bell. The Bell around her neck, untouched, danced and sang softly in cheerful accompaniment.

"It's like background music filled with harmonies I can feel rather than hear," Maggie observed.

Arrendel nodded his head. "I wondered if the sound would begin to grate on your nerves, or mine, but I don't think this will, do you?"

Maggie was enchanted by her birthday gift. "Not at all. Not ever." She gave him a greedy, anticipatory smirk: "Now—where's my birthday cake?"

After cake (which had been purchased from the bakery in the village), they sat on the couch together as the autumn evening flowed toward full night. Maggie played with her Bell, making it ring over the quiet, steady chime it was already sounding.

"Well, I can see you aren't going to be bored with that anytime soon," he teased, settling against her with a cheerful wriggle. "Now, are you sure about not wanting your own Spriggan? Because if you change your mind—"

Giggling, Maggie climbed on to his lap. "In case you haven't noticed, I rarely change my mind about anything, and I'm usually right, too.

Especially about this. No extra Spriggans, thanks, Arrendel. Sometimes I can barely cope with the one we've got."

He spoke before he thought. "Then it's a good thing he's going with me, isn't it?"

They were both stunned at the words. "Oh, Maggie," he said, his eyes apologizing at once. "It just came out. I never meant—"

"No, no, it's all right," she whispered, hoping he didn't hear the small quaver in her voice. "Actually, it's a good thing he's going with you, since I don't know what I'd do with him here, really...he's been teaching Tristan some very bad habits." Rambling, Maggie moved out of Arrendel's lap and went over to the stove, shaking. "I'm going to make some tea. Would you like some?"

In a heartbeat he was beside her, his arms around her, holding her close. "I'm sorry. This is torturing you." The anguish in his voice made her look up at him.

"I wonder how many ways this is torturing *you*," she said with sad concern. "This is the longest you've ever stayed with me. Are you sure you're all right?"

Arrendel held her tightly. "I'm fine. Thinning a bit, I think, but that's something that happens." She tightened her arms around him anxiously, as if measuring his body. He chuckled; he couldn't help it. "Not 'thinning' like that. Thinning, kind of like 'fading,' although that's a little overly dramatic." He met her eyes seriously. "I've been away from Home longer than I should be. I'm well enough, but I can feel that I'm weakening. It's a little harder to breathe," he gasped and then laughed as she reflexively squeezed him tighter. She immediately released him, and he looked at her with more tenderness than she could bear. He tilted her head up to meet his eyes. "It's only a *little* harder to breathe, and my appetite's waning, but I'm not unwell. There's no danger. Don't worry."

She studied him closely, comparing what she knew of him physically with what she saw in front of her now. His eyes were still beautiful. Was it her imagination, or was their deep blue brightness muted just a bit? His hair seemed as healthy as it always was, right? She noticed, finally, that he looked dry somehow, literally as though his body desperately needed water.

And then the thought struck her, as sharp as a physical blow. It had never occurred to her before: he was a Water Faerie, a Water Faerie who looked dry, almost hollow, beneath the beloved features. She very nearly staggered under the weight of belated awareness.

As if he'd seen or even felt the force of the blow behind her realization, he grabbed her arms and held her tightly, looking into her face. "Maggie, what is it?"

She felt sick; she couldn't stand it. "Arrendel, Sweetheart, you have to go." Her eyes met his, emphatic in their demand. "You need to go now. Right now."

He just looked at her. "What?"

"You heard me. You've stayed too long. I don't know what the repercussions are, you can tell me the next time you're here, if you want to. But I don't want anything bad to happen to you because you stayed...because I wanted you to stay." She was frightened and worried, trying hard not to cry.

He pulled her into his arms and surrounded her with all the caring and gentleness he had in him. "My Maggie," he whispered as he smiled into her hair. "There's so little middle ground with you. Sometimes I wonder how you get through a week."

She laughed jaggedly at that, but told him: "I manage, quite well. And you know it." Her eyes were ferocious with love. "Arrendel, you have to get back to Elvenhome."

Releasing her from his embrace but still holding her at arm's length, he met her gaze, challenging the fear in her eyes with a look of intense determination he didn't usually show her. "I am not leaving you on your birthday. Tomorrow, or even the next day, will suffice."

She knew he would never lie to her; the Fair Folk do not lie. But just like mortals, they can sidestep the truth easily enough. She did not want him to have to sidestep to spare her, especially over this. She wondered if it wouldn't be better to simply stay silent and let him decide what he wanted to do, and when he wanted to do it, and let it go at that, no matter how she felt about it. It was certainly the way mature, sane people handled the business of their lives, each individual taking responsibility for his own issues. She wanted to let go of her fear for him. She would shut up, and let him tell her himself when he should leave her. Yes, that was the best and most loving thing she could do. And she would tell him just that. She stepped a little away from him and opened her mouth.

"I want you to go *tonight*," she told him, her commitment from only seconds before evaporating in the face of her raw need to protect him. She didn't want it to be this way, but there was no help for it. She knew that she'd have plenty of time to think about all of this later, when he was gone for weeks or months...

Arrendel turned and walked to the couch, and sat down. If he hadn't looked tired before, he certainly did now. He reached out a hand to her. "Come, Maggie."

She couldn't help it. The look in his eyes melted what little resistance she thought she had. She went to him, took his hand, and sat close beside him. "I love you," she sighed.

"I'm very glad to hear it, because I love you, too."

The Bell around Maggie's neck chimed a bit louder, as if jubilantly underscoring their words.

"Well," Maggie said a little bitterly, "at least we all have that part settled."

He kissed her hand. "It's a good thing to have settled, all things considered. Now let's go upstairs." She stared at him, surprised. "Please, Maggie, I'm not dead, I'm only leaving for a while!"

Afterward, they decided that he would in fact leave late that night. She knew that he was not feeling as well as he wanted her to believe he was. Still, she noticed that he did not lie to her, nor did he attempt to evade answering any of her careful questions.

Arrendel would leave with Menace at moonrise. No, they did not need anything from the cottage for the journey. Yes, he would be strong enough to return safely to Elvenhome. Yes, he would come back to her as soon as he could. And yes, he would miss her terribly (Maggie didn't ask this, but Arrendel said it anyway).

"Once I kiss you and close the door, I want you to stay inside, and find something to keep you busy," Arrendel instructed, his eyes searching hers. "Don't watch me go. It will be hard enough on both of us.

She had never actually seen him leave her before; he generally left when she was asleep. "But..." she began.

"No, Maggie. Let it be. I'll leave at moonrise, and I'll be back," he promised.

Her jaw was hard and set; she had made up her mind. "Arrendel, I want to watch you go, this time."

"No," he said firmly.

"Yes," she said, just as firmly, but with an edge of steel that made him smile in spite of himself. "Please?" she asked.

Arrendel sighed. "You have a good idea about what it will look like," he protested, "and I'm not certain that it won't bother you. I'd imagine it looks very strange, and maybe frightening, to mortals, my love. I'd prefer not to have you upset by it."

Her hands shook slightly. "I'm going to be upset anyway, what with missing you and wanting you and worrying that you're safe. Oh, come on, basically I know what to expect, Sweetheart. Let me watch."

He felt a piece of his heart shatter, along with what was left of his resolve. "Oh, why, Maggie?" he asked.

She couldn't help it. Her eyes filled with tears. "Because I will always, always want one more look at you."

The night was clear and cold. They walked toward the loch together in the darkness as the moon rose brightly above them. Bundled in her favorite shawl, Maggie had stopped crying, but her eyes and nose were red, felt hot in the chilled air. Arrendel wore a long woolen cloak, under which he was sky-clad for the journey. They held hands and talked of small things. She imagined that the Bell around her neck chimed now with a muted sadness.

Maggie stopped, and looked around. "Wait a minute, where's Menace?"

"Don't worry about him. He'll turn up."

"What could he possibly be doing?"

"I believe he's saying goodbye to Tristan and Abbey," Arrendel answered.

Maggie made a dry sound that might have been a laugh on another day. "He's going to give them fleas," she observed.

There was a grin in Arrendel's voice. "I think he already has, Love."

She squeezed his hand. "Don't tell him, but I'm going to miss him, too."

He squeezed back. "I know it. Shall I make sure to bring him back with me next time, then?"

"Do I have to answer that right now?" she replied as tartly as she could, and they both managed a weak smile.

They walked in silence for a time, holding hands. When they arrived at the loch, Arrendel looked up at the moon, bowed his head, whispered something soundless into the air, and then met Maggie's eyes. "It's time to go."

Unable to speak, she nodded bravely as they slowly unclasped their hands.

He kissed her with infinite care, imprinting the taste of her on his lips. At last he turned away from her, and handed her his cloak. His naked body was beautiful in the moonlight. She found herself wondering how long it would be before she could touch him again.

Arrendel cleared his throat and called: "Come, Spriggan! It's time!"

In the small space between Maggie and Arrendel, Menace appeared a heartbeat later. He was crying, and he was covered with two different colors of cat hair. Seeing him, Maggie nearly snorted in spite of herself, but showed a little mercy in the face of his sadness.

"Good Journey, Menace," she said. "We will miss you here."

"*Merry meet, merry part, and merry meet again,*" Menace said, speaking the ritual solemnly, and meaning it.

"*Aye, Friend,*" replied Maggie, completing the round of the blessing.

Menace looked up at Arrendel. Eyes focused on the water, Arrendel said, choking on the word, "Now."

Menace disappeared at once in a bright flash of yellow light.

Arrendel did not turn around. "You can still leave, and not watch," he suggested.

"I'm staying." Her eyes were dry, but her voice was ragged. "And by the way, Arrendel, I love you."

"I love you," he murmured, stepping into the freezing loch.

As he walked toward the deeper water, the moonlight kissed his hair and shoulders, making him completely visible to Maggie. He moved through the loch with a grace and ease that startled her; she knew how very cold it was. The farther in he went, the more elegant and fluid his movements were. Her throat caught at the radiant loveliness of him.

He didn't turn around to look at her.

She didn't expect him to.

He walked until the water came up to the center of his chest. After that, he seemed to glide forward toward the center of the loch.

When he reached the center, his skin began to shimmer and glow in the moonlight, slowly at first, then faster and more brightly.

Maggie stood on the shore in miserable but fascinated silence.

It was unclear to her whether Arrendel was trembling violently in the water, or if the water was somehow reacting to his glittering presence. All Maggie knew was that the water and the faerie in it were both vibrating, tapping into some energy she could only guess at.

And then, without a sound, Arrendel's body lurched forward, and melted into a swirling arc of crystal-clear water, and blended into the loch as he changed form and was gone from her.

Her Bell stopped its chiming, grieving and silent against her heart, under the folds of her shawl.

The ordeal over, Maggie gasped in spite of herself, and closed her eyes, her heart beating too hard.

She was not sorry she'd seen the process of his departure, or, at least, she didn't think she was. She forced herself to take a few breaths for Arrendel. All she cared about was that he would be all right now. It didn't matter a damn that she was already missing him.

She began to shiver as she walked woodenly back to the cottage with the cold comfort of Arrendel's cloak in her arms. It was only when she let herself in the front door and closed it behind her that she allowed the tears to come.

ten

RIDING IN THE semi-darkness, through pockets of alternately thick and then light fog, lit regularly by varying degrees of streaming rays of moonlight, Thomas had an unsubstantiated sense that their trip to Faerie was not exactly what it seemed to be. He was certain that the wood behind The Queensgate Inn hadn't been this large, but all in all, he didn't mind. The huge horse plainly knew where he was going, and Thomas had the distinct impression that if Callie were riding Cassane alone tonight, the white-gray stallion would be galloping homeward rather than trotting through the night.

Thomas' arms were comfortably around Callie's waist as they rode. Her back rested against his chest, and he could smell all the fragrances that she carried with her: the green earthiness that he loved, some musky personal scent that he couldn't specifically identify except as part of her, the faint whiff of fresh rosemary in her hair, the warm wool of her cloak mingled with the fragrance of night jasmine and, underneath it all, the subtle but unmistakably heady smell of sex. He inhaled deeply, memorizing the redolence of her. Enchantment or not, he decided that he could be willing to breathe her into himself like this forever.

He sighed. When she turned her head at the faint sound, he kissed her ear lightly.

"That's nice," she murmured, her hand moving back to squeeze his thigh when his arms tightened around her waist.

"Mmmmmmm," he said, and she laughed.

"We're almost home," she said. "Do you want to stop and rest for a few minutes before we get there?"

"That would be good," Thomas replied with an air of practicality. "I've been arguing with my bladder for a while."

In a small area of the woodland, untouched by the fog, where a small group of trees stood protectively in a semicircle facing east, Callie halted Cassane. The stallion stood patient and still as Thomas slid from his back, and then reached up for Callie to help her dismount. "Good call," she commended him with a wink. "I have been, too."

Ten minutes later, Thomas and Callie walked together in the thicket, stretching their legs. "If we're almost to Faerie, I think you've gotten some bad press over the years, Callie," he teased.

"How so?" she asked.

"In most of the literature that I'm familiar with that generally relates to the journey to Faerie, when the Queen takes the man out of his world and into hers, it takes a long time, days or weeks, depending on which story you're reading." She watched him, eyes bright with interest, but she made no comment. "There are usually heavy moral choices involved," he continued, warming to the subject, "and literal and archetypal roads to choose. Long explanations from the Queen to the hapless, helpless enchanted mortal about the meaning of life." Hands stuffed in the pockets of his jacket, he raised an eyebrow inquisitively as they circled back toward Cassane. "So, where's my series of life-affirming, cosmic metaphors?"

Smirking, Callie slipped her arm around his waist as they walked. "No metaphors, Thomas. There never really were any, apart from a storyteller's poetic license, and whatever truths he needed to tell for his own edification. The journey is now what it always has been, mostly. And how someone writes about it, whether he's actually taken the journey to Faerie or only imagines it, is up to him. I never interfere with the story that anyone elects to tell, be he mortal or Fey. Despite a person's private moral dilemmas, sometimes the story itself is what's important, right?"

"Well, then," moaned Thomas, with mock wistfulness, "there goes my last chance to do battle with classical medieval metaphysical devilry and come out on top."

She laughed merrily. "Perhaps, but perhaps not. You can find your moral dilemmas any place you choose to look for them." She met his gaze with kindness shining from her eyes. "The trick is in not needing to look for moral dilemmas. And also knowing when to look at them, and when to let them go."

"Uh-oh," he said. "We're getting into metaphorical territory. Back away, Ladies and Gentlemen, and do it slowly," he joked. "No, really, though, Callie, according to the literature, the journey to Faerie traditionally has been long, and sometimes difficult, chock-full of blood and suffering and death imagery, with the requisite pointers to the bliss of heaven and our worst fears of hell...and I've got to tell you, sliding into Faerie after a jog through the woods on horseback with you is a lot easier on mind and body. The soul, too, I'd imagine. Maybe it doesn't make as great a story, but I'll take relative comfort over heavy-handed archetypal fiction in this case. Which is unusual for me—I'm always happier if I've got a little extra fiction rolling around in my life."

They were close to Cassane now. Callie stroked the horse's head and face, praising him, before she responded to Thomas. "Well, then, perhaps this is exactly the right adventure for you, Thomas. I trust that the fiction your brain needs won't obscure your ability to see the facts your heart needs while you're living in Elvenhome."

Her words jolted him, but before he could consider whether they'd stung him or not, she gave him a smile that softened the seriousness of her tone. Stepping away from Cassane and closer to Thomas, Callie took his hands and stared hard into his eyes, all but forcing him to hear and heed her words.

Unspoken ritual danced with enchantment in the air, but Thomas would not realize this until much later. All he saw was beautiful Callie standing beneath the moon and the stars as she spoke to him:

"We're ready to go now. **Remember**: do not eat any food unless you know exactly where it has come from. You must not eat faerie food by mistake. The water of Faerie is safe for you, faerie ales and wines are not. **Remember**: do not speak to anyone at all, even when they speak to you, if you are not in your own rooms, or if we are not alone, unless I have specifically given you leave to speak. And if I should bid you to be silent, you must be silent at once, regardless of anything else." She squeezed his hands tightly, and her smile brightened. "You will be my Court Singer, and you shall come to me when I call for you. You will be mine for the space of a year and a day. I will do with you as I will, when

I will. I want you to write songs, and I want you to sing them to me in the long, dark nights. Will you do that for me, Thomas Lear?"

The solemn scrutiny in her warm, steady gaze was so beautiful to him that he thought his heart might break. In that moment, he knew he would do anything she asked him to, whether he knew himself to be capable of it or not. His breath seemed to be caught in his chest, around his heart; he had trouble finding words to tell her exactly how much he was willing to do for her.

Callie understood. Her eyes told him so, as surely as if she'd spoken the words. She caressed the side of his face with a soft hand. "For your part, you can do as you please, when you please, provided that you recognize that my will takes precedence. You will see that I am not a hard taskmaster. You will find that the work you will do for me will give you pleasure as well.

"Are you ready to come with me? Your understanding of the world is about to change forever, you know."

He was ready, very ready. Mute with emotion, he nodded, trying and failing to match Callie's regal level of gravity. He felt a smile of acknowledgement sneaking across his face, and he gave himself up to the pleasure of it.

"So be it," she said, more of a pronouncement than an acknowledgement. She kissed him, softly for a second, then harder and more forcefully as her hand lowered to his hip. He responded by sliding one hand over her shirt, caressing her while he slid his finger gently along the long tip of her ear. They both trembled in the woodland moonlight, their need for each other undeniable.

"Do we have time for this?" he muttered against her lips, shrugging out of his jacket.

"Probably not," she answered, smiling. "But I am, after all, the Queen. I'd imagine they will all have to put up with waiting a little longer."

CASSANE CARRIED CALLIE and Thomas through the moonlit night. The silver bells on his harness jingled merrily, marking his movements as his hooves made contact with the forest floor. Then, without warning, he moved into a hard gallop and ran headlong toward a small glade some fifty feet in front of them. Without warning, the stallion stopped in front of two large standing stones at the far edge of the glade, which was ringed by a watchful group of tall rowan trees.

"We're here!" Callie cried.

Thomas looked around. "We are?" he asked.

Callie pointed to the stones. "Yes. Faerie is through there."

The stones were about five feet tall, far older than the forest, and stood approximately seven feet apart. In moonglow they looked almost fierce. Thomas suppressed the urge to ask her if they were alive.

"Okay," he said, instead. "Let's do it."

Callie sat up straight, and gently slid Thomas' arms from around her waist. "I need a moment," she said. "Stay there, only move back a little. All is well, Thomas. But please don't touch me until I'm finished."

Puzzled, Thomas moved away, giving her as much room as he could without falling off of Cassane.

She held her arms straight out from her sides, and took a deep and peaceful breath. Exhaling, she made a nearly inaudible humming sound, which was almost a laugh, while a strong and earthy green fragrance surrounded her. There was a strange, silent fluttering of movement under Callie's cloak; Thomas felt it but could not see anything. Under them, Cassane stood patient and unperturbed by the activity. It was as though bed sheets were being fluffed, moved and straightened all around Callie's body. There was no actual sound, but something was happening. Callie was not troubled by it so Thomas took a long, confused intake of fresh air and waited.

And then as suddenly as it began, the fluttering stopped.

"All right," she murmured to both Thomas and Cassane. "We can go."

"Callie," Thomas said, sliding back toward her as she reached for him and replaced his arms around her waist, "What the hell was that?"

"That, Thomas, was what you might call 'protocol'." She laughed merrily. "Oh—and you should close your eyes now, too—I don't want you to get disoriented and fall off Cassane. He hates that."

The horse nickered his agreement.

Thomas closed his eyes when Callie leaned back against his chest.

"Cassane," she commanded. "*Now!*"

The stallion sprang toward the standing stones in the longest leap that Thomas had ever felt. He tightened his grip on Callie, and peeked out of one eye.

Energy crackled in the air. Thomas expected the recognizable sight of waves of electricity—he had seen too many bad science fiction movies—but there was only a green glow mingling with a blue mist around them as Cassane continued his leap. Thomas was certain they were sailing through the air. He had no sense of anything firm and steady under the horse, although there was an odd, subtle feeling of down that he had not expected. Breezes danced at him from all directions, but he felt neither cold nor wet, only the sensation of movement through, under and between something he could not quite fathom.

He heard and felt Callie's laugh against his chest. "You're holding us up. It all looks pretty much the same as this. Close your eye."

Caught, Thomas snapped his eye shut, and a fraction of second later, Cassane's hooves touched on solid ground...

...the solid ground of Faerie.

Thomas opened his eyes, and was nearly blinded by brilliant sunlight. As his vision adjusted, he looked around and saw a dense forest behind them and to his right, and a short, stone-paved road in front of them. The road led to an arched entranceway through a tall stone wall. Thomas realized slowly that the stone wall was in fact part of a castle wall. They were in Elvenhome.

At a gentle nudge from Callie, Thomas slid down from Cassane's back, and then he reached up to help Callie down. As he did so, he was so startled that he nearly dropped her. She no longer wore the black slacks and white blouse he had helped her out of not too long ago, when they'd made love in the forest prior to the leap into Faerie. He had watched her put the same clothes back on again afterward.

She was still wearing the woolen cloak, but under it now she wore a medieval-looking wide-sleeved gown. Long and flowing, it was made of rich, deep-green silk. As her feet touched the ground, he noticed that her boots were gone, replaced by soft green leather slippers.

On her head sat a delicate golden circlet crown with shining leaves worked into it, which was loosely woven into her hair. She was altogether beautiful, and he nearly gasped when his eyes met hers, as much from her radiant loveliness as from his surprise at the sartorial change.

"Sorry to do that to you," she grinned. "And thank you for not dropping me." She laughed out loud then, and he couldn't help but laugh with her.

Something was wrong, though. No, it was simply different. His eyes darted around the contours of her face in confusion.

"What is it?" Callie asked blithely. She looked as though she might burst into giggles, as if some bizarre joke was being played on him before he could get his bearings and figure it out.

Repulsed, Thomas found himself unaccountably angry, speechless for a moment. When he could form words, he stammered them:

"What is that? Where did it come from—and when? What the hell happened to your beautiful face?"

There were tattoos (*tattoos?*) on her face—many tattoos. A chain of astonishingly tiny blue flowers and their even tinier leaves lay across the bridge of her nose, and ran cheekbone to cheekbone, disappearing under her hair just below her temples. At the point of her left jawbone, a small but distinct trine moon glowed white and yellow and blue. It looked so impossibly real.

Callie lifted her hand to his face to pull his focus, calm him. Alarmed, he took a full step back and away from her. The hand still extended toward him was tattooed as well: small green leaves decorated a series of long, languorous swirls that ran down her index finger, across her hand, wrapped her wrist, and slid down the arm that came out of the long, wide sleeve of the gown she wore.

What was this? How had it happened? Why—

Her voice was steady, and entirely regal, accustomed to commanding obedience. There was a kindness in it, too. Perhaps that was why he did as he was told: "Thomas Lear: pull yourself together. Take a breath, and find your words."

Exhaling the deep breath he'd taken, he studied the designs on her face, with a bit less hostility this time.

"Why would you have your skin tattooed, Callie?"

She laughed in earnest. "No tattoos. This is my skin. The designs are my Fey birthright and my delight. They announce me. The Folk anywhere in the Worlds immediately know who I am because they can read the shapes and colors I am blessed with." Gazing into his eyes, she raised both of her eyebrows, as if to help his brain open enough to understand and appreciate what she was telling him.

Thomas didn't get it. "This is what you look like? Not...the other way?"

Callie considered this, and chuckled, kindness flowing from her proud smile. "I have found it easier to move around Upworld without my regal Fey markings. I seem to attract enough attention without them. And more attention would be...unseemly...for my purposes, would it not?

"This is who I am, Thomas."

His eyes were darting across her face, her hands, her hair, her clothing. He put his right hand on Cassane's flank, as if testing for solidity, reality. Suddenly nervous, he looked at the castle wall, the trees from which they'd just come, and then tilted his head back to get a good view of the sky above them.

Oh my God, Thomas thought, going weak in the knees. *Sweet screaming Jesus...*

She had seen this countless times before. She waited patiently as he lined up the words and the realization.

He was not going to Spain for a vacation when he got bored with her; he was going to be with her, here, in this place, for a year and a day. Each of the implications was staggering, and he struggled to take it all in. She had told him the truth from the beginning, the impossible truth: "You're the fucking *Queen of Faerie*, Callie!"

"High Queen, actually. It is an honor to meet you again, Thomas Lear."

The world spun around him, much too fast. In panicked self-defense, he inhaled long and slowly to keep himself from falling over. He muttered something indistinguishable, but she got the general idea, and helpfully patted him on the arm.

"I guess we'll wait a little while before I show you my wings," Callie said under her breath.

Male voices were coming toward them. Still trembling, Thomas looked around and saw seven men, of various sizes, dressed in green and brown livery, moving down the road from the castle on foot. At the head of the group was the man he'd seen in Edinburgh, the man who'd brought the Fiat to Callie on the street below Calton Hill. He was dressed in a black tunic with tiny bright yellow and orange stars dancing over his right shoulder, and he wore loose, flowing black trousers and short boots. He gestured for the others to wait while he walked directly up to Callie and Thomas.

Thomas opened his mouth to say something, and Callie turned to him quickly. "Remember, Thomas—be silent. He knows you aren't to speak to him. Say nothing—the game has begun! You're in Faerie now, and you know your obligations!" Thomas closed his mouth at once, took a long step back from Callie, and watched.

The man bowed to her deeply, and then nodded at Thomas before he spoke. "Welcome home, Your Grace," he said.

"Hello, my friend," she said, touching the man's shoulder.

"We waited, Your Grace…quite patiently," the man said with a twinkle in his eye that was not wasted on The High Queen of Faerie. She shrugged, and they both laughed.

"I am not *that* late," she chided him.

The man cleared his throat, and continued: "All is as you commanded, and all is ready. There are, however," he lowered his voice, "several, ah, sensitive matters which may require your attention…soon." He looked at her, his dismay communicated by the faint tilt of his head and the intensity in his gaze.

"I see," Callie said, seriousness creeping into her voice and across her face. She was quiet for a moment, reading something vaguely uncomfortable that Thomas did not know how to gauge from the other man's silence. "Very well," she said, with a hint of sadness. "I shall deal with that while Thomas is getting settled. Will that do?"

The man nodded, and gave her a small smile. "It is good to have you home, Your Grace."

She beamed at him. "Thank you."

The man gestured at the group waiting at the end of the road, and they moved toward Callie and Thomas. "The Court is assembled in the Great Hall to welcome the High Queen home," he told her, and then added with a wry grin and a knowing wink, "The Fair Folk are eager to see their new Court Singer."

He then nodded a silent order to the liveried men, who dispersed at once: two moved directly to Cassane, and led the stallion back up the road to the castle. Three men, who were rather short and stout, marched back toward the forest, in the same direction from which Callie and Thomas had just come. The remaining two men moved to a position five paces behind their Queen and Thomas.

Callie turned to Thomas, and rolled her eyes in cheerful self-deprecation. "Actually, the Folk are eager to see Her Grace's new lover. Oh, let's not keep them waiting any longer." And with that, she rested her hand delicately on Thomas' arm, and they followed the older man up the road toward the castle.

He'd seen castles before, of course. He'd visited the ruins of many of them during previous trips to Europe. He'd also been in mansions in Los Angeles that could pass for castles. Yet nothing in his experience had prepared him for what he saw as he walked through the archway and into Callie's castle.

This was a not a ruin held together by memories of time long past. This was not a contemporary mansion pretending to be a castle. This was a live, active, medieval *castle*.

They'd come in a back entrance, and Callie strode down the wide corridor, talking softly but insistently with the man who'd greeted them, as hurried along beside her. Thomas couldn't hear their conversation, but that was all right; he was too busy looking around while he tried to keep up.

The castle walls were high, and felt thick, strong and secure. Sunlight poured in from windows cut into the outer walls. Thomas noted with some surprise that most of the windows had glass in them, and they could be opened. The stone walls and floors were relatively clean, too, which he hadn't expected. There were iron-wrought sconces on the walls at intervals. Some of the sconces held huge, multiple-wicked candles. Others supported what he recognized as torches, although he'd never seen ones exactly like them. There was light everywhere, it seemed, dispelling his unspoken anticipation of dank, chilly, airless darkness.

As the corridor led them toward the center of the castle, Thomas got fast glimpses of some of the people who lived here. Keeping up with

Callie, he was moving too quickly to settle on one person and take a good look. The flurry of motion gave him a comfortable sense of dashing through a large, safe crowd.

Callie slowed her pace, and turned to get his attention. "Remember to be silent," she said, "and all will be well." She nodded at him, waiting for acknowledgement.

He nodded acquiescence, and she smiled before she turned away from him and kept walking.

The thinning crowd was moving in the same direction that Callie did. The buzzing sound of people gathering was getting louder. A blast of horns coming from the direction in which they were heading cut through the noise, and announced the return of the High Queen of Faerie.

With infinite grace, Callie moved into the Great Hall. She radiated the smooth elegance of experienced regal homecoming as she walked through the massive room, toward the large carved chair which stood atop a three-step dais at the far end of the huge Hall.

Thomas followed her, trying to take in the room and its assembled inhabitants all at once. The high-ceilinged stone and wood chamber had easily over ten thousand square feet of floor space, he reckoned dizzily. The bright hues of the innumerable banners on the walls mixed with the dazzling colors of the clothing of the Folk who parted and bowed to make way for the Queen. Sound and color blended in a surreal visual, harmonic blast. The din of a hundred conversations in the room made the colors come alive. The myriad scents of floor rushes, peat, and the perfumes and sweat of the individuals who had gathered in the Hall combined in his nose and lungs, and nearly took his breath away.

There were trestle tables stacked in twelve sets of three against the far wall, and Thomas saw long benches piled six high beside them. He remembered that castle Great Halls were multipurpose rooms, used for eating and sometimes for sleeping, and for gatherings and general business. He looked around, almost stumbling into Callie as she paused to greet what could only be described (Thomas gulped to himself) as a Dwarf. He had seen drawings in books of fairy tales, and had seen Dwarfs in movies, but the words and pictures he'd been familiar with were not even close to the breathing reality that stood a few paces in front of him.

He was staring at a Dwarf; Good God. At least the Dwarf wasn't staring back at him. The short, barrel-chested creature was running a hand through his metal-gray beard and nodding stiffly, listening to something Callie was whispering into his ear.

Before Thomas could think clearly, Callie was on the move again, striding toward the dais. He worried about getting separated from her in the midst of the throng. There had to be several hundred people in here, and he did not want to get lost. He quickened his pace, and felt a childish relief when he caught up with her.

Just before she reached the dais, she turned to Thomas and pointed to a simple dark-colored wooden bench that sat beside the dais steps. "Sit there, please, Thomas, and when I call for you, stand up and do whatever I ask, all right? And without saying a word, please. Remember!" she admonished him, making sure he saw the seriousness in her eyes.

He nodded to show her that he understood, and sat down, watching her climb the three deep steps up the dais. As she turned around and looked at the Court, invisible horns sliced through the air again. The buzzing conversations quieted.

Callie lifted her hands in greeting as well as in blessing. "Fair Folk of Elvenhome, as you see, I have returned." There were general cheers of approval; she waited until the happy noise died down before she continued. "I have brought someone with me. We once again have a Court Singer, from Upworld," she announced. The crowd offered up more vocal endorsement, and Callie raised a hand for silence. She got it.

"His name," she added, "is Thomas Lear." Callie beckoned Thomas, who stood at once, and walked up the steps, stopping on the middle step and turning to face the Court when Callie put a hand on his arm. "He is a poet and musician, and he is ours for a year and a day."

A mirthful, aged voice rose up from the assembly, its Highland accent broad and deep. "Well, Your Grace, I'd be thinking he's *yours* for a year and a day, and we get to borrow him for special occasions, aye?"

There was much laughter from the Court. Thomas, startled by the remark, glanced up at Callie, and was surprised to see her laughing.

"That may well be true," she said, her eyes shining with merriment as she looked out at the assembled Folk. "As for the subsequent business at hand, I'll be brief—"

"—since she has a new mortal toy to play with?" roared a gravelly voice from the crowd, brimming with amusement. There were many such comments, mostly drowned out by good-natured peals of laughter. Callie sent Thomas back to his bench with an approving smile.

"He is very pretty, Your Grace," crooned a silky feminine voice that Thomas couldn't locate. "If you decide you don't want to play with him, I suppose I could find time for him."

"I'll be certain to let you know," Callie countered sportingly. "Now: for the business at hand." She slowly swept her gaze over her subjects in the Hall. "We have had new Court Singers with us over the years. All of the same rules apply. For those of you among us who may be forgetful, I will remind everyone of how this game is played.

"Thomas Lear will be our Court Singer, and he will sing, and play and will share his music and write new songs. Whatever else he does here will be mostly my own business," she smiled, and was rewarded with some guffaws, "but when he is not functioning as Court Singer, and is not spending time in my own service," and there were cackles here, "you may approach him and spend your time with him, as you choose. You will each see to it that he is ever and always accorded the respect due the Court Singer of Elvenhome.

"He understands the rules of this game, my friends, but they are new and strange to him. The rules are these: he is not to speak a word outside of his own rooms unless he has my leave to do so. He is not to eat the food of Faerie, or drink anything of Faerie save water. Be kind to him as he learns his new life with us."

"Send him over to me, Your Grace, and I'll show him what he needs to know," interjected another feminine voice—low, sultry and sensual. Thomas got a look at the speaker this time, and was jolted when he saw her standing at the front of the crowd. She was short, green-skinned, completely naked, and devastatingly hideous to look upon. She was a Pixie; ancient, dry and gnarled, the breathing personification of a small, wholly unattractive tree stump. Her bumpy scalp was covered with thin wisps of black hair underneath a tall, yellow, pointy hat that was taller than she was. She had a beaklike nose that was half the size of her head, and long, hooked fingernails that seemed to sprout directly from her wrists. She ogled Thomas toothlessly, her intent unmistakable, but this was not what made him feel faintly sick. The creature's feet were pointing backward on her ankles; the rest of her was facing forward, toward the Queen. Thomas felt himself begin to sweat.

"Thank you for your willingness to educate Thomas, Dear One," Callie said, chuckling. "And if it should be that I am the one who needs the lessons, I'll come to see you as well!"

The aged Pixie snickered gleefully, and the Court howled with bawdy laughter again.

Callie waited for the noise to die down once more before she continued. "As is the duty of all new Court Singers, Thomas has named me. From today until the day that Thomas leaves us, my new name is 'Callie'." The High Queen waited while the gathered Folk repeated the name, then continued: "If you are in the habit of addressing me by my given name in public, the name you will use now is 'Callie.' Is that understood?" The Court responded in the affirmative. "Very well. Soon Thomas will also name all of you with whom he will be in contact, either for necessity or pleasure. As is our way, be reminded: any name that Thomas chooses will be the name you will wear, and you will address each other by those names. I will risk no one's True Name. To that end, if you do not wish to play this game, you know which options are open to you, and you may act on your choice at once." There was no dissent, Thomas noticed, only murmurs of eager acquiescence.

"Remember that he is mortal. It is well if you do not immediately expect that he will be able to maintain our natural levels of energy and activity." Callie's voice now took on a more subtle shade of seriousness. "Let memory serve you, Fair Ones, especially those of you with wings, and those of you who shift your form at will, remember this: use kindness and discretion when you fly or change. Thomas has never met the Fair Folk in his world, and you would not wish, certainly, to alarm him overmuch."

A young Bogie, surrounded by a small group of his fellows, looked decidedly disappointed. "A wee bit of fun won't harm him, Your Grace," he suggested. The others around him agreed vociferously.

Callie contained her chuckle. "You are always free to be and do as you will. This is your birthright, and you all know it well," she assured the rowdy Bogies. "But consider this: if you alarm or worry the new Court Singer, the cost of the anxiety that you cause him may be the very music that he is here to play and sing. It would be a great loss to us, would it not?"

There was instant agreement and urgently murmured comments from the gathered Folk. A female Dwarf standing near the Bogie group leaned over and poked the ringleader with a thick, firm finger. "There'll be none of your mischief to harm the Singer's music!" she warned him with narrowed eyes. "Else I'll be visiting ye, aye?"

Immediately chastened, the Bogies nodded, promising to behave. Callie had to take a moment to smooth her hair out of her face and gracefully rub her chin to cover the laugh that nearly escaped her. "You know the apartments in which the Court Singer traditionally resides. Do not be afraid to approach him. I believe you will find that he is a good man. Come to know him, and learn his music. Be ever kind, and also mindful of the limitations of mortals."

"Have you met his limitations yet, Your Grace?"

"Do you know yet whether this one prefers females or males, or perhaps sheep, Your Grace?"

"Does he need some Ladies-in-Waiting, Your Grace?"

Amid the Court's ribald comments, Callie stepped down from the dais, took Thomas' hand, and walked with him through the crowd, nodding and chatting as she acknowledged individual remarks. Observing her, Thomas was glad that he had not been given permission to speak; he had no idea what he would say to the people around him. He wasn't shy, he was overwhelmed just beyond the point of endurance, and he knew it. He gave Callie's hand a squeeze. She returned the pressure with a calming look. "We'll be out of here in a moment," she whispered, "and then you can get some fresh air and a little quiet."

He gave her a grateful nod.

Before they could take ten more paces across the room, a creature (whose face instantly reminded Thomas of the toy trolls that had been a fad in the United States some ten years earlier) swept up to them, bowed to Callie and nodded at Thomas. He was a Goblin and, based on his clothing, he appeared to be a rather high-ranking Goblin at that. He was four feet tall, and was dressed in what Thomas could only imagine were robes of state. The Goblin also wore a decorative bronze chain across his chest, attached at the shoulders. Despite his pointed ears, orange hair with white streaks, and almost cartoonish features, he had intelligent brown eyes, and a respectable snow-white beard, which he wore close-cropped.

"Your Grace, I'm afraid there is a matter of some urgency that is of grave concern to certain members of the High Queen's Council," Thomas heard the Goblin tell Callie in a hushed, somewhat shrill voice. "They beg you to meet with them in the Presence Room at your convenience, Your Grace."

Callie bit her lip. "Very well. Tell them that I will attend them presently." Satisfied, the Goblin bowed, and scurried away.

Thomas raised an eyebrow, concerned by her reaction. He wanted to ask her what was wrong.

She exhaled, and shook her head when she saw his face. "Do not worry. I doubt that it's anything terrible, but I do have to talk with them."

He nodded. He would not know what to do or where to go if Callie left him here in the Great Hall. Reading his eyes, she gave him a warm, easy smile, and touched his hand.

"I'm going to have you escorted to your rooms. You'll be safe there, and can speak freely once you're inside. You will be able to relax and begin to get acquainted with your new life." She glanced around the room, clearly looking for someone. "Now, where is—"

The man with the stars on his tunic appeared quite literally out of nowhere, materializing close enough to her left arm to almost touch her. "Your Grace?" he said, with a glimmer of amusement in his eyes that belied his serious, respectful demeanor.

Callie gave him a mock scowl and rolled her eyes, but smiled at him nonetheless. "One of these days you're going to knock me over when you do that."

"I doubt it, Your Grace," the man replied, and Callie sniffed at him. "How may I be of service?" he asked her, ignoring her with much dignity.

"Escort Thomas to his rooms, please, and help him to settle in. Send for food from the kitchens, and be certain that it is safe for him to eat. Remember to name everything you give to him." The man nodded. "Remain until I come. Do not leave him unwarded. You are fully aware of the obligations imposed upon him, and there must be no misadventure." Protect him for me, her eyes urged him.

The man bowed, and turned to Thomas, his eyes soft with deferential courtesy. "All will be well."

Callie reached out and touched Thomas' face. "I will come to you as soon as I may," she promised. "You will be safe with him."

Thomas looked from Callie to the older man, and back at Callie again. Putting as much communication as he could manage into a single gesture, he shrugged blithely and smiled at both of them.

The other man turned, and Thomas, with a last quick smile for Callie, followed him from the Great Hall and into the depths of the castle.

He did not mind admitting to himself that he was overwhelmed. Everything Thomas saw was a blur as he tried to take in as much as possible. Led by the man with the stars on his tunic, they moved through the corridors, past wide stone staircases and beyond heavy, arched wooden doors.

"Too much, too quickly, Thomas?" the man asked, watching Thomas struggle to absorb his surroundings and still hold onto his waning sense of direction. "And, nod, please, if I may call you 'Thomas'?" he added hastily.

Thomas had opened his mouth to speak, immediately shut it tightly, and nodded, grateful for the reminder.

"You nearly forgot, didn't you?" remarked the man, not unkindly. "Her Grace wants me to continue to prompt you so that you do not forget. It is difficult in the beginning, but I have seen that it gets easier. Do not be discouraged, Thomas."

His escort now led Thomas through a narrow passageway, which in turn led them into a large, open courtyard. There were fruit trees growing tall along one side of the peaceful, quiet area. Thomas couldn't decide what the fruit was, and stopped to get a closer look. He saw roundish bunches of what could have been huge, dense, shiny-skinned, apricot-colored grapes. He had never seen anything like them, and looked to the other man to explain.

"Goldenfruit," his companion offered. "The taste is something of a cross between a melon, an orange and several different varieties of berries. They're quite delicious, very rich, but absolutely not for mortal consumption. One of the many delicacies of Faerie you can appreciate from a distance, but should never touch."

Thomas nodded grudgingly, showing that he understood.

They crossed the open courtyard, leaving the goldenfruit trees behind. The older man took Thomas through another confusing series of corridors, and at last stopped in front of a wide oak door at the very end of a hallway.

"These are your apartments now, Thomas. Welcome home."

Thomas gave the man a grateful look, and at the other's gesture, Thomas opened the door and went inside, followed by his escort, who closed the door behind them.

The room they entered was bright, large, airy and spacious. This was only the first thing that surprised Thomas as he looked around. He had expected that interior living space in a castle, particularly a medieval castle the size of this one, would be cramped, dark and damp. He saw sunshine, and felt the glowing warmth of the afternoon sun. One wall of his room was entirely windows, and he could see part of the forest through which he and Callie had come to Faerie. He pointed, and gave his companion a questioning look. For all the walking and stair-climbing they had done to get here, he was amused when he realized that this room was on the ground floor of the castle. He shot the other man an ironic grin that didn't come close enough to communicating what he wanted to say.

The man chuckled. "You're in your own rooms, Thomas. You are free to speak."

"Oh," Thomas said, readjusting his thinking, "That's right..." He laughed, and cleared his throat. "I wasn't expecting windows." He looked around. "Nice place."

It was furnished as a living room and dining area. A fireplace stood in the wall, to his right. In front of it was a very comfortable-looking overstuffed easy chair. Near the fireplace was a large round wooden dining table, with three sturdy chairs around it. To his left, by the wall of windows, he saw a large gray couch, another smaller easy chair, a writing desk, a simple wooden stool, and a wide and tall cabinet with two glass doors on top and two wooden doors below it.

"Her Grace particularly wanted you to see that cabinet," his escort said, with invitation in his voice.

Thomas walked past the couch to the cabinet. His eyes lit up in amazement before he even opened the glass doors. Inside stood an exquisite six-stringed guitar, made of mahogany, with what looked to be the most intricate mother-of-pearl inlay he had ever seen. The small flowers that were inlaid around and along the neck of the guitar were identical in shape, size and color to the designs on Callie's face.

He knew a good deal about guitars, but he had never seen one quite like this one. It was both familiar and unfamiliar—a blend, he chuckled to himself, that he'd better get used to for a while. He took a deep breath and lifted the beautiful instrument carefully out of the cabinet, sat down on the stool, and touched the strings. He was not in the least surprised that the guitar was in better-than-perfect tune. The voice that flowed from the guitar was heartbreakingly sweet, dynamic, rich and full.

Thomas looked at his companion.

"This is really something," he said, knowing the words were inadequate.

"Her Grace hoped that you would like it," the other man replied. "There are also a few other instruments you might be interested in, down in the bottom."

Almost reluctantly returning the mahogany guitar to its stand in the cabinet, Thomas opened the lower wooden doors and saw a Renaissance-era lute and a small harp. He had never played either of these instruments before, and said so.

"That may change, Thomas, you never know," said the other man with a wink.

"True," Thomas said, touching the strings of the lute. "Very true."

"If you will excuse me for but a moment," the man said, "I will arrange for your dinner. In the event that someone knocks on the door while I am away, please do not open it."

"Okay," Thomas said. He hadn't thought about visitors yet; he was relieved that someone else already had.

The man with the stars on his shoulder disappeared in the next instant. Thomas jumped only a little. "I am not going to get used to that," he muttered to himself as he turned and walked toward a closed door he assumed was a large closet. He opened the door and was startled and pleased to see that he had found his bedroom.

The wall of windows continued in here, with heavy green damask draperies pulled back to reveal the sunny view. The room had a dresser, a comfortable chair, and a very large bed. Thomas smiled in spite of himself as a clear image of Callie and her sumptuous hips played stirringly across his mind. He hoped she would get here soon.

His musing over Callie's physical virtues was distracted by what he saw beside the bed.

It should not have startled him, but he felt a jolt anyway: his guitar case and the leather overnight bag waited for him in front of a small nightstand, beside the bed. The last time he had seen them, they were in the back seat of the Fiat, and then they were not. He walked over to them, and, lifting them, reassured himself of their solid weight as he dropped them on to the bed. He opened the guitar case, and there was his cherished old friend—familiar, safe and grounding despite its location in another world. Thomas shuddered and decided not to think about that very much.

A thought whipped into his mind; he acted on it at once. Opening his overnight bag, he pulled out the small plastic bag that held a plastic lighter, and two joints. Taking one out of the bag, and sliding the lighter into his hand, he kissed the bag with a wry grin, and dropped it back in the overnight bag.

Lighting the joint, Thomas lifted his guitar out of the case, sat down on the bed, and played a whisper of an elusive melody that had been teasing him for months, sneaking around somewhere in the back of his mind.

"That's lovely," said the older man as he materialized by the inside of the bedroom door, genuine appreciation on his face. "Your evening meal is on its way here," he added. "Ah, and I see you have found your things. Is everything in order?"

"Yes," Thomas said, toking deeply, deciding then that it was.

"Thomas," the older man suggested, "It occurs to me that since you will have a great deal of naming to do shortly, you might wish to practice a bit." Thomas stared at him, without comprehension. "On me, I mean."

"Oh," Thomas said. He frowned; he was tired. "I don't know. It was hard enough coming up with a name for Callie...for Her Grace," he admitted with a frown.

The man nodded. "I understand. But it will be easier now that she's been named. You needed to please her with your choice, and I believe you have done so. You only have to point to the rest of us, name us whatever you wish to, and that will be that."

Thomas groaned. The other man smiled. "You'll know why we have to be renamed. Her Grace is quite clear on the strict boundaries between mortals and faeries. Well," the man reconsidered, with as much dignity as his amused and knowing smile could allow, "Most boundaries."

Thomas hoped he wasn't blushing. "All right, then. I'll give you your new name. Here goes." He looked at the other man, wishing that a stunning flash of inspiration would strike, but it did not. He frowned, feeling defeated as he studied the man to find some clue that would help him. The cannabis was not all that inspirational at the moment.

"I like the design on your tunic," Thomas finally blurted.

"I am privileged to be Her Grace's Lord High Chamberlain. The stars are signs of my office."

Sign. Stars. Inspiration smacked Thomas on the back of the head. "I've got it...I think. How would you like to be 'Zodiac'?"

The man thought it over for a fast second, his amusement evident. "'Zodiac'," he repeated, his smile growing. "I would like that very much. Thank you, Thomas."

"Two down, and way too many to go," Thomas groaned, thinking about the crowd in the Great Hall.

A knock on the front door took Zodiac out of the bedroom. Watching him go, Thomas finished his doob as he turned and noticed more doors he hadn't explored yet. There were double glass doors at the far end of the room, to the right of the bed. Through these he could see a stone path that led, when he walked over and looked, to a walled garden. He put his hand on the door knobs to go out and explore, then thought better of it. It might be wiser to wait until Zodiac was with him, so he didn't make any mistakes.

The other door, arched and only a little taller than Thomas, was made of a light oak with wrought-iron framing and a handle. The door was in the corner of the wall opposite the bed, on the same wall as the exit to the garden. He opened this door, and found himself staring into the small privy. He was glad that Callie had prepared him; he was not certain that he wanted to live without plumbing, although he recognized with a mental shrug that he had little choice in the matter.

The privy was lit by a small, square glass window, which was currently open. The seat was a slab of stone with a smooth, round hole cut into it; it was cool but not cold to the touch, at least not now. If it got cold enough, and the presence of the big fireplace in the living area implied that it could, using the facilities might be somewhat bracing, to say the least. Oddly enough, it didn't smell in here. Thomas wondered if that was because the castle's privy systems were well-constructed and maintained, or if it was that no one had occupied the Court Singer's rooms for a while. He assumed he'd find out. There was no sink, naturally, since there was no plumbing, and no tub. He wondered about bathing, and had another spontaneous lusty mental vision of Callie.

Zodiac entered the bedroom as Thomas stepped back and closed the privy door. "Your meal has arrived and is waiting."

eleven

CALLIE STRODE THROUGH the heavy oak double doors into the Presence Chamber. The three sets of large recessed windows to her left were open wide, and she felt a cooling breeze as she moved past them. Each window's half-moon recession was richly-cushioned, and draped for privacy, should that be required; today all the draperies were held back by white satin ribbons, as they were on most days. Four of the Queen's Ladies, who attended her from several paces behind, settled decoratively in one of the window seats and continued their quiet but animated conversation. Callie heard Thomas' name mentioned, and smiled to herself, but kept walking through the middle of the room.

The Presence Chamber was long rather than wide. At the far end stood two massive, joined thrones. They had been carved from a huge, single piece of ancient oak, and each was inlaid with gold, silver, and stones. The thrones were positioned on top of a dais, which stood seven wooden steps above the floor. The steps were also of carved oak. There were several large silk banners and chivalric crests on the wall above and behind the thrones.

This was the room where she formally and officially met with her Council or with lesser Kings and Queens when they visited Elvenhome. Traditionally, petitions from Fair Folk all over the kingdoms were also heard here. Regally impressive, the walls were dark blue, purple and gold, the curtains a deeper purple and matched the window seat cushions. The wall opposite the open windows held dozens of ancient weapons, shields, and swords from famous battles. Fierce-looking, even from a slight distance, they spoke of hard-won victories and heroic feats of chivalric bravery. Today there were no chairs or tables set up. Callie moved easily across the floor, skirts swirling.

Double doors of blonde oak stood below and to the left of the dais, and through these walked the four Folk who urgently needed to speak with their Queen. On their sleeves, each wore the badge of state, a golden seal bearing the likeness of an ancient tree with a harp beneath it. Three long, golden ribbons hanging from the badge indicated that the bearer was, indeed, a member of the High Queen's Council.

"Lady, Gentlemen," Callie said in casual greeting, tempering the growing gravity in her eyes. "A full half of the Council. This must be serious."

"Your Majesty," they said in turn, bowing.

Callie was quiet until they were each looking her in the eye. "I am here. What is it that cannot wait?"

A youngish Dwarf, wearing brown breeches, a tan vest and a white shirt, tugged nervously at his Council badge. "Lord Arrendel has not returned from Upworld," he said.

Callie looked from the Dwarf to the three others who stood above and beside him; each of them looked concerned. Callie frowned. "He was due back the day after I left for Edinburgh."

"We know that, Your Grace," replied a tall, red-haired Elf. She looked worried, but her voice was steady. "He has been away too long."

"He was planning to be somewhere in the Highlands, but we don't know exactly where," added a handsome Naiad, a medium-built Water Faerie, beside her. "He was, of course, obeying your Grace's request to visit the Upworld Folk. We have had word that he spent several days with some of his Glaistig friends, in one of the more remote spots in the northeast, but there has been no word of him since."

Callie's eyes narrowed as she frowned. "Is he alone?"

"No." The answer came from a lean, yellow-haired Sprite with deep blue cat's eyes and large, iridescent wings. "There is a Spriggan with him."

Callie arched an eyebrow. "*Which* Spriggan?" she asked, although she already knew.

The Sprite swallowed hard, as if trying to find a way to delay the inevitable. He looked at the floor as he answered her. "Swiftaine, Your Grace."

"Swiftaine?" Callie growled. "Am I mistaken, or was not Swiftaine forbidden to venture Upworld after his last misadventure?"

"He was forbidden, and by Your Grace," confirmed the Dwarf, "but it seems he left when Lord Arrendel did, only we were unaware of it at the time."

"Arrendel knows that Swiftaine is not careful," Callie said with an irritated sigh. "But Arrendel can take care of himself—and of the Spriggan as well, I daresay. Are we certain they're together?"

"It would seem so," the red-haired Elf answered. "The Glaistigs said that the Spriggan was present when Lord Arrendel was with them. And they were certain that he had plans to travel elsewhere, but he did not tell them anything specific."

The Naiad cleared his throat. "We should not immediately assume that Lord Arrendel is in some sort of trouble, although we cannot rule it out, of course. What, besides visiting friends and performing his duty for her Grace, could keep him Upworld, or at least, away from Elvenhome?"

The Sprite scratched his chin. "He has no tie to the mortal world, Your Grace. His personal interests are focused on Elvenhome. I believe he was only doing what you sent him to do, to visit the Upworld Water Faeries."

The red-haired Elf had a startling idea. "Could he be in love?" she asked, eyes wide. "Could he be staying Upworld to be with someone?"

The Naiad nodded. "It had occurred to me, but I do not know it for an absolute fact."

Callie considered this. "It's possible. He has not been in love for a very long time. Perhaps he has found someone who makes him happy." She smiled at the thought, and then jolted as another thought occurred to her. "Could he be in love with a mortal?"

"Absolutely not!" the Elf blurted out, and then blushed hotly. "I am sorry, Your Grace. But Lord Arrendel is a Water Faerie, noble by birth. Mortals might be temporarily interesting to him for their strangeness, but he would be bored before very long. Mortals are as tedious as death. Who would know that better than Your Grace?"

The three males gasped in shocked amazement at her audacity, and then looked at Callie, who was chuckling. "You speak your truth with little gentleness and less tact, but you do speak your truth, and I value you for it," she laughed. "Not all mortals are tedious. Many are, perhaps most are, but some are not, and the ones who are not," she smiled, thinking of Thomas, "are often worth the trouble of discovering and caring for them.

"As for Arrendel, it is possible that he has indeed met someone, either Fey, or mortal—which would be difficult, and not only for the tedium factor," Callie pointed out for the outspoken Elf's benefit, "and that may be keeping him away voluntarily, although, as you have said, he has been away from Elvenhome for longer than may be wise or even safe for him."

Callie was thinking. They studied her in an uncomfortable silence.

"What are we going to do?" asked the Sprite at last, tension evident in his voice. "His delay could very well mean that he is in some danger, and we will not be able to help him easily, since we do not know precisely where he is."

The Naiad said, "Still, Your Grace, Lord Arrendel knows his way around Upworld, and he does not take foolish chances—"

"—unlike a certain Spriggan—"interrupted the Dwarf, still tugging at his Council badge.

"—So," continued the Naiad, "there's a good possibility that nothing is truly amiss, other than the fact that Lord Arrendel is somewhat overdue on his return." He met Callie's eyes, trying to sound confident. "He may merely be late, and not in any real difficulty. He knows how to take care of himself."

Callie agreed. "That is true. And so here is what we will do: we shall wait one more day for him. If he does not return before moonrise tomorrow, send three water faeries to search the rivers and lochs in the Northeast Highlands. Also send some smaller Folk to search for him in areas closer to the mortals—they are less likely to be seen. I want no incident, but I want Arrendel back swiftly."

The decision made, and the command given, the tension in the room dissipated. The Council thanked Callie.

Callie nodded in kind dismissal. "And when Lord Arrendel returns," she commanded, "with a certain Spriggan, send them both to me at once." The Dwarf, the Sprite and the Elf bowed once more then departed, leaving Callie alone with the Naiad.

Callie moved to the dais steps, sat down heavily, and stretched her arms and legs with a long, luxurious groan. The Naiad watched her for a moment, and then sat down on the steps near her.

He smiled at her. "You have brought your new Court Singer back with you from Upworld, and instead of spending time playing with him, you are confronted with things you should not have had to think about the very moment you arrive home," he frowned. "Duty seems to be forever in the way of pleasure, does it not?"

"Apparently so," Callie conceded. When he didn't respond, she eyed the Naiad, and groaned. "I take it there's more?"

"Only one other thing," he said, glancing across the Chamber at the Queen's Ladies to confirm that he was not being overheard. "It is my sad duty to inform you, if you do not know it already, that Terena is fading. She is in no immediate danger, as far as I can see, Your Grace, but you need to be aware that she is slowing down. And her mind may be slipping a bit. She has been somewhat difficult to locate of late, more than she has been before."

A rush of sadness took Callie's breath away for a moment, and showed in the depths of her brown eyes. "I can admit to you that I have tried not to think about it, and by not thinking about it, have pushed the inevitable as far away as I dare. Is she well otherwise?"

The Naiad nodded. "She seems to be." He paused, and then met Callie's eyes. "I am concerned about the reaction when Terena—when he hears of it..."

Callie put a hand on his arm to silence him. "Do not say it." It was not exactly a command, but it sounded nearly like one. The Naiad sat very still, and was silent while the Queen considered the situation. "Is he at all aware that she is fading?" Callie asked.

"That is hard to say, Your Grace. I would like to think that he is aware of it, for not knowing and then finding out that she was *dy*—that would be a harsh thing. But I do not know if it is better that he knows, or not, for her sake." He grimaced but faced his duty squarely. "What would you have me do?"

She patted his arm, a deep fondness shining in her eyes. "Nothing. I will talk with him."

The Naiad raised his head and looked at her in blatant surprise. She almost laughed, but didn't have the heart for it. "Keep your shock to yourself," she chided. "After we deal with Arrendel's return, and I thoroughly chastise one wayward Spriggan, then I shall go and talk with *him*." She wrapped her arms around her chest, hugged herself, and looked away.

The Naiad's smile was forced, and it wobbled, but he did his best. "Thank you, Your Grace. I confess that I did not wish to be the one to tell him."

"I know it." She looked at him after a moment. "All is well. Do not fret about it."

They didn't speak for a short while, instead listening to the sounds of muffled conversation and hushed laughter coming from the Ladies by the windows.

He turned to her. "I do not suppose you might be in the mood for some strong Elfish ale and a relaxing game of chess with an old friend, Your Grace?" he teased.

Callie laughed then. "I take it that you were not in the Great Hall when I introduced Thomas to the Court?"

"No," he told her. "I was in the library, looking at maps of the Highlands and wondering where Lord Arrendel might be. But I have heard about him already. Why?"

"You have not *seen* Thomas. He is quite handsome, almost devastatingly so, and has a very beautiful form. And an alarming number of ladies are already pondering ways to get his worthy attention."

The Naiad gave Callie an easy, conspiratorial smile. "I see. In that case, perhaps we can play another day. You beat me soundly the last time, and I would like the opportunity to earn some of my waning dignity back." He winked at her mischievously. "Your Grace, may I wish you a good night."

She nodded at him, her dazzling smile telling him that it was certainly going to be a good night, once she got to Thomas' apartments. He grinned back at her, stood up, and offered her his arm. They walked out of the Presence Chamber, and planned another time for a game of chess, while the Queen's Ladies fell into place behind them.

For an hour and a half, Zodiac had talked and answered questions while Thomas ate an early dinner of roasted pork and potatoes fried with rosemary, and drank two glasses of Upworld ale. Yes, the castle was old, even older than it looked, but was well-maintained and was a very good place to live. In the brief Faerie winters, it did get cold in some of the Northern Kingdoms, but not often here in the South, so Thomas didn't have to worry much about sticking to the seat in the privy.

There were nearly five hundred Fair Folk living inside the castle at any given time, and there were about that many in the village of Elvenhome. Elvenhome was the capitol of the Faerie, which was comprised of eight individual kingdoms. Callie ruled the entire land, as well as the kingdom of Elvenhome. The seven other kingdoms were each ruled by a Faerie king, who reigned in his own land in his own fashion. Each king was duly subject to Her Grace, who was the High Queen of them all.

The inhabitants of Faerie were, as Thomas was no doubt aware, known as the Fair Folk, the Good Folk, the Fey, and so on. The Fair Folk were made up of many different kinds of faeries. The Elves, who were in the majority in Elvenhome, were all relatively tall, human-looking and almost always very beautiful to look upon; this group included the Water Faeries and the Glaistigs. There were also the Dwarfs, the Spriggans, the Goblins and Hob-Goblins, and Knockers, Pixies, Brownies, the Sprites, Bogies, the Sidhe and the Leprechauns, Kelpies, Selkies, Giants, and other perhaps lesser-known faeries.

"And I have to name them all?" Thomas cried bleakly, dismayed at the enormity of the task ahead of him.

"No, Thomas. Just the ones here in the castle, and of those, only the ones you might have to speak with or need to refer to," Zodiac replied, managing a straight face. "More or less."

Zodiac continued his instruction. The Queen had eight Ladies-in-Waiting, each representing one of Faerie's seven smaller kingdoms, and one from Elvenhome. These Ladies attended Her Grace almost constantly, sometimes one or several at a time, sometimes all at once, depending entirely on the Queen's good pleasure.

"I wish you good luck in naming the Queen's Ladies, too," Zodiac advised. "They are somewhat competitive among themselves. If one name you bestow outshines the others, I would say it is a fortunate thing that you live under Her Grace's protection." He raised both eyebrows in meaningful warning, and Thomas smiled half-heartedly, eyes widening.

"I am going to get beaten up," Thomas sighed with conviction. He poured himself more ale from the stone pitcher on the table.

"We have an apothecary who will be able to bandage you up quite nicely, should the need arise." Zodiac chuckled. "He will need a new name, too."

"Very funny," Thomas grumbled.

The sound of voices outside his door startled Thomas for a moment, until he recognized one voice in particular. Callie was on the other side of the door, dismissing her Ladies.

"But are you certain, Your Grace, that at least one of us should not attend you here?" asked one breathy feminine voice (a touch petulantly, Thomas thought).

"I believe I can manage well enough," Callie told them.

"But how will you arrange for your disrobing for the night, Your Grace?" demanded another feminine voice, higher-pitched, and sounding somewhat affronted. "Your gown must be changed and hung away. It is my duty, and my privilege, Your Grace."

Callie's tone was firm but Thomas could hear the amusement glittering behind it. "I am quite hopeful that I will find someone to help me remove my clothing. Now, Ladies, if you please, I will join you in my rooms in the morning. I am certain that you will be able to occupy yourselves for the remainder of this day and into the night. Good evening."

The Ladies, with audible resignation, were bowing and leaving. With a glance at Zodiac, Thomas rose from the table and moved to the door, expecting either a knock or an entrance. He reached for the doorknob, ready to open it.

Nothing happened for a long moment. Thomas froze, uncertain in the silence.

The knock, when it came a second later, caught him off-guard. He opened the door with a sloppy mix of surprise and mollification on his face.

He stepped aside as Callie moved gracefully through the doorway. She saw the relief still written in his eyes, and stopped mid-step. "Thomas, is something wrong?"

For some reason, he was embarrassed. "No, no, not a—nothing's wrong at all," he stammered, frustrated with himself.

Callie shot a puzzled look at her Lord High Chamberlain, who had risen from his chair as she entered, and now shrugged. She returned her gaze to Thomas, who had regained most of his composure. "What is wrong?" she asked again, eyeing him.

"Nothing, now," he smiled. "But for a split second it was so quiet out there that I thought you'd left with them. What were you doing out there by yourself?"

Callie smiled back at him. "I was attempting to hold myself silent so I wouldn't laugh out loud before they got far enough down the corridor." She leaned toward Thomas and kissed him on the mouth. "They were disappointed that they would not be sharing the pleasure of your company this night, Court Singer," she chuckled.

"Oh," Thomas said, looking into her face and running his hands through her long, dark hair. On impulse, he lightly caressed the tip of one ear, and she beamed at him.

The sound of a throat clearing separated Thomas and Callie. She took a step away from Thomas, then nodded at her Chamberlain. "Yes?"

"If there is nothing else, Your Grace..." he said with infinite poise, "I shall go and attend—"

"In a moment," she told him, lifting a hand as if to stop his leaving. She walked farther into the room, now addressing Thomas. "Are your rooms suitable?"

"Very much so," he said.

"Have you been out to see the garden?" she asked, turning to him.

Thomas shook his head.

"Good. Perhaps we can go out and see it together. It has been some time since I was in that garden." She glanced around the room, and returned her gaze to Thomas. "You found your guitar and your bag?"

He nodded. "Yes. Thank you."

"And the other guitar?" she inquired, her eyes sliding to the cabinet where it sat waiting.

"Callie, it's beautiful," he said.

"I hope you will play it for me later," she murmured.

"Your Grace..." the Chamberlain whined, his patience straining.

"Oh, very well," Callie said, making a face at him. "Thomas, would you excuse us for just a moment, please?" She inclined her head toward his bedroom, and he nodded, then went in and closed the door behind him.

Straightening his tunic with great care, The Lord High Chamberlain moved to stand beside her. "What happened with the Council, Your Grace?"

"I am going to wait one more day for Arrendel's return. After that, we'll search for him until we find him."

"Are you worried?"

She pursed her lips, her mouth tight across her teeth, her eyes determined. "Not as worried as I'll be if he is not here tomorrow."

There was a discreet pause. "And what of the other matter?"

"I shall focus on Arrendel first." Callie's response was firm, her eyes fixed on him as she sat down at the table where Thomas had eaten his dinner. "Do you disagree?"

"Not I, Your Grace."

"Good," she said, almost to herself. "Do you have anything to tell me?"

"Only that Thomas seems to be adjusting, and that I think he will be able to live easily enough within the bounds of his obligations."

"That is well," Callie told him. "Anything else?"

He grinned at her. "Thomas has named me, Your Grace."

"I would have expected that. You have been with him for two hours, and he will have had to call you *something*. You are looking rather pleased with yourself, too. Out with it."

"I am now 'Zodiac', Your Grace," Zodiac announced.

"'Zodiac'?!" Callie burst into good-natured laughter.

Zodiac assumed a look of complete imperturbability. "Yes, Your Grace. By virtue of the sign of my office," he added, pointing to the starry shoulder of his tunic. "'Zodiac'."

"'Zodiac'?" she said again, choking, her eyes wide as she gaped at her friend. In a matter of moments, Callie was laughing hard, her face red, tears streaming down her cheeks. "But that's...that's..." Giggling, she gave up on the attempt to comment.

"I am so very pleased this amuses you, Your Grace," Zodiac told her, narrowing his eyes at her. He gazed fixedly at his Queen while she calmed herself, as though he had no idea what was so funny to her. "I was thinking, Your Grace," he went on, "that as I like the new name so well, I may make a point of requesting it specifically from now on, through *all future iterations* of Court Singers." He flared his nostrils at her to underscore his gross impertinence, and she dissolved into another fit of giggles. "Just so," he said frowning as he bowed to her before he vanished into the air.

Still smiling as she wiped her eyes, Callie rose from the dining table and walked to the bedroom door, and knocked. Thomas let her in at once.

"You were laughing," he said.

"I was," she agreed, with a twinkle in her eyes. "'Zodiac' is committed to maintaining his position as a primary source of my perpetual entertainment." She chuckled to herself as she moved toward the one door he had yet to open. "Have you looked in here yet?"

He shook his head. She motioned for him to do so. When he did, and saw the contents of the closet, he took a step back in surprise before he turned and smiled at her.

The closet was filled with clothing, the clothing of Faerie. There was a dazzling array of colorful tunics made of various textures, all of which were soft and inviting. There were half a dozen pairs of loose-fitting breeches, several pairs of tighter-fitting leggings, two pairs of soft slippers, and a pair of tall, bronze-colored, soft-leather boots. There were two robes, one black and one green, hanging on the inside of the closet door.

"If you prefer to wear your Upworld clothing, I will understand. I can easily arrange for more jeans, sweaters, shirts, and the like. But I thought you might find it intriguing to dress as we do," she said. She met his gaze, not certain that she could read it accurately. "Thomas, I will not be offended if you choose not to—"

He put a finger across the curve of her lips, and beamed at her. "I have no objection to the clothing. I meant it when I said that I was ready for this adventure, all of it. Thank you."

Callie's delight in his willingness to play the game fully was evident in her eyes. Pleasing her in this way was easy, and he couldn't help but burst into laughter. He touched her face, letting his fingers play across the flowers on her cheekbone. "You are so very beautiful," he told her.

Hand in hand, they walked through the walled garden behind Thomas' apartments as the late afternoon wore on. The garden sat on nearly an acre of land, and was the home of two ancient rowan trees, one of which, Callie told him with pride, she herself had planted when she had first come to live at the castle. He wanted to ask her about that, but decided against it before he opened his mouth. There were too many questions, and he wondered how much he really wanted to know. He would think about it all, but later. Right now he only wanted to be here with Callie.

There were large beds of fragrant flowers everywhere they walked. She showed Thomas a good-sized scatter-garden of wildflowers, and expressed pleasant surprise at how much they'd grown and spread since her last walk here.

They also talked of other things.

"You are always free to speak when you are out here, to anyone you choose, within the confines of the walls of this garden," Callie was saying. "That means your rooms, your garden, and beyond that, whenever I give you leave to speak. I promise you, Thomas, this is for your safekeeping."

"I understand that," he replied, repeating her words in his mind so that he would not forget to keep his mouth closed outside his boundaries. "It's been fine so far. Zodiac kept me from answering a question, and I was glad about that."

"You will find that most of the Folk will help you in all things—when they remember to be helpful," she observed. "We Fey have our flaws, in the name of fun and sometimes brashness, and have been known to make mistakes and errors in judgment. Always remember to stop and think first, Thomas."

"I will," he assured her, squeezing her hand for emphasis. He moved the conversation to another level. "Callie, you know things about me, the official stuff as well as some of the unofficial stuff. Tell me about you. I don't know anything about you other than that you're the High Queen, you're beautiful, you're smart, you're busy, you're an Elf, and you can make guitars and leather bags disappear at will."

She was quiet for a time, gathering her thoughts. She made several attempts, and smiled at him each time she changed her mind. "Perhaps it would be more helpful if you asked me something you'd like to know."

She bent down and picked a small orange flower that was growing alone in the grass, held it up to her nose, enjoying its sweetness as she waited for his reply.

Thomas settled on a question. "Okay. Tell me: what is the most difficult thing in your life?"

"What an interesting idea," she said. "Do you know, I don't believe anyone has ever asked me that." They walked in easy silence for a few minutes while she thought about it.

"In this moment, Thomas, I think the most difficult thing in my life is maintaining my private sense of balance, and translating that into the balance of Elvenhome and its people. Sometimes that means balancing all of Faerie, which is no small task. There are, as you have noticed, many things that require my attention. I have had to learn which things I can put in this hand and deal with later," she gestured and indicated an abstraction of a scale in the air with her hands, where a shimmering ball of silver glitter danced for a few seconds above one side of the imaginary scale, "and which things, too heavy by far, need to be dealt with immediately, before..." and she let her other hand fall, its shining silver glitter spilling fluidly to the grass at her feet. She shrugged, her smile wistful. "I think queenship has a good deal in common with the honorable art of juggling. I am good at it, but keeping everything in the air where it is supposed to be is not always a comfortable vantage point from which to find and maintain my own balance. And I cannot give of myself what I cannot find for myself. That is the most difficult thing."

He was amazed at her unaffected response.

"What?" she asked him. "Too much bad melodrama?"

"No, not at all," he answered. "I don't know what it was that I thought you were going to say, but I know this wasn't it." He lightened his tone as another question occurred to him: "What's the thing that makes you happiest right now?"

"Oh, that's easy," she said. "Having you here. Being with you. Touching you. It's what I want, and what I need, in this moment. You."

He shook his head, not so much in disbelief as in wonder at her. "You're...remarkable," he told her, finding no other word that could begin to express what he was feeling.

"Perhaps not so much 'remarkable' as merely aware of what it is that I was born to do."

"No," he disagreed. "You're remarkable." Taking both of her hands in his, he bent his head and kissed her, his lips touching hers with a sense of reverence he'd never experienced before, the awareness of which made his chest ache with wanting to draw her completely into and around himself, to be her protector as well as to be protected by her.

Sliding her hands out of his, she poured herself into the warm circle of his arms and gave him a measure of the shelter he sought.

By the time they went back into his living room, the dishes from his meal had been removed. There was a pitcher of cold water on the table, beside which sat a carafe of wine, two goblets, and four large pears. There was a note beside the fruit, written on a small piece of beige paper. Thomas reached for it, looked it over, and handed it to Callie with a question in his eyes.

"So much for your degree in Medieval Literature," she taunted him with a rather lovely smirk. "I am not impressed."

"That's not Middle English—and I should get points for knowing that," he said in his own defense, pointing. "But even if it were, I'd never be able to read it. What does it say?"

"It's in Elfish, of course," she chided, harassing him. "It says *The wine is French, as are the pears.*" She put the note down, and nodded, satisfied. "Everyone who works in the Kitchens is aware of your mortal dietary requirements. You will be safe as long as you are careful and avoid anything you're not certain of."

Sitting down at the table, she glanced up at Thomas, and indicated that he should sit down beside her. "How is your energy? Are you getting tired?" she asked, watching him intently.

Thomas smiled expansively. "Is that a subtle invitation for sex, Callie?"

She laughed. "No. When I want to initiate sex with you, I make it quite clear, don't you think?"

"I don't think I can disagree with that."

"I'm asking about your energy, and how tired you are, because you've been awake and active for the better part of twenty-four hours. You've made the journey to Elvenhome, and that takes some physical adjustment, although not as much as merely being here does. And the only way mortals can make the adjustment—to our air, our water, the light, most everything—is to sleep."

"So you're asking me to go to bed," Thomas teased, giving her an exaggerated wink. "I think I see the difference. Like I said: subtle, Callie, very subtle."

She grumbled at him good-naturedly. "You're going to try to come very close to exasperating me, aren't you?"

"Okay, I'll behave." He put his hand over hers and told her the truth. "I'm not tired at all. Which means," he grinned, "that maybe we should go to bed?"

She laughed; she couldn't help it. "Later. Why don't we close this day with some of your music? Play for me, Thomas, would you, please?"

He smiled as he rose from the table and walked to the glass-fronted cabinet. He removed the mahogany guitar from its place, then went over to the sofa, sat down, and closely examined the flawless, well-crafted instrument as he tuned it.

Callie poured them each a goblet of wine, and after handing him one, moved to the chair on the other side of the couch so she could watch him.

The sounds that flowed from the guitar filled the room with a rhythmic sweetness; it was less "music," more the introduction of Thomas and the instrument. He realized without thinking about it that he wasn't ready to play his own songs for her, not yet. He felt himself internally grasping for some kind of emotional, creative distance from her and from this surreal adventure. He needed a buffer for his soul, even if only for a little while longer, until he got his bearings.

The music decided for him. He began to play the song that always been the buffer he most trusted. It was one of his favorites, written by a close friend who had been dead for some time. Thomas had never played it for anyone else.

Pulled inward, in the moment, Thomas played only for himself, incidentally for Callie. He was lost in the richness of the sounds his fingers called from the strings. As always, the purity and sureness and truth of the melody he played brought him closer to the fragile parts of himself that he secretly wanted to know and learn to love. He closed his eyes, and nearly forgot about the Queen seated less than ten feet in front of him.

He played the piece twice.

When he finished, and came reluctantly back to himself, he slowly opened his eyes and glanced at Callie. Tears spilled freely down her cheeks.

"Oh, it wasn't as bad as all that, was it?" he teased, and gave her a look of mock horror until she laughed at him.

"You made it sing, Thomas," she whispered, pointing at the guitar. "Make it sing again. Only play something for me that you have written."

He did—or, rather, he meant to. He began to play one of his first hit songs, got as far as singing the first two bars, and stopped. Callie stared at him but said nothing. He made a face, changed his mind, and started to play a different song. After a couple of bars into the second song, he stopped again, ran a hand through his brown curls in agitation, and tried again with a third song. This too was halted before he sang much of it.

Perplexed, Thomas glanced at Callie. "I can't do it," he informed her.

She didn't understand. "You can't? Why not?"

His troubled look smoothed itself into a glimmer of self-amusement; he realized what was happening. "I can't do it right now, Callie. Later, but not right now."

"Why?"

His amusement grew; so did his smile. "I've sung these songs hundreds of times, and rarely think about the women I wrote them about. But for some reason, each of the songs reminds me of them now, and it's pretty intense." He stopped speaking, considering this.

"I don't mind it, Thomas. Wherever the music and the poetry came from is where they came from. Unless it hurts you to sing it..." Callie kept any sign of disappointment or alarm from her voice, her gaze steady.

"I can sing them later, and will, any of them. All of them, if you want," he assured her. "But right now, sitting here, I don't want to think about any woman but you."

Quietly, she sipped her wine, her eyes glued to his, her expression passive and open, waiting for him to do whatever he wanted to.

"There are a couple of tunes I've been working on that I haven't written lyrics for yet," he offered. "I can play you one of those."

And so he played for her, watching her face light up with pleasure as she listened to him.

He played his newer compositions with an energy he hadn't experienced since the beginning of the tour. He felt strong, free, and complete. The music had always connected him to himself in the best ways, but this was different, somehow.

The Monster In His Head rolled over and went to sleep. Thomas knew it would leave him alone for a while, and the overwhelming sense of relief and even gratitude he felt about this would have shattered him, but for his focus on the music.

When at last he finished playing, Callie beamed at him, glowing, her pleasure and respect for the work shining in the warm depths of her dazzling brown eyes. An unexpected thought occurred to him: *perhaps, for the very first time in his life, had he come all the way home?*

It was a perfect night for making love. Incandescent moonlight poured in through the open windows and the garden doors of Thomas' bedroom. The heady fragrance of exotic night flowers floated in from the walled garden on an occasional calm and soothing breeze.

On the bed, Callie's cinnamon-brown eyes were barely visible above the dark curly hair that nested Thomas' genitals. She raised herself up on her elbows and grinned lasciviously at him, her hair sweeping across him softly as she firmly placed a hand where her mouth had just been; he shivered in response.

"Thomas, are you religious?" she asked playfully, extending her other hand to tickle his twitching hips with a definitely lecherous sparkle in her eyes.

"What?" he gasped through clenched teeth, opening his eyes and looking down at her dazedly.

"Religious," Callie repeated, pointing her chin at him by way of clarification. "You." She nipped at Thomas' upper thigh, since it happened to be in the vicinity.

He made a noise deep in his throat and had to take a breath before he could answer her. "Not...not really. Why?"

She tightened her hand and continued stroking him deftly. "Well, you've been saying 'Oh my God' somewhat fervently for quite a while now, so it was only natural that I would wonder about your religious proclivities," she chuckled, and returned to the business of licking him.

A sharp and delicious tremor went through him. He groaned, and muttered "Oh my God, Callie..." then laughed when he realized what he'd said. "Okay, you may have a point there. But I can't help it—I'm feeling close to heaven," he told her, closing his eyes again and struggling to control his ragged breaths. "Wait, Callie, slow down—religious conviction notwithstanding, it's all I can do to keep from rolling you under me and 'worshipping' the life out of you..."

Callie let out a spirited shriek as, in one sudden and relatively fluid motion, he slid away from her mouth and hands, flipped himself over on the bed and grabbed her, kissing her long and hard as he pulled her against him and up over the entire length of his body.

"Now," he whispered, tasting the pointed tip of her ear, "let's see how religious you're feeling, My Queen." He rolled her on to her belly, and lay on top of her, waist to legs, bracing his weight on his left arm. Taking her left ear captive, he sucked on it at first gently and then with increasing force. She arched her back against him; he took the opportunity to reach around for her right breast, which he fondled, his fingers rubbing over the tightened swell of her nipple.

She moaned, pushing upward toward him, her body frantic for contact.

"You were saying, Your Grace?" Thomas observed, hand and tongue moving a little faster.

"Mmmmmmmmmmmmmmm," Callie managed, her bottom pushing against his lower abdomen.

"What?" Thomas teased, enjoying the sharpening of his own body's arousal again. He squeezed her aching nipple and she groaned. "You were saying?"

She writhed against him, feverish with wanting him. "Thomas, please!"

"As my Queen demands," he said, his own voice tight and breathless with wanting her.

Keeping their bodies together, he rolled them onto their sides, and gathered her against him, holding her close. His hand grazed the soft brown hair between her legs; he felt the slippery evidence of her arousal on his fingertips. Unable to hold back any longer, he pushed himself into her.

Callie's hand was on his buttock and thrusting hip, moving in the rhythms his body chose. One of his hands cupped and caressed her breast, and the other stroked between her legs. Impaled and on fire, she rocked her body against his. Her breath came in sharp, jagged gasps as she tried to wriggle away from him and ram herself into him at the same time.

Thrusting home, he felt the initial ripples as pleasure began to take her. Moaning, Callie clenched Thomas inside her, riding the first sharp, exquisite climax.

He couldn't wait now; he was too close to the edge to hold back any longer. Her final orgasm squeezed and jolted his cock. Hips bucking, he pushed himself into her, deep and hard and fast.

Arching his back, body rigid, he stroked into her one last time, and the delicious explosion came. Crying out her name, his body convulsed and he flooded her, his release coming in long throbbing spurts that took his breath away.

Shaking, she turned to face him, and kissed him, caressing his trembling chest with infinite tenderness.

It took a long time for their breathing to slow down. By the time it did, they were sound asleep, sated and content in each other's arms.

The moonlight slowly faded from the room, leaving only the intoxicating scent of night flowers to keep watch over Callie and Thomas as they slept.

MIDMORNING OF THE next day, Callie stood in the center of her wide clothing chamber and endured the studied regard of eight pairs of inquisitive eyes as her Ladies dressed her in a burgundy-colored silk gown.

She had arrived in her own apartments nearly two hours before, ready for a long and leisurely bath in the oversized soaking tub that stood in the corner of her private bedchamber. She had commanded the two Ladies who attended her bath to silence. She soaked in warm, lilac-scented water and remembered the long, sweet night with Thomas without the interruption of talk.

Once she was fully clothed, Callie sat on a tall, golden hassock while her hair was dried, brushed, and braided. The Queen had answered the Ladies' questions about her night in the bed of the new Court Singer. They would ask her questions all day if she let them, she mused, gazing at them with affection.

"Is he as beautiful with his clothes off as he is with them on?" asked one of the Ladies, a pretty Elf. She sat on the bench beside the Queen's dressing table, straightening combs and brushes. She was nearly as tall as Callie, with long blonde tresses. She held the beaded end of her tail in her hand, stroking it absently during the conversation. Like the hair on her head, her tail was blonde, long and thin; it sprang from the base of her spine. It was not always noticeable, because she wore gowns most of the time. In the relaxed presence of the Queen and the other Ladies, she'd reached for the tail and held it in her lap with her skirts pulled up to accommodate her. "He looked rather beautiful to me, Your Grace."

Callie pretended to stop and consider this before nodding in the affirmative with a big smile. "Yes, he is quite beautiful, clothed or otherwise." The Ladies collectively burst into giggles.

"Is he well-endowed?" inquired one of the youngest Ladies. "It was hard to tell when he walked past us in the Great Hall!"

"He is," Callie confirmed with a wink, and the Ladies tittered.

"But does he know what to do with his endowment, Your Grace?" asked another, more seasoned, Lady, arching a thin eyebrow.

Her Grace patted her chest theatrically, as if to calm her racing heart. "So it would seem," she confessed. "It is a wonder that I can still walk!" The Ladies squeaked and squealed.

"Oh, Your Grace, did he sing for you?" sighed yet another of the Ladies, a very small, purple-winged creature who darted around above their heads; she was more interested in the rapture of music than that of physical love at the moment. "We have yet to hear him speak, so we do not know for ourselves if he has a lovely voice," she added, hovering for a moment close to Callie's face.

"Perhaps we can visit him in his rooms and hear his voice for ourselves," suggested the Lady with the blonde tail.

"His voice is lovely, whether he's speaking, singing, or..." and here Callie batted her eyes, "...whispering!" The Ladies roared at this, laughing so hard and making suggestive comments about Thomas' overall fitness that no one heard the first anxious hammering on the outer door of Callie's apartments.

The pounding continued until the Lady with the tail scurried out of the Queen's bedchamber, down the staircase, and through the spacious living area to get to the door. The Queen and the rest of the Ladies followed.

The door was opened, and a hairy Knocker of middle years, dressed in Queen's Guard livery, bowed when he saw Callie descending the staircase with her Ladies.

"Your Grace," he announced, "Lord Arrendel has returned."

twelve

DESPITE THE FACT that his body ached terribly, Arrendel attempted a casual smile as Zodiac helped him into a soft robe. "You like the new name, then?" he asked his old friend, his voice barely above a whisper.

"Strangely, I do, My Lord," Zodiac said, "and it mightily entertains Her Grace."

"I can see that it would," Arrendel replied, forcing himself to move across his bed chamber and out into the main living area to wait for the Queen. She had been informed of his return; he knew she would come. He was not looking forward to the reunion.

"Did I already tell you that she is now to be called 'Callie', My Lord?" Zodiac spoke from behind Arrendel, ready to catch him if he stumbled. "'Callie', indeed," he chuckled under his breath.

"You know you did, 'Zodiac'. I appreciate your subtle efforts to distract me, but I'm well enough, or will be, once I've rested."

The Lord High Chamberlain genuinely hoped so. Lord Arrendel did not look as though he would be well any time soon; his eyes were bloodshot, glassy and fevered, his hands shook, and his color was bad. He looked brittle and starved, and it was apparent that he was in some pain, although he had not mentioned it.

Zodiac masked his concern by telling Arrendel, "I have arranged for food. It should be here soon."

Arrendel blanched a little as he dropped himself into a comfortable chair. "I am not convinced that I can eat at present, my friend. That may take me a while—after I've slept, perhaps."

"I think Master Snick would not like it if you waited too long, My Lord. And if I may be frank, My Lord, you look like you could use a good meal and a cask of wine or two."

Arrendel almost laughed. "A good meal, 'Zodiac', might well finish me, at least today. And as for the wine..." He turned and caught Zodiac's worried glance. "I am only very tired, truly. I will mend. I swear it," he murmured. "If I do not, she will most likely kill me," he added with a sudden flash of smile.

"I think you may confidently rely on that, My Lord," Zodiac agreed. They knew their Queen.

They considered this in companionable silence before Zodiac asked, "Is there anything else I can do for you, Lord Arrendel?"

Arrendel shook his head. "Nothing, thank you. I shall wait here for her—for 'Callie', and then I shall rest in my bed."

"An excellent idea, My Lord." Zodiac turned to the outer door of Arrendel's rooms, and opened it to leave.

Behind him, Arrendel's weary voice came quietly, with a hint of mirth: "Provided she doesn't slay me when she arrives."

Zodiac smiled, nodded at Arrendel, and closed the door behind him. He decided to have a talk with Master Snick on his way back toward the Great Hall.

"I know you're here. Don't make me look for you." It took a great deal of energy for Arrendel to speak.

Menace, known in Faerie by his True Name, which was Swiftaine, instantly appeared at Arrendel's feet. The Spriggan tilted his hairy head back and stared at Arrendel, his eyes wide, hands twitching with concern. "Do you feel as terrible as you look?" he asked in something close to horror.

"That's hard to say. I don't know how I look, so I don't have to think about it," Arrendel said, dismissing the Spriggan's visible anxiety with a wave of his hand. "The Queen will be here soon—you know she now answers to 'Callie'?"

"You're as bad as 'Zodiac' is. Of course I know it. I heard it all four times he told you, and I heard it this time, too. I never call her by her given name anyway," Menace pointed out. His mood moved from irritation to tension in the blink of a nervous eye as he thought about what the Queen was going to do to him for once again disobeying a command. "Her Grace is going to be somewhat angry with me for going Upworld."

Arrendel nodded. "You knew that when you followed me."

"You needed me," Menace insisted.

"I tried to send you home," Arrendel argued, dizziness forcing him to abruptly give up when he met Menace's obstinate glare.

"What shall I do?" Menace asked, nervous now. "What shall I say when she arrives?"

"Just stand there and tell her the truth. And don't disappear. She hates that."

Menace pondered this, frowning as he weighed his options.

"One thing, though," Arrendel said, trying to focus on the Spriggan, who had begun to pace in agitation in front of Arrendel's chair. "I do not want you to mention Maggie, for any reason or under any circumstance." He was startled at how much the mere saying of her name made him ache. The grief was almost too much; he was having trouble breathing around his broken heart. He shook himself mentally and warned the Spriggan: "I mean it, Swiftaine."

"And what shall I do if Her Grace asks me?"

Arrendel sighed. "She won't. If she wants to know anything, she'll ask me, not you. I do not want you to speak Maggie's name to anyone. Do you understand?"

Menace nodded, not knowing what to do or say in the presence of Arrendel's pain and sadness.

"Do I have your word?" Arrendel whispered.

"You do, My Lord," Menace swore. He gave Arrendel a sad half-smile. "I shall miss her, too, you know," he said. "She has the most beautiful ankles."

If Arrendel could have laughed at that, he might have. Menace couldn't be certain either way. Arrendel covered his face with his trembling hands and was silent.

Less than five minutes later, Callie knocked on the door to Arrendel's rooms, and at his soft call of "Come," she opened the door and strode in.

He was standing, more or less, when she entered. The Spriggan was standing on the table beside the chair Arrendel had been sitting in.

"Your Grace," Arrendel began with a bow. "Welcome home. I hear you have a new Court Singer, and a new name." He smiled faintly and the gentle look in his eyes invited her to smile too.

Callie was startled at how frail and ill and sad he looked. She ached to comfort him, but she had stern duties to perform first. Glancing at the clearly worried Spriggan, she forced herself to keep from smiling. She cleared her throat, pressed some irritation into her voice, and threw it vigorously at both Arrendel and Swiftaine.

"You both have caused a good deal of worry and concern," she snapped, leveling a fierce glare at them. "I trust there was an important reason that you were not here when I returned from Upworld?"

Arrendel's calm gaze was as steady as he could manage; he said nothing. She masked the fact that she could see that his hands were shaking. She bit her tongue hard to keep from saying anything to him about it.

The frightened Spriggan spoke up. "Your Grace, My Queen, I—"

"Yes, let us deal first with the Spriggan. The Spriggan who was forbidden further journeys Upworld because of yet another capricious lark." Her eyes narrowed and she stared him down. "I hope you are not going to tell me that you are the reason that Arrendel stayed so long Upworld. Because if that is what has happened, I—"

"Swiftaine is not the reason I was a bit overdue, Your Grace. That fault lies only with me. He persisted in urging me to return home, but..." Arrendel ran out of words and energy.

Under her scrutiny, he knew that his misery was obvious to her. He tried but failed to hide the broken sadness shining in his eyes. He looked away from her.

So, Callie thought, he is in love. "The Spriggan was somewhat less of a hindrance than I am persuaded to believe, this time?" she asked, eyeing both of them.

Arrendel nodded. "It is so, Your Grace."

More for effect than anything else, Callie glowered at the nervous Spriggan. "Do you deny that you willfully sidestepped my forbidding?"

Swiftaine looked fearful, but he met her eyes and shook his head. "No, Your Grace. When I knew that Lord Arrendel was going Upworld,

I chose to follow him, against your express command." He stole a look at Arrendel, and then returned his twitchy gaze to meet Callie's powerful glare. "I am prepared to face punishment for my disobedience," he mumbled.

Callie shook her head at him. "Very well. I should banish you, you know," she noted. She was rewarded with an immediate shriek of horror from the Spriggan, which she considered was probably punishment enough for the exasperating creature. She kept a regal scowl firmly fixed on her face as she continued: "Your punishment is this, Swiftaine: from this night until midnight of the day I rescind the command, you will live in the Library, and you will serve Master Snick by carefully dusting every book on every shelf, and by doing whatever else he asks of you, without fail. You may read, and you may talk and be merry with anyone who enters the Library. But you may not leave that place until I am convinced that when I forbid you to do something, you will heed me and obey. You will take your meals there, you will sleep there, and you will work there, beginning one hour from now. Do you understand?"

The relief on the Spriggan's face made him even less attractive, if such a thing were possible. "I understand. Thank you, Your Grace." He bowed.

Callie allowed herself a small smile. "Go now," she told the Spriggan.

He glanced up at Arrendel, who was still standing beside him, swaying slightly.

"Now, Swiftaine," Callie commanded. "Go."

The Spriggan instantly evaporated into the air, leaving only a few shaggy hairs behind.

Callie flew to Arrendel's side, and helped him sit down in the chair. "I am sorry, Cousin. I dealt with him as quickly as I could. I had not been told you were this ill!"

Seated now, Arrendel took a deep breath, and tried to control his shivering. "I'm well enough, Your Grace, I'm merely tired."

"Stop 'Your Gracing' me, Arrendel. We shared a wet-nurse when we were babies. And I'm 'Callie' now."

"So I hear."

She knelt on the floor beside the chair, and took Arrendel's hand, willing his trembling to stop. It did, after a few minutes, but he seemed weaker for the effort spent controlling it. "Tell me," she urged.

Arrendel smiled at her. "You'll be pleased. There are more Fair Folk in the lochs, streams and ponds in the Highlands now than there have been in two hundred years. Families. Babies. The Water Faerie population is growing slowly, which is amazing, considering how careless the mortals are about polluting the waters."

"That's excellent news," Callie said.

Arrendel nodded, and closed his eyes.

She looked up at him, biting her lip, her concern for him winning out over tact. "You look just awful."

He grunted at her, a sound that blended pain with a flicker of humor.

After a moment she squeezed his hand to remind him that she was there. "Did you come up beside the castle?"

"Yes," he answered, eyes still closed. "It's a good thing it's not far from the loch to the castle gate, or I'd still be out there. The water gave me the last shred of energy to make the walk. It almost wasn't enough. Swiftaine got help right away, so that by the time I almost made it to the gate, others were already there to help." He frowned, his voice revealing how ill he was. "I am not certain that I could have managed it on my own."

He was silent after that. A few long minutes passed, and Callie wondered if he had fallen asleep. She considered getting up and leaving, but his hand moved toward his head, smoothing his hair away from his face. He rubbed his thumb gently against the space between his eyes in an attempt to relieve the pain there.

"Are you going to tell me why you truly stayed away too long?" Callie prodded.

Her voice startled him. Arrendel's eyes shot open, but he didn't say a word. His lips tightened as he worked to steady himself.

She waited, and then asked, "Is she Fey, or is she mortal? Is she even a she?"

Caught out, he groaned, forced a very tired smile, then gave in. "She, Cousin, is mortal."

"And, if I put the pieces together, I'd say you've seen her every time you've gone Upworld over the last two years? Or is it nearly three now?"

Arrendel nodded.

"That's a long time to keep a secret, especially around here. Why did you not say something to me? I have no small experience in this. Loving mortals is very different from loving Fair Folk."

"So I've learned," Arrendel smiled, in spite of himself. "She's a very different kind of woman."

Callie moved to the arm of his chair, sat on it, and put her arms around him comfortingly, much the way she'd done when they were children. "Oh, Arrendel, how can I help you? What can I do?"

He patted her on the back. "I don't think there's anything to do. She has a good life, she's happy. The only unhappiness is when we are apart. I can't bring her here, or, I won't. She has a place in her world that satisfies her, and she must have it. But I do love her, Cousin."

"And you can't stay in her world, although you've certainly tried, at quite a cost. You can't live Upworld, Arrendel, it doesn't work for us," Callie said, her voice trailing.

"I know. I keep hoping that I'll think of something to change that." Exhausted now beyond the point of conversation, Arrendel slumped in the chair.

Callie stood, and helped him up. "I'm going to take you to your bed. You can argue later about when you want to eat." His fevered eyes met hers. "Yes, I saw Zodiac. I told him you'd eat when you felt up to it. I expect that you'll let yourself rest and get strong again, Arrendel. Perhaps we can discover a way to..." Her voice faded into dust as she realized the utter uselessness of the words.

He leaned on her as they walked in halting, tentative steps out of the living area and into his bedroom. Once there, she gave him some water to drink after she eased him into his bed.

Kissing Arrendel on the forehead, Callie brushed his hair out of his face, careful to not let him see the worry in her eyes as she assessed just how unwell and unhappy he was.

"I don't know anything at all about your mortal lady,'" she murmured, turning to leave. "What is her name?"

"Maggie," Arrendel whispered, and his voice broke at last. "Her name is Maggie."

IT SEEMED TO Callie that her beloved Tower Room was one of the few remaining places in the castle where she could find peace. Her duties as High Queen had occupied more of her time than usual since she'd returned to Elvenhome. She needed the soul-replenishing solace of her own thoughts, and the happy comfort she found in the company of her small collection of personal belongings.

She glanced at the delicate sketch of Elvenhome Castle at sunrise, which hung on the wall above the fireplace. Her precious Rabbie Burns had drawn it for her; she felt a warm, vibrant glow at the memory of him. He had made her laugh, often. In this moment she blessed him for this gift again. She thought of his poems—how he'd read them to her late at night, how she'd wake sometimes to find him out of bed and across the room, writing new verse by candlelight. She remembered every story he'd ever told her. She closed her eyes, felt his arms around her, and found herself waiting for his kiss. It didn't come, of course. Still, when she thought about it, she could remember his kisses well. There was nothing to do about it but smile, and smile she did—the open, generous smile that she saved for the people who were most important to her.

It was good to be here alone in the Tower Room, and to be quiet. She could think clearly; she also didn't have to think at all. She could simply look around and feed her soul.

Over on a table by the door, there was a large, hand-wrought bronze-and-stone chalice that one of her Dwarf friends had given her a century or two ago, in which she kept some of her favorite jewelry. These were pieces she no longer wore, only liked to look at and remember every now and again. A glass-fronted bookcase held some favorite, cherished books, penned by friends, mostly written and bound by hand, some written by the Fey, others by mortals. They were poems and stories that had been privately published, or bound solely for her own pleasure, and she cherished them.

The High Queen's Tower Room also contained several pieces of furniture from Upworld that she'd acquired over the years, like the small carved rosewood table with the pearl-and-amethyst inlay that she loved. Upon that table sat a small hand-sized casket that she hadn't touched, let alone opened, in more years than she was willing to count. The casket held her most prized possession, also one of her most painful memories. She was faintly surprised when she realized that the thought of it and its precious contents did not break her heart, or even catch at her throat. She was glad it didn't hurt any longer. She gathered strength and courage from that gladness.

The Tower Room was silent. She closed her eyes and felt its comfortable, familiar stillness. She needed this quiet, and, more than that, she desperately needed to not be needed for a while. Earlier this morning, she had given her Ladies leave to amuse themselves away from her presence for the remainder of the day. She wanted to be alone, to revel in some of the things she couldn't readily do in any other part of her home.

Here, there were no eyes on her; she liked the temporary sense of anonymity. While she was accustomed to being a constant focus of attention much of the time, she basked now in the tranquility of her rare and precious solitude. She almost did not know what to with herself— almost.

She crossed the room, and opened a cupboard in the massive walnut sideboard that housed more of her favorite possessions. There was a small stereo system inside. She touched a small lever on the turntable, and it sprang to life. She placed the player's needle on the outside edge of a vinyl record album, and music spilled cheerfully into her Tower. It was Vivaldi's *The Four Seasons*.

Callie stretched happily, enthralled by the music. Dancing across the richly-carpeted floor, she moved to the window that faced East. There was window at each elemental direction of the Tower; each window had stained-glass shutters bearing images artfully relevant to the quadrant it represented. The East window's breathtaking view was by far the best in the castle. From this vantage point, Callie could see the large central courtyard, a bit of the great, green forest beyond the castle walls, the small loch that shimmered with life near the main gates, and a portion of the largest of the castle's formal gardens. She could see the busy Folk of Elvenhome move around far beneath her window. Relaxing, she sighed, entirely content in the moment.

Something occurred to her now that she had momentarily forgotten. With a wide grin she walked to a tall cedar bureau, and opened a drawer. Digging through it for a moment, Callie beamed as she found what she'd been looking for: a box filled with a dozen different colors of fine silk thread, several golden needles, and a length of bone-colored Irish woven cloth. She collected a small pair of silver scissors and a golden thimble from another drawer, and took her armload of treasures back to her favorite chair, which was near the East window. She sat down cheerfully, and sorted through the box of thread as *The Four Seasons* spiraled around her.

Callie was peacefully working a needlepoint stitch when she heard a hesitant, discreet tapping on the heavy oak door. She was tempted to ignore it. She had only been in the Tower Room for three hours, and was not ready yet to address any of the issues that waited impatiently for her on the other side of that door. She was enjoying her solitude and the music (Praetorius' *Terpsichore* at the moment), and did not want to acknowledge any intrusion.

Only one person knew for certain where she was, and that was Zodiac. He would not have disturbed her unless he believed that an interruption was necessary. She put her needlework down and rose from her chair: something could not wait.

She opened the door only far enough to be able to see Zodiac standing there.

His face was impassive as usual. *Good*, she thought. *Nothing too terrible. Yet.*

"Your Grace," he said.

"Zodiac," she acknowledged, not opening the door any farther.

"There is something you should know at once. I am very sorry to disturb your privacy, Your Grace, but—"

Her stomach lurched and dropped a few inches, but she kept her voice calm. "Is Thomas—?"

Zodiac's almost imperceptible smile reassured her at once. "Still asleep, Your Grace," he said, the words playful despite the ever-dignified composure of his face. "While I would never remark upon either Thomas' staggeringly mortal need for sleep, or my own personal amazement of, and deep respect for, the no-less-than-Herculean effort that went into whatever strange and undeniably carnal things you did to the poor man to require almost four days to sleep it off, Your Grace, it occurs to me that—"

She chuckled. "Ah, yes. I see. I suppose I should be grateful that, unlike the rest of the Court, you would never deign to comment, either favorably or unfavorably, on anything so exalted as the Queen's sex life, eh, Zodiac?"

The Queen's Chamberlain allowed himself a brief but hearty guffaw, his eyes twinkling. "That is correct, Your Grace." A split-second later, his face was composed again, although a hint of mirth glittered in his eyes. Callie opened the door only a little wider.

"Is this about Lord Arrendel?" Callie whispered to mask the tension in her voice.

"No, Your Grace," Zodiac answered. "But I can report to Your Grace that Lord Arrendel has eaten today, and is certain to recover over time. Master Snick has examined him thoroughly and has ascertained that Lord Arrendel was indeed undernourished and of course dehydrated. He had simply been too long away from Faerie. Master Snick has insisted that Lord Arrendel submit to a quiet convalescence. The patient seems content to comply. And so that I could personally reassure Your Grace of Lord Arrendel's condition, I looked in on him on my way here. He was sleeping soundly."

Callie gave him a grateful look. "Excellent." She pursed her lips together, and eyed Zodiac. "That means that you're here about the other matter?" She took a breath, held it, and then blew it out hard and fast as she said, "He has returned, then?" It was not really a question.

Zodiac nodded.

"Do you know where he was?"

"Apparently he and his Men traveled West for some stag stalking."

"I see," Callie replied, her words tight and clipped. "Where is he now?"

Zodiac frowned, but his voice remained neutral. "If he is no longer in the stables with his men, seeing to the horses, he will be in his rooms, or else—"

But Callie already knew. "—I know, I know," she said, suddenly weary. "He'll be walking in the garden."

"Shall I send word that he is to attend you? When and where would you—?"

She shook her head, interrupting him. "No," she said, her voice low and determined. "I'll go and find him myself."

Her Chamberlain raised an eyebrow in surprise. "Will you need anything else then, Your Grace?"

She shook her head again, but gave him a tiny, ironic smile. "Only the one thing I don't seem to have, and which no one can give to me: a long string of hours dedicated to quiet time for needlework." The corners of her mouth twitched upward, but the smile she gave Zodiac was humorless. "Thomas should awaken soon. When he has done so, send someone for me."

"Yes, Your Grace."

Callie walked through the Tower Room door, and closed it ruefully behind her. She moved past Zodiac and hurried down the Tower stairs.

The Lord High Chamberlain followed her descent with his eyes. "Go gently, Your Grace."

IT OCCURRED TO HER as she walked into the formal private garden at the west end of the castle that it had been much too long since she'd last been here. She had once known this garden well, knew every tree and flower that lived and thrived in it. Callie looked around and slowed her pace to a stroll. There were many beds she no longer recognized, and a quiet, fragile part of her wanted to take in as much of the garden's now-unfamiliar beauty and fragrance as she could hold.

It had been such a long time.

As ever, the garden was well cared-for. It was more than merely beautiful; she liked that it carried many varied perfumes, and that it gave the impression of being slightly wild and random, despite its clearly formal overtones. There was no point in denying that she had always enjoyed spending time in this garden. Once, she had been happy here. Very happy.

And so had he.

Thoughts whirling, her chest felt tight. Callie stopped abruptly for air. Perhaps coming here to talk with him had not been one of her more clever decisions. Certainly it was a better choice for everyone else; not many at Court were comfortable when the two of them were in the same place at the same time. No one, not even the boldest of the Folk, wanted to be present when they crossed words.

He himself would not have any objection about wherever they met. It was likely that he would not speak with her at all; he rarely did. She in turn spoke only occasionally to him, and only then when there was some explicit need, when duty or courtesy demanded it. She wondered which reason this particular occasion called for.

Here in this garden, she would not have a single emotional safeguard, and she knew it.

Steeling herself, and ignoring an insistent impulse to turn and run, she sensed him before she saw him. She forced herself to walk calmly as she moved deeper into the garden in the bright afternoon sunshine.

He was standing before a tight ring of white thorn trees, his back to her. She walked toward him, and stopped ten feet away. He turned his head slightly to the side, sensing her.

Neither of them moved or spoke for several eternal heartbeats.

Eventually, he turned to face her. Her eyes met his in mid-stare, her own steady and focused, his slightly blurred, as though he were near-sighted and couldn't see her clearly. She saw at once that he was, as usual, mildly drunk; she had rarely seen him any other way. She grimaced to herself, suddenly half-missing the man he'd been before, feeling the beginnings of a sharp ache of inconsolable sadness…and then she swept the thought and its unwelcome emotion away while she took a good, hard look at him.

He was tall, and well-built. His hair was long and dark, tied back now with a leather thong. His eyes were steely gray in color, the shade of restless water in a cold winter storm. His nose was long, and his chin had a slight cleft. His mouth was wide and generous, and his lips were full and sensual, or rather, they should have been. He should have been handsome, and he had been, once, but now he was not. There was a large, glaring, ugly scar that ran from his right cheekbone and down to what had once been a very attractive mouth. The entire right side of his face was cruelly affected by it. Beside the end of his nose, the scar had puckered and tightened his face, made it rigid, giving him a constant look of pinched, angry bitterness.

His still-beautiful gray eyes rested on her, dully anticipatory. With a chilled detachment, he studied her, his eyes unreadable and his mind closed to her.

Callie forced herself to ignore who he was and, at the same time, to remember who she was. "I hear you've been hunting stag," she opened, pleased at the surprising lightness of her tone.

He nodded his head once, watching her.

"Did you do well? Will there be venison for the Court?" she asked.

His voice was quiet when he finally spoke. She almost had to strain to hear him. "Let us say only that there are a dozen fewer stags in the forests below Elvenmere than there were a week ago," he answered.

She nodded but did not smile at him. "I would imagine your praises are being sung in the Kitchens, then." This was merely a polite observation, without warmth.

"Very likely," he agreed neutrally, his voice barely above a whisper.

Callie moved immediately to the point. "I've come to talk with you about Terena," she began.

She sensed a quick, uneasy stir in him, but it was not evident from his face or in the way he held his body. "Terena is not your concern, Madam," he told her.

"That's where you are wrong, or, rather, one of the places where you are wrong," she assured him, her confidence building. "I am the High Queen of Faerie. As such, Terena is under my care and protection, which is well, since she does not seem to be under your care and protection any longer. Nor has she been, I understand, for some time."

His eyes traveled through several different flickers of inner emotion, but his voice was dispassionate when he responded. "I will not discuss Terena with you, Madam."

"Discussion is not necessary, My Lord," Callie said, bringing herself up to her full height, falling now into her comfortable role as High Queen. "There are some harsh facts about which you need to be made aware. If you are already aware of them, I regret having to bring them to your notice again. But the facts are these: Terena is old, she is not well, and her mind appears to be…fading. I am sorry to tell you this, for I know how you have felt about her." Callie's eyes and her voice softened fractionally; she took a short step closer to him. "It did not seem kind to have you ignorant of her situation. I did not think you had spoken with her in a long time, so it was possible that you did not know. I confess that her state was not brought to my attention until quite recently. It seemed only right that you were told."

He made a gruff noise that might have been a bitter laugh. "No one else wished to tell me, did they, Madam?"

Callie shook her head. "No. No one wanted to cause you pain."

He smiled ironically, but the gesture made him look wild and fanatic rather than amused. "No one but you, Madam."

She took a breath and let it out between her teeth. "I am sorry that you think so, My Lord. I should assure you that that is not the case, but I elect not to waste my breath." She took one last look at him, and turned to go, agitation rising despite her efforts to control it. "I have told you what I know of Terena. If you were not aware before, you are now. Do take a moment to transcend yourself, My Lord, and for love's sake, be kind to the woman!"

Callie took two full steps away from him before he commented. "I hear there is a new Court Singer, Madam."

She stopped, but did not turn around to face him. "True."

His voice was deceptively light. "I understand he is handsome, and gifted. And that he seems to please you."

"Also true," Callie said.

"You are going to put all of us through the childish diversion of living with new names for the benefit of yet another of your mortal Court Singers. By the gods, Madam, how many new names—and new lovers—have we had to endure over the long years?"

Callie nearly turned toward him, but stopped herself an instant before impulse became action. She mentally clenched her fists, and answered him with the cool confidence of a reigning monarch. "We have had as many as I deemed necessary, for my own purposes as well as for the good of the Folk. There is no harm in having him give us names, for his ease. Or would you have him know your True Name, My Lord, to use as he wished, if he were clever and knew what to do to thus control you?" She sniffed at him. "Now that would be a diversion."

He was silent then, as she knew he would be.

"I did not think so," she continued, not missing a beat. "When he meets you, if he meets you, he will rename you as he chooses, and you shall abide by it."

"Just so, Madam," came the frosty reply from behind her.

Heart slamming against her ribs, Callie pitched her voice low, calm and only a little patronizing. "Was there anything else, My Lord?"

"Only that the pathetic sobriquet 'Callie' does not become you at all, Madam, and you are a fool to continue to play this game." His voice bit her.

She had nothing else to say. She took a step away from him, and then another, her ribs and chest aching from the furious pounding of her heart.

She was nearly out of the garden when she heard his voice moving toward her. She did not turn around or alter the steadiness of her pace.

"I have no stomach to meet this pretty Court Singer of yours. I am going Upworld tomorrow or the next day," he informed her as he approached.

She stopped, and whirled around to face him; he was only four feet away. She met his bitter gaze, matched it, and hurled it back at him. "Is that how you dare ask leave of the High Queen of Faerie, My Lord?" She spat the words out, clear and distinct, the frozen fire of royal command unmistakable.

His glare wavered in the face of her undeniable authority. He looked away, testing himself. When at last he raised his eyes to hers again, his growl was rough and angry. "Will you grant me leave to go Upworld for a time, Madam." It was not framed as a question or a request.

Her eyes were still blazing icicles. "Who is going with you?" she questioned, teeth clenched.

"I will go alone."

"Very well," Callie said. "Go." The Queen turned and walked away without a backward glance.

thirteen

"*JANE KEPT HER knowledge of the visit by the Queen of Faerie to herself for most of her long life,*" Callie read aloud to Arrendel from a small green book. The High Queen of Faerie sat in the chair beside his bed, entertaining him as he recovered from his illness. "*She eventually inherited the family farm, married a good man, and raised a family with him. She told her daughters the story of the night the Queen of Faerie and her magnificent stallion stayed in the barn.* Oh, Cousin, Cassane would approve of this."

"You should read it to him, then," Arrendel suggested with a smile.

"He is vain enough already, I daresay. All of this praise would make him insufferable," Callie smirked, and continued reading:

"For the whole of her life, she kept a watchful eye and a safe, ready room for an unheralded visit from the Queen and her royal stallion. Jane never gave up her dream of welcoming the Queen, who might well move to and from Elfland on her mysterious journeys through the world.

"Jane's youngest daughter, Jeanne, was enthralled by the tale of the rainy-night encounter; the child grew up waiting for the Queen's unexpected visit. With that in mind, Jeanne, when she grew up and eventually inherited the farm and raised a family of her own, had a small cottage built near the barn as a guest house intended for use only by the Queen of Faerie.

"And who is to say that, over the generations, the Queen did not come to stay from time to time?"

Callie gently closed the thin, hardbound book, nodding her approval. "Your Maggie wrote this, eh?"

Arrendel nodded with pride.

"You tell her tales of Faerie, and she turns them into faerie tales! How clever of her! She's quite good, I'd say."

"She is, Cousin," Arrendel agreed. "You'd like her, Callie. She doesn't just rewrite stories I tell her, though. She dreams up some wonderful stories on her own. She's like no one else you'd ever meet. Smart, gifted, beautiful, generous, kind..."

Callie gave his hand a squeeze. "And she has your love. Lucky lady." She turned the book over, opened it to the last page, and looked again at the author's photograph. "She is lovely indeed. And I like the way she writes. May I borrow the book and read the other stories at my leisure?"

He pretended to be worried about that, but they both laughed before he could get the words out: "You want to take the book away with you? It's the only copy—can I trust you not to misplace it?"

Callie raised a regal eyebrow, and they laughed more.

"Take it, you will enjoy it," Arrendel told her, yawning as he watched Callie slide the book into her pocket. "I know the words in each tale by heart. But bring it back to me when you are finished, so that I can look at her."

"You need to sleep now," said Callie, as she kissed his cheek and adjusted his blanket. "I will come back when you awake."

She was nearly to the door when he remembered to ask, "And how fares your Court Singer this day?"

The High Queen beamed a knowing smile at her cousin. "He is still sleeping, as you should be. Now, close your eyes, my dear; welcome healing sleep. Dream of your sweetheart."

A warm, green light shimmered from her words, surrounding Arrendel. He breathed it in as he fell asleep and, in his dream, was reunited with Maggie.

WHERE THE HELL was Thomas Lear?

Only Jack Grandberg, Susannah Rickert, the two people who took care of Thomas' home, and Stan Williams (still sore about losing the bet) had any genuine information about Thomas' location, and that intelligence was nearly a week old, now. He had called from a hotel in

Edinburgh, Scotland. All parties had agreed that if Thomas contacted any of them, the information would be shared in the interest of Thomas' business welfare and overall safety.

After a somewhat heated private conversation, Jack and Stan had agreed to keep the whole "Lear Disappears" thing low-key and manageable; they were both masters at this sort of activity. The trick, they knew, was to keep Thomas' career options open despite the fact that he'd closed the door on everything for the moment. He'd done this before, and there had been no permanent negative impact on record sales, his celebrity or on the work itself. Together, Thomas' producer and his business manager could weather any storms, control the story (if and when there was a story), and keep the singer-songwriter from entirely flushing his career and his income, both personal and for the label, down the drain.

Once again, Susannah mentally replayed the phone conversation she'd had with Thomas Lear, and found herself wondering if he were still in Edinburgh, or if he had moved on. She didn't think he was simply vacationing or in need of a break from the pressures of his career, although she couldn't have said why. She had the impression that whatever had made him leave (*no, whatever had made him run away*, she corrected herself) had not been resolved.

A veteran in the music industry, and a vice-president at the record label, Jack produced platinum albums for other musicians, too, and stayed busy with them. As Jack's assistant, Susannah was busy as well, but the work, while creative and rewarding, didn't give her whatever it was she got from dealing with the music—and, okay, with the maddening bullshit—that seemed to wrap itself around her favorite songwriter.

All in all, Susannah knew she spent far too much time thinking about Thomas Lear.

THE NIGHT WIND blew a cool breeze in through the open windows in Callie's bedchamber. It was very late. Despite the fact that she was exhausted, Callie could not wrap herself in the comfort of sleep tonight. She had come to her bed four hours ago; she'd been weary enough to believe that she would fall asleep the minute she was settled, but it hadn't happened.

There was too much on her mind.

She wished that she could talk with Thomas. The very thought of it made her smile a little, even though she knew that he was still sleeping. She had looked in on him earlier in the evening; she knew he would not be completely awake until sometime tomorrow. She had seen countless mortals adjust to Faerie in this way; the adjustment took time. There was no need to hurry it along. She supposed it was just as well; she couldn't tell Thomas most of the things that were preying on her mind, anyway.

Still, to have him close by, to play for her, to be able to listen to him talk to her about anything at all would be comfortable right now. When she thought about him, the other issues tugging at her seemed lighter, less disturbing. And when she thought about him touching her...

She turned over onto her stomach, and decided that in her present mood it was better not to think about Thomas. With an effort, she let thoughts of him go.

The very moment she released the delightful, vivid images of him from her mind, the things she didn't want to think about rushed into the waiting void.

She saw Arrendel, pale and tired, sitting in his favorite chair in his chamber, trying to talk with her. She ached for him as she considered the hopelessness of his feelings for the unknown mortal woman, Maggie—a woman Arrendel felt he could trust with stray bits of Faerie history. It was a fact that this writer had a sparkle of her own; her words created something quietly profound and true, yet gave a sense of tangibility to the variations of the tales that Arrendel had chosen to tell her.

Callie grudgingly admitted to herself that she was enjoying reading Maggie's book of tales, *Memories of the Fair Folk*.

"That would please you endlessly, Cousin," she murmured, her lips set in a tight line as she thought again of Arrendel, sleeping fitfully at the other end of the long corridor.

He was still unwell; this tore at her heart, and at her sense of justice as well. The fiendish logistics of Arrendel's love for Maggie made Callie groan aloud. Arrendel's broken heart was not helping him get well, and this worried her. His color was better, and he was resting and eating, but there was a haunted torment in his eyes that was nearly unbearable to behold. Sad, fretting and frustrated, Callie could do nothing for him, had no means by which to solve the problems and alleviate the pain of one of the people she loved most in the world. She did not give herself room to wonder too much about the mortal woman Arrendel had fallen in love with; it would not serve any purpose now.

Her complete inability to help Arrendel made her want to lie in the bed and howl with rage and hopeless sorrow.

No wonder she was awake tonight.

And then there was the problem of the scarred man who was even now planning to go Upworld. She sighed, rubbing her hands over her tired eyes. Few at Court, especially the High Queen herself, minded when he left Elvenhome for some other part of Faerie, and passed time away from the castle. She was keenly aware, though, of her own unspoken levels of tension whenever he went Upworld.

She knew he could always take care of himself. He was not stupid; he was careless, though, and he drank to what she was sure he considered a glorious excess. Suddenly, irritably, she rolled over onto her side, as if to move herself physically away from thinking about him. Her stomach tightened, and then knotted.

To be fair, some of his trips Upworld had been uneventful, with no cause for concern. Some others, however, were not so benign. Callie struggled to quell her apprehension of the trouble he could cause or the damage she knew very well that he could do Upworld. He had only gone Up this morning; if she began to fret about it now, she would not be able to function. He could be absent for weeks. No, it was better not to think about it. It was better still not to think about *him*.

Her mind traveled over the smaller stream of pressing responsibilities she had to deal with tomorrow: one of the subject Kings was coming for a visit (she suddenly hoped that nothing had gone amiss with a certain recent stag-hunting trip); there were several petitions she needed to hear and rule on; and a clan of angry Bogles who lived just West of Elvenhome were feuding with an equally angry clan of Boggarts, and were arriving the day after tomorrow as commanded, to work out their differences or to be dealt with by the High Queen.

On top of all of this, Callie did not want to give herself any room at all to think about Terena...

She was so tired. She considered getting up, dressing quietly so as not to disturb the Ladies, and slipping up to her Tower Room to do some more needlework and perhaps lay her own petitions for peace—and a fervent prayer for the grace to keep going—humbly before the Moon Goddess. Callie always felt centered and peaceful in the presence of the Great Light.

No. The dawn would come in a few hours. It would be wisest to try to get some sleep.

No. No. She lay there, her mind whirling, her stomach tight, her hands curled into cold fists. She got up from the bed, agitated, feeling lost and terribly alone.

If she dressed herself, the Ladies would be roused from their own sleep; she did not want to wake them. She did not see the point in sharing her frustration with them; they would not know how to comfort her. Still in her light shift, she moved to her closet and took out her favorite wrap, a soft, lilac-colored shawl that was long enough to keep her entire body warm when she walked alone through the castle tonight.

She paused at the door, listening to reassure herself that her Ladies were sleeping soundly. There were several separate sets of snores. Callie cracked a smile of amusement. She put her hand on the doorknob, pulled the door toward herself, and slipped through the doorway.

The hushed voices were so low that, had she not caught a tiny sibilant sound on her way out, she might have missed the conversation altogether. She paused just beyond the doorway, and faced into the blackness of the large alcove where the Ladies usually slept, situated just to the left of her bedchamber door. Ears pricking at the whispers, Callie listened.

"Do you know whose turn it is to get the Court Singer if Her Grace discards him?" asked a wistful voice.

"Yes, of course. It's your turn, and we all know it," replied a sleepy second voice. "You've reminded everyone a hundred times—since before he got here."

"Do you think Her Grace remembers that he'd be mine this time if she didn't want to keep him for some reason?" pressed the first voice, breathless with concern.

"Her Grace doesn't forget," assured the second voice. Callie raised an eyebrow but said nothing.

The first voice took on a tone of wistfulness. "Oh, do you think there's a chance she won't want him?"

"I don't know. She hasn't spent that much time with him yet; he's not awake. She seems happy enough with him, but who's to say? You should be content in the knowledge that if she doesn't want him, he falls to you. I got the last one, and that was lovely for a while. I'm so happy when Her Grace is happy, aren't you?" the second voice said around a sleepy yawn.

"Yes, of course," came the reply from the first voice. "But if he doesn't make her happy, having him myself could make *me* happy."

The second voice sighed. There was some rustling of bed linens, followed by another long and heavy sigh, and then silence.

After a thoughtful moment, Callie moved without a sound past the alcove, through her rooms, down the staircase, and out the door into the chilly corridor.

THE GLASS-FRONTED music cabinet was catching a streak of starshine through the windows. Tendrils of light flowed across the smooth body of the mahogany guitar, giving the impression that it breathed. Callie sat on the couch in Thomas' living area and stared at it, and decided that this was not so far from the truth: in Thomas' hands, the gorgeous guitar was most definitely alive.

She was a little surprised to find herself sitting here. She had had every intention of returning to the private comfort of her Tower Room. Somewhere she'd taken a different turn and, perhaps not all that surprisingly, found herself in the dark on Thomas' couch. She sat in the stillness, and struggled to align herself with a serenity she could not find.

A hot tear made its way down her cheek, and landed on her hand. She stared at it in the bleak dimness, ran a finger across it, and shivered as sudden rivulets of unbidden misery rolled down her face and fell like autumn rain from her trembling chin. She wrapped her arms around herself and held on tightly as rasping sobs shook her.

She was lost, fragmented and isolated; it was too much to bear. She was weak, cloaked in failure she felt helpless to prevent, and could not find the power to remember the best of who and what she was. The burdens of a High Queen were heavy tonight, too heavy by far.

Callie stood up, dropped the lilac shawl onto the couch, wiped her eyes with the back of her hand, and walked toward and then into Thomas' bedroom.

He was lying peacefully on his side. She got into the bed, and slid her body into the long, inviting curve of his sleeping form. She lifted his arm and slid herself into a loose embrace. Snuggled against the warmth of him, she felt herself begin to relax, soothed by the sound and sensation of his quiet breathing.

Sleep was still elusive. She lay quietly under the protection of his arm, but she could not settle her mind. She tried to focus on how she would speak her heart to Thomas now, if he could hear her, but the unspoken words that cascaded through her were only a retelling of all the things that had been torturing her all night.

"Callie?" Thomas mumbled through the haze of a dream, in a feeble attempt to grope toward wakefulness.

She turned, still trembling, and kissed his face, soothing the mild lines of confusion settling on his forehead. "You're dreaming, Thomas. Go back to sleep. All is well. Sleep."

"Callie…" he said again, smiling this time, curling his arms around her before sighing and sinking back into slumber.

"Oh, Thomas," Callie whispered against his shoulder, "how I would dearly love to hear you speak my True Name in the dark…"

Running her hand across his beard, she kissed him again gently, grateful for his partial presence.

Only then did the necessary soul-healing tears that she needed this night come, hot and silent, soothing and cleansing.

And after a while, she slept.

The dawn came early, and Callie woke as the first full rays of sunlight flowed in through the windows and streamed bright and welcoming across the bed. She hadn't slept long, but she had slept well.

Smiling, she rolled onto her back, and untangled herself from Thomas' sleeping embrace.

Tentatively, he woke, too. He stretched himself, and grinned when his eyes came into focus on her beautifully naked body. He smiled at her peacefully, and watched the markings on her face move ever so slightly as she came fully awake. "Good morning, Your Grace," he said, startled by the unaccustomed gruffness of his own voice.

"Good morning," she greeted him. "How did you sleep?"

He stretched again, and yawned. "That was the best night's sleep I've had in years," he admitted with a contented sigh.

She chuckled. "It should have been the best night's sleep you've ever had in your life, Thomas. You slept for five days."

He gaped at her in disbelief. "What? No... Five days? You're kidding."

Stunned into silence, he stared at her as she got up, and then bent down to pick up her shift, which lay discarded on the floor, several paces from the bed. She pulled it on over her head, adjusting it down her body. Her eyes glimmered with amusement.

Thomas was trying to absorb the information. "Wait. Wait a minute, Callie. The last thing I remember was...was...making love with you after we came in from the walk in the garden."

She stuck her tongue out at him playfully. "Good. It was rather memorable, wasn't it?"

"You're telling me that was *five whole days ago*?"

She nodded, sitting on the bed now, watching with interest as he tried to process the facts.

Thomas was clearly bewildered. "What's happened since then?"

It was Callie's turn to look troubled; all of the things she had forgotten about in her sleep came rushing back. He caught the grim expression in her eyes and repeated "What's happened? What did I miss?"

He looked so concerned that she had to smile at him. "Oh, nothing terrible. I've had a lot of things to deal with, that's all."

He raised an eyebrow. "You've been doing 'Queen Stuff'?"

She laughed out loud. "'Queen Stuff'! The very thing. I've never thought about it that way, but that's the best way to describe it."

Absently raking a hand across his beard, he was shocked when he found himself measuring approximately five days' worth of additional facial hair. It struck him that she was, of course, telling him the truth: he had slept for five days. His eyes widened.

"Don't let it worry you," she told him. "I told you this was going to happen. It's the way most mortals process being in Faerie and acclimating. You probably won't sleep this much at a stretch for the rest of the time you're here."

"What else happened when I was sleeping?" he asked, feeling a distant need to stay connected to whatever she'd been doing this week.

"Let's see...I got out of bed that first morning, spent most of the day with my Ladies, dealt with Court matters, spent some lovely time alone doing nothing at all, dealt with more Court matters the next day, and the day after that, and the day after that," she laughed again, "and made a point of checking on you myself at least once a day. Zodiac and some others checked on you as well." She saw that he was feeling exposed and defenseless, and put her hand on his arm to comfort him as he lay looking up at her. "You were perfectly safe, Thomas, at every moment. Everyone is glad that you are here. Don't fret."

He sighed, accepting the words as calmly as she delivered them.

"You should be gentle with yourself today. Your energy will build on its own. Stay in bed for as long as you choose to. I'd suggest a trip to the privy soon, as it's been five days since..." her words trailed off. "I expect you'll want to shave. And I'll have Zodiac arrange for a soaking tub to be brought here for you. A warm bath will help your muscles. Zodiac will also take care of arranging a breakfast for you. Eat slowly at first, but you can eat as much as you want. Just remember, it's been five days."

"Are you going to stay and have breakfast with me?" he asked, hoping she planned to linger, despite the fact that she was no longer naked.

Callie shook her head. "I left my apartments late last night; I need to get back, dress, and deal with a few small matters while they remain small."

He nodded. "So you snuck out and came here in the middle of the night?" he asked, his voice shining with approval.

Her smile grew. "Actually, I did. I left the Ladies without telling them where I was going, although I'd imagine that they know. I passed a few guards on duty in the corridors and by the Great Hall, so anyone who needs to know where I am has likely been informed." She shook her head, only marginally sarcastic. "Such is the life of a High Queen."

"Poor Callie," Thomas commiserated, only marginally teasing. He reached for her, and pulled her to him, then kissed her. He faked a pout as she gently pulled away and got up from the bed again.

"I'll see you later," she promised him, and turned to go.

Something tickled the back of his mind. "Callie?"

"Yes, Thomas?"

"I had a wild dream," he told her.

"Dream?" she asked, turning around and looking at him.

"Yes," he replied, struggling to remember. "I dreamt that you slid into bed, and we...we...um...did we...?" He made a subtle gesture that clearly indicated what he had dreamed that they had done.

"Hmmmm," she said, as if trying to recall. "I suppose you were much closer to being awake than I thought, then."

He didn't understand. "What does that mean?"

The suggestive gaze she turned on him was brighter than the bedroom's beaming streaks of sunlight as she answered him. "When I fell asleep in here with you, I still had my shift on, Thomas," she pointed out. "Perhaps three hours ago, you seemed to want my shift *off*, very much. You were rather insistent about it, as I recall. And when I didn't move quickly enough for you, you took it off *for* me." She was winking immodestly. "With a surprising amount of energy, too."

Dazed, he ran a hand through his hair and listened in amazement. "I don't remember," he said in a strangled voice. "Are you telling me that I... that I...?"

Callie blessed him with a distinctively catlike purr of satisfaction. "You did. And it was very nicely done, too." She gave him a lascivious wink. "Twice."

She chuckled when he, to his infinite surprise, began to blush.

"And you weren't going to mention it to me?" he demanded, embarrassed into changing the subject a little, his face flaming red. "I'd have told you." He folded his arms across his chest and shot her what he hoped was a withering look.

"I'll see you later," she repeated merrily as she whisked out of the room, taking her light laughter with her.

After he heard the front door to his apartments close behind her, he rubbed his eyes, and grinned, all at once insufferably pleased with himself.

Two hours later, Thomas was up and, thanks to the ever-efficient offices of Zodiac, he had also shaved, trimmed his scraggly beard, bathed, dressed, and eaten. As he came out of the privy for the second time that morning, he thought he heard a voice out in the living room.

Curious but not alarmed, he walked toward the couch. He saw no one. He had been told by the Pixies who had brought breakfast that Zodiac would come to collect him sometime before noon, and he knew it was likely that someone would come to retrieve the breakfast dishes that were still sitting on the table. He returned to the bedroom and dug a book out of his leather overnight bag, which was put away on the floor of his closet. On his knees in front of the bag, he was startled when he heard the glass-fronted doors of the music cabinet in the living room rattle, as though they were being opened. He turned his head to listen, and heard a quiet and clearly feminine voice say:

"Pretty."

"Who's there?" Thomas called, jumping to his feet with the book in his hand and rushing out into the living room. "Hello?"

There was no one there; he was hearing things. Thomas scanned the area, then shrugged and sat down with his book while he waited for Zodiac.

Precisely at noon, Thomas answered the tapping at his door. As expected, it was indeed the Lord High Chamberlain. He carried a heavy wooden box the size of a milk crate. This he took to the writing desk, and set down.

"What's that?" asked Thomas.

"Her Grace indicated that you enjoy certain Upworld potables. I took the liberty of procuring some for you. If you find there is something missing that you would like, I trust you will let me know." Zodiac lifted the lid of the box, and Thomas peered inside. A bottle of tequila, four bottles of various excellent single-malt whiskies, several bottles of Very French wine, good gin, decent vodka, and a tall bottle of tawny Australian port filled the box.

"What's the occasion?" Thomas asked, smiling down into the box at some of his oldest and dearest friends.

"I thought this would be a good time to bring them for you. You may find that you need them later on."

Thomas wasn't sure he understood what Zodiac was saying. "Why? What's happening?"

Zodiac's face was benign, but there was more than a hint of mirth in his voice. "Perhaps you've forgotten, Thomas. Today you begin to meet the Court and give everyone new names."

"Oh, no..." Thomas protested. "Are we sure that I have to do this?"

"Quite sure, I'm afraid." Thomas noticed that Zodiac didn't look like he was afraid at all. "We are to go to Her Grace's private Reception Chamber just off the Great Hall. There you will meet many of the Folk of the castle, and will give them their new names."

"Oh, great," the new Court Singer muttered. "I can hardly wait." He looked down again at the bottles in the wooden box. "You'd better be here when I get back," he warned them. "I'm going to need you."

THE BEST THING, Thomas thought, about Callie's Reception Chamber was that it was not much larger than five hundred square feet; not too many of the Folk could be in here at once. He was seated in a comfortable-enough chair in the center of the room, waiting for Zodiac. After dutifully warning Thomas to stay silent, the Queen's High Chamberlain had gone to fetch Callie. To ensure that Thomas remembered not to speak to anyone, Zodiac had posted a guard outside the door.

Thomas was grateful for the quiet. It was going to be a noisy, busy and largely taxing afternoon. He was not at all certain he wanted some of the less human-looking of Callie's subjects getting too close to him. He shuddered, and glanced around.

There were several windows in the wall to his left, and these were open wide, letting in brisk fresh air and September sunlight. The walls, which were painted a deep shade of blue, held banners and chivalric crests similar to the ones he'd seen in the much-larger Great Hall. A dozen long benches, brought in from the Hall, had been placed against the walls. Two chairs and a small writing desk flanked Thomas' own seat.

He had been alone for less than five minutes when the door opened and Callie strode in, followed by Zodiac. Thomas stood, and smiled at her. Before she reached him, she stopped, raised her hand at him in warning for silence, and flicked her fingers in the air, aimed at Thomas. There was a flash of bright green light, and Callie said hurriedly:

"Thomas, you have my leave to speak in this room until such time as you cross its threshold when your task is done."

Thomas realized with a start why she had spoken so quickly. She had known even before he did that he had nearly called a greeting to her the instant she had entered the room.

"Thanks," he said, taking a nervous breath. The relieved expression in her eyes told him that she understood.

She walked to him, looking him over. "Very nice, Thomas," she approved, noting with satisfaction how good he looked in the loose black breeches and light amber tunic. "You're a picture," she told him. "And I daresay you look better in the clothing of Faerie than some of the Fair Folk do!"

He smiled at her, happy that she was pleased. Indicating the chair beside the one he'd been sitting in, he asked "Are you staying?"

Callie shook her head. "I can't, I'm sorry, Thomas. I will try to be here later in the day, but..."

"...but I will be here, Thomas," Zodiac interjected with a bright smile. "I wouldn't miss this for the world."

Callie laughed, and Thomas glowered at Zodiac. Unruffled, Zodiac addressed Callie. "Will there be anything further that you need from me, Your Grace?"

"Not at the moment, Zodiac. But I'll know where to find you if I think of something."

"It's going to be a very long day," Thomas grumbled, and sat down.

Callie blessed him with a sweet smile, and then turned and left. Zodiac settled in the chair to Thomas' left, rubbing his hands together.

"We should get started," Zodiac said, his cheerful tone taunting the Court Singer.

There was no escape, and Thomas knew it. "You're right. The sooner we start, the sooner it's over."

Zodiac nodded. "My thought exactly. Here is what is going to happen: Folk will come in to greet you, you will name them, and then they will either stay here for a while and chat politely, or leave and go about their business."

"Great," Thomas said without a shred of enthusiasm.

"Oh, it will be fun, Thomas," Zodiac chuckled. "And the first thing you will do, which will make everyone's life much easier, will be to name the scribe who will sit with us and record all the names you give to the Folk, so we can keep everything organized. Her Grace wants no mistakes made."

The guard outside leaned his head into the doorway, addressing Zodiac. "My Lord, the Folk are coming."

"Splendid," laughed Zodiac. "Send in the scribe, please."

A very tall young Elf with unfortunately oversized pointed ears protruding from a cap of pale brown curls walked into the room, carrying a large book, several quills and three bottles of ink. These he set on the writing desk, which he moved in front of the vacant chair beside Thomas. He smiled in greeting.

"Thomas," Zodiac said, "this is one of Her Grace's finest scribes." The young Elf bowed his head toward Thomas. "Give him a new name," the Chamberlain urged, "and we can get started."

Thomas looked at the young Elf, and at the large book, which was now open with an ink-coated quill poised over it. The Elf looked back at Thomas in anticipation.

Zodiac looked at him, too, an annoying expression of unbridled mirth dancing in his eyes.

Searching for cosmic inspiration, Thomas found it in a matter of seconds. "Your name will be 'Scribe'," he announced lavishly to the scribe, who nodded, and wrote his new name carefully in the book in bold Elfish characters.

Shooting a blithe look at Zodiac, Thomas was rewarded with the barely audible sound of a deep moan. Complete surprise and profound disbelief announced themselves vividly on the Lord High Chamberlain's usually neutral face.

Thomas swallowed a chuckle, and managed to keep his own face straight and serious as he and the older man stared at each other, then at the doorway of the Queen's Reception Chamber, which suddenly seemed crammed with Fair Folk waiting to approach Thomas for new names.

Zodiac sighed, but he couldn't help but smile. "You were right, earlier. I fear this is going to be a very, very long day."

"YOU SHOULD HAVE seen your face!" Thomas laughed, pouring himself and Zodiac yet another cup of whisky. It was well after midnight, and they had been drinking together in Thomas' rooms for some time. "You looked like you were going to have a full-blown stroke!"

The Chamberlain nodded his thanks, accepting the cup. He took a long drink. "I most assuredly did not," he said crisply.

"You did, man. It was beautiful! You were this close to having a fit, and we both know it!" Thomas choked, trying to drink and laugh at the same time.

Zodiac snorted with disdain. "You, Thomas, are drunk."

"I am," agreed Thomas. "And, my friend, so are you."

"You have a point," Zodiac conceded, and began to laugh in earnest as they recounted the daunting task of the renaming of Callie's people.

IT HAD BEEN quite a day. No less than four hundred of the Fair Folk of Elvenhome had come to the Queen's Reception Chamber that afternoon to meet Thomas and receive a new name from him.

He met Folk from most of the various Faerie races, and had had the leisure to talk with three hundred or so of them briefly, a familiar situation not unlike the innumerable press junkets he had endured to promote his albums and concert tours. Throughout the day, Thomas had been able to take in more than he had when he'd been in the Great Hall the first time. What made everything easier was that Zodiac pointed out some things to him that he might not have noticed right away on his own.

The Woodland Elves, for example, who made up the largest group of the Fair Folk at Elvenhome, were generally tall and thin, and had elongated pointed ears like Callie's. Some Elves had other (additional), non-human-looking body parts, and these had surprised Thomas at first. By the end of the day, however, he had grown more or less accustomed to seeing Folk of all shapes, shades and sizes, webbed feet and toes and sometimes fingers, large and colorful butterfly wings, back-to-front feet, disproportionate noses, huge eyes, and cows' tails. (During a brief lull in activity, Thomas had thought about Callie for a long and happy moment and tried to imagine what she would look like with a tail, and what he might be able to do with it.)

Zodiac was a good ambassador. His deep, melodious voice verbally sketched the varieties and vagaries of the Fair Folk that paraded up to Thomas to receive their new names.

Playful, but also hard-working when the moment demanded it, Pixies were obsessed with hats, the taller and pointier the better. The Water Faeries, who were all nearly breathtakingly beautiful, were closest cousins to the Woodland Elves, and had varying degrees of soft webbing between their fingers and toes. Female Dwarfs were as barrel-chested and stocky as their male counterparts, and laughed even more readily. At first glance, Goblins were unattractive as a race, but seemed to have quick minds and shared a characteristically lewd sense of humor. According to Zodiac, they loved secrets and complex plots and schemes more than nearly anything else and therefore made marvelous spies, both in Faerie and Upworld. Their closest cousins, the HobGoblins, were similar in looks but on the whole tended to be far less intelligent and far more likely to cause havoc.

Although everyone he met in the Reception Chamber was polite and made him feel welcome, Thomas could not help but realize that the Fair Folk were definitely not mortal, in any sense that mattered. As he met the sometimes surreal eyes of his potential new friends and neighbors, he understood that, while the permanent lines between the Folk and himself were blurred for a time, there would always be subtle shadows, deep shading, things he would not and could not understand, behind every interaction. As he was introduced again and again, Thomas was indirectly barraged with the truth of his own inescapable, unavoidable feelings of the faeries' strangeness, their otherness. He was not certain why he was not afraid; he elected not to consider this until he was back in his own space, preferably drunk. This thought made him laugh and wince at the same time.

The colorful markings on her skin constantly reminded him that Callie was different. He understood that the differences were much deeper than he knew how to understand. Regardless of how he interacted with anyone, including Callie and Zodiac, he would not be able to forget for very long that these people were not mortal, and therefore, somehow, could not be wholly trusted.

His best move, for now, was to not think about it. He needed to stay focused.

More than a quarter of the Fair Folk Thomas had met that afternoon—the ones who looked human as well as those who clearly didn't—had been casually naked. His puzzled look, and occasional shock, entertained Zodiac.

""Dressing down' is as common here as 'dressing up', Thomas," Zodiac explained. "We don't need clothing so much as we like clothing, when the whim takes us."

Surprised, but unsure why, really, Thomas raised an eyebrow. "You Folk walk around naked?"

Zodiac nodded. "Unless it's not practical, I suppose, like Dwarfs in the mines or while blacksmithing, Hobs in the Kitchens, things like that. We don't give it much thought, Thomas. Why should we? It's nothing. Clothed or not clothed, is there a point? Most of us prefer to live sky-clad."

Thomas tried to take it in, but it wasn't easy. He indicated the clothed people around him with a discreet nod of his head. "So then why—?"

Zodiac's smile was kind. "Her Grace felt you would be more comfortable if the Folk who are going to be around you regularly were clothed. She thought the distraction might confuse or trouble you."

"Oh," Thomas said. He supposed that she was right. Dammit, he chuckled to himself.

A moment later, he gasped as an extremely tall, gorgeous, red-haired Water Faerie made her way toward them to get her new name, her magnificent nakedness only technically contained in a transparent light blue gown. Zodiac suppressed a laugh and nudged Thomas back into breathing. "You've lost an eyebrow on that one, my friend...I believe it shot straight up your forehead and into your hair!"

"Shut up," Thomas whispered to a thoroughly amused Zodiac as they watched the redhead approach.

Over the course of the day, Thomas had met and named most of the Queen's Guard, everyone from the Kitchens, both groups of Court Musicians, all of Zodiac's staff, the castle's farmer and gardener families, the blacksmithing families (mostly Dwarfs), the royal Scribes (there were ten), the master tailor, master barber and master shoemaker, the Lord of Hounds, the Court juggler and acrobat troupe, the jewelers (mostly Dwarfs again) and the members of the High Queen's Council. The Elf now known as "Scribe" had dutifully recorded each name change in his book, with Zodiac occasionally looking over his shoulder with approval.

"IT WAS APPARENT to me early on that you had no intention of straining yourself with the task of naming so many Folk," Zodiac chortled, finishing off his whisky again. "I think you did well with the Queen's Ladies, however."

In a shimmering cloud of multiple complementary colors, textures and scents, The Queen's Ladies had arrived in the late afternoon. They were perfectly coiffed and gorgeously dressed, the very picture of individual as well as collective loveliness. Thomas had risen from his chair at Zodiac's covert signal. He had bowed and smiled at each of them in turn, after looking for Callie and hiding his disappointment that she was not with them.

"Ladies," Zodiac said formally, rising to his feet as he spoke, "It is my pleasure to present to you the Court Singer, Thomas Lear. Thomas, these are The Queen's Ladies. They attend Her Grace in all matters." He bowed to them, and sat down.

A tiny, slight woman that Thomas recognized now as a Pixie took a step closer to Thomas and smiled up at him. She bore a frightening familial resemblance to the old woman who had teased Callie in the Great Hall that first day, the one who had volunteered to teach Thomas whatever he needed to know to please the Queen. The difference was that this woman's features were softer, her coloring closer to a pretty light brown than green, and she looked to be in her late twenties. Her hair was black and pulled up into a loose bun on her head, from which elegant black curls cascaded. "We attend Her Grace in only *most* matters, else you would have seen all of us before this," she chirped with a wink.

"You should be careful," taunted the Lady behind her. "Behave, or he'll name you 'Bawd,' and it would serve you right, too!"

The Ladies giggled.

The Pixie smiled at Thomas again. "You'd better hurry and name us. As a group, I fear we only get worse. Ask our friend 'Zodiac'."

Thomas turned to look at Zodiac, who put his hands up as if to ward off the suggestion. "I know nothing of the inner workings of the minds of the Queen's Ladies, who only have the most respectable and demure reputation," he said, tightening his face to keep from laughing. "Hurry," he told Thomas with a sly grin.

"All right," Thomas said, sitting down and scrutinizing them as group. "You're all very lovely. And you smell wonderful." The Ladies giggled merrily. Suddenly, an unbidden but not unwelcome, vivid yet long-ago memory of his grandmother's flower garden in San Francisco slid cozily into his mind. He grinned; this was going to be easy.

Thomas pointed to the Pixie in front of him. She was wearing a rich pink gown and a tall, tapering pink hat whose pink-feathered point came to the same level as Thomas' nose. "You are 'Rose'."

Pleased, Rose giggled and clapped her hands. Scribe's pen scratched across the page.

"Dahlia" was a Dwarf whose royal father ruled the kingdom at the northernmost tip of Faerie. She was nearly four feet tall, was broad-chested, and had wide, silver eyes.

"Iris," the Lady who had attended Her Grace longer than anyone else, was descended from Irish Banshee royalty, but she was a Scot by nature, temperament, and inclination. She was Callie's domestic right hand, and Callie counted on her as much as did the Queen's Ladies, with whom she had a distinct one-to-one and one-to-many relationship. Iris had a whimsical maternal side that only appeared to offset her sharp mind, quick wit, and deeply-ingrained sense of duty and service.

"Will you play for us soon, Thomas?" whispered the shy, middle-aged Goblin that Thomas named "Carnation."

"Perhaps he will, when he has stopped for breath after playing with Her Grace!" smirked a Glaistig, one of the several types of Water Faerie. Dressed in a fully-transparent rust-colored gown with sleeves that fell to the floor, she was just over six feet six inches tall, and her rich golden hair tumbled loosely to a point somewhere below her waist. She tilted her head and eyed Thomas seductively. "Juniper," he said, swallowing hard. Juniper slowly touched the tip of her tongue to her upper lip, and then turned away, sliding her hips in unmistakable invitation as she moved.

"Orchid" was a small woman with soft, liquid black eyes, small and perfect teeth, and dark brown hair. She was from the waters off the Orkney Islands. She told Thomas proudly that she was a Selkie. As she spoke, the intense impression of a small, warm, sweet seal flashed into his mind. She smiled then, and he knew that she had put the image there. He smiled back at her.

There was a humming in the air over Thomas' head. He looked up, and saw what he first thought was a cross between a big butterfly and an even bigger hummingbird. It swooped and dove through the air much too close to his head, so he did the only thing he could do: Thomas ducked.

The airy, rippling laughter that came from the flying thing sounded the way a waterfall would—if it could manage an animated giggle with a delicate, feminine voice.

When Thomas stood straight again, the tiny faerie was still laughing, but she hovered in the air in front of his now-very-wide brown eyes. Her dark purple wings fluttered sensuously, and Thomas got a close look at the smallest of the Queen's Ladies.

Her size in no way detracted from her stunning, electrifying beauty. She was not quite eighteen inches tall, and she was perfectly formed. Her dark purple hair, which fell in long, straight wisps below her tiny waist, matched the purple of her layered butterfly wings. Her eyes were black as a lost midnight, her skin a solemn shade of lightest tawny brown. Her tiny body was completely covered with the proud, decorative designs not unlike those that Callie wore. The winged Lady's markings were thin, lazy tendrils of purple and green, with, Thomas thought, a suggestion of tiny buds at their ends.

"I would like to know my new name, Court Singer," she declared breathlessly, fluttering her dark eyelashes along with her wings.

Zodiac had to nudge Thomas in the ribs twice before he could stammer some words out. "You're very pretty," he blurted, looking at Zodiac for support, which was, alas, not forthcoming because the Lord High Chamberlain was laughing so hard he could barely catch his breath. "Also, really violet...Violet!" Thomas sputtered. "Your name is Violet!"

"Violet" curtseyed in a fashion that seemed far more erotic than polite, and shot through the air above the assembled Folk and out an open window, laughing as she went.

Thomas was sweating. He rubbed the sleeve of his tunic across his face. "Holy shit," he whispered.

"Indeed," nodded Zodiac, wiping his eyes.

The last of the Queen's Ladies was a startlingly beautiful Elf that Thomas instantly named "Lavender," since the color violet was still very much on his mind, and the pretty Elf was wearing a lavender-colored gown. Lavender's hair was long and blonde, her ears pointed and seductive. Her eyes considered him carefully, almost wistfully, before she spoke. When at last she did speak, her voice was low, pleasant and playful. "Hello, Thomas. I hope that you will grace us with your music soon. We have need of the beauty of your songs."

"Have you heard my music before?" he asked with an easy courtesy. It had not occurred to him that anyone but Callie was familiar with his work. He couldn't help it; he was pleased in spite of himself.

"Of course we have heard it," Lavender continued with a grin. "Her Grace has many of your recordings. We love to listen to them. There is a magic in your music that gladdens us. But you knew that already, else you would not be with us now." She softened her smile and pressed on. "If you have need of anything from me...from any of us," she amended, "I hope you will call on us."

The Queen's Ladies giggled.

"I'll, uh, do that," replied Thomas, shooting a quick look at Zodiac, whose face was mercifully blank.

In one sweeping movement, the Queen's Ladies bowed to Thomas, then to Zodiac. They smiled, tittered among themselves, and departed as group.

"Good God," Thomas mumbled to Zodiac. "I feel like I've just met the in-laws."

Zodiac chuckled behind his hand. "Quite so. I trust it did not escape your notice that several of them seem to be willing to get to know you extremely well." He saw the uneasy astonishment in Thomas' dark eyes. "Poor man," Zodiac said, with no sympathy whatsoever.

A band of fifteen nasty-smelling, dust-streaked, hairy Spriggans had been waiting for new names impatiently behind the Queen's Ladies. The one closest to Thomas was staring hungrily at his leg, as the Spriggans moved, *en masse*, toward Thomas and Zodiac.

In a slight panic, Thomas took a deep breath and named the next dozen Folk randomly after the American Presidents whose names he could immediately remember.

"Shame on you," Zodiac scolded in mock disgust when the Spriggans, once named, collectively disappeared into thin air in front of a very startled Thomas. "You've simply run amok."

THOMAS HICCUPPED, AND waved his empty cup at Zodiac, who was still chortling in delight. "I knew I wasn't going to have to remember any of the names later on, but *they* were. I threw caution to the wind, and went to town," he laughed.

"Several towns," Zodiac corrected. "And whatever possessed you to name the members of the Queen's Council after cities?"

"Couldn't help it," Thomas answered, opening the last bottle of whisky. "I'd already run out of names of cars, units of measure, fruits and vegetables, mythological characters, islands, literary heroes and heroines, animals, movie stars and authors, holidays, days of the week, flowers and fish."

In his present state of immoderate intoxication, Zodiac was prepared to be magnanimous. "All in all, I don't think you did too badly, despite your somewhat inauspicious start."

"'Scribe' likes his name," Thomas said in his own defense. "He told me so."

"I doubt that you asked 'Squid' if he likes his very much," Zodiac countered.

"Well," admitted Thomas, "It was the end of the day. You should be glad that it didn't occur to me to start in on diseases. Even 'Squid', which is certainly not my best work, was better than 'Hangnail' or 'Appendicitis'."

Zodiac's shudder made Thomas laugh. "I think we are definitely going to need more whisky," Zodiac observed with a groan.

"I'm certain that you're right," Thomas agreed, and then passed out in the chair.

fourteen

HE LAY ON the couch in his living room, smoking his last joint. He had planned to ration it until he could get more weed, but was smoking it all, of course.

He thought hazily about the songs he would play at the Feast tomorrow, one to be held in his honor. It would be Elvenhome's official introduction to the music of the new Court Singer. There was much speculation about what Thomas would sing for the Fair Folk.

The event would take place in the Great Hall. He found himself wondering about the Hall's acoustics. Sitting straight up, he suddenly wished for microphones and professional sound checks. He took another hit, lay back down on the couch, and shrugged.

This would be the first time he'd performed here for anyone but Callie, and he smiled as he realized that he was looking forward to it, microphones or not.

But he needed to find some weed. And some coke, too, while he was at it.

Zodiac was heading to Thomas' rooms to drink and talk sometime that evening. Thomas would make his request then, Zodiac would get him the stuff, and all would be well.

Zodiac arrived with a bottle of seventy-five-year-old single malt. After he'd poured their second round and finished telling the Court Singer a startling but funny story about a Gnome who was currently in the infirmary after an attempt to fly ("...he failed to include the necessary existence of strong gusts of wind in his calculation..." Zodiac reported almost sadly), Thomas broached the subject of getting more weed. The Monster In His Head reminded him to ask about coke, too, and so he did.

"After all," Thomas pointed out, "Callie told me before I got here that all of my needs and desires would be met, that I can have whatever I want to eat and drink. I enjoy weed and cocaine, and I need more now. That was my last joint, and I haven't had coke since—"

Zodiac's response was kind, but it was also firm. "Her Grace has informed me that, while you may certainly have any kind of alcoholic beverage you desire, and as much as you choose, you may not consume any other substance that might compromise your music, neither the creation of it, nor the performance of it."

"You don't understand, and that's cool. But I need the drugs if I'm going to write songs for Callie." Thomas went for the first idea that occurred to him. "I can't write without them. They're part of the creative process. It's hard for people who don't write to get that."

Zodiac stared at him, his face unreadable for several long seconds. Thomas tried to stare back, but didn't do so well; he found himself staring at his shoes.

He tried again. "There's magic in what cocaine does with the way an artist's mind works. The weed helps to—"

"No, Thomas. I am sorry, but no."

"Look, I'm not an addict, but I do a lot of shit, and I need—"

"Stop." Zodiac's blunt, single-word interruption startled Thomas into an obedient if moody silence. It was becoming evident that he would not be getting any candy or weed from the Lord High Chamberlain. Thomas considered launching into some sort of defensive positioning, but instead sat quiet and wide-eyed, as though he'd been slapped.

"Her Grace was clear on the matter, my friend. I never disobey my Queen, especially when she is right. You shall not have access to, or need for, marijuana or any other so-called recreational pharmaceutical while you are here with us."

Thomas may have gasped. Zodiac continued. "You will find that the water you drink in Faerie does much to heal, repair and nourish a mortal body. You have been drinking Fey water since you arrived, and it has been, for want of a better word, 'protecting' you from the maladies associated with detoxification. You don't physically need your drugs at present, Thomas; your addiction merely wants them. But you may not have them, so you might want to adjust your thinking about that."

Without warning, The Monster In His Head growled and glared fiercely at Zodiac through Thomas' eyes. Its effort made Thomas' stomach hurt.

"Go away," Zodiac scoffed at The Monster, wiggling a finger at him.

In a flash, The Monster dissolved into a condition not unlike sleep. Thomas closed his eyes and watched in amazement, but said nothing. In a few moments, his stomachache disappeared.

Zodiac waited while Thomas found his balance and opened his eyes. "Her Grace commanded me to tell you this: she wants you to allow yourself to be free of the things that truly distract you from your music."

With a nod of his head to punctuate the end of this particular line of conversation, Zodiac waited a long moment, let a conspiratorial smile slide onto his face and said, "Thomas, remember that gorgeous redheaded Water Sprite you met at the Naming? The one who was almost wearing the light blue transparent gown?"

Thomas' eyebrows went up.

Zodiac looked around to make sure he wasn't being overheard, and poured more whisky into their glasses. "Well...I just heard the most astonishing thing..."

Thinking about it later, he wondered how he'd gotten off so easily about the drugs. He hadn't had a single withdrawal symptom, not even a headache. Nor had he felt the need to feed The Monster—or try to hide from it—for the first time in several years. What had Callie done to clean him up, take the need away? He wasn't sure he wanted to know the particulars. Easy rehab, though, he grinned to himself. Rehab without a price...

THE FEAST HONORING Thomas Lear's arrival in Elvenhome was held in the castle's Great Hall.

The Folk loved to celebrate; even the simplest occasion called for a party. Welcoming the High Queen's latest Court Singer, and the gift of New Names for everyone, was ample motivation for an event that would go on for several days.

Merry-making was the order of the evening. HobGoblins who managed and worked in the castle's kitchens carried large, heavy trays of food, and served roasted pork, venison and fowl to the Folk seated at the long common tables that filled the Hall. The Boggarts, whose families had tended the Faerie vineyards for generations, served wines and ales and other spirits from huge casks that were stacked precariously against the far wall. Jugglers and acrobats performed, dogs chased cats under trestle tables, and a small group of Spriggans planned a raid on the kitchens when the HobGoblins were away, busily serving the meal's next course.

An assorted band of faerie musicians, made up of three Bogles (fiddlers), a Sprite (harpist), a Pixie (piper) and four Goblins (percussionists on tambourine, cymbal, Jews' Harp, and drum), played mad, wildly whirling melodies as the Folk danced with untamed exuberance, laughed long and hard with delight, ate and drank with abandon, and talked animatedly with their neighbors. Pandemonium gleefully reigned; it was a gathering worthy of the Fair Folk.

Raw, happy chaos filled the Great Hall, with one notable exception.

The Guest of Honor, Thomas Lear, watching the festivities all over the Great Hall, ate Upworld food and drank Upworld wine—and did so without making a sound, by strict command of the High Queen of Faerie. He sat on her right, at the royal table, which stood a little above and apart from the general flurries of activity that occupied much of the Hall. On Thomas' other side, Zodiac was deep in a conversation with two of the Queen's Ladies, the newly-named Iris and Orchid. Callie was, at the moment, talking with her most senior advisor on the Queen's Council, the handsome, dark-haired Naiad who now bore the name "Boston," and sat on her other side.

Conversations buzzed all around him, but Thomas didn't mind in the slightest; he was listening to the music, watching the band play, and marveling at the strange place in which he found himself, both physically and metaphysically. He was relaxed, and was enjoying himself more than he had been able to in ages. The absolute surreality of his present situation was a blast; if this was a drug dream, he didn't want to come out of it anytime soon.

A smile softened his face as the band started playing music that sounded a bit like a strange modulation of some classic American Swing tunes.

Wait... Thomas thought, that's a Sinatra standard...it's "Fly Me to the Moon"! Almost it, but it's not...wow... The musicians are good; they play the song well, but still...

When he took the breath that would have resulted in a hearty laugh and clever side comment, he was surrounded by a nearly invisible, quieting web of flickering green light, which spotlighted his obligation to remain silent. He let the air out of his unreleased chuckle and pithy remark, and was rewarded with a light touch on his left hand. Callie's approval glowed in her eyes.

"That was well done, Thomas," she complimented him. "Is it very difficult to not speak when there is so much speech around you?"

Thomas shook his head. It was actually a relief to not have to talk tonight, strange as that was.

Callie understood. "Good. I did not wish for you to miss the feast honoring your presence among us. That seemed like poor form."

"And no challenge at all," Zodiac added, with a wink at the Court Singer.

Smiling, Thomas shrugged, and reached for the near-empty bottle of wine that waited patiently beside his goblet as he pointed several times toward the musicians, who were still playing an eerie medley of songs that Sinatra, Bennett and Martin had made famous decades before.

Zodiac and Callie watched Thomas for a moment, and then burst into merry laughter.

"Where did they learn that music?" Callie framed Thomas' question for him.

"Why does it sound like something you recognize, but doesn't sound like anything you recognize?" Zodiac anticipated Thomas' other question.

Thomas nodded his head, and sipped his wine.

"Well asked," Callie smirked, and Thomas took a silent bow.

"Our last Court Singer was quite fond of something called "Swingie" music, and he taught us many songs when he was with us," Zodiac began.

"He loved them, and wanted to write songs like that, but didn't really have it in him. It wasn't his style, although he gave it a try. He was—is—a Scot," Callie added.

"Down to his toes," Iris chimed in, and everyone within earshot cheered at this.

"Anyway," Callie continued, "he was a marvelous storyteller with his songs, but he couldn't make it work in the Swingie genre. He wanted to write for Sinatra and Clooney..."

"He wasn't experienced enough about life yet," Iris concluded, abruptly but not unkindly.

"But," Callie said, sidestepping the interruptions, "he played many instruments, and taught us to love the music of the Swingies. He also experimented with other kinds of music, right here in Elvenhome." Callie finished. "It was quite a lot of fun."

Zodiac nodded. "He taught us well, and he brought not only this American music to us, he gave us his own songs too."

Orchid, the Selkie with the dream-deep, liquid brown eyes, leaned into the conversation and said to Thomas, "We love music, any music, all music. We learn it the first time we hear it. It becomes part of us, and then we can sing it or our musicians play it, and thus it is shared with all the Folk, and belongs to us always."

Thomas lifted an eyebrow in inquiry.

Orchid looked at him, frowned, then looked to Callie for clarification.

The High Queen smiled. "Thomas, we can only play music that we've heard elsewhere. We Fair Folk do not create music; that is not in us, remember what I told you? We can only repeat what we have heard, and that repetition shines through the one singing or playing the song. So what we hear is somewhat different from what you hear. We hear 'music.' You hear 'Faerie Music.' Faeriekind and mortalkind can both hear it, but we do not necessarily hear the same things. Does that make any sense?"

Thomas nodded in the affirmative, then, thinking this over, shook his head instead. After a few seconds, he shrugged, and grinned as his dinner companions laughed. Zodiac clapped him on the shoulder and admitted, "It gets easier, or so I hear, my friend."

After the HobGoblins had cleared away the food and dishes and taken everything back to the Kitchens, other Folk worked swiftly to remove the trestle tables from the floor and stack them neatly against the far wall. Meanwhile, still others repositioned all of the benches to face the small, elevated stage built for Thomas' performance.

There was an almost electric excitement as the Fey audience found seats and waited for the music to begin.

At the High Table, Callie turned to Thomas and smiled as she took his hand. Squeezing it, she said quietly, "Thomas, you have my leave to speak in this room, from this moment, until you leave it to return to your apartments. Sing to us, and show us your heart." A flash of green light sparked quickly around Thomas' face.

He gave her a questioning look, and she laughed. "Go on, you may speak now. Exercise your voice so you can sing, and go up there and show the Folk why I chose you." She nodded toward the stage area at the opposite end of the Hall. Both of his guitars were waiting for him there.

Obediently, and with a wry grin, Thomas cleared his throat theatrically, and kissed Callie's hand. "Here goes," he said, and cleared his throat some more. He grabbed a bottle of French wine from the table. He also picked up a large goblet of water, which he drank as he moved through the crowd toward the stage, working his voice as he walked.

Thomas Lear, Rock Star, sang his songs for the High Queen of Faerie, and for all the Fair Folk of Elvenhome. He started with two of his earliest love songs, and the Folk, delighted with what they heard, applauded wildly.

The audience drank in Thomas' music as it left his guitar and surrounded them. Some winged sprites, Violet among them, hovered beside the Court Singer as he sang and played, humming in interesting harmonies that, Thomas noted, worked pretty well.

He'd done this for so long that he could do just about anything else in another part of his brain while he performed, and never miss a note, a beat, or a well-practiced visual expression. His eyes scanned the audience of Gnomes, Elves, Goblins, HobGoblins, Sprites, Dwarfs, Pixies, "Flyers" (his own name for the winged Folk), Naiads, Knockers,

Spriggans, and a Giant. He marveled at how well he'd adjusted to the many races of faeries he'd met, then wondered in self-directed amusement if something was wrong with him. He was taking the whole year-and-a-day—the full-on *Thomas the Rhymer redux* thing—mostly in stride.

Catching Callie's eye, he smiled as he slid into *What I Need Tonight,* and nodded at her as her smile broadened in appreciation of the song. It pleased him to please her. He hoped he would be in a position to please her later that night as well.

When he finished the song, loud and merry applause from the Folk pulled his attention from thoughts of Callie and back to the Great Hall. Even so, the next time he looked at her from the stage, she winked at him.

He gave her his best smile, and retuned a string on his guitar as he addressed his audience: "Thank you. Thank you very much. This next song is one of the last I wrote and recorded, and it's becoming a favorite of mine. It's called *'Dangerous Blue Eyes'*. I hope you like it."

As he began to play, he decided that the drug thing was, strangely enough, no longer an issue. It didn't have to matter now. Maybe he could learn to face himself with the same sense of approval and genuine welcome as he saw in the hundreds of eyes that watched him as he stood on the stage.

Thomas Lear, Court Singer, stepped away from his own thoughts, and at last focused his mind and heart entirely on his music, and on this audience.

And there was magic.

Before the festivities in the Great Hall concluded that night, Thomas was honored by a gift from the High Queen of Faerie.

The formal presentation was in keeping with the significance of the occasion. After Thomas' final bow to the audience, once the wild applause wound down, the Lord High Chamberlain stood up from his seat at the High Queen's table, and announced: "Her Majesty the Queen has a Gift of Welcome and Thanks for her—and our—Court Singer."

The Folk murmured their approval.

Intrigued, Thomas placed his guitar in the stand behind him, and watched as one of the Queen's Ladies, Lavender, the pretty blonde Elf with the tail, moved through the crowd toward the stage. She carried a large box, the contents of which were speculated upon in hushed, excited whispers.

When Lavender approached the stage, she stood in front of and below Thomas, and raised the box to him, shifting the lid so he could lift the gift out for all to see. It was an elegant thigh-length velvet jacket, the color of *goldenfruit*.

Callie was glowing with pride and pleasure.

Honored by the gift, and satisfied by his own performance, Thomas bowed to the High Queen. When he straightened, he smiled and mouthed the words to her across the Hall, over the heads of the audience: *Thank you, My Queen.*

As the torchlight and the softer candlelight flickered together in the Great Hall, the jacket in Thomas' hands glittered in response. Enchanted by the sparkle that danced on it, Thomas put the jacket on. It was comfortable; it fit like a charm.

The Folk cheered again, and Thomas found himself laughing, his pleasure fueled by their enthusiasm.

When they began to disperse a few minutes later, talking and laughing as they made their way out of the Hall, Thomas thought he heard stray snippets of some of the songs he'd sung for them. He had to admit to himself that *Dangerous Blue Eyes* sounded a little strange coming out of a high-pitched Pixie voice. Hearing bits of *I Don't Think I Can Love You* from the throat of a Giant was a more-than-sobering experience that he decided that he'd attempt to forget about as soon as possible.

He didn't think he'd ever had this kind of entertainment after a show before. He couldn't wait to be alone with Callie, to talk with her about it, and wind down from the performance. He glanced at the High Table; she was still seated there, talking with two of her Ladies. Laughing now, she did not notice that he was watching her. Once again captivated by her beauty, he was also fully aware that there was so much more to her than her lovely body, her dark eyes and her sensually-decorated skin. He wanted to know all the layers of her. He chuckled to himself when he realized that he didn't care how long that took.

His reverie abruptly dissolved when a sultry feminine voice skidded across his awareness.

"Does the Queen's gift please you, Thomas?" Lavender asked, wide-eyed, from his left. She was still standing beside the stage. The box she'd carried was at her feet. She was gazing up and over at him, and at the jacket. "It is so very beautiful!"

He had forgotten that she was there.

"Yes it does, and yes it is," he replied, smiling at her. "Thank you for delivering it."

Lavender's tentative look grew into a wide, beaming grin. "I was honored to do it."

He turned and picked up his guitar, ready to call it a night.

"I loved listening to you sing, Thomas," Lavender said. "I love your songs."

"Thank you," he said. He stepped down from the stage, jacket glistening, guitar in hand.

She stood motionless, unable to take her eyes off him as he took two steps away from the stage. "Thomas?"

He turned and met her eyes, eyebrow raised in distracted inquiry. She was a pretty thing, and he had not forgotten about her tail.

"I am so glad you are here...to sing for us."

"I'm glad too, Lavender." Thomas Lear, Rock Star, flashed the pretty Elf his famous smile. He said goodnight, winked at her, and walked into the crowd.

From that moment on, and through all the days of her long life, she would hold the precious memory of the Court Singer winking at her that night. For it was in that random fragment of a mere fraction of a second that Lavender fell completely, irreversibly in love with Thomas Lear.

AS IF IT had never disappeared (and it had, Thomas warranted with a barely-suppressed shudder), the famous Lear Magic was back; he was a songwriter again, and the work was as intense and satisfying as it was brilliant. The sweet, heady awareness of this was intoxicating. It was possible that Thomas was higher on the utter delight and relief of his jubilant return to creativity than he'd ever been when feeding The Monster In His Head. If he realized that The Monster hadn't stirred since Zodiac had all but banished it more than a week ago, he hadn't taken the time to consider the change. Thomas' energy was, at long last, focused on the work that allowed him to be the best, most glowing version of himself, and he poured himself into the process. His consuming passion for writing music and poetry was not lost or dead, as he'd feared. It was more than alive in him; he felt it all as his words and his hauntingly beautiful melodies came together, sang and danced in his mind.

With the guitar Callie had given him, Thomas sat on the stool facing the windows in his living room, and played one of his new songs to the trees outside. As he played, he listened to the cadence of the notes. At one point, he stopped, and considered a different phrasing. He played the changed phrase three times, decided he liked it better. He strolled to the dining table, guitar in hand, to note the change on the staff paper on which he'd drafted the melody.

There was quiet knock on the front door.

When Thomas had made the change, he rested the guitar against the table, and went to the door.

Orchid, the Queen's Lady, gave him a shy smile as he let her in. Once the door was closed, and the Selkie and the singer stood facing each other, she brightened, and bowed to Thomas. Her soft brown eyes were alight with merriment.

"The Queen's Grace asks if you would join her in her private chambers in four hours' time." Her smile widened as Thomas' eyebrow went up surprise at the request. "And she bids me point out to you that the High Queen of Faerie doesn't often ask for the companionship of her Court Singer," Orchid continued with a chuckle. "But as Her Grace is aware that you are composing new music, she chooses to show respect by honoring your work time. She hopes that you will have something to play for her this night." Orchid bowed again.

Thomas nodded. "Tell Her Grace that it will be my pleasure to serve her."

The knowing look in Orchid's eyes made him laugh, and she laughed with him. "I believe that is quite true, Thomas!" Orchid noticed the mahogany guitar propped against the dining table. "Oh...you were playing! I do not wish to disturb you. But..." her voice trailed off wistfully.

"Would you like to stay for a moment? I just made a change in a song, and need to play it for a while."

She looked so pleased that he nearly burst out laughing. "Truly?"

"Sure," he said. "Have a seat." He indicated the couch. She moved across the room, brown eyes wide with wonder and a growing excitement, then sat down on the couch, watching him.

With practiced elegance, Thomas lifted the guitar, then the stool, and moved to a spot in front of Orchid.

And then he began to play.

The music seemed to whisper from the heart of the guitar. The melody was simple, sad and sweet, reaching for stars it could not touch, aching for love it needed but could not find. As Thomas began the second line of "She Sings Sad Songs," the guitar's voice deepened beside his own, and seemed to weep for the woman Thomas sang about, the woman with the open yet still empty heart.

Orchid was enchanted. The lyric brought tears to her gentle, seal-like eyes while the music held her captive. She drank in the experience as though she had been thirsty for longer than she'd realized; she gave herself to Thomas' passion and artistry. Song and singer were the only true things in the moment.

When he was finished, and could take a small step away from the recital, he looked at her to gauge reaction to his work. Her approval trickled down her cheeks; her bottom lip trembled when she smiled at him.

For a flash of a second, Thomas wondered if the song, although he knew it was good, might be too much. It had moved him when he was writing it, and it tugged at his heart while he sang it, taking him perilously close to tears of his own. Should he tone it down a little? He started to ask Orchid about that when she asked, interrupting him: "Thomas, could you play that for me again? Please?"

Later, when Thomas and Callie were alone in her private rooms, the High Queen's reaction to "She Sings Sad Songs" was much like Orchid's had been. She made Thomas sing it to her four times. When he finally put the guitar aside, and stood still, watching her, Callie found that she couldn't speak. Instead, she took a deep breath, and pondered the love and pain that infused his song. She had immersed herself in the beautiful spell he'd woven as he sang his heart. She had opened her heart fully to the emotion of it, and savored the experience. Her reward for losing herself in his music was that, as she listened to Thomas sing, she had had no room to think about the handful of serious concerns that weighed on her mind. Whatever was she going to do about—

"Callie?"

Mentally, she pulled herself back, and focused on the man who now stood in front of her, questions forming in his dark eyes.

She smiled at him; she couldn't help it. "I always like it when I'm right," she said.

In soft light from fireplace and candles, they dined on warm bread and butter, cheese, fresh fruit and a robust red wine, all safely provisioned for Thomas from Upworld. (*"Eat and drink, free from care,"* Callie spoke the ritual before he reached for a knife to spread the butter.)

"I cannot help but to be equally fascinated and frustrated by the creative act of composition," Callie confessed with a sigh, sipping wine from a silver goblet.

"How so?" Thomas wanted to know.

"I have spent much time with mortals who are unimaginably creative, gifted, who practice their art with devotion and delight. I have learned how their minds work, how their hearts fill and spill over and fill again. I have watched their souls dance in wild pleasure and writhe in silent pain. I can see where and how the magic that only mortals make comes into being. I remain fascinated in the presence of it." She frowned. "And frustrated, too, because I understand something of the fiery energy, the why behind the act of true creation –and the knowledge makes me yearn to share in the making of something new and beautiful. But, being faerie-born, I do not have a connection to the inner fire that gives light and life to music or poetry. I cannot dream stories that touch the very heart of the world—like you can, Thomas."

She rose from the table, and walked past the staircase, and across to the glass doors that opened to her gardens. Once there, the High Queen of Faerie gazed at the trees, which were bathed in moonshine; she reveled in the beauty around her. Looking up, Callie smiled at the moon, which was full and slightly red, as she continued: "We are different from mortals in this, as in so many other things. I think of it this way: we Fair

Folk can accurately reflect dazzling starlight back into the night sky—but we ourselves are not the light, nor are we the stars."

"Tomorrow," Callie promised, "I'm going to show you the oldest trees in Elvenhome. They're wise, and strong, and most of them are quite pleasant to be around."

Thomas had not been outside of the castle since his arrival. He liked hiking, although he hadn't had time or inclination for it over the past few years. He welcomed the idea of a walk in the woods; it would be even more enjoyable with Callie.

They were sitting in a large golden tub filled with herb-scented warm water. Thomas watched as shy Carnation washed and rinsed the Queen's hair, and wondered why it didn't strike him as too strange that he and Callie were not alone as they bathed and talked. Just then, Dahlia, the Dwarf princess, entered the chamber with another bucket of hot water; this she added to the contents of the tub with a satisfied nod. Violet flittered above their heads, sprinkling rosemary and comfrey leaves into the water. Iris stood in the doorway, overseeing the Ladies as they served the Queen.

"You're much lighter when you've been writing," Callie observed, sloshing water at Thomas. "I think I prefer you this way. You're quite handsome when you're not scowling."

"I do not scowl, Your Grace." Thomas sloshed an impressive wall of water back at her.

"You do. Every photograph I've seen of you, and on every one of your album covers, there's a scowl on your face, or in your eyes. You are more than a little moody, and you are selfish." Busted, Thomas raised his eyebrows but did not argue. She saw his unconditional surrender, and laughed. "I recognize a deep selfishness in you, Thomas, because I also can be selfish, in my way." She looked around, glanced at Iris, and subtly inclined her head. In seconds, all the Ladies had bowed and left the Queen's presence; in a moment, they could be heard speaking in cheery but hushed voices as they walked as a group down the staircase.

He had never considered the notion that he was selfish. As he thought about it now, he had to agree that she was right. The funny thing was that it didn't bother him all that much.

"See?" she said. "You recognize it."

Thomas shrugged. "Part of the artist personality?"

"Absolutely," replied Callie. "If you were not always turned inward to look at yourself, and very likely scowling while you did it, too, you would not be able to tell your stories, and write your songs in such a personal, intimate way. There would be no magic in the music of Thomas Lear, and that would intolerable. That you can sing so beautifully only makes the music that much stronger."

He tilted his head and laughed. "So I'm a selfish bastard, but it's okay because I'm incidentally doing something good with it, and you like what you hear?"

She laughed too. "Something like that."

Standing up, Thomas reached for a large towel that Dahlia had placed on a bench beside the tub. He climbed out of the tub and dried off. "How are you selfish, Callie?" he asked.

She thought for a moment, a wry smile sliding onto her face. "I am selfish in that I do not bring Court Singers and their stories and songs to the Folk for their happiness alone. I do it for myself, when it pleases me to do so, not based on the needs of my people. In this I am self-serving, hungry, and perhaps greedy. I use the music, the stories, the man, to feed and fill needs that I carry. And somewhere in the experience, I get to almost touch creation."

Thomas gave Callie his hand, and she raised herself up out of the water. She slid into the dry towel he held for her.

"It doesn't seem at all selfish when you put it that way," he murmured, rubbing the towel against her back and watching the tiny leaves on her skin tremble as he did so.

"As you said, I too am 'doing something good with it,' yet it is still about me, and about what I want. It may be a creative selfishness, but it is selfishness nevertheless."

They walked hand in hand toward her bedroom with other, less intellectual, intimacies in mind. It occurred to him that talking with Callie was proving to be a constant game of Truth or Dare. He wasn't entirely comfortable with it; he was even less comfortable when he realized that he didn't really understand what might be at stake.

Callie turned her head and blessed him with a very pretty yet enigmatic smile. *Did she know what he was thinking? How did she do that?*

The allegedly selfish High Queen of Faerie burst into a lusty giggle, and bolted for the bed.

Naked, he had no place to pocket his many carefully-crafted, safe personal fictions, the notions about himself that mostly kept his mind, heart and soul together, and the fears that kept them all alive. So he consciously let them go—for now, anyway—and eagerly darted after Her Grace.

fifteen

THE CORNERS OF Lavender's mouth turned down as she watched them leave together, Callie's hand on top of Thomas' as they walked away, through the castle's main gate. The blonde Elf's eyes narrowed as Callie laughed at something Thomas said.

"Come, Lavender," said Iris. "We have embroidery to finish while The Queen's Grace is off with Thomas."

Lavender wasn't listening. She was watching the man she loved stroll with her Queen along the stone path toward the wood, their intention unmistakable to anyone who had seen the hungry sparkle in the Queen's eyes. Lavender felt her face and jaw tighten; her hands clenched as her eyes followed them until they were out of sight.

It was simply not fair.

"Lavender?" prompted Iris.

Sighing, Lavender turned and met Iris' gaze. "I am coming," she muttered.

She straggled behind a bit as she walked with the other Ladies through the castle to the Queen's Chambers, keeping a little distance to let the others move ahead so that she could think.

Thomas. Oh, Thomas! Even though he had not been granted leave to speak to them as they waited for Her Grace to arrive, he had not needed to speak to make her pulse race. He looked especially attractive today; the gold tunic and leggings were wonderful on his beautiful body. Entering the courtyard, he had smiled at her, and melted her heart all over again. All right, to be honest, he had smiled at all of the Queen's Ladies, but she had been included in that smile. That counted, didn't it?

She remembered the expression on his face when Her Grace had first joined them, followed by Iris, Rose and Orchid. His eyes had sparkled, bright as new fire, when the High Queen stepped onto the stone-paved yard. Thomas had smiled, then, shooting a suggestive look at the Queen that hinted at the intimacy between them.

Seeing that private smile had sliced Lavender's aching heart into painful ribbons.

So complete was his focus on the Queen that he hadn't noticed the Ladies at all after her arrival.

And that's as it should be, Lavender thought, trying to be reasonable. *Except that he could be, should be, mine when she's finished with him!* she reminded herself in the next heartbeat.

She had waited so long for it to be her turn again. Juniper had had the last gentle cast-off, several Singers ago, toward the end of his time in Elvenhome. In truth, Her Grace had not been all that fond of that particular Court Singer. She had been quite busy with her royal duties at the time, rather than bored with the handsome mortal, but it worked in any case. The Queen felt that he needed more attention than she could give him just then, so she offered Juniper the opportunity to play with him instead. It was, after all, Juniper's turn. Naturally, Juniper took him to her bed and was happy with him until he left, then she went back to her other lovers, everyone was merry, and all was as it had been before his arrival.

Now, at last, it was again Lavender's turn to have the Court Singer as her lover, finally, finally! It had been such a long time in coming. Her Grace was ever patient with her mortal lovers, and gave them plenty of freedom to do as they wished. It was understood that if the Court Singer was not in Her Grace's presence, he could be anywhere he wanted to be, including someone else's arms.

Lavender could not help but wish that the other arms the present Court Singer would choose would be her own.

Unfortunately, Thomas Lear seemed to see only Her Grace. And for her part, although the Queen did not spend every night with Thomas, Lavender knew that Her Grace was happy with him. And, oh, the look in Her Grace's eyes when she spoke of him...

Not for the first time since Thomas' arrival in Elvenhome, Lavender wondered dismally if there was a chance that Her Grace would not tire of him.

She felt herself die just a little. She had much love to give...

Her thoughts were interrupted as she nearly collided with Carnation and Dahlia, who, with the other Ladies, had stopped walking and turned to look back at her.

"Lavender! Watch out!" Violet laughed as she zoomed past Lavender's right ear.

Lavender froze, eyes still glazed over as her mind cleared. "What?"

Orchid's smile was kind and sympathetic. "You were very far away."

"She was not so far away," Rose taunted lightly. "She was only as far away as the wood!"

Lavender glared at the Ladies collectively, but said nothing.

"Come along, my dear," Iris said in a soothing voice, moving back through the group to stand beside Lavender. The Banshee patted the sad Elf on the arm. "We shall send for musicians to come and play for us while we work, to take our minds off our troubles, aye?"

Giving Iris what she hoped could be interpreted as a grateful nod, Lavender joined the other Ladies and tried, without success, to put Thomas out of her mind.

In the afternoon sunshine, they talked only of small matters as they walked together through the forest.

Thomas found the fresh air, the sounds of small animals and talkative birds, and the smells of the grasses, the flowers, the trees and the dirt under their feet nothing short of exhilarating. "This is great. It's like hiking through a vivid dream," he suggested.

"A happy dream, I hope." Callie made a scary face at him, and he smirked. "Do you walk with trees at home in Los Angeles?"

"God, Callie, I haven't been hiking in six or seven years. When I was younger, and was less busy, less noticeable, I would get in a couple of good hikes every month. There were lots of places not too far from where I lived then that are great for day hikes. Later, when things started happening with my career, I'd try to take vacations where I could do some serious hiking, but I didn't seem to get any time to go off by myself, and I stopped doing it."

"Perhaps not a good decision, since you enjoy walking in the woods," she replied, without malice.

"Yet *another* not-good decision," he admitted and frowned as he thought about it. He heard a noise in the nearby undergrowth, and brightened when he saw a small, red fox dart directly across their path and into the trees.

Callie pointed out her favorite birches and rowans, and introduced Thomas to a gathering of white thorn trees that guarded a wide ring of ancient oaks.

"They pay far less attention to me than I do to them. The spirits in these trees must outrank me," the High Queen chuckled as they walked past.

"Impossible, my Queen," Thomas assured her with a bow and a grin.

"He learns quickly!" Callie announced to the birds that nested in branches overhead. "Handsome as well as intelligent," she added, addressing a massive rust-colored rock, which she touched as she led Thomas deep into the wood.

The vibrant energy behind the silence of the trees subtly enveloped them. Their conversation faded away. Thomas opened himself up to the glory that was the heart of the forest: the dignified trees, the sweetly-scented grasses, the soothing sound of birds calling to each other, the dappled light dancing in long, sparkling beams.

He stopped, then stooped to examine some bright-white flowers he'd never seen before. When he stood up again, Callie reached for his hands and, kissing them, backed him up against a huge alder.

Much later, they came out of the cool shadows of the wood and into the dazzling sunshine, talking and laughing. Callie carried some stray wildflowers that she had picked along the way.

Moving along the stone road that led back toward the castle, they made their way up to and past the main gate, and walked in the general vicinity of the loch that shimmered several hundred feet to the west of the castle. The loch was small; it barely took up a full half-acre. The water was bright blue, and sparkled in the sunlight. It smelled fresher than any loch water he had ever encountered, and he said so.

"I'd imagine so," Callie said. "They keep it very clean."

"*Who* keeps it very clean?"

"The Water Faeries that live there," she answered. "There's a good deal of traffic through it from other parts of Faerie," she added, by way of explanation.

It was not a real explanation as far as Thomas was concerned, but he wasn't sure he could phrase his next question, so he shrugged it off and attempted to approach the issue from another direction.

"What's the lake – I mean the *loch*—called?" Thomas asked.

"Elvenhome."

He stopped, and looked at her in amazement. "The loch is called 'Elvenhome'?"

"Yes," she nodded, taking his arm and propelling them on their way.

"Elvenhome the Loch, Elvenhome the Province, and Elvenhome the Castle?" he teased her. "Someone was a little short on originality, I'd say."

She rolled her eyes becomingly. "Well, I suppose we could have left the naming of loch, province and castle to you, Thomas, if we were willing to live with a possible selection from lists of tall buildings or board game titles."

He chuckled. "You know, 'Loch Monopoly' has a certain ring to it."

She grimaced at the thought. "That's terrible."

"I know. That will teach you to make poor bedazzled mortals name the Fair Folk, so there." He sniffed at her in mock indignation, she sniffed back at him, and then they were laughing again. They reached the top of the fragrant knoll that stood above the edge of the loch.

From the corner of his eye, Thomas could see a rippling in the center of the sparkling blue water. He turned his head to watch it for a moment, assuming that it was a pretty trick of the light. When the rippling continued and then seemed to move faster, he halted at once and pointed to it. "What's that, Callie?"

Callie turned and looked. Thomas stiffened, but said nothing as he realized that the ripple was getting larger, and it was coming toward them.

She felt his tension, and squeezed his arm. "It's nothing harmful, Thomas, don't be alarmed. It's only a Water Faerie, and perhaps it is someone you already know. We shall have to wait for a moment and see."

In a matter of seconds, the ripple was less than ten feet from the loch shore. Thomas took a step back, Callie took a step forward, each watching with interest.

He rose up out of the loch, beautiful in his nakedness, long, wet, golden-blond hair falling around his shoulders and plastered against his head, revealing elongated, delicately pointed ears. Lost in his own thoughts, he was oblivious to Callie and Thomas watching him. His eyes were as bright and blue as the water, but even from twenty feet away, Thomas could see that there was deep, sharp pain in them.

Thomas glanced uneasily at Callie, who was watching as the tall Water Faerie moved away from the loch; her eyes filled with tears. Her chin trembled and she barely held back something that sounded very much like a small sob.

"Callie?" Thomas whispered in concern. He knew he'd never seen this man before. Still, it was obvious that Callie had feelings for him.

"He's my cousin, Thomas," she whispered, not taking her eyes from the Water Faerie. "He has not been well, and he is so very sad. If he speaks to you, you may speak until he takes leave of us. If he does not, say nothing."

Thomas nodded, put his arm around Callie, and then looked from her to the Water Faerie, who was now walking up the loch side of the knoll toward them, toward the castle. In a matter of seconds, he was standing in front of them. Callie threw her arms around him, hugged him hard, and then took a step away from him. When she did, Thomas could see that she looked composed; there was no outward evidence of her distress. He also noticed with some surprise that the Water Faerie was no longer dripping, as he should have been; his skin was dry and his hair was damp rather than wet.

The Water Faerie smiled at them; the profound sense of pain that had been visible in his eyes only moments before was gone now, buried.

"Cousin," Callie said, greeting him. "Swimming, bathing, healing, or visiting?"

The blond Water Faerie smiled. "A little of everything," he told her. His eyes met Thomas', and he reached out a hand to him. Thomas noticed delicate webbing between the other man's fingers just as their hands met in greeting. "You'll be Thomas Lear. Your music is most beautiful. I trust that Callie has made you feel…welcome?" he said, with a rakish lift of eyebrow.

"Everyone has a rude comment about the Queen's social life," Callie muttered. "Thomas, this is—this is someone who needs a name," she smirked. "And, please, do better than names of American cars." She looked at her cousin and gestured her mock dismay. "You will not believe some of the names the Folk now carry. I would tell you, but I cannot even think about some of them without begging the assistance of some very strong ale."

Thomas looked askance at Callie, and said to the Water Faerie, "She only says that because it's true. I panicked. Was that so hard to understand?"

Both males smiled, liking each other at once.

"Go on, then, Thomas, do your worst. Callie has probably not mentioned to you that once I was named 'John Smith the Elder', though I never did find out why…or if there even was a why…"

Thomas looked at the Water Faerie. Perhaps it was because he'd just come from the water; Thomas was reminded of a graceful but powerful lifeguard. *Lifeguard?* But that wasn't quite right somehow. This man looked as though he could protect anything by the sheer force of his will, even more than he could protect it with the obvious strength of his body. *What a strange thought*, Thomas said to himself. He rolled a few sounds around in his head, and then said: "'Guardian'—but I don't know why. It feels right, I guess…" He looked from Callie to the Water Faerie. "God, is it too awful?"

But they were both smiling, first at each other, and then back at Thomas.

"Well done, Thomas!" Callie cried, beaming at him.

The newly-christened "Guardian" nodded. "I like it; it will do nicely. Thank you, Thomas."

Thomas breathed a sigh of relief, and tried unsuccessfully to look as though it had been no effort at all.

Callie touched Guardian's face, and met his eyes. "Are you well?"

"Well enough," he told her. He winked at Thomas. "Women."

"I have nothing to say," Thomas declared.

"That will be the day, Court Singer." She made a face at him.

Guardian straightened, and with a brisk energy he did not feel, he told them, "I have many things to accomplish before this day is over. I should return to my rooms. It was a pleasure meeting you at last, Thomas. Be welcome in Elvenhome." A thought occurred to Guardian. "Do you play chess?"

"I do," Thomas said.

"Excellent," Guardian smiled. "Perhaps we shall meet for a game soon."

"I'd like that."

Guardian raised a hand in farewell, walked several steps past them, and then turned back to face them. "Cousin?"

"Yes?"

Guardian bowed his head slightly. "Is my friend still at work in the library?"

There's a library! Thomas thought, but he stayed quiet and listened.

Callie matched Guardian's look. "Yes, Cousin."

"Do you think he has spent enough time there yet, Your Grace?"

Callie licked her lips and pretended to consider this. "I suppose so," she said after a moment, now feigning intense boredom. "I suppose that you may tell him that my command has been rescinded. Which means he will be free to leave his confinement at midnight. And I mean midnight, 'Guardian'!"

Guardian bowed again, amusement flickering in his blue eyes. "Thank you, Your Grace. He will be delighted with the news. I believe he had begun to think you had forgotten him."

"We should all be so fortunate," Callie grumbled. Guardian and Callie exchanged a visual message, and then Guardian turned to walk toward the castle alone.

Before Thomas could ask, Callie looked up at him and explained succinctly: "Queen Stuff." The menacing look in her eyes made him laugh out loud.

She turned on him, but it was mostly in fun. "What are you laughing at?"

"Me?" he asked, mock innocence written all over his face.

"You!" she hissed.

"I'm not laughing," he laughed.

"I'm glad to hear it. Just as you'll be glad to hear that, once that exasperating creature is out and about again, you've got to give him a new name."

Thomas stopped laughing. He groaned instead.

Victorious, Callie arched an eyebrow, and looked at the now-placid loch. "And I'd suggest you work from a list of 'types of headache'."

"YOU'RE RIGHT. I don't see any way around it, either," Jack agreed with Stan. They had been sitting in Jack's office for an hour or so, discussing the source of their own mutual headache, and attempting to come up with a way to manage him and his career while he was maddeningly *in absentia*.

Tired, Stan rubbed his eyes. "Will she do it?"

"She has to. She works for me." Jack shrugged and pushed a button on his telephone. "Susie, come in here for a minute, will you?"

Susannah walked into Jack's office and looked at the two men who were studying her far too closely for comfort. "What do you need?"

Jack indicated with a wiggle of his fingers that Susannah should sit down and join the discussion. Then, after two false starts, he glanced at Stan for assistance. Stan was no help at all; he was looking out the window, staring down at Los Angeles rush-hour traffic with excessive fascination.

"What?" Susannah prompted Jack.

He intended for it to come out sounding playful and tantalizing; instead, it came out as something just short of a direct order from a frazzled admiral. "Guess who's going to Scotland to track down Thomas Lear and get him to come home?"

THOMAS WAS TIRED tonight, but he was in a good mood as he lay on his back on the deep, comfortable couch, content as he looked out his windows at the night sky. Dining with Callie in the Great Hall in the company of the rest of the Court had been more fun than he'd expected. He had perfected the habit of not speaking at all when he was away from his own rooms, and everyone around him understood and was agreeable about it. He was getting the hang of communicating with others, like Zodiac, the Queen's Ladies, and his potential new friend,

Guardian, without words. The notion fascinated him. It was a game, and he was learning to play it well.

He was amazed at how much listening he'd done since he'd been in Elvenhome, and how differently he processed information now. Had he ever truly listened to a conversation he'd participated in before he got here? He was beginning to believe that he hadn't ever taken the time to listen to much of anything at all; he'd been far too focused on whatever he was going to say next in every conversational exchange. In his new life here he was learning things on levels he didn't know how to contemplate. The thought amused him even as it pleased him. He was changing, and for the better; he was as close to being happy as he could imagine he could possibly be. *This is strange, very strange*, he told himself. *But I like it.*

Congratulating himself with a wry smile, his mind wandered and he thought about the group of musicians who had played during dinner. The lively music was performed on pipe, flutes and harp. The four somewhat nervous young Goblins were quite good. They got even better when they'd each downed a large mug of ale or two.

Stomach full, body warm and relaxed, Thomas snorted in amusement as he drifted toward a light sleep.

A book, which he had left lying on the table beside the couch, hit the carpeted floor with a dull thud, and Thomas was certain he heard a sharp intake of breath that was followed by a whisper of mild but sincere profanity.

He froze, instantly wide awake, more curious than alarmed. He lifted an eyelid only wide enough to take a surreptitious look at the table upon which the heavy book had sat only seconds before. Then he stealthily checked the room. There was no one there.

Closing his eye again, listening hard, he was sure he could hear something or someone breathing by the front door, less than fifteen feet from him.

Someone was there.

Perhaps it was the same someone, he remembered, who had been in here the morning of the day he'd spent naming Fair Folk in the Queen's Reception Chamber with Zodiac. He had forgotten all about it. He had forgotten about her; the memory of the single word she'd spoken reminded him of the very feminine voice.

Keeping his eyes closed and his body still, he said, just above a whisper, "I know you're there. If you're frightened, don't be. I won't hurt you."

Several long minutes passed before he heard her voice, small and nervous, come from just beside the door. "I did not mean to disturb you," she breathed.

"It's all right," he said. "Will it bother you if I open my eyes?"

She hesitated for a moment, then let out a breath. "No."

"Good," Thomas said, and opened his eyes, looking toward the front door. She was not standing there. "I don't see you," he murmured.

"Of course you don't," she chided, a small laugh forming behind the words. "I'm invisible, of course."

"Yes, I can see that." Thomas made a face. "Or, I mean, I can't."

The voice laughed in earnest now. "You're funny."

Thomas took his time sitting up so that he would not frighten her. "You may be one of the few people alive who thinks so," he replied, thinking of his too-serious life Upworld, and shaking it off with a careless shrug. "You can show yourself, if you like."

"I can't," she replied. "But thank you."

If this confused Thomas, he didn't take the time to ponder it. "What are you doing here?"

"Well..." she murmured, "I wanted to hear you make the guitar sing.'"

Thomas pointed to the mahogany instrument in the glass-fronted cabinet. "That one?"

"Yes," she said. "It is said that when Her Grace is not here with you, you play it in the night when you are alone, and you make the sweetest and saddest, most beautiful music."

Thomas raised an eyebrow. "'It is said'? Who says it?"

"Everyone," the voice admitted. "Guards in the corridors. The Queen's Ladies. Folk who happen by to hear you. Everyone listens. They ache for the music you carry in your heart."

Thomas was stunned into silence for a moment. "And so you came to hear me play?"

"Yes, of course".

He had a thought. "Some of the Fair Folk, like Zodiac and those odd little Spriggans, kind of pop in and out of places. It's a little unnerving, but I'm getting used to that. Is that how you got in here?"

"No," she confessed. "I do not possess those gifts. I followed you inside when you came back from the Great Hall. I was waiting by the door. But you did not touch the guitar. I was going to wait until you were asleep before I left, but then I saw the book on the table, and picked it up to look at it, then I dropped it, and..."

"And that's what has us talking now," he finished for her. "I'm glad you dropped the book...um...do you have a name?" He had a dismal thought. "Or am I supposed to name you, too?"

Her laugh was genuine and utterly charming. "Oh, no, Thomas, you do not have to name me. And I am just as glad about it as you are—you created quite a stir with your naming of the Folk. I do not think I would want to be named for days of the week or kitchen spices!"

He frowned, but he chuckled. "It seems that everyone is a critic. Why don't I have to name you? I was told I had to name the Fair Folk that I communicate with. Is it because you're invisible?"

"No. It is because I am not faerie. At least, not really."

This had not occurred to him. "You're not? What are you, then?" He couldn't think of what she could possibly be, which race she could belong to. One that he hadn't been introduced to yet? It crossed his mind again that it was a damned good thing for him that he'd had more than a passing acquaintance with psychedelic drugs, or he would be spending most of his time in Elvenhome more or less freaked out. "What are you?" he asked again, trying to be ready for anything.

She gave him the only answer he wasn't prepared for. "Why, I am mortal, of course. I am as mortal as you are."

"You're an invisible mortal?" his question felt stupid to him, but he was trying to grasp the concept.

"Not exactly, Thomas," she explained. "I am a mortal who has been made invisible."

"Is there a difference?"

"I should like to think so," she replied, the ironic smile evident in her voice.

"What's your name?" Thomas began, and was interrupted by a brisk knock at the door.

Her worried voice was immediately beside his ear, and she was breathing fast again. "Please do not say I have been here. Please. I will go when you open the door. Please," she begged.

"I won't say anything," he promised. "Will you come back some other time?"

The knock came again, a little louder this time. She gasped, but she was not going to answer him now.

Thomas rose from the couch, and strode to the front door, which he opened. Guardian stood there, carrying an ornately carved box which could only hold a chess set. "Are you in the mood for a game?" the Water Faerie asked, challenge flickering amiably in his blue eyes.

"It's been a while since I've played," Thomas admitted, although a smile was creeping across his face.

"You may remember how it's done once you begin," suggested Guardian.

"You may be right," Thomas replied, swinging the door wide and moving aside to allow Guardian to enter.

Guardian grinned, and waved a bottle, which he held in the hand not carrying the chess set. "And if you've truly forgotten how to play, Thomas, after a while, neither one of us will mind it very much."

When Guardian reached the center of the room, Thomas felt something solid move past him and out the door into the corridor. He wondered if she would come back, and if he would ever find out who she was. What had she done, that someone had made her invisible? Wait a minute, someone made her invisible? And who was the someone who...

Guardian's voice pulled his focus. "Thomas? Is something amiss?"

"No. It's fine. I was just trying to remember the difference between a bishop and a castle," he chuckled, and closed the door.

Guardian took Thomas' black king in nine moves.

If Thomas was perturbed by this, he didn't show it as he saluted Guardian with his goblet before he drained it for the third time. "I can see you're going to be all kinds of fun to play chess with," he grumbled.

Guardian stretched and poured himself more faerie wine from the bottle he'd brought with him. He smiled across the table as Thomas tried to pour himself more French wine into the now-empty goblet he still held in his hand, eyeing the multitude of black chess pieces lined up beside Guardian's left hand with feigned suspicion.

"I wasn't even a challenge for you, was I?" Thomas groaned, realizing slowly that the bottle from which he was pouring was empty. Shrugging, he put it down, reached for a second bottle—Italian this time—and filled his goblet to the brim with a flourish.

The blond-haired man tried not to smile wider. "Untrue. I found it quite challenging, since you were playing so badly. At first I thought you were playing to some Upworld strategy that I have never encountered, and I had to work to keep up with whatever it was that you were doing."

"...until you began to realize that my strategy was that I really stink at chess," laughed Thomas.

Guardian's heartfelt grimace made Thomas laugh harder. "I hate to say it, Thomas, but, in truth, you do. It was close to unbearable!"

They chuckled together, drinking their wine.

"You don't want to play again now, do you?" Guardian asked with a pained expression.

"Hell, no!" Thomas exclaimed.

"Thank the gods...I don't think I could stand it," gasped Guardian with apparent relief. "Maybe you should read up on chess before we attempt it again," he added.

"Shut up," Thomas retorted with a smile. "But I probably will."

They left the sad remains of their first chess encounter on the table, and moved toward the couch and chairs on the other side of the room, wine goblets in hand. Guardian settled into one of the easy chairs, and Thomas dropped himself a little dizzily onto the couch.

"It's been about thirty years since we've had a resident, mortal Court Singer. It has been too quiet in Elvenhome, for too long a time. We are all glad that you are here with us."

"Your musicians are good—the group tonight was fun to listen to. I've heard there are a couple of Pixies who play some mean fiddle."

"We have forty local musicians, and over the course of the seasons we get minstrels from all over the kingdoms. They play the music they've learned from all of our Court Singers, and from other mortal interaction, and they play it well enough. By the way, the Bogle you'll hear tomorrow (I believe you recently named him 'Hemingway') plays the lute quite well – he also sings sweetly enough to break your heart.

Callie's probably told you this already: the problem is, most of the Fair Folk can only reproduce and reinterpret music they've heard, music they've learned, until over time it becomes something else, what mortals have come to think of as 'Faerie Music.' We don't seem to be able to create it, not wholly original compositions, anyway. I don't know why." Guardian grinned, he couldn't help himself. "I'm not sure that the average mortal would recognize 'Happy Birthday' if played and sung by the majority of Fair Folk. It would sound too Other-Worldly to them, far too Fey to be discernible as anything but Faerie Music." The Water Faerie chuckled.

"But it explains why you have Court Singers. It keeps your music from going stale, or getting boring," said Thomas.

"Callie insures that we get new music on something of a regular basis," Guardian pointed out. "Her own love for it is immense, of course. We all know well that her quest for Court Singers is about far more than keeping her bed warm, although, of course, there is that. It's also about warming the hearts of the Fair Folk with something we all need as much as we need air and water and light."

In a flash, Thomas had a clearer idea of why he had been so readily accepted by the Court, and why Callie was able to banter away with the Court about her physical relationship with Thomas, often at her own expense. He nodded as the realization struck him.

He turned and looked at Guardian, who was staring back at him. "Let me ask you this, Guardian…how do you fit in around here?"

The blond man thought for a moment, and then smiled. "You already know that Callie and I are cousins. Our mothers are sisters."

"So, you've known her forever."

"Well, not quite forever, but for a long time; I've always known her. She's a couple of years older than I am, but it's best that we don't mention that to her too often," Guardian remarked with a wink, and Thomas laughed.

"Everyone around here always seems to be busy doing something. What do you do?" asked Thomas, interested.

Guardian's eyes glittered, as much from the faerie wine as from amusement. "Well, I act as Queen's Emissary when she requires it. I am an ambassador of sorts, to the native Water Faerie population Upworld. I spend a good deal of my time in the Library conducting research for

Master—for Master Ocelot (I cannot fathom how you named him 'Ocelot', Thomas!) because there is so much to learn and so much to know and so much to pass along to our people." Guardian grinned at Thomas' groan. "Oh, yes...and I'm Heir Presumptive to the High Throne of Elvenhome."

Surprised, Thomas gaped at his new friend. "You're next in line to be the King of Faerie? The High King?"

"A true but unlikely thing," Guardian nodded with an easy shrug.

"You're Callie's heir?"

Guardian nodded. "Something none of us will have to address for a very, very long time, if ever,"

"But what if Callie has a child?" Thomas blurted.

"She won't."

"How do you know that?" Thomas was curious.

Guardian eyed the Court Singer. "Thomas, have you not noticed that there are no children here at the castle?"

Thomas had to admit that he had not noticed. Children, and the idea of children, had never been of any importance to him; he had never paid much attention to whether they were present or not.

"No one here has children," Guardian explained. "To find them, you must go outside of Elvenhome, into the other kingdoms of Faerie, like Elvenwood or Elvenstone or Elvenmere..."

"No children? So Elvenhome is like an Adults Only vacation resort?" Guardian looked completely blank. Embarrassed, Thomas waved the lame comparison away. "Never mind. No kids, that's fine with me. And you're the heir. That's great." Thomas caught a flicker of something cross Guardian's face. "Isn't it?"

"It is, I suppose," Guardian said seriously. "It is a good deal of work, which I am most honored to do, of course, but with it comes huge responsibility, and a degree of personal sacrifice that sometimes I would not mind passing on to someone—perhaps anyone—else."

The fleeting wistful, almost pained look in Guardian's eyes reminded Thomas of the way his new friend had looked in the moments before Thomas had first met him the week before.

"Guardian? What is it?" Thomas didn't have to ask; he knew exactly what it was, having seen that look in his own eyes more times than he ever admitted to anyone but his guitar.

The Water Faerie forced a small smile. "It's nothing. I just thought of someone I miss."

Thomas nodded. "I'm something of an expert in this area. You have the undeniably miserable look of a man who is very much in love." He rose from the couch, walked over to the table, collected the bottle of Spanish wine and the bottle of faerie wine, which he handed to Guardian as he passed him on his way back to his seat on the couch, and poured more from the Upworld bottle into his own goblet. "You, my friend, are in love up to your fucking eyebrows."

The eyebrows in question lifted, but Guardian said nothing as he poured the last of his wine.

Thomas was still talking. "And my guess is that since you look unhappy in the extreme, you've got some nasty complications someplace. All things considered, those have to be way off the scale." His tone softened. "Callie says that it's sometimes a challenge to love a mortal, and I guess she should know. I'm only beginning to understand a little of what she means by that." Thomas scratched his chin, considering this.

"Have you fallen in love with the High Queen yet?" Guardian redirected the conversation.

"In love with her, as in wanting to stay with her forever? I don't know, and that's the truth. When we're together, it's great. When we're not together, and I'm writing songs, or walking around outside, or playing music, that's great. I do have feelings for her, sure, but I don't know what that means, yet." He met Guardian's gaze. "I think I could love her. She might turn out to be the love of my life, who knows? I'm not sure how much of what I might be feeling is left over from the initial enchantment. You know what I mean: the whole 'Faerie Queen meets unsuspecting mortal, and casts an enchantment on him so he will follow her to her castle and do her bidding' thing. I have a Master's Degree in Medieval Literature, you know, and I get some of this stuff. But does the enchantment fade over time, or does it stay part of the energy around Callie and me until my year is over?"

Guardian shook his head. "I don't know."

"I like being with Callie, but I don't think I'd die without her. I'd miss her if I didn't see her again, but I'm not sure I'd look as wretched as you do right now," Thomas observed, filled with sympathy for his new friend.

Guardian almost smiled.

"Come on, man," Thomas urged. "We've had more than enough to drink. If the wine you've been drowning in is as potent as what I've been drowning in, then I'll wager you can hardly see me sitting across from you. I don't think I can stand up again. So you're pretty safe; you can talk about her."

Guardian closed his eyes.

"It might help," Thomas suggested. "Of course, tomorrow I probably won't even remember what you tell me."

Opening his eyes, Guardian studied Thomas for a moment, then groaned before he drained his goblet.

"You may well be right. It might ease me to speak of it. To speak of her." He took a breath. "I am in love, very much in love," he began, gripping the bowl of the empty goblet tightly. "She lives Upworld. She's mortal. Defiantly, delightfully mortal." He stared at the goblet in his hand as he continued. "Her name...is Maggie. Margaret. She's the most remarkable, most loving, most exasperating, most beautiful, most exciting...I met her more than two years ago, and I go Up to be with her as often as I can, which of course is not as often as I wish to." He was silent for a moment. He did not look over at Thomas, who was staring resolutely at the mahogany guitar in the cabinet as he listened. "She has a good and happy life Upworld that I would not ask her to forsake for a life with me in Faerie. She loves me, as I love her. There is not a way for us stay together Upworld, because I am faerie and cannot survive there for longer than a very few months at a time."

When Guardian finally raised his eyes to look at the Court Singer, he had a half-hearted smile on his face. "So you see, Thomas, you and I are both in very dire circumstances, are we not?"

Thomas, who had listened and was feeling drunkenly wistful and sad about Guardian and Maggie, was stunned by this declaration, and he met his friend's eyes. "Both of us? I'm not in 'dire circumstances', man, I'm doing just fine," he frowned in wine-soaked confusion.

But Guardian shook his head, his internal balance somewhat restored, courtesy of the wine and the talking. "Dire circumstances indeed: me, with my impossible situation with my sweet lady—and you, my friend, cursed as you are with your unbelievably bad chess game."

sixteen

DANCING IN THE air along a wide corridor on the second level of Elvenhome Castle, high above the heads of other Folk who moved toward business of their own, a merry Violet chatted with the two large black and gold butterflies who fluttered along beside her.

"There he is!" cried Violet, pointing to the man with dark brown curls who was walking casually with the Lord High Chamberlain, now known by everyone as "Zodiac." Zodiac was dressed in his regular official attire; the man with him wore loose-fitting black trousers and an ivory-colored tunic. "That," the breathless Violet announced, "is Thomas Lear, our Court Singer. Isn't he delicious?"

The butterflies giggled and gasped when they got a good look at his face. Zodiac pointed to some military artifacts hung high on the castle wall, and Thomas turned to examine the swords and shield his companion was telling him about.

"That sword belonged to Her Grace's great-grandmother, and was used during the battle of—"

Violet dipped and flew over to Thomas, hovering by his left shoulder. Thomas bowed his head in wordless greeting.

The fluttering Queen's Lady grinned at the Court Singer as the butterflies made a delicate, almost shy, glide to the space directly behind her. "Good morning, Thomas! Good morning, Lord Zodiac! These are my cousins, visiting from the Western Forest."

Zodiac bowed in welcome, and Thomas did the same. He thought he heard the butterflies titter, but he wasn't sure.

"You see? I *told* you he was beautiful to look upon!" Violet chirped to her cousins with lascivious pride. In a flash, she was soaring up and through the air, with the butterflies close behind.

Zodiac watched their departure with amusement, and said to Thomas, "We should continue our walk to the Library; Her Grace will be waiting." He took a couple of steps, then glanced back at the Court Singer, who hadn't moved; confusion and wonder were evident in his eyes.

"Oh, do not be alarmed, Thomas," Zodiac told him with a knowing wink. "I'm certain that, concerning being beautiful, the Lady Violet was specifically referring to me, not to you."

THE LIBRARY AT Elvenhome Castle was a huge and spacious series of rooms that housed not only thousands of books but also large apothecary cabinets filled with herbs and other medicinal and gardening paraphernalia, a dozen various-sized work tables, and a generous number of chairs and couches. Bookcases lined the walls, floor to ceiling, and each wall had a ladder that reached nearly that far.

About a third of the books shelved in the Library were relatively contemporary; many others were easily several hundred years old and more. Most of them were hand-written, never commercially published. The Library also held scrolls, tapestries, and ancient rolls of parchment where poems were written in Ogham, Early French, Late Latin and Middle English. Elvenhome Castle held the best and most treasured books in all of Faerie, and Folk came from all over the kingdoms to read them.

Smaller chambers bordered the vast main area of the Library, and were sometimes used to tend the injured or sick; there were beds in several of these. Bundles of dried or drying herbs hung upside down from the room's heavy mid-ceiling open beams. The scented air, and the warm sunlight that poured in through the many windows, bathed the Library with a natural feeling of both reverent and playful tranquility. Magic and intellect whispered together here, and the Library and the Folk who entered it felt this keenly.

The Library was the domain of the recently-renamed Master "Ocelot," a tall, weathered Elf who had nurtured and managed the Library as well as the castle's main herb garden immediately behind it.

Master Ocelot—Thomas had been running through a mental list of wild cats at the time of his naming—had worked as the chief apothecary to the castle and village of Elvenhome for as long as anyone could remember. He supervised the planting, growing and harvesting of medicinal herbs; these he used when he was visited by Fair Folk and mortals alike for cures for everything from hangovers to broken bones and bruised wings. He was well-read, greatly revered, highly organized—a living repository of knowledge for, by and about the histories, cultures and wisdom of Faerie.

He had short gray hair, and twinkling blue eyes that were lined from centuries of wonder, discovery, and laughter. His was a strong, contemplative, intelligent and playful soul. He loved his work with books and herbs, and was rarely found far away from the Library; he was both its revered master and its humble caretaker.

At this moment, there were about fifty of the Fair Folk moving around the place, some reading, others talking quietly, several serving as librarians. In the center of the busy area, Master Ocelot himself stood at his massive maple desk, gently digging through the desk's many compartments to find a specific piece of paper. Beside him, looking understandably anxious, stood a HobGoblin who worked in the Kitchens. After an unfortunate encounter with a meat cleaver, the Hob had managed to cut off his right hand, which he now held protectively in his left hand, pressed against his quivering chest.

"Can you truly fix it, Master?" asked the Hob for probably the fifth time in as many minutes.

"Of course I can fix it, you fool. I need to find the right incantation, though, or you will end up with an extra hand, and we do not want that. You did not do all that well with the two you have got, did you?" Laughing generously, he continued to pull small bits of paper out of the desk and scanned them as he spoke. "Alchemy takes time, my friend. It does not do to rush it. Ah! Here it is; I was right, of course, but it never hurts to check. Come along, we shall get you put back together."

Satisfied, the Master strode across the wide space toward one of the smaller side-chambers, the HobGoblin scurrying close behind.

Far across the library, the High Queen sat at one of the smaller tables, talking with Guardian. Lavender and Carnation attended the

Queen's Grace from several tables away, engaged in a serious conversation about buttons.

Callie sighed. "He has been gone for nearly a fortnight. I have had no word of him, but I would imagine he is up to some small mischief."

"That is not necessarily so, if you will forgive my saying it," Guardian frowned. "That he left in anger is true. But he does not behave badly Upworld. He never has, and you know it well." He smiled reassuringly at her, and patted her arm. "You see only the harshness in him, because that is all he allows you to see."

"That is all I have seen for a long time, and you know that well." She studied his eyes, and looked into his heart, seeing gentleness and vulnerability there. "You have been caught between us from the beginning, and for that I am sorry. I never intended it."

Guardian smiled in response, as he always did when this discussion came to this point, as it always did. "What do we say when we get to this place in the conversation? *'Intention is everything, and nothing'*?"

Grudgingly, Callie smiled too. "All right, we can move to a more pleasant subject."

"I think that is a good plan."

"Good. I have a small surprise for you."

Guardian raised an eyebrow in anticipation.

Shifting in her seat, Callie stretched and pulled two sturdy paperback books out of the pocket of her gown. "I asked Sheila to collect these for me, for the Library, where they will live with us until the end of days."

She placed the books on the table in front of Guardian: *Dreams of the Fair Folk* and *The Faerie Queen's Mirror*, two collections of stories written by Margaret J. Forrest.

"These tales are also somewhat familiar," the Faerie Queen observed with a wry smile, "but they are beautifully written, and told with a true affection for the Fey that I have rarely seen in printed form. She's talented, and has a great heart. I daresay someone has been talking to mortals about things they perhaps should not, Cousin," Callie attempted to frown imperiously at him, "but she has been selective about telling the stories she has heard, and I believe she has been discreet in how much she reveals, which is more than I can say for you."

Happier than he had been in days, the blond Water Faerie grinned. "You like the stories."

"I like the stories."

Guardian's face took on a look of childlike innocence even as he teased her. "Is it that my Maggie writes very well, or is it that the High Queen of Faerie simply likes to have her life and her world talked about in books again and again? I think it is not appreciation of Maggie's talent, but vanity that motivates your royal approval, Your Grace..."

The cousins burst into spontaneous laughter at each other.

With a nod from Callie, the attending Ladies approached the table, standing close by as Her Grace laughed and talked with Guardian.

Coming from the opposite direction, one of Master Ocelot's librarians, a male Pixie with a bright green pointed hat that matched a bright green robe, came over to the table as well, and, bowing, accepted Maggie's books from Callie. These he took to the Master's desk to catalog.

"In any case, Callie," Guardian continued, "I am always glad to have Maggie's words near me."

She had to ask, and did so in a rueful whisper: "Did you have to tell her *that* particular story, though?"

He knew which one she meant. Guardian was incapable of deceit, so of course he told the truth. "It was on my mind late one night, and I found myself revealing the tale."

"She was kind in the telling of it."

"She is kind in most things, but doesn't know it." He looked at the High Queen with concern in his eyes. "Does this hurt you?"

Callie shook her head. "No. And the fact that it doesn't hurt makes me a little sad somehow." She took a breath, and let it out with a fresh smile as dazzling as the afternoon sunshine that danced in the room. "Foolishness. Old stories cannot create new wounds. We won't let them."

"Majesty?" Lavender asked, concerned. "Is all well?"

Her Majesty nodded in the direction of the librarian, who was now meticulously shelving Maggie's books. "Yes. It is only that I encountered a telling of a sad tale, one that we have never seen written before. Guardian's lady has re-told the tale in print, and done is done."

Lavender watched as the books slid into their new places on the shelf, and the librarian scurried off to deal with other business. She did not have to wonder which story the High Queen had referred to; it was a story they all knew too well. And the mortal woman had written about it?

It took Lavender a second or two to realize what this could mean, and to wonder if it might be a piece of something larger, something useful, something that could make her own dreams come true.

"Ah, there you are, Your Grace!" Zodiac's strong, clear voice interrupted Lavender's thoughts, and dragged her back into reality.

The reality was standing right in front of her: Thomas Lear, the handsome mortal who unknowingly held her heart. He was close enough for her to touch, except he was looking at Her Grace, his cheerful smile making him all the more desirable.

"We have walked through much of the castle today, Your Grace." Zodiac was telling Callie, "and we met some very charming butterflies. I think, though, that the Lady Violet has shaken our Thomas' fragile sensibilities."

Callie and Guardian rose from their chairs, and greeted Thomas, each in their own way: the Water Faerie touched the Court Singer's arm in amusement, and Callie kissed him.

"I believe," Zodiac added, chuckling, "that today, Thomas was right glad of his obligation to silence." He winked conspiratorially at Thomas. "One must be very careful about what one says to butterflies."

Everyone laughed, and Thomas wore a bemused skepticism on his face, which made everyone laugh harder.

Everyone, that is, except Lavender.

Several minutes later, Callie instructed Carnation and Lavender to gather the other Ladies and attend her in her private chamber within the hour. Carnation left at once to find Iris, and Zodiac went with her. Then, after a brief exchange with Master Ocelot about a HobGoblin recently injured but ultimately blessed with the correct number of hands, the High Queen left the Library with her own hand happily wrapped in Thomas'.

Watching Callie and Thomas walk away, Lavender stood alone, wishing that her hand was in Thomas', too. She sighed, and started to leave the Library to find Dahlia, Orchid and Rose.

Then she stopped, her mind whirling in a direction it had never taken before. She made her decision in a heartbeat.

No one was watching when Lavender strolled over to the bookshelf where Maggie Forrest's books had been placed. She pulled one of the books out, opened it, and skimmed the table of contents for the titles of the stories.

It wasn't there.

Replacing the first book on the shelf, she reached for the other one, quickly read the table of contents...

...and there it was.

The clever idea sparkled in her mind. Truth was truth, after all, and faeries do not lie. They can—and do—however, shine light on specific pieces of truth, often for their own mischievous purposes.

Happy now, Lavender slid the book into the deep pocket of her gown, and wandered out of the Library in search of the other Ladies.

SUSANNAH RICKERT SAT alone in a small sandwich shop near Greyfriar's, finishing the soup of the day and a slice of warm, fresh bread. She'd walked all over Edinburgh New Town for the past two days, and was no closer to succeeding at her mission than she had been before she'd started.

Where in Edinburgh is Thomas Lear? she moaned to herself. *Is he even still here? Where in the world did he go? And why?* The hot Scottish tea she sipped as she considered these things did not comfort her very much.

Susannah did not like mysteries, nor did she appreciate mental puzzles. She sighed with irritable resignation, and carefully reconsidered her facts. There was so little to work with.

The night concierge at the Caledonian, who had been working at the front desk when Thomas checked out, told her politely that Thomas had looked quite well when he'd paid his bill and left his luggage and further instructions. Was something amiss?

No, Susannah had reassured him. The record company was simply trying to track him down, and would do so shortly. This was not a serious problem— *American celebrity musicians and their craziness, right?* It was an inconvenience, to be sure, but nothing to be genuinely concerned about—and she'd prefer to keep the fact that he was being searched for out of the press, please. She felt certain she could rely on the Caledonian's discretion.

The concierge had reluctantly given Susannah the name and phone number of the cab company that he had called to assist Mr. Lear. It had not been difficult to find out where the cab driver had let him out. The name Thomas Lear, and the brief interaction the singer had had with the cabbie, had been added to the cab company's collection of celebrity encounters. Everyone at the dispatch office, and nearly everyone at nearby pubs, knew that Thomas Lear had asked to go to the top of Calton Hill, and got out of the cab a few minutes before midnight, carrying a guitar case and a small piece of luggage. He'd smelled a bit like whisky and marijuana, she was told; he had been quite courteous, and had given the cabbie a handsome tip.

The Rock Star had not been seen or heard from since. And that had been nine days ago.

The concierge confirmed that Mr. Lear's luggage had been placed in storage, waiting for someone with proper identification to collect it and take it back to America. Susannah was able to prove that she was employed by the record company, and that she had been directed by Mr. Jack Grandberg and Mr. Stan Williams (whose names were specified in Mr. Lear's instructions) to take possession of said luggage. It was now in her suite at The Caledonian.

She did not want to hunt through Thomas' suitcases; the notion made her edgy and uncomfortable. But she'd hit a dead end, and she was supposed to call Jack and report in. She had nothing substantive to tell him other than that the quiet search for the pain-in-the-ass musician was not going well. She did not want to talk to Jack about it, but she would have to tell him something.

It occurred to her then that, apart from the concierge and two people at the cab company, she hadn't had a genuine conversation with anyone since she'd left Los Angeles.

She blamed her nervous jetlag for her reticence to speak to anyone, even though she'd been in Scotland's capital city for three days, walking up and down the High Street, strolling around Greyfriar's, and visiting the Scottish National Library because she knew that Thomas loved books and read a lot.

She blamed her upset stomach and her anxiety on the jetlag, too. She wanted to blame Thomas for all of it; he was such a selfish bastard. She wanted to find him and give him all kinds of hell for making her life miserable.

Instead, she worried about him, and about the likely repercussions of this latest disappearing act. The Label was no longer amused. In another couple of weeks, they'd be furious if he didn't turn up. *The Dangerous Blue Eyes Tour* had gone well and the talk shows were starting to clamor for Thomas to make the requisite appearances. To have Thomas missing, unavailable, "in seclusion," to have him miss the Label's big PR push of the live album that would release next month, was more than irresponsible. It was courting disaster.

It was typically Thomas, though, flipping The Finger and evaporating on a whim, no matter whom or what else was affected by his actions. Selfish bastard.

As she walked back to the hotel in the light drizzle that seemed to be a subtle part of Edinburgh's autumn landscape, she found herself pondering the same things that had crossed her mind more than once since Thomas had vanished: what if he had not disappeared voluntarily?

There had been no indication that this was the case. Jack and Stan had ruled it out almost at once and they were most likely right. They had teased her about her mission to Scotland: Rock Stars, they agreed, didn't get kidnapped. Overall, as a breed, they were such pains in the ass that any self-respecting kidnapper had to know that no one would ever pay to get a rocker back. Thomas' producer and his business manager thought they were funny. Susannah wasn't so sure about that.

If Thomas had been injured, it would be news. If he'd been found dead, it would be news. She shuddered at the thought of the drug overdose she knew was likely waiting for him. He had been known to drive his cars when drunk.

Not kidnapped, then. And not injured. Not dead, either. Just missing. AWOL. Oh, hell...

The most credible likelihood was that, as usual, Thomas had met a woman and was off with her somewhere. He would play until he was bored; naturally, he wouldn't strain his pattern enough to grow up. If she was right, and he'd met a woman and was shacking up with her for a while, he'd surface whenever he felt like it. And not until.

Susannah nodded as she walked past another concierge behind the desk at The Caledonian and walked toward the elevators. Those who knew him understood that Thomas was terrified of commitment, no matter what his beautiful songs sang to the contrary. He also got bored very quickly with women in general. How many had he been involved with since she had first met him? The numbers must be staggering.

She was so frustrated and overwhelmed that she almost walked past her suite. She didn't want to, but she was going to open his suitcases to see if she could find a clue about where he might be right now.

Thomas Lear, Rock Star and Unbelievably Selfish Asshole, was fine, despite her worries. He would turn up soon enough, and would naturally charm his way back into everyone's good graces with very little effort.

She hated him.

And she thought she might love him, too, so much that it hurt.

Opening the door, she sighed, mentally preparing herself to do the unthinkable. With purpose, she would invade someone else's privacy. She would go through the suitcases fast, get it over with. She would call Jack with her report late tonight (it would be morning in Los Angeles). After she was finished with the luggage search, she was going to go shopping.

And after that, she was going to find a pub and drown her need to love Thomas Lear.

She almost wished that she could drown him instead—but she understood too well that, all things considered, it wouldn't change a damned thing.

There were three pieces of luggage positioned beside the fireplace in the living room of Susannah's suite. They were made of dark brown leather, and probably cost a small fortune. One of the pieces was nearly as big as she was and, when filled to capacity, probably weighed more than she did. There was a key taped securely to one of the three heavy handles on the long side. The huge suitcase was elegant and very sturdy despite its somewhat tired and scuffed appearance. It had seen some active, noisy travel, and there was a small, deep tear on the front. This was most likely the infamous suitcase that Thomas had allegedly used as backstage fuck furniture during the *Dangerous Blue Eyes Tour*. The bag was becoming legendary, a topic of gleeful discussion among performers, the press, and fans alike. It had acquired its own reputation on the road. Rumor hinted that this bag had a rude and possibly disgusting name, Susannah remembered, but she hadn't heard what it was. Probably just as well.

Rumor also had it that Thomas had lifted this heavy suitcase and hurled it at his lead guitarist in a fit of drunken rage during a furious argument an hour before one of the shows in Chicago. The guitarist ended up with a seriously bruised back, and Thomas had had to perform that night and the ones following it with a badly-strained shoulder. Ah, rock and roll...she did not know whether to chuckle or shudder.

The second suitcase was a far more manageable size. It sat beside and a little in front of the largest one (which Susannah decided she was a little afraid to touch). The third suitcase of the ensemble was small, probably held toiletries.

She bit her bottom lip, took a deep breath, and with a determination she did not feel, walked over to the waiting luggage.

"Okay, Thomas Lear, what kind of clues did you leave behind?"

With a loud, satisfying ripping sound, she freed the tape from the biggest suitcase, and immediately turned her back on it. She picked up the middle-sized bag instead, and carried it over to the very comfortable white-and-blue striped sofa, and sat down. Laying the suitcase on the coffee table in front of her, Susannah unlocked and opened it.

She searched through the assorted clean, folded clothes, with no idea what she was looking for. She hoped she'd recognize anything important. Among the clothing were stray things that he must have picked up while walking around and shopping on the High Street. She saw brochures and small bags with shop names that she'd seen near Edinburgh Castle. Feeling guilty, she peeked in the bags and saw postcards, a box that held a pretty gold necklace with a thistle hanging from it, and a couple of tee shirts that bore unfamiliar Scottish phrases. She found a penny whistle with the price tag still on it, a deck of cards, and a small, intricately-carved box.

So he had gone shopping, like every other tourist in Edinburgh. There was nothing here to hint at where he had gone after that.

She closed the suitcase, locked it, and walked it back to where the others stood waiting.

The smallest of the three bags was next. Its leathery shell carried the masculine scents of dark musk, sweat, alcohol, and a faint hint of cannabis. It also smelled of Thomas' cologne—*Aramis*, she thought, but wasn't sure. Still, it conjured him as she breathed it/him in. She tried to shrug him off, even as her heart stubbornly skipped a beat.

As she'd assumed, this bag was filled with toiletries. She noted aspirin, multivitamins, a blow-dryer, mouthwash, a small bottle of rubbing alcohol, a tiny first-aid kit, and a package of over-the-counter sleeping pills and another of laxatives. She saw several books of matches, an electrical adapter, a crushed pack of cigarettes. The pocket inside the bag held a handful of unopened condoms, a couple of honey-flavored throat lozenges, and a Swiss Army knife.

However, there was no toothbrush or toothpaste, no chewing gum, comb, brush, razor (electric or otherwise), no shaving cream, aftershave, cologne, soap or shampoo. He had definitely packed those things in another bag and taken them with him. Still, nothing pointed to what he had planned to do or where he had chosen to go.

Like it or not, it was time to address the largest of the bags.

Susannah pushed it over on its side, and sat on the floor next to it, unlocking and opening Thomas Lear's Infamous Tour Suitcase.

It smelled of dirty clothes and (or did she only imagine it?) dirtier sex. Inside, there were two wrinkled sports jackets, five wadded-up shirts, about a dozen tee shirts, four pairs of jeans, stray socks and assorted underwear all in need of a washing machine. Two handsome dress shirts, and a rather stunning three-piece suit, black with gray pin-stripes. A pair of heavy logger boots, a pair of worn-out sneakers, a belt, two pairs of sweat pants and a hooded sweatshirt completed the random sartorial inventory. Last month's *Rolling Stone* sat under two guitar magazines and a copy of an old *Variety*, a folder holding blank paper, a box of blue pens. Silk pajama bottoms wrapped around an empty Scotch bottle. There was nothing here that told her anything helpful. She wondered if Jack or Stan, or anyone else they brought into the picture, would see something revealing that had eluded her.

She was about to close the suitcase, already mentally composing her report for Jack, when she realized that she was absently, gently running her hand across the vest of the pin-striped suit. Apparently he had taken off a dress shirt without first removing the vest; it was still in place, around the shirt.

Susannah involuntarily lost herself in the moment. There was no one to see her, so she pulled the shirt and vest out of the Infamous Suitcase, raised them to her face, hugged them close, and breathed in the personal scent of Thomas Lear.

She ran her hands over them and, to her surprise, discovered that he had returned cufflinks to the cuffs when he'd taken the shirt off. She would not remember later actually removing them from the cuffs, but she did remove them, holding them in hands that trembled in horror at what she was doing, and strangely in longing for the man who had worn them.

The cufflinks were square, only a little larger than a quarter. They each had three fleur-de-lis designs on them, which sat on three deep horizontal lines. The back of the cufflinks had the initials "TL" engraved in the bottom left corners. They were beautiful, and probably terribly expensive, but that was not what drew her to them. That he had worn them, that they belonged to him, made them precious to her, precious beyond reckoning.

Susannah held the cufflinks in her hand, and struggled to breathe as tears filled her eyes and ran down her cheeks. Kissing the cufflinks, she closed her eyes and made a tight fist around them, squeezing so hard that their corners bit accusingly into her hand. Clutching harder still, she slammed her guilty hand into her pocket and began to cry in earnest.

She would not call Jack tonight. He could wait for his damned report.

Rose street in Edinburgh's New Town was paved with smooth terra cotta-colored bricks, and Susannah kept her head down, watching her feet carefully so she wouldn't misstep and fall off her platform shoes. It was an October Friday evening, just getting dark, and Rose Street and its cheerful pubs were brimming with people hunting for a pint and relaxation with their friends.

Susannah liked the hustle of bodies moving around and through the pubs, restaurants and shops. She didn't object at all to swerving and weaving past people who had a better idea of where they were going than she did. She was grateful that Rose Street was a pedestrians-only area; she only had to watch her feet and the swirling movements of other people. She was grateful that cars, and which side of the street they were coming from, were not an issue at the moment.

She wasn't hungry, and she didn't especially care where she went; she was content to be part of a crowd, anonymously. She felt guilty about Thomas Lear's silver cufflinks, which were now tucked away in one of the pockets of her single suitcase, in the bedroom closet at the hotel.

It surprised her, and annoyed her too, when she realized that she was scanning the faces here on Rose Street, looking for him. There wasn't any way he'd be strolling toward one of the pubs; he'd had to give up that kind of easy visibility years ago.

Susannah wondered again if she could have said something during that last phone call to get his attention, refocus it on his career, and get him back to the States. He had seemed distracted, but in a good way. He'd been almost friendly to her, and had sounded genuinely relaxed, which had not been in the makeup of the man she'd had to deal with at the record company. She was willing to bet that whatever he was doing right now, it was selfish and would probably require someone else's effort to get him back on track. On the other hand, she hoped his disappearing act wasn't going to ruin his career. A practical soul with a sharp—if somewhat drugged—mind for business, Jack would only be patient for so long, even though he and Thomas had been friends for a long time. Would the record label, Jack's bosses, be patient? Would the public be forgiving, and welcome Thomas back?

A scruffy man in dirty jeans darted in front of her to move into an open door, and she nearly collided with him, momentarily lost her footing, twisted her ankle, and only barely managed to avoid tripping over her shoes and falling. *Damn you, Thomas*, she thought. *Why the hell should I care about your damned stupid career, if you don't?*

The pub she limped into a few minutes later was dimly-lit, filled to capacity with bodies, loud music (some local radio station playing contemporary rock piped through huge speakers mounted on the ceiling), deafening chatter, and a huge, dense and malevolent cloud of sharp cigarette smoke.

Over the noise, she could barely hear herself demand that she to go back to the quiet of the hotel. She doubted that she would be able to breathe in here at all. Standing just inside the door and looking around, she nearly turned and fled.

Instead, she forced herself to stand still, breathe deeply, and calm down. She looked around at the inside of the pub again and grimaced; this was the last place she wanted to be. Her snap decision to find a place to sit down and order a pint of ale brought a hard and wholly artificial smile to her face.

When she realized there were no unoccupied tables, she scanned the long bar for an empty stool. She saw one at the end, by the far wall, and headed toward it, trying not to inhale the acrid smoke as she made her way through the boisterous crowd in the semi-darkness.

The man sitting on the stool next to the empty one she was about to claim was not talking to anyone. He seemed oblivious to all of the good-natured rowdiness around him. She scooted her stool away from him, a little closer to the wall, and sat down, relieved that he did not bother to acknowledge her. She was thankful that he didn't glance in her direction. His mind was elsewhere; he stared straight ahead, and drank his whisky in a private, somehow sullen, silence.

Settling on her seat, she rubbed her still-throbbing ankle, and forced a smile at the tired, middle-aged barmaid when she leaned over the bar and asked Susannah, in as thick a Scottish dialect as Susannah had ever heard, what she'd have.

"A pint, please," she said, conscious of how whiningly, pathetically American she sounded, and how lost, lonely and shy she felt. The realization annoyed her, and made her want to pound her fists on the strong, solid surface of the bar's heavy wood, but she knew she could never do such a thing. Frustrated by yet another disappointment, Susannah was instantly determined to drown at least her loneliness in the ale, and to do so as soon as possible.

By the time she had finished her second pint, it occurred to her that she should have eaten something. She was getting a nice buzz on, and she was having a little difficulty focusing on the posters on the wall beside her. She looked around the pub covertly, and watched people eat. When the barmaid came back with Susannah's third pint, she also brought fish and chips.

She ate her meal in a grateful, though somewhat hazy, silence. Despite the addition of the food, the ale was having a mellowing effect on her, and she found that she didn't mind at all.

Suddenly, the man on the stool beside her jolted, as if roughly awakened. The unexpected movement startled her. She gasped, and dropped the piece of fish she was eating.

They both watched as the greasy cod filet hit the floor with a wettish thud.

He glanced over at her. "I did not mean to startle you." He had a nice voice. Deep, and nice. His accent sounded Scottish, but not only Scottish. She was unable to place it.

He was tall; long, she decided. His hair was dark, and fell loosely past his shoulders. He was gray-eyed, and, from what she could see of him in the murky dimness of the pub, rather attractive.

She was a little drunk, and he had not turned all the way toward her to look at her when he had spoken. That was fine with her; she was not good at prolonged eye contact anyway. But she had to say something, didn't she, since he had?

She met his eye, and then looked away, ducking her head as she croaked, "Not a big deal."

"I will replace what you dropped," he said mildly.

"No, that's all right, I'm finished eating," she told him. "But I think I will have another pint," she added, addressing the barmaid with a tentative smile as the older woman approached.

The next round of ale seemed to have a settling effect on both of them, and they found themselves talking casually, without the strained awkwardness that Susannah usually carried into non-business conversations with strangers. Her companion, too, had relaxed. The distant and unhappy look in his eyes and the tension in his body seemed to dissolve slowly as he emptied his glass again. He turned his head only slightly when he looked at her; she had yet to see much of his very handsome face. She wondered if he had had a neck or back injury that kept him from turning his head too far in her direction.

"Do you know," he remarked, "that we have been sitting here talking for an hour, and I have failed to ask your name?"

Startled, she laughed in amazement; she couldn't help it. "I think I've heard variations of those words a hundred different times, and this is the very first time they did not come out like a bad pick-up line!"

He bowed his head, and gave her a small smile. "Just so," he said.

"Susannah," she told him. "Susannah Rickert. And you are...?"

An unexpected chuckle bubbled out of him, followed by an unmistakable secretive look in his eye, but before she could wonder about it, it was gone. "I have been called many things," he admitted with a flash of a smile. "'Rex' will do."

"Nice to meet you, Rex," she told him.

"What brings you here, Susannah?"

"To Edinburgh, or to the pub?" she replied, lifting her glass and sipping to give herself time to think how to respond. She had known that he would ask the question. It was a basic, natural, logical and non-threatening one, but she didn't know how to answer it now without launching into a pathetic monologue in which she would reveal the mess she knew she was. He looked at her, waiting patiently. It seemed to her, for the space of a heartbeat, that he would be able to read words she wasn't about to say. She fled from the idea, composed her thoughts, gave him as nonchalant a shrug as she could muster, and told him "The company I work for sent me here to handle some business. I'm finished, though, and I'm going home."

He nodded, recognizing and accepting the evasive nature of her answer. "What is it that you do?"

Susannah could talk about the music business all night and feel very safe. "I'm a senior production assistant for a major record label in Los Angeles." He did not look as impressed as most people did when she told them what she did for a living. "What do you do?" she countered in self-defense.

The amused look on his face as he considered her question was, she thought, extremely charming. "Hmmmm," he replied, "I suppose I work in government."

"Wow," she blurted, fascinated in spite of herself. "I don't know much about Scottish politics. You're in public service—or maybe even something Top Secret?"

He drained his glass, and there was a twinkle in his eye. "Perhaps a little of both," he admitted, and he laughed.

Intrigued, she turned on her seat to look at him in the dimness. "So that means what? What is it that you actually do? Do you—?"

At that moment, from the other end of the noisy pub, the music from the too-loud radio was cranked up, drowning out myriad conversations, smoke and hectic traffic. Susannah felt suddenly dizzy, and found it almost impossible to take a breath. Focusing hard, she fumbled for some money in her purse and, shaking, dropped it on the bar. Rex's head had turned upward and toward the sound coming from the nearest speaker. He frowned, first in surprise and then in growing annoyance.

Susannah put her hand on his arm for less than a fraction of a second, to get his attention. "I need to get out of here, Rex. Sorry." She heaved herself off the stool, and made her way out of the pub, bumping into too many people to apologize to as she struggled past them.

Eyes narrowed, Rex scowled for reasons of his own and then, dropping his own money on the bar, gracefully moved through the now-dancing crowd after her.

The radio was playing a song called "Dangerous Blue Eyes," and the voice that flowed through the pub belonged, of course, to Thomas Lear.

When Rex caught up with Susannah a few minutes later, she was leaning against the outside wall of a pub three doors down from the one they'd just been in.

"You did not get very far," Rex murmured. "Are you all right?"

In the flickering lamplight, Susannah was pale, and her voice shook despite her best efforts to keep it steady. "Oh, I suddenly didn't feel well. I needed some air."

"Is it better now?"

"I just needed to get out of there," she breathed unhappily.

"Is it better now?" he repeated, watching her face.

"Yeah, yeah, it is," she insisted. She met his eyes and tried to smile. "Thanks, Rex. It really is better."

They both knew she was lying, but it didn't matter.

In the autumn darkness, he escorted her back to her hotel.

"I'm fine, you know, and I'm not too drunk to walk back by myself," Susannah told him, with a feigned grumble. "Too drunk to drive, absolutely, but not too drunk to walk."

"True enough," Rex said, reaching for her arm to steady her as she nearly collided with more of Rose Street's pub-crawling pedestrian traffic. "But I will accompany you home, all the same."

"You didn't have to come after me, you know. You could have finished your drink."

"I did finish it," Rex said. "You looked as though you needed some able assistance, and since I was recently acquainted with you, it seemed to be the thing to do."

Something in the way he spoke made her smile in spite of herself. "Well, thank you for that. It may not seem like it, but I do appreciate the company, more than I can tell you."

"What happened to you, Susannah? Why did you rush out of the pub?"

She sighed, long and laboriously, as she walked beside him. "It's nothing. Really. It's just that...oh, the music, that song, came on out of nowhere, and upset me for reasons too stupid to ponder. It made me think of someone I don't want to think about, and that made me angry, and sad, and..." she stopped before hurling herself from a too-familiar emotional precipice. "Oops. Too much to drink...that always makes me talk too much, and then I say really dumb stuff. Sorry, Rex. No need to go to dark places with new friends, right?" This she punctuated with a self-deprecating, mildly-intoxicated giggle.

They were quiet for the space of half a block. Susannah was grateful for the dark and the silence, and wrapped herself in their familiar protection.

"Are you very much in love?" he asked, after some minutes had passed.

"Love? Not me," she denied with a gruff chortle, digging her fingernails into the palms of her hands in the hidden safety of her coat pockets. "I was only caught off-guard. Music has a way of taking you places you don't want to go sometimes, and you're powerless to do anything but go there, no matter how much you—"

"Hmmmm," Rex interrupted, a quirky smile growing in his rich, deep voice. "So you find yourself in love with someone who hasn't got the good sense to love you back?"

She stopped then, and tried to look up at him in the darkness. All she could see was the reflection of the moonlight in his gray eyes. "How could you possibly know that? You don't know me. I never said—"

His smile was kind and his voice was sympathetic, and it held her, calm and safe, for a moment. "I recognize the feelings, Susannah. Unrequited love, in all its many variations, brands each of us in similar ways. We can see it and sense it in others once we've tasted the harsh bitterness of it for ourselves."

Moved by the evenness of his tone and the sad smile in his voice, Susannah found she could meet Rex's bright eyes without fear or embarrassment. She searched for and read the truth in them.

Rex offered her his left arm, she took it, and they resumed their walk toward Susannah's hotel.

Ten minutes later they stood in shadow in front of The Caledonian, at the end of Princes Street. The silence between them was a friendly, comfortable one. Susannah didn't want to break it, but she forced herself to by clearing her throat.

"I know this sounds all wrong, but...would you like to come up to my suite and hang out for a while? We could have coffee or tea. Rex, I haven't had anyone to talk to for days, and—"

His face was all but invisible in the shadows. "I would like to, Susannah, but..." his voice trailed off before he admitted "I'm afraid that if you got a good look at—"

"What? The scar on your face?" she said with an ease born of a world-weariness that seemed somehow older than she was. "The scar? Is that it?"

Rex nodded, surprised into speechlessness.

"Good Lord, Rex, I saw it in the pub. It's a scar. A big one. Were you concerned that it was going to freak me out or ruin the ale or become a topic of conversation?"

He looked at her with eyes that held something very close to amazement. He said nothing.

"Come on, then," Susannah prodded. "I make really good coffee."

She patted his arm matter-of-factly, and turned away, walking as steadily as she could into the lobby of The Caledonian.

After exactly two of the longest heartbeats of his life, Rex took a deep breath and followed her.

seventeen

THE HOTEL SUITE was warm and spacious. The two large bedrooms, the oversized bathroom, the kitchenette and the large living area could comfortably hold a gathering of twenty-five or thirty people.

Susannah shrugged as she made coffee while Rex looked around. "The Label is paying for it. They usually get large suites so they can do their PR stuff and party stuff with a minimum of hassle. I told my boss I only needed a single room, but arranging that seemed to be more complicated than just going along with the way they always do things, so I'm here in what's practically a castle!"

Rex chuckled at the irony, but said nothing as he continued to look around. He judged that the artwork on the walls was not only bad, it was singularly unwelcoming. The neutral, drab colors of the place, and its tedious décor, were far too sterile for his taste. He was pinched by a sudden ache for the warm richness of the tapestries in his Tower Rooms at Elvenhome and Elvenstone, for the comforting scent of the books in his personal libraries, and the vibrant, sensuous colors that lived in his gardens. This place is unreal by comparison, he thought, and chuckled again.

She carried a coffee pot, two cups, sugar, cream, spoons and a small plate of chocolate chip cookies on a large tray, and placed the tray deftly on the coffee table. "Coffee, as they say, is served," she said, dropping herself neatly on the white-and-blue-striped couch.

Rex seated himself at the other end, and watched Susannah as she poured coffee into a cup, concentrating around the buzz she still had from the ale in the pub. "Cream? Sugar?"

"No, thank you," Rex said, smiling as she handed him the cup. The coffee was warm and smelled of cinnamon. He took a small sip, and his pleasure at the flavor was evident on his face.

Susannah poured herself a cup, and stirred in some cream. "I *told* you I made good coffee," she murmured without looking at him.

"So you did," he laughed, and then, so did she.

She kept the conversation safely within the boundaries of her own small level of comfort. He did not push her anywhere she did not want to go. She found herself grateful for his kindness.

"You mean, why did I start working in the recording business? Why am I in production?" Susannah asked. "Easy. I love the music. I can't get enough of it, can't live without it."

"So why work in the industry instead of in the art?" Rex wanted to know, shaking his head when she offered him another cookie.

"Because...oh, because working in the industry allows me to be around it, in every way, sometimes from the moment of inspiration all the way through global distribution. It's a very interesting business, Rex, and it's exciting sometimes. I love it."

He tilted his head and looked at her. "Do you play? Or sing? Or perhaps write?"

"Not me," Susannah admitted. "I'm not gifted, not at all, unfortunately. I can't carry a tune, but I know how to hear one, and that's what makes me good at my work. One of these days I'm going to be a very big producer on my own, and introduce the world to lots of new music—and to musicians who've never been heard before."

"A noble goal, that."

"A fun goal," she corrected him with a giggle.

"And what about family? Children?"

She sipped her coffee. "No family. I've never been married, so, no kids." Their eyes met, and she narrowed hers at him as playfully as she could. "Rex, I'm only twenty-five! Anything can happen. I may run into Mr. Right one of these days. And when I do—"

"When you do, you can make him coffee like this and he'll be yours until the end of days," he told her, and looked at her with such shrewd appreciation that she couldn't help but laugh with shy delight.

Another hour later, perhaps as a result of the earlier ale and the coffee and the things they had in common, the talk had moved to other, perhaps less comfortable, topics.

"Yes, I am married, but I have been...separated from her...for a very long time," Rex said, his words spoken thoughtfully, as though he chose each of them with deliberate care.

"Why aren't you divorced, then?" Susannah asked. She shocked herself with the bluntness of the question. "How can you move on with your life if—"

"I am afraid that for the most part, she is my life, for good or for ill." His sigh was a little sad. "We encounter each other on occasion, and I admit that we do not bring out the best in each other, despite temporary gentle intentions. We have not loved each other for a great deal longer than we ever loved."

Susannah nibbled the remains of the last cookie and then pointed it at him. "Deep down, you're still in love with her, aren't you? Deep down, is she still in love with you, do you think?"

Rex closed his eyes. "No. She does not love me any longer. She cannot forgive or forget." He opened his eyes and looked at Susannah with a ghost of a smile. "Not that I blame her. I have not forgiven or forgotten, either."

"So you love her, she doesn't love you, and you live like that every day?"

He grinned now; he couldn't help it. "Something like that, apart from the drama of it. We generally ignore each other, and live peacefully apart. When we do speak, it is either cold or hot, but it is rarely pleasant. I have been known to go well out of my way to make her angry, for the pure joy of seeing something in her eyes other than unspoken contempt."

"You've got it bad, Rex. Is she worth all that?"

Rex nodded, and looked away for a moment. "Oh yes. She is worth all of that, and much more."

Susannah sighed. "Unrequited love is the pits, Rex."

"That it is, Susannah." He closed the door on his bitter and aching heart, and changed the subject. "So what of this fool who has your heart?"

She pulled her legs up on the couch and crossed them under her. The combined effect of the ale, the coffee and the easy talk had, to her surprise, completely relaxed her. She discovered that she wanted to tell this stranger in her hotel suite about her stupid, wistful feelings of unrequited love. "Oh, I don't know. He's...an amazing musician. I've always fallen for musicians; I can't seem to help myself. And *this* one, he has it all, damn him. He's got an immense talent – he writes the most beautiful songs, and he sings them well. He's gorgeous, he's sexy, he's rich, he's too famous for his own good. And now," she went on, almost to herself, "he seems to have taken the world on a wild goose chase— Los Angeles to Edinburgh to who knows where? It's like he vanished from the face of the earth...and Rex, he's the most arrogant, self-centered, egomaniacal irresponsible son of a bitch I've ever met."

"This is the man you love? A man whose love you want?" Rex, for all of his worldly experience, was mystified by this, even as he suddenly put all of the pieces together. *Great gods! It is Lear! Susannah bolting at once when Lear's voice filled the pub. The clear identification of the mortal who was currently enchanting his Queen...*

Rex thought he could not resent the new Court Singer more than he already did, but listening to Susannah now, he made plenty of room to loathe the man on Susannah's behalf as well as his own.

"To tell you the truth, I think I hate him even more than I love him," Susannah continued with a self-directed scowl. "I'm not saying it makes any sense, and I'm not saying I'm happy about it. But I love him. I see him at work, or, well, did, until recently. I'm not happy if I don't see him. I'm not happy if he doesn't talk to me, even though I'm not happy sometimes when he does. He can be such a mean bastard. But he is the music, and the music is so..." she struggled for a word to describe it, and gave up, opened her hands in the air and made a vague gesture. "I love him, I care about him, I want to take care of him, see him succeed, make him happy...and that sounds like so much syrupy garbage, even to me. I hate the way I feel about him, I hate that he doesn't notice me, and I hate myself for even thinking about him. He's a terrible waste of my time and energy, but I can't seem to help myself. I wish I could find a nice guy, fall in love with him and settle down so I could forget the bastard, but I don't think I can...he's connected somehow to the way I breathe, isn't that ridiculous?!" She looked over at him, frustrated. "Do you know what I mean?"

The bright, sad and empathetic look in his eyes told her that he understood.

"At least I deal with rejection better than I used to," she muttered with a grim finality.

Later, Rex stared at himself in the bathroom mirror as he washed his hands. He studied the scar that marred the entire right side of his face; it had been a long while since he'd inspected it this objectively. It was as hideous as it had always been. Still, Susannah had been able to see it without any interest at all. She had looked past it, without a flicker of pity, a trace of fear, a comment or a question.

He did not know what to do with the strangeness of her non-reaction. He had lived with the unbreachable barrier of his scarred face set firmly between himself and everyone he'd come into contact with it since she—

He shuddered, driving the memory—and its related trains of thought—away with a sharp, stubborn turn of his head. He straightened, gave himself a forced, dour smile in the mirror, and dried his hands.

When he walked back into the living room, Susannah was still sitting on the couch, watching him. He felt himself rise to an internal challenge he would not have believed could have occurred to him in any other setting. Silently he blamed the ale and the timing.

He sat down beside her and, pointing to the right side of his face, confessed: "I have never discussed this with anyone. It would not haved served me...but may I ask you something?"

Susannah nodded, and waited as Rex framed his question and then asked it: "What does this look like to you?"

She did not miss a beat. "It looks to me, Rex, like you had a really bad day, once upon a time."

The unflinching honesty of her answer nearly destroyed him. He had to fight to keep his chin from trembling.

"Tell me, Susannah, why you are not frightened by this. Everyone is, of course—most look away, or stare, or ask unanswerable questions or..." He stared at her, unable to understand. "Why are you not frightened? You have not pitied me over the damned thing—why?" he demanded, perplexed now. "What makes you different from everyone else?"

Her lovely hazel-colored eyes looked into his as she reached over and laid her hand on his for a moment. "I'm only sorry that you had to suffer at all. You seem like such a great guy," she stated, calm as she raised her hand from his, and with her finger gently traced his scar from top to bottom.

Rex shook his head in uneasy wonder at himself. He could not believe that he was talking about this with her. More than that, he could not believe that he was allowing her to touch his face this way; with a shock, he realized that no one ever had. By the time he fully grasped that she had caressed the very thing that had become his long-standing, private symbol for the worst part of himself, and would have pulled away from her, she had already moved her hand back to rest on top of his.

Overcome by the gentleness of her spontaneous act, he swallowed hard, his eyes searching hers for something he sensed in her but couldn't see. "I am accustomed to dealing with the damnable pity of others, and responding by making them frightened or uncomfortable," his words flowed in a fast whisper. "I have mastered the knack, although it has had some ill effects on my popularity. You confuse and confound me. I do not understand why you are untroubled by the sight of it. By the sight of me," he amended.

Looking away, she moved her gaze to her hand on top of his, and seemed to be studying it very carefully.

"Susannah?"

With an effort, she looked up at him. "It seems to me," she said in a voice so quiet that he had to lean in closer to hear her, "that scars aren't who you *are*, they're...they're where you've *been.*"

Staring into his eyes, using her right hand, she unbuttoned her left cuff and rolled the sleeve back, holding his questioning gray eyes captive with the sudden, fearless intensity in her own. After a minute she nodded her head, looked down for a fraction of a second, and finally turned her face away from him.

Following her gaze downward, he nearly cried out when he saw what she had chosen to show him: there was an uneven thirteen-inch gash, a jagged pink and white scar on the inside of her forearm that ran from wrist to elbow. It reminded Rex of a small but still-angry mountain range.

"This is how I once dealt with unrequited or broken love," she said simply, without apology, or the need for pity or sympathy. "Like I said: it's not who you are, it's where you've been."

In silence, more deeply moved than he had been in centuries, Rex gently lifted Susannah's arm to his lips, and kissed the long scar with slow and infinite tenderness.

IN THE COMFORTABLE living area of Callie's royal apartments, five of the Queen's Ladies sat on couches and worked on their personal embroidery projects. Her Majesty had left several hours earlier, in the company of Rose, Carnation and Violet, to meet with her Council, and was expected to be occupied for the remainder of the morning. The Ladies remaining in the Queen's apartments had completed their morning duties, and were now at leisure.

"I have been fiddling with this peacock design for about ten years longer than necessary," Iris chuckled as she pulled a long needle with bright-blue silk thread through the linen in her lap. "I can't seem to make myself finish it. Something always needs doing, or re-doing. I take out as many stitches as I put into it."

"Maybe you are not willing to give it away once you finish it," Juniper suggested, studying her own design of a captivating, dark-haired Merrow, the male equivalent of a mermaid. Juniper's Merrow had a few extra and substantial body parts but none of the Ladies objected too strongly. Every time someone tells you how much they like that peacock, you tell them you will give it to them when you finish it."

Iris raised her heavy eyebrows. "Nonsense!"

"Oh, it is true, and you know it," Dahlia, the Dwarf princess, teased Iris. "I distinctly remember you promising that to Her Grace, to Lord Guardian, also to that minstrel from Elvenmere last year, who said it was so beautiful that he would have to find a perfect song for it. Then there was the horse master, the one from Ireland..."

"Which? The old Leprechaun, or the young Brownie?" Orchid wanted to know.

"Both, I believe," laughed Juniper. "And who knows how many times she has promised it to the Lord High Chamberlain!"

"Be still," Iris grumbled amiably, then laughed with the others, even as she noted again that Lavender, who sat alone on a couch a little removed from the two the other Ladies occupied, had not spoken since they'd pulled out their needlework an hour before. Iris attempted to catch Lavender's eye, but failed. The pretty blonde Elf appeared to be fully focused on the guitar pattern she was stitching, oblivious to all else. "Actually," Iris continued, "I have likely promised it to Zodiac a dozen times or so, for reasons that," and here she winked wickedly, "escape me at present."

The Queen's Ladies were still giggling and teasing each other when a half-awake, distracted Thomas Lear came down the stairs from the Queen's bedroom.

"I hope we did not disturb your rest, Thomas," said Iris, who stood up when she saw him. The other Ladies rose from their seats as well.

The Court Singer, under obligation of silence, shook his head and smiled. Barefoot, he wore a wrinkled gray tunic and brown trousers. His hair was tousled, and he looked tired, but then, he'd just spent the night in Her Grace's bed. He gestured to the Ladies to return to their embroidery and conversation while he searched for his footwear.

Juniper, Orchid and Dahlia sat down again and reached for their embroidery. Iris watched Thomas for a moment, and then sat down as she told him, "Your boots are beside the front door."

Thomas nodded his thanks as he walked to the door, and slid into his boots. With a polite wave to the Ladies, he opened the door and left.

Everyone noticed, with some surprise and discomfort, that Lavender was still standing, needlework in hand, staring at the door through which the Court Singer had exited.

"Lavender," Iris offered, "Come and sit by me, and show me your needlework." She glanced at the other Ladies, her authority unquestionable. "We shall talk about needles and thread, and you can tell me to whom I should give my peacock."

"If you ever finish it," Orchid interjected, and the conversation picked up where it had left off, with the Ladies teasing one another and tacitly giving Lavender space to regain her composure.

Realizing her situation, the uneasiness she had caused, and the kindness of the others, Lavender took a breath and went to sit beside Iris.

"Poor Lamb," Iris whispered to Lavender as the others talked and giggled about Juniper's embroidery work. "I am sorry for your heartache, we all are, but you must put him out of your mind. I do not believe Her Grace will cast Thomas aside. She has feelings for this Court Singer, in her way, so that's an end to it, my dear. Your turn will come. You must wait until next time, and see what's what then."

Lavender nodded her head in tearful resignation, and tried to smile at Iris' kindness. The others included her in the conversation about the prowess of Water Folk, and she cheered up a bit and participated. But beneath the merry chatter, she wondered how she was going to do her duty to her beloved Queen and to her trembling, hungry heart at the same time.

TWENTY MINUTES LATER, Thomas sat on the bench under the shady tree in the gardens outside his apartment and played his guitar, the one he'd brought with him from Upworld. Callie's gift—the mahogany masterpiece that he was more than a little in love with—was inside, in its cabinet. He wanted to play his old friend this morning. He had had disturbing dreams, nightmares set in his other life in Los Angeles, and he'd awakened feeling anxious, out of sorts, and unsocial as he worked to regain his balance through his own music on his own guitar. He'd been grateful for the forced silence that had protected him from interacting with the Queen's Ladies at Callie's place. He was even more grateful that he'd had the dreams after Callie had gone off to do Queen Stuff. He had awakened alone, sweating and shaking. He might have cried out, he wasn't sure. He didn't want to think about it again, but of course he did.

He couldn't help it.

In his dream, he'd been performing at the Universal Amphitheatre in Studio City, in the San Fernando Valley. There were easily 5,000 people in the audience, and when he walked on stage to start the show, there were no guitars waiting in their stands for him, and his band-mates weren't around. There were no amps, no lights, no microphones.

When he opened his mouth to ask what the hell was going on, he had no voice; a dry brown wind had blown from his mouth, with no sound. There was only Thomas Lear, empty and alone, standing before an audience to whom he had absolutely nothing to give. Even now, in the safety of the sunlight, his guitar making soothing music, he shuddered at the troubling memory.

Another dream had followed immediately after the first, and that one was even more upsetting. He had been snorting an endless line of cocaine, under the approving eyes of The Monster In His Head. Thomas kept breathing the line in, and the line got longer and longer until his lungs, mouth, and nose were filled with the bright white powder. Instead of getting deliciously high, which had been the point, he had smelled and tasted what he knew was his own blood. He had wanted to stop, but his inhalation went on and on. He ingested more cocaine than he could handle, tasting rivers of blood.

Sitting alone in the morning sunlight, he could still taste the blood in his mouth. He was having a hard time shaking off the tension. He knew that if Callie had been in the bed when he had the nightmares, she would have wanted him to talk about them. He did not want to discuss the bad dreams with anyone, not even with the beautiful woman who had become one of his closest friends, among other things. No, better to keep his mouth shut and just get over it. No one needed to know how messed up he really was.

So many doors in his life were better left closed, locked, and ignored.

For the next hour, he played his old songs, and found comfort and safety in them. His breathing relaxed. After a while, his tension melted away, and so did the power of the nightmares. Calmer now, he thought about new songs.

Thomas was absently playing a piece of a tune he was currently writing for Callie when he felt a subtle shift in the air behind him. He recognized it, almost—but not quite—soon enough.

"Pretty," the voice said, and he nearly jumped out of his skin.

"Don't do that!" he exclaimed in surprise. "You'll scare me to death!"

"I am sorry," she said, apologizing at once. "But it is pretty."

Thomas laughed. "Thanks." He turned to face her or, rather, to face the direction from which the voice had come, but he gave up. "You didn't tell me your name," he reminded her.

"I thought I had, before." She sounded uncertain.

"You were about to. Or, I thought you were about to, and then Guardian came to the door, and you left, remember?" Thomas prompted.

She was quiet for a moment, and then clapped invisible hands and laughed. "Yes! And I asked you not tell anyone I had been there, and you did not."

"That's right, I didn't," Thomas agreed. He thought about this for a second. "How did you know that?"

"Easy," she said. "No one said anything to me about it. 'Out of sight' is not 'out of mind' here. At least, not with everyone." Her voice sounded strange as she said it, but Thomas didn't know what to do about it, so he moved on.

"Since you aren't Fey, I don't have to rename you. You can tell me your real name," he urged. "If we're going to talk to each other, I have to call you something." Perhaps she was considering this; she was silent. Thomas continued to strum the guitar. "You already know mine," he teased her. "Fair is fair."

Another minute passed before she answered him. When she did, her voice was little more than a whisper on wind. "I am Terena."

"Terena. Pretty name," Thomas replied.

"Why are you sad?" Terena asked him, her voice serious and concerned.

"Do I look sad?"

"Yes," she told him. "What is wrong?"

Thomas shrugged. "It's nothing. I didn't sleep well. Or, I did. I just didn't dream well, I guess."

"I am sorry." Terena's voice took on a sadness that touched him. "Bad dreams are harsh." There was nothing from her after that, and he wondered if she'd walked away, until her voice came from the other side of him. "Sometimes good dreams are harsh, too," she sighed.

"What do you mean? How could a good dream be harsh?"

"Sometimes, when you dream a good dream, you wake up and realize that you can never go back and touch the thing that made you happy when you were dreaming." Her voice was soft and low, tinged with a depth of melancholy that made his throat ache with a sense of kindred sympathy. He had had many such dreams, and he knew how much they wounded the heart.

Thomas put the guitar down, leaned it against the bench. "What good dream do you dream?" he asked, hoping to cheer her up.

Her tone was wistful, but her voice didn't waver. "I dream of my beloved one," she told him with pride. "I dream that he is yet with me, and that he loves me still, despite..." Terena's voice stopped for a moment, and she took a deep breath before beginning again. "In my good dreams, he sings to me still, and dances with me, and tells me stories. He speaks his heart and mind to me, and loves me. Oh, how he loves me!" She sighed then, her troubled mood of seconds before faded away, replaced by a smile that glowed in her voice. "Love is the only thing that matters, you know."

"I know," he murmured, shifting his eyes to take in the colors of the garden, since he couldn't see her anyway.

"Are you in love, Thomas?"

"Me?" he whispered, more to himself than to her.

"With the Queen? Or perhaps with one of her Ladies? Or is there another?"

He smiled. "I think it's fair to say that I have feelings for the Queen."

"That is good."

He grinned then. "And I'm rather fond of you, too."

Laughter bubbled in the air around him. "Oh, you, you are as silly as an old Pixie with a new hat. But I am flattered just the same."

"Tell me about the man you love," Thomas suggested. "Do I know him? Oh God, have I given him a terrible name?"

Terena was silent for several long minutes. When she spoke at last, her voice came slowly, each word delivered with a wistful, brave sadness. "I do not see him often. He is busy, of course, quite busy. I sometimes wait for him outside his private chamber, just to have a glimpse of him as he passes by. He is terribly handsome, you know."

Thomas felt another stab of pain for the invisible woman beside him. "What happened? What went wrong?"

"What went wrong?" she echoed, as if from a great distance. "Life changes. People change. Desire changes. The whole world changes. The only thing that does not change is love that is true, love that knows no boundaries, love that exists for its sake alone, love that gives much and asks little in return." Her voice was steady and sure, but Thomas felt tears. Were they hers, or were they his?

"I must go," she said abruptly.

"Terena..." Thomas reached his hand out to the place where he gauged that her voice had last come from, but touched nothing.

She was gone.

IN THE SLOWLY-growing brightness of dawn over Edinburgh, Susannah watched Rex as he slept beside her.

She lay pondering the fact that, after they had found comfort in each other's bodies and later drifted off to sleep, they had ceased to touch each other. Rex and his dreams and his pain rested, almost self-contained, at least ten inches from Susannah's body on the bed now, beneath the sheet, the blanket and the duvet they shared.

She didn't mind, though; she was not in love with him, despite the fact that she liked him very much and felt that she trusted him a little. And he was not in love with her, nor did he pretend to be. Although he had not said his wife's name last night in the delicious, sizzling heat of several very intense moments, she had seen the look of raw hunger mingled with distant grief in his eyes; she knew that while he took pleasure in her body, it was very likely that he was also far away from her, making love in his mind with the woman who ruled his heart.

"That's so very sweet, Rex," she whispered. She found herself wishing that she was whispering to...to...well, all right, to Thomas Lear, she groaned to herself, shaking her head to toss the stupid thought away.

A soft ray of the morning's new light streaked in through the bedroom's unshaded window, and within minutes inched across Rex's face. She thought for a moment that the beam might wake him, but he only breathed more deeply, sinking into another layer of a dream she knew she couldn't share.

He turned his head, and mumbled something. Asleep, he looked both powerful and vulnerable to her. She was startled when she realized that, looking at him now, she was seized with the impulse to laugh and cry at the same time. She didn't know why, precisely, so she put the thought away with the hundreds of others she had never known what to do with, tucked safely away—for good—in some useless filing cabinet in her head. She sighed and rubbed her eyes with the back of her hand.

The sunbeam caught something in his hair; she saw a quick metallic flash, and recognized that the light had sparked a glow against the small gold earring he wore. She watched the light while it lasted, and tentatively moved a few strands of dark hair away from and behind his ear.

And then she saw it. She stared at it, straining her eyes to make sure she was seeing what she thought she was seeing. And she was.

Rex had a long, pointed ear. It was likely that his other one was pointed, too. Why hadn't she noticed it before? Something out of Star Trek, *very Vulcan-ish ears*, she told herself. Her stomach tried to do a little flip of alarm, but she ignored it.

The longer she stared at the tip of his ear, the less it looked like Mr. Spock's. It was long, delicate-looking, and, yeah, very sexy. If he wasn't a Vulcan (*Yeah, right, Susannah*, she grimaced at herself), then what was he? She'd never seen anyone with ears like that. Her mind flooded with possibilities. It couldn't be a deformity, it was too, well, pretty. Or maybe...

In seconds, with a dull certainty, she knew that she would never ask Rex about his ears. She was not comfortable with any form of personal confrontation, never had been, and found it unlikely that she would cozy up to it anytime soon. The very idea of asking him directly made her tremble with sudden anxiety, even though she felt certain that if she did ask him, he would tell her about his ears, and somehow the explanation would be the truth. She did not feel any better for realizing this, however.

He would never have to explain it, because she would never, could never, ask.

She sighed at herself and closed her eyes, annoyed at yet another acknowledged interpersonal ineptitude.

"So heavy a sigh for so beautiful a morning," Rex said softly.

Caught, Susannah's eyes flew open and met Rex's peaceful gray ones watching her with interest. "Is something wrong?" he asked with an easy smile.

"Not a thing," she said, slipping deftly into her favorite version of herself—the competent, worldly, sophisticated one—and offering him what passed for a lustful invitation. "Good morning, Rex."

"Good morning, Sweet Susannah," he replied, reaching for her.

It crossed her mind as she slid willingly into his welcoming embrace that—just maybe—it was far better to be the casual breakfast of someone who was kind and gentle, even if he would rather be dining somewhere else, than it was to be Thanksgiving Dinner for the one you secretly loved, especially since he would never be coming to the table at all.

Later that day, they rode through Edinburgh in a black cab that made its way toward the airport; Susannah would fly to London, on to New York, and then to Los Angeles. Thomas Lear's luggage, and Susannah's, too, had been sent to the airport earlier in the day, so, apart from her purse and a tote bag filled with snacks and reading material for the long trip, Susannah was unencumbered for the flight.

"You didn't have to make the trip with me, Rex, but it was so nice of you to want to," said Susannah.

"I am honored to see you safely on the first leg of your journey home." He looked out the window and indicated the city, pride shining in his eyes. "Edinburgh is especially beautiful today."

In this moment, dividing her glances between the Edinburgh streets and the gentle, gallant man with whom she had shared her body and random fragments of her life, Susannah felt better about things than she had since she'd first arrived in Scotland. If she had been the kind of person who spent much time in deep self-reflection, she might have realized that, in fact, she was happier and more at ease with herself—and with the world around her—than she had been in years. She still had strong yet opposing feelings for Thomas Lear, whose name she'd never mentioned to Rex. The inconvenience of loving someone that far out of her league would always be daunting, and the helpless vulnerability of wanting him, and wanting the best for him, and wanting to run him over with her car a few times, still made her ache with diverse varieties of feverish frustration.

Yet somehow she had discovered her balance today; this was something of a mystery. She hadn't done anything in particular to effectively manage the immensity of her multi-level Lear problems, but the conflicting emotions that surrounded the pain of her unrequited love seemed to have been delicately resolved, and kindly laid to rest.

For the first time in ages, Susannah's heart didn't hurt.

She had feelings, but she was giving herself permission to feel all of them, at the same time. An unexpected light had burned through darkness and she could see her emotions very clearly. All was well, and this confused her a little; she knew she was going to learn to be at peace with herself and her choices. When and how had that happened?

It might have had something to do with Rex, and their conversations—and other, more tangible interactions—last night and throughout this day. She'd have to think about that later.

She looked over at him now, and her smile a touch wistful. "I don't know you as well as I'd like to, but I think I'm going to miss you, Rex."

"I am grateful we met, Susannah," he told her as he reached for her hand. "You have given me a most precious gift. I thank you, Sweet Lady, for your kindness and your grace." He kissed her hand, then winked at her slyly, chuckling when she blushed. "I have a small gift for you. I hope you will accept it, as a reminder of our brief time together...two friends who shared a lonely night and gave each other some much-needed warmth and comfort."

She was searching the depths of his shining gray eyes, wondering what she should say to him, so she did not see the fast puff of golden light that slipped through the fingers of his closed right hand.

"A gift? For me?"

"For you, Susannah. With much affection and many thanks."

He opened his hand.

A delicate gold chain sat there, curled around a small gold charm in the shape of a detailed willow tree, surrounded by a protective circle of small oak leaves. The oak leaves were subtly carved with mysterious, Celtic-looking designs (or were they letters forming a word she couldn't read?).

The necklace was beautiful. It took her breath away. She told him so, and Rex smiled as she slid her blonde hair over her shoulder so he could fasten it around her neck.

"You are a not a lost leaf in the wind, my dear Susannah. You never were," Rex whispered as he touched the charm before he let it fall into place on the chain, and then sat back and smiled at her. "You need no longer be blown around by circumstance or the storms of others. You are a willow tree, and your heart is your own. You are strong enough to face the world on your own terms. You are wise, and, like the willow, you will know when to bend with the wind, and when to stand strong and let the wind pass without incident. This is my gift to you."

The chain was long enough for the willow to rest close to Susannah's heart. She imagined that she could feel the willow in its golden circle instantly settle in and become part of her, but she shrugged the strange notion away as quickly as it had come to her.

The cab stopped; they had arrived at Edinburgh Airport. The cab driver turned toward them, and slid the glass between the front seat and passenger area open. Rex paid the man, and tipped him well.

Susannah and Rex stepped out of the cab, and they watched it pull away.

Dropping her purse and her tote bag on the pavement, Susannah flung her arms around Rex. "Oh, Rex! Thank you for the beautiful necklace. The tree is amazing. I love it! Thank you so much...for, oh, so many things!"

He put his arms around her, and held her close. "You are welcome, my dear, for all of them," he replied, and then whispered into her hair, "I will always remember you."

They held each other for a long moment, and then separated slowly. Susannah looked at her watch.

"I've got to go, or the stupid plane will leave without me." She'd attempted levity, but the lump in her throat got in the way. "It's time," she said, a little sadly.

He tilted her chin up, and kissed her. "It's time for many things." He laughed, and she laughed too, although she couldn't have said why.

One last hug, and Susannah, with purse and tote bag in hand, turned and walked alone into the airport. Rex remained where the cab had left them, watching her go. She turned back to look at him one last time, and waved. He waved back, they smiled at each other, and then she hurried toward the airplane that would take her home.

He stood unmoving for a moment, considering the past twenty-four hours. "There is magic, Susannah," he murmured into the air, "And it is everywhere!"

With a bemused grin, Rex vanished in a sparkling flash of golden light.

eighteen

ALONE IN THE moonlight, Lavender walked in the arbor behind the High Queen's apartments. She had spent the evening with one of her lovers, a handsome and fun-loving Elf who currently answered to the unfortunate name of "Buick." They had danced wildly, shared Faerie wine and pleasure. Lavender had tried to listen while Buick told her a story he'd heard that was in one of the books written by Lord Guardian's mortal lady. There was much conjecture around the castle about which stories Lord Guardian might tell Maggie Forrest next, and how she would retell them to other mortals...

She'd had a difficult time keeping her mind from wandering, even when they had danced in Buick's bed. It was not until Buick spoke the Court Singer's name that Lavender's focus had darted back to the conversation.

"...I thought that Thomas Lear might know Lord Guardian's lady, since they both know Lord Guardian, but my father said he doubts it. It must not be so. My father is right about most things."

Lavender's eyes fixed on Buick's, waiting for more.

"Ah, there you are!" Buick teased. "I could talk for a day, and your eyes would not light up...unless I said 'Thomas Lear' or 'guitar' or 'Dangerous Blue Eyes' or..."

"Stop it," Lavender retorted, looking away and fidgeting unhappily with her beaded tail.

Buick put his arm around Lavender's shoulders. "You spend too much time thinking about Her Grace's lover. That can only lead you down a sad road, and we have no need of sad roads, right?" He'd nudged her until she finally looked up at him, tears spilling down her cheeks. "Oh, you are offering your heart, and you should not, this time. Poor Lavender. This will come to no good. Leave it."

As she walked under the stars, she thought about how kind Buick had been, her Faerie-born lover holding her while she wept for helpless love of a mortal she could not have.

At least, not tonight.

OVER BREAKFAST IN Thomas' rooms, Callie sipped hot water and lemon juice and watched her Court Singer eat Upworld bacon, eggs and brown toast.

"So," Thomas goaded her, "King Arthur: fact or fiction?"

Callie groaned. "Don't you ever tire of this game, Thomas?"

"Nope," he grinned.

"I must meet with the Council in half an hour. I should go."

"You're avoiding the issue, Callie."

"And deftly, too." She rose from the table.

"Chicken," he muttered, loud enough for her to hear him and laugh.

She kissed him on the top of his head, and then smacked it lightly. "You're asking about a fictitious king, around whom is as much mythology as history. Allow me to point out that you are speaking with the fictitious Queen of fictitious Faerie. What do you think?"

Studying her dazzling brown eyes and accepting the notion that she would never tell him all the secrets that lived behind them, he sighed. "Forget I asked."

"Asked what?" Callie giggled as she swept out the front door.

"She doesn't play fair," Thomas grumbled, and bit into his toast.

FROM THE SADDLE of the huge black stallion WindRunner, the scarred man arranged and rearranged his thoughts as he rode toward Elvenhome Castle. He'd left Edinburgh Airport in a flash of light the previous afternoon, and had reappeared at Queensgate Inn in the Highlands for some sleep, a meal, and time to think before returning to Faerie.

He'd slept well last night, and was pondering the notion that, while nothing had truly changed, everything had in fact changed. He would have laughed out loud, but he found the prospect of assimilating his new perspective somehow daunting. He had much to do, now, and he had no idea how to do it.

He murmured a comment to the horse about the edible treats in store for him if he moved a bit faster. The stallion had had several days of leisure and the Lord teased him about laziness and the dangers of equine fragility. Sheila and her family always took excellent care of WindRunner whenever his owner spent time Upworld; the stallion was in fine form this morning as he reared to get his master's attention, indelicately threatened to drop the Lord on his arse, then, with a cheerful nicker, galloped them homeward.

A short while later, the scarred man left a rather smug WindRunner in the stables with the castle's Master of Horses, and was immediately met by the group of men who served him. These men, one from each of the eight kingdoms of Faerie, followed him as he strode through a wide courtyard, into the castle, down a corridor toward his private apartments. He did not acknowledge anyone he passed along the way, more from habit than from his present mood. He had much on his mind, and he told the men who accompanied him, "It is true. They are there; I saw them in Glasgow and Edinburgh. I mean to have them back."

"It will cause some mischief, My Lord," commented a gray-haired Dwarf who walked beside him.

"Not necessarily, Dwindor," his master replied as they entered his rooms. He waited until they were assembled in his living area, a spacious chamber with large, comfortable chairs, a huge dining table, and a wall of bookshelves. He addressed an ancient-looking Elf with long, gray hair and youthful, laughing eyes. "Emmel, I want them back, and soon. Take care of this for me, with no mischief. Is this understood?"

Emmel bowed in acknowledgement, looked at his fellows thoughtfully, and vanished into the air.

A handsome, auburn-haired Water Faerie handed the scarred man a goblet of wine. "The Queen's Grace will know by now that you have returned." He winced ever so slightly, and was surprised when his master chuckled.

"I would imagine that is so, Wyand."

The others looked at each other in amazement, and then looked at their leader in disbelief as he sat in a tall-backed chair and took off his boots.

He gave them a mock frown, and narrowed his eyes. "One would think, Gentlemen, that you have never heard me laugh."

"Not when you are sober," said a Goblin while he reached down to collect the boots. "And we would know."

At this, the scarred man laughed harder, and was joined by the others. "Ah, yes...it is good to be home."

That night, he lay alone in his bed, and considered the time he'd spent Upworld.

He thought about Susannah, and smiled. His encounter with her, the physical as well as the conversational, had moved him. Until now, he had not seen a reason to change, and on his own, he could not have found the road that led to a desire to change. A night and part of a day with the sweet mortal lady had opened his eyes, his heart and mind as well.

He wondered how Emmel was going to manage the task set before him, but he was not concerned. Emmel had served him faithfully for hundreds of years, and was a master at organizing Folk to do what needed doing. He decided to be patient and let Emmel supervise the retrieval of—

Without warning, his thoughts flew in the direction of the woman he had loved, who no longer loved him. But in this moment, as he saw her in his mind, and let memories wash over him, he noticed that he wasn't feeling angry, or sad, or bitter, or lost, or any of the other intense emotions that he usually choked on when he saw her, heard her speak, or thought of or dreamt of her.

It took no real effort to imagine himself telling her his mind, as he had done at their beginning. He saw himself showing her that he was capable of changing, finding his way back to the man she had once loved deeply—all because of the gentle acceptance he had found when he was with Susannah. He could almost feel the remembered touch of his wife's hand in his own; his breath caught in his throat. He had never stopped loving her, not really, despite the years of empty rage and silent bitterness he had carried. If they could set the past aside, even for only a few hours, and simply talk for a while...

Almost wistful now, he allowed himself to ache as he thought of all the things he would have liked to tell her.

And then he had an idea.

"I fear this is a bad idea, My Lord," Wyand said quietly as he and a thin young Brownie walked on either side of their master two hours after dawn.

"Perhaps. Perhaps not," he replied. He had bathed and dressed carefully, and now moved quietly through the corridors away from his rooms, and toward hers.

"Wyand may be right, My Lord," added Annodin, the Brownie, unhappily.

"Wyand's rarely right," retorted the scarred man, attempting playfulness to cover his nervous excitement. "Wyand, don't have a wind change and be right for once. Not today."

The Water Faerie and the Brownie exchanged a pained look, but kept pace with their master as he turned a corner and strode down another corridor.

A few minutes later, he stopped, took a long-stemmed, shimmering white rose from Annodin and told them, "Wait for me here. I mean to deliver this myself, to her door. No words, just this rose. For now."

Without a sound, he moved down the corridor, and prepared to turn one last corner when, further down the hallway, he heard a door creak open in the early-morning stillness. He stopped, still holding the rose.

Thomas Lear came out of the High Queen's apartments, followed by the High Queen herself. She was robed in nothing but a green blanket, and her hair was tousled rather beautifully. She spoke to the Court Singer, but the scarred man couldn't hear the words; he could only look at her.

Then she comfortably leaned into the musician, and kissed him, long and lazily.

The white rose shimmered as it fell to the floor, unnoticed and alone. A moment later, it faded away.

THOMAS SAT ON a wrought-iron bench in the tranquil afternoon shade of a maple tree in the arbor, which stretched along the outside of the lower level of Callie's apartments on the quiet northern end of the castle. He was completely absorbed in writing music, entirely content and enveloped in a solitary, wholly-introspective frame of mind as his fingers caressed the strings of his new guitar.

He had very nearly finished the melody line he'd been working on all day, and he was experimenting with it here in the shade, wrapped in his creativity, comfortable with and aware of his imposed silence. Callie was busy, closeted again with her Council in the Queen's Presence Chamber; he did not expect to see her until dinner, which was still several hours away.

Every so often he could hear giggles and an occasional sigh from the second-story windows of the Queen's rooms that looked out over the arbor. Several of the Queen's Ladies were watching him, listening as he worked. He chuckled to himself when Carnation, the shy—and strangely pretty—Goblin who seemed to live only for music and for serving Callie, let out a long, breathy gasp and whispered, "That was the loveliest chord I've ever heard!"

Thomas scribbled a notation on the pad of paper beside his lap, bending and reaching his arms around the guitar, rather than moving the magnificent instrument that sat on his thigh. He was so focused on getting the transcription down accurately that he did not notice that someone was standing several yards behind him, leaning against a fruit tree.

By the time Thomas realized that he was not alone, his observer had been present there for several minutes.

Reminding himself to be silent, Thomas moved the guitar from his lap, and rested it against the trunk of the tree behind him. He turned. He knew instinctively that it was not Callie. Most likely it would be Zodiac, or perhaps Guardian; for obvious reasons, few others came looking for him when he was anywhere in the vicinity of Callie's place.

He twisted around and encountered the steely-gray gaze of a man he hadn't seen before.

The man was tall, and powerfully built. He had long hair, dark and straight, which fell loosely just below his shoulders. He wore a flowing white shirt, fitted black leather gloves, and tight black breeches. Dark, knee-length soft-leather boots accentuated the strong legs that were, at present, crossed idly as he leaned against the tree trunk. He studied the Court Singer.

Thomas noticed the man's long nose, and the arrogant lift of his chin. Thomas' eyes were drawn to the ghastly scar that marred the right side of the other man's face from mouth to cheekbone. It was by far the worst scar Thomas had ever seen, and even as he rose and stood beside the maple tree, he could not move his eyes from the long deformity for some seconds. Then, embarrassed, he forced himself to meet the man's steady gaze straight on.

The gray eyes scrutinized him keenly, in a silence that was nerve-wracking and oppressive. Thomas' self-contained peacefulness of only moments before evaporated under the alarming force of the man's unwavering stare.

Because he was not in his own rooms and did not have Callie's permission to speak, he could not say a single word to this man, whom he had spontaneously dubbed "ScarFace." Thomas conscientiously did two of the very few things he could do right now: he stood still, and he waited.

ScarFace's laugh was rough as he saw Thomas' resolve. The laughter came as a coarse, straining sound that left Thomas uneasy. He forced himself to stand still as the larger man took a few long strides toward him.

Startled gasps came from the open upper window of the Queen's apartments. The Queen's Ladies were instantly unsettled, apprehensive about this man's presence. ScarFace narrowed his eyes into menacing slits and made a delicate gesture with his left hand. "Fly away, Little Birds!" he called to them with a deceptive lightness. The Ladies moved away from the windows, and they were pulled closed at once, but not before Thomas thought he heard Iris order in an anxious voice, "Dahlia and Juniper: find Zodiac at once, please. Lavender, Rose: inform Her Grace. Daisy: to Guardian. Go! Go!"

Thomas had been watching the other man, but at the unmistakable note of tension in Iris' voice, he looked up just in time to see Orchid shoot him a worried look before she stepped fully away from the closed windows. A very worried look.

Thomas was a little afraid to wonder what that look meant.

He turned and faced ScarFace, who was grinning with bully-like amusement at the reaction of the Ladies. Thomas gave the man an inquisitive look and hoped he would be able to make himself understood without the benefit of words.

"Yes, yes, Court Singer, I am fully aware of who you are. And you have no idea who I am. That may be a good thing, for all I know." ScarFace understood Thomas' intention, and spoke with a polished condescension that rankled Thomas. On the other hand, it occurred to him that the man might just as easily be talking to himself as to Thomas. Thomas realized with a jolt that ScarFace was more than a little drunk, and carried the subtle, weary air of someone who had probably been so for some time. This stranger bore an unspeakable sense of bitter frustration that was as familiar to Thomas as the underside of his own soul. Intrigued by the depths of dark and tacit kinship, Thomas met ScarFace's gaze with less alarm than he'd felt seconds before.

There was nothing else to do; Thomas shrugged at the man and kept his mouth shut.

"I know well that you cannot speak, Thomas Lear," ScarFace said, as if testing the notion and considering pushing it further. Then, without warning, his tone changed, the threat of roiling anger only barely contained behind his cold gray eyes. "You are not the first, nor will you be the last, brought here to serve, and service, the High Queen of Faerie. Remember that, in the event you feel yourself begin to believe that you love her. You are but one in an endless chain of Court Singers who perform in her Court as well as in her bed. Do not believe that you will ever hold her heart, not for your year and a day, and certainly never for a moment beyond it."

Thomas stared hard at ScarFace. Who the hell was he? He looked human, and had once been handsome—striking, even—before that huge scar had all but destroyed his appearance. ScarFace turned his head, and a ray of sunlight caught a shining object, a small golden earring. Thomas' eyes flickered slightly upward, and he was able to make out the delicate point of a positively Elven ear peeking through the dark, straight hair.

"Yes, Thomas Lear, I'm Elven born. That may be all you need to know about me. I have been known as 'Hunter,' and 'Father,' and "Defender," and 'Dark Knight," and even once as 'Satan,' called so by a rather cowering Court Singer who was somewhat alarmed by my presence. Whatever name you choose for me means nothing. Do not anticipate that you and I will have words to say to each other, even on those rare occasions when you have leave to speak."

If Thomas had been able to speak, he would not have known what to say. He frowned at the scarred Elf. Thomas himself was well-built, and had always considered his own body strong. But looking at ScarFace, at his size and his elegant muscles and his graceful ease of movement, coupled with the sullen drunkenness and the smoldering rage burning behind the gray eyes, Thomas knew he did not want to cross this man.

"Are you assessing my strength? Or perhaps my position here? I suggest that you do not waste your time; the knowledge will not serve you. Gifted Singer or no, you are no match for me, and you would do well to be mindful of that.

"You would also do well, Thomas Lear, to stay out of my way. I am dangerous when provoked, and your presence begins to vex me." He eyed Thomas speculatively. "Do you have something to say to that?" he asked, the subtle, mocking confrontation lighting his eyes in a parody of gleefulness.

Annoyed now, Thomas did have something to say, but he bit his lip hard to keep from saying it.

"I warrant there is wisdom in silence, especially in your case," ScarFace said. "You may survive yet." With a dismissive turn of his body, the arrogant Elf called over his shoulder as he walked away, "Make sweet music, Thomas Lear, and play it well. That is primarily why you are here. Dallying with the High Queen, regardless of her enchanting hold on you, is only a secondary pastime. Remember that. Ease the hearts of the Folk with your tunes and your voice, and you will have little trouble from me—for as long as I choose to bear the distasteful knowledge of your presence among us."

There was no mistaking the bitterness in his voice.

Thomas watched as ScarFace walked back through the arbor. Once he was completely out of sight, Thomas took a deep breath and made himself relax. He hadn't realized how tense his shoulders and hands had become during the confrontation with...who was he? The names didn't mean anything. There was no mistaking that he had to be a person of some noble rank, like Guardian. That was it; maybe he was a relative of Callie's. But he wasn't at all like Guardian. There was something unnerving about this guy.

Exhaling long and deeply, he refilled his lungs with fresh air, steadying himself as he let the breath out. Then he went back to the maple tree and retrieved the guitar. Bending down to pick up the notepad, he saw Zodiac hurrying toward him from the opposite direction that ScarFace had come and gone. At the same time, skirts and sleeves flying wing-like behind her, Callie came running from the north end of the castle, her eyes wild and predatory, giving her a surprising look of ferocity rather than panic, which, Thomas realized hazily, was what he'd expected, based upon the earlier reaction of the Queen's Ladies.

Rushing toward him, Callie seemed dangerous and feral, maddened and powerful, as though she could and absolutely would draw blood, without mercy. The naked savagery on her face almost frightened him.

She reached Thomas only seconds before Zodiac did. She all but slammed her fingers to his lips to keep him from speaking as she demanded, "Did you speak???"

Thomas shook his head once, stunned by the force of livid anger in her.

"That's good," Zodiac sighed in relief from somewhere behind Thomas. He felt Zodiac's hand on his shoulder, as the Lord High Chamberlain took careful custody of Thomas' guitar. "Are you hurt, man?"

Thomas shook his head once again. At this, both Callie and Zodiac let out deep breaths in simultaneous blasts. Callie lifted her shaking fingers from Thomas' lips, and ignored the questions taking shape on his face as she jerked herself away from him.

Agitated, she paced back and forth, struggling to control her fury, flexing her fingers in a way that made Zodiac blanch under the cover of his returning composure.

"Thomas, I'd like you to go back to your rooms, please, until dinner," she hissed, her voice low and straining as she tried for a courteous tone. "You may dine in the Great Hall with the rest of the Court if you'd prefer, or have food brought to you. I will join you later, in any event."

Her wrath was not cooling as she paced. She moved in longer, faster strides and addressed Zodiac in a clipped, anger-ravaged voice, although she did not look directly at him. "Zodiac, please escort Thomas. I do not want anyone else accosting him today."

Zodiac bowed at once, and gave Thomas a tug on the arm to get him moving. He did not want Her Grace to have to repeat herself; she was not often this angry, and he knew his Queen well, had served her long enough to know that this would be an exceedingly bad time to cross her. "Come, Thomas," he urged.

Thomas looked from the furiously pacing Callie to Zodiac, uncertainty in his eyes.

Zodiac tugged Thomas' arm a little harder. "She is only very angry, and was more than a little frightened for you. Come, let us leave her to cool her mind. She has commanded it so. She will come to you later, as she said," he whispered, sneaking a furtive glance at Callie.

But Thomas wanted to do something, anything, to comfort her, to assure her he was all right, to help her to calm down. It slowly dawned on him that there was much more going on here than he understood. He knew then that there was nothing he could do for Callie. Still, he hated to leave her like this. And who was that scarred Elf, anyway? He was someone important, or someone who at least thought he was...

Zodiac tugged at him again, so hard that he nearly dropped the notation pad.

With aching reluctance, Thomas let Zodiac lead him away through the arbor, and back into the cool safety of the castle, leaving Callie fuming and swearing under her breath as she stormed back and forth, seething in a maddened rage that showed no sign of dissipating anytime soon.

It was well after midnight when Callie finally knocked on Thomas' door. He let her in at once.

She smiled at him, her usual equanimity restored. She glanced around the room, and saw the remains of his dinner on the table. "You've eaten. Good."

"Orchid and Lavender brought it," Thomas told her. He touched her on the shoulder. "Are you all right, Callie?"

She nodded, and kissed him with tenderness to prove it. "Yes, Thomas. I am sorry that you were accosted today, and I am sorry that I allowed my anger to get the better of me."

"I asked the Ladies about the man," Thomas said, his tone cautious, "but they didn't want to talk about him. They seemed to be a little frightened of him. So we talked about music instead, and what it's like to live Upworld, and the last book Orchid read. Still, I would like to have heard about him—"

"And what did you have for dinner?" Callie asked, changing the subject.

Thomas had to stop and think about it. "Roast beef—that was from the north of England—Upworld carrots, some excellent Stilton cheese, and a baked potato with everything on it." He laughed. "I've gotten so used to the recitation of where the food comes from that I can't imagine starting a meal without it. Kind of like saying grace: Eat and drink, free from care. Strange, isn't it?"

"Not at all," she answered, the look in her eyes serious. "Knowing where everything has come from will keep you from eating anything you mustn't."

She moved to the couch and sat down in the middle of it, making a show of arranging her skirts with great care and attention. He sat down beside her, and took her hand.

"Callie, who is he?"

She looked Thomas directly in the eyes, took a slow, even breath, and said, "He was once a great Lord, with immense responsibility in Elvenhome, and in all of Faerie, as well." She looked down at her hand, sitting in his. It was a long moment before she spoke again.

Her voice was calm and steady, despite its quiet hint of something close to pain. "He met with a cruel tragedy, and was never able to move beyond it. He began to lose himself in drink. In time it was his most constant companion. Thus, he made wrong and sometimes dangerous choices, and was forced—by virtue of his deep sense of duty and his profound love for the Fair Folk and his guilt for wrongs he could not amend—to forsake his rightful place among us. He still fulfills many of his former duties, as is his right and his pleasure, but he no longer truly holds the hearts of the Folk the way he once did." She met Thomas' eyes again, and studied them. "He is strong, and powerful. But he cannot harm you. He can attempt to make you uneasy, but you are safe." Callie took another deep breath, and let it out; the last of the tension in her shoulders eased. "Now tell me, Thomas. What did he say you?"

"He said several things. He reminded me that I'm not unique in my position as Court Singer." He grinned when Callie rolled her eyes in what would have been exasperation, except that Thomas shook his head, indicating that it had not offended him. "He told me some of the names he'd been given by other Court Singers during their own time here. He also told me that he would tolerate me, for as long as he could, for the sake of the Fair Folk."

She frowned. "That is more or less what Iris told me. Did you know that she remained by the windows and watched over you?" Thomas shook his head. He'd been so focused on the scarred man and his anger that he hadn't looked back up at the windows. "Was that everything he said?"

Thomas replayed the conversation in his mind before he continued. "That's the gist of it. He seems to be very angry with you, and he was not kind." He stopped, waiting for her to ask him for details. When she didn't, he continued. "And he said that he didn't care much about the name I gave him, since he and I would not be talking to each other much."

"Oh," she said, taking this in. "And have you named him yet? I know you did not speak to him, and rightly so, since you were in the arbor, but did you name him to yourself?"

Suddenly Thomas felt like a nasty child caught behaving cruelly. His dismayed expression told her that he had indeed named the scarred, gray-eyed Elf.

"Out with it, Thomas," she ordered, her voice tired. "We have to call him something. I suspect that he may come up in conversation from time to time."

Thomas cleared his throat, feeling awkward. He could not lie to her, even though he really did not like what he was about to say.

Callie caught his eye, and looked wary. Could she know what he was thinking? Perhaps she didn't, really, maybe it was just that he felt vaguely guilty and more than a little bit rude. "Well, Callie, to tell you the truth, once I got a look at him, I started referring to him in my head as 'ScarF—'" The pained horror on her face closed his mouth in the middle of the word, and he never finished speaking it aloud, startled by the way she tore her hand from his and put it over her eyes. "Callie, Callie, I'm sorry. It's just that…" he began miserably.

She looked back at him when she heard the contrition in his voice, and gave him a patient, ironic smile. "Do not fret, Thomas. It is not so terrible a thing, and you actually saved it a little at the last. He shall be known now as 'ScarF', and there's an end to it."

Thomas did not look convinced. "I didn't mean to hurt you," he apologized.

She leaned her head against his shoulder. "I know it. It's all right. It was not what you said so much as it was what it made me think of. But all of that was long ago, and of no true consequence." She sat up then, and looked at him. "Do not dwell on it, Thomas, for I shall not.

"Now," she added, "I have been told that before you met 'ScarF' today, you were composing some very beautiful music. My Ladies were most taken with it. Might I, as your demanding patron, be permitted to hear it?"

Forgiven and relieved, Thomas felt playful. "I suppose, Your Grace, that I can force myself to present the unfinished piece for you, as you command," he sighed theatrically, and was rewarded by an amused smirk from Her Grace.

Eyeing him up and down, Callie lowered her voice, and gave him a mock pout. "What if I ask you to play it for me, not as your demanding royal patron, but as your enthralled and most eager lover?" Her eyes grew warm and intense as she showed him the depth of her desire, wrapping him in a familiar delicious heat.

"I'll get the guitar," he said with a lustful grin.

SEVERAL DAYS LATER, the High Queen of Faerie, attended by the Ladies Carnation, Dahlia and Rose, swept purposefully and unannounced into the scarred man's private library, which was located near the broad staircase that led to the castle's southernmost tower.

Her entrance silenced the active, masculine conversation. The Lord, seated in a large, comfortable chair, watched as the four men he'd been talking with bowed to Callie, then looked to him for instruction. He gestured, indicating that they should stand behind his chair.

The scarred man moved his somewhat blurry gaze from his men to the face of the High Queen.

"I understand that you are planning to remove yourself to Elvenstone Castle," she said, without preamble.

"That is so," he confirmed with a lazy nod.

"You are obliged to inform me—yourself, directly—when you plan to leave this castle. Yet you sent vague words through others instead."

"So I did."

It was apparent that he was, as usual, more than mildly drunk, and now she was, as usual, both frustrated and bored by the familiar and likely unpleasant encounter. "You and I have something of importance to discuss," Callie told him.

He closed his eyes, and his attention drifted. "As you wish."

"It is about your accosting of my Court Singer."

"I presumed so."

She waited a moment, watching him, as her irritation grew warm and moved toward hot. He kept his eyes closed, floating in wine-inspired reveries that nearly made him smile.

Callie saw the beginning of his smile, and her irritation grew prickly. Wisps of green light began to flicker around her hands as she let anger in.

"My Lord..." Wyand began, leaning across his master's chair to whisper in his ear. "My Lord, the Queen's Grace is—"

"Likely beginning to turn green?" A smirk spilled across the scarred face.

Callie raised her right hand into the air, green light wriggling around it. Without turning around to her Ladies, she commanded: "Go."

Rose, followed closely by Dahlia and Carnation, exited immediately and without a backward glance.

The green light around Callie's hands was burning brighter now.

The men were growing nervous. "My Lord, please," Wyand pressed beside his master, and spoke in as calm a voice as he could manage. "The Queen's Grace requires your attention, if you please..."

"Oh, very well." The scarred man slowly opened his eyes, and shrugged. "Finish the preparations for our journey, and I will remain here and face the Queen's ire alone."

Wyand and his fellows hurried out of the room, with abbreviated but sincere bows in the direction of the High Queen.

Ignoring their departure, Callie observed the Lord with a critical eye. From the look and the smell of him and the men who attended him, he might well have been drinking heavily for several days. The notion perplexed her; occasional wine and ale in excess was often playful and fun, but those who all but drowned themselves in the wine barrel did themselves no good, and could do others harm. She knew her objections to drunkenness were pointless when applied to this man, but she objected nevertheless.

"Madam," he said, slurring his words, with a bow of his head, "I go to Elvenstone. There I shall remain until you have finished debasing yourself with this new Court Singer."

"An intelligent plan," Callie conceded, eyeing him with her teeth clenched. "I do not want you to cross his path again. Such action on your part will have dire consequences, My Lord."

He heard the threat, and raised an eyebrow. "Indeed?" The scarred man rose from his chair, wobbling only slightly. "You threaten me, Your Grace?"

"You are drunk; you forget yourself, and you forget to whom you are speaking."

He smiled, amused by something she could not identify. "Yes, I am drunk, and drunk I am." The smile on his face vanished as quickly as it had appeared. "I do not forget to whom I am speaking. I do not forget anything."

The High Queen and the drunken Lord found themselves glaring at each other. Green light danced around Callie, and golden threads of luminous energy sparked from the Lord's fingertips.

Callie took a breath and inched toward control. The green light faded away. "You accosted Thomas Lear. You attempted to force him to speak, and to break his obligation to silence. You put him at risk, against my express command to all the Folk."

The scarred man's eyes narrowed, but the golden light glowing around him faded away, too. "Untrue. I spoke to him, yes. I did not give a thought to whether he would choose to speak in turn. I did not care. But I did 'encourage' him to give sweet music to the Folk, which is, if I recall correctly, one of my own obligations, Your Grace." He set his face in a stubborn scowl, and watched her.

"I regret to inform you that he has named you 'ScarF," Callie said, with only a hint of tacit challenge in her voice.

"So I have heard," ScarF said. "It is of no consequence, as there will be no reason for conversation between us."

"In any case, you will bear this name throughout Thomas Lear's year and a day, whether you are present in Elvenhome or not. Further, you are to leave him alone, unharmed, untouched, regardless of where you find yourself."

"So I shall, Madam, as you command." Something stronger than annoyance flashed in his eyes as he acknowledged Callie's orders. "I will not cross his path, in any way, in accordance with the wishes of the High Queen of Faerie."

She was tired this conversation, and of all the other similar ones they had endured. "Why," she asked, suddenly weary of him, "year upon year, why do you choose to live your life in this pathetic, useless way, when you have had so much time to—"

He stared at her, his scarred face filled with more emotion than Callie could read. She did not look away, her brown eyes searching for something unreadable in the maelstrom in his gray ones. "Why?" she repeated, knowing he would never give her a true answer, but asking anyway. She turned, and walked toward the door.

The irony of the moment was not wasted on the man called ScarF; he embraced it, without much bitterness, knowing that telling her the truth would cost him nothing. He spoke the words under his breath, but she heard them clearly enough as she moved away:

"This time, I confess, it was all for the loss of a pretty white rose."

THOMAS LEAR WAS, by now, so accustomed to spending time with Terena that he was no longer alarmed by the fact that she was, well, invisible. He found her to be charming and funny; he enjoyed spending time with her when she visited him in his garden, or knocked shyly on the doors of his apartments. They had developed a light and easy relationship where he teased her, and she teased him back. Generally, they left talk of serious things to other Folk, and basked in the fun of their growing friendship.

"I am too wearing a pink gown," Terena was telling Thomas as he sat in his living room restringing his guitar.

"I don't think you are," he said, testing the D string.

"You are going to have to take my word for it, I suppose."

"Hmmmm. I think you are not wearing a pink gown. I also think you are not wearing a gown at all," he taunted.

"Great gods!" Terena gasped. "Do you think I'm standing here in my shift?"

Thomas shrugged dramatically. "I would not be surprised if you were standing here stark naked. Who would know?"

She was speechless for a matter of seconds, and then started to chuckle. "I daresay if I were stark naked, I'd freeze to death."

He liked hearing her laugh.

"Now...prove it!"

"Prove what?"

"Prove that you're wearing a gown."

"You are impossible, Thomas!" she countered. "And I will warrant you have heard that said about you more than once."

He laughed with her, and a moment later, felt a satiny material brush against the back of his hand and forearm. He sat, unmoving, feeling the proof of her otherwise undetectable presence...fully clothed.

"Are you sure it's a pink gown?" Thomas prodded. "It's invisible, Terena, so how do you know what color it is?

"It was pink when I put it on this morning, quite a pretty shade. It is still pink."

He set the restrung guitar aside. "You can see it?"

"Of course I can see it, you strange man, or how would I be able to find it, and dress?"

Thomas frowned, trying to logically navigate his way toward a viable understanding of Terena's invisibility. He had spent some time on this since their first meeting, but had not yet found any explanation that he could get his head around. He had not mentioned Terena to anyone, not Callie, or Guardian, or even Zodiac, for reasons that he hadn't fully formulated. He accepted that there were many things afoot in Elvenhome that he did not know about.

"All right," she sighed, and he could feel her sit down beside him on the couch. "I will attempt to explain it to you – again. Are all Upworlders as thick as you are, I wonder? I can see myself in direct sunlight, and in direct moonlight. Without sun or moon shining on me, I cannot see myself, which is why my windows always face the sunrise...a gift from the Queen's Grace."

He could hear the pride and gratitude in her voice. Still, no matter how many times he made her tell him, he still couldn't get it. "Even when I can see myself, no one else can. All that I touch becomes invisible. If I touch an apple to pick it up and eat it, it becomes as I am – invisible. You might have seen the gown I chose to wear this morning, when it was hanging untouched in my closet. You would have known it was *pink*," she added with a cheerful laugh. "Once I touched it, it became invisible when I stepped out of the rays of sunshine that bless my chamber every morning."

"If I had seen the gown hanging in your closet before you put it on, we might be having an entirely different conversation, Terena," he teased her with a wicked wink.

"You are shameful. I am a Lady."

"In a pretty pink gown...or so I hear," Thomas pointed out, and they laughed together.

He felt her hand rest on top of his, firmly enough for him to observe that she wore no rings or bracelets.

They sat together until Terena patted his hand and stood. "For all your *unspoken woes*, Thomas Lear, you are a good man. And a good friend, too."

Unspoken woes?

He did not stop to think before opening his mouth. "What are you talking about? I don't have any 'unspoken woes,' Terena," he protested, sliding into the comfort of Thomas Lear, Enigmatic Rock Star, where he could be anything he said he was, and no one could challenge the truth of it.

"You carry woes, and we both know it. It is in your poetry and your music, and it is in your eyes. You only *think* it is invisible."

He looked around, very much wanting to make eye contact with her so he could convince her that she was wrong. He couldn't see her; he groaned instead. "I don't know what to say."

"Then say nothing, my dear, and listen." She waited until she saw the conflict flicker away from his eyes, and his face softened. "I do not wish to make you angry or sad, but it hurts my heart to know that you carry heavy burdens alone. I can see you, do you not know that? You hide your woes in your songs, in wine, in other things...

"You, Thomas, pretend your fears are not standing behind you, and your worst enemy —whose presence seems to be less clear to you than it is to those around you—is the power behind most of the things you do. Yet you do not speak the true name of the troubles, and in not speaking of them in a true voice, their lies consume you. You do nothing, and in that 'nothing' resides much needless suffering."

"I am happy here," he said, in his own defense. Determination was the only thing that kept his voice above a whisper.

"I am glad of it," Terena replied, tenderness welling in her sweet voice, "but do you not think it wise to begin to step away from the lies your enemy tells you? It is good that you are happy here; Faerie can be a safe place for you to tend to yourself. Perhaps it is in the safety of Elvenhome, dear Thomas, where you can learn that you are entirely worthy of the blessings in your life."

Thomas, who had visibly paled, felt soft lips place a kind kiss on his cheek.

Then Terena was gone.

nineteen

Once upon a time, in the Highlands of Scotland, there lived a crofter and his wife. They were poor, and their cottage was small, but they were happy together. Their child, a small and perfect baby girl, was a month old.

The crofter and his wife adored their new daughter. She was lovely to look upon, and stared back at them wonderingly with wide, magnificent violet eyes, the shade of rich, shimmering amethysts.

"Surely this girl is meant for something special," they told each other with pride several times each day. "Else the gods would not have given her eyes of such rare and royal coloring. She is going to be a beauty, of this there can be no doubt. She must have been born to gaze upon kings!"

One starry summer night, the crofter and his wife sat at their table and talked as usual about their beautiful daughter, delighting in her fabulous eyes and sweet smile, dreaming dreams for her future happiness—and through her happiness, their own as well.

"And a king will fall in love with her, and will beg to carry her off to his castle, and will make her his wife," the crofter's wife said, with a touch of wistful romance in her voice.

"And when the king asks me for her hand, I will grant it, and in his joy the king will gift us with a new plow and two horses," murmured the crofter, weaving his own daydream as he smiled down on his small daughter, already savoring the wealth her matchless beauty would bring.

As they talked, a solitary moonshadow shimmered in the darkness just outside the cottage. Sparkling flecks of golden light fell softly across an open window.

The moonshadow listened as the two continued to praise their daughter's rare loveliness. Intrigued, the shadow, bathed in subtle starlight, slipped into the cottage and observed the month-old child. She was, as her parents had said, very beautiful indeed.

When the moonshadow furtively bent over the cradle and beheld the child's exquisite violet eyes, he nearly staggered at the force of the intensity with which she stared back at him. This is meant, *her eyes told him.* I know you, and this is meant.

The moonshadow shook his head, not wanting to believe what he saw in the child. He had been wandering the night, waiting for a sign of some kind, of any kind, to lead him to the remedy for his private loneliness. He did not want to believe that this newborn girl could be the hope of his heart. He had had daydreams of finding a woman to love, who would love him in return, but he had assumed that he would find her ready to love him, as he had found women before. All he was certain of was that the woman he had dreamed of had violet eyes—these violet eyes.

He groaned then, in his yearning, the sound coming like a whisper of the wind. The crofter and his wife, still congratulating themselves on the child and her future, did not notice him, or the soft shifting of the moonlight that he wore.

So I wait, *said the moonshadow sadly to himself.* I wait; so be it. *He looked at the infant. Her eyes were still locked on him, watching for an answer. Slowly, he smiled at her, and offered the only response he could:* This is meant. I know you, and indeed, Child, this is meant.

Shaking, his emotions barely in check, he reached an invisible finger down to her tiny hand, and was elated when she beamed back at him , confidence shining in her violet eyes. She wrapped her infant fingers around his. He recognized without hesitation that she could see him clearly beyond the guise of the moonshadow; the relief of it made him almost giddy. Resolved now, he winked at her, his gray eyes twinkling merrily as he disappeared, leaving only starshine marking the spot where he'd stood only a moment before.

Early the next morning the crofter woke to anguished screams from his wife: The baby was missing from her cradle. In her place was a life-sized, crudely-carved wooden doll, wrapped in the child's blanket. The doll had two huge gold coins for eyes. Beside the doll was a note that carried a stern warning: Tempt not the Fair Folk with boasts of mortal beauty, lest they steal it away from the unworthy.

The crofter and his wife never saw the child again. They grieved forever after, and took the warning fully to heart. They never boasted of beauty again, for fear of losing anything or anyone else of great value.

And the moonshadow, who was in truth a gray-eyed faerie in disguise, took the child, whom he named Terena, to his home among the Elven people. He immediately provided her with a wet-nurse, and a doting faerie foster-family. In due time, Terena grew to be a healthy, sturdy child. As the years passed, she became an educated and kind young woman, with eyes for only one man—the man who had captured her heart as surely as he'd captured her from her cradle years before.

She always knew that she was mortal-born; being mortal is no crime in Faerie. She had never known the mortal world, and thus did not miss it. She never ached to return to it. She had friends and her foster-family, and a life of her own in Faerie. She ate faerie food, danced and played and feasted and sang; there was no question that she belonged with the Fair

Folk. More than that, she knew she belonged with the man who still sometimes cloaked himself in radiant moonlight.

She could only think about him with love and awe, and remember how much she had always adored him. Terena was by choice—as well as by nature—continuously focused on him, and so she understood him. He made no secret of his deep feelings for her, and within the private sphere of those feelings, she sensed a degree of almost humble gratitude for her affection, which she never questioned, but which made her love him all the more.

She never doubted that she'd been born specifically to love him and him alone, not as the child she had been, but as the woman she came to be because of his constant care and attention. She could not recall a single day of her life that he had not taken some part in, even if it had only been to bring her a small gift, kiss her forehead fondly or blow away childhood injuries to body or heart, approve of her lessons, or help her foster-mother tuck her into bed at night. She took her first halting baby steps directly to him, and when she was eight years old he taught her to swim as well as any Water Faerie. It was he who sang songs to her, taught her to ride horses and to read. She was enchanted by him, and worshipped him, and did not realize until she was at last a woman that he had brought her to Faerie so that he could, in his way, worship her in return.

The day came when she was old enough to choose to exchange the unconditional love of a favored child for the passionate love of a woman for the man who holds her heart.

And so Terena chose him, willingly, and they shared their lives with each other, inseparable, for a time out of memory. She loved him joyfully and faithfully every day, and so she lived, happily ever after.

IN HIS SUN-DAPPLED garden, Thomas Lear stood in the shade of an ancient rowan and played a much-requested song to the Folk gathered there.

The audience was comprised of Her Grace the High Queen of Faerie, all eight of the Queen's Ladies, The Lord High Chamberlain of

Elvenhome, The Heir-Apparent to the Kingdoms of Faerie, and some kitchen HobGoblins, who were taking their time filling goblets with water or wine as required, and clearing away the remains of the festive picnic held in Thomas' honor. Despite the nobility of most of those present in the garden this afternoon, the atmosphere was informal, relaxed and, as always where Fair Folk of any ilk are concerned, playful.

Seated comfortably in the grass, Callie watched Thomas as his fingers moved on the strings of the wonderful faerie-made guitar. Her eyes glowed with both delight in the music and desire for the musician. He smiled at her as he moved out of the smooth opening riff and into the lyric:

> *She's midnight-mad at fever pitch*
> *When the full moon starts to rise*
> *She's dream and cat and queen and witch*
> *The woman with the Dangerous Blue Eyes*
>
> *I found her on a starless night*
> *She saw through my dark disguise*
> *Kissed me with scented candlelight*
> *She held me with her Dangerous Blue Eyes*

Violet hovered in the air above and behind Callie, fluttering delicately as Thomas sang. At the mention of "scented candlelight," the tiny faerie nearly wept at the romance of the moment as she let her emotions control her luxurious purple wings. Thus distracted, she was startled when she realized that she'd very nearly flown herself into the face of the equally-distracted Zodiac, who was at that moment whispering into the ear of the Lady Iris as he took her hand in his. Everyone in the group saw the near-collision; jolts of surprise and alarm, then relief and laughter, punctuated Thomas' performance. He grinned at his friends, and kept singing.

> *On her thumb a silver ring*
> *Her touch brought me to flame*
> *I wanted to tell her everything*
> *She wouldn't say her name*

I'm thirsty for her hungry fire
Each touch holds a surprise
Takes me deep into her desire
I lose myself in her Dangerous Blue Eyes

Thomas caught Guardian's eye, and grinned acknowledgement when the blond Water Faerie flashed him a solemn nod of approval. He wondered in passing if Guardian's cherished Maggie had blue eyes. Then he laughed to himself even as he honored the magic he'd made: whenever he sang this song, to whomever he sang it, every woman had blue eyes. Sometimes he couldn't believe how great he was on paper. The trick was not letting anyone know that he was as moved by it as everyone else was.

She binds you with her sapphire stare
Or she can set you free
Her laughter lingers in the air
When she gives her love to me

Carnation, sitting in the grass, was closest to where Thomas stood playing. She could not take her eyes off the guitar; she was fascinated by it and by the music that Thomas coaxed out of it. Her long, green-gray fingers twitched, a sure sign that she either wished she could play the beautiful instrument herself, or that she wanted to hold the guitar and talk to it, the way she imagined Thomas must have to.

Framed in sunlight, Juniper and Lavender stood together as they listened to Thomas sing. Instead of her usual gaze filled with calm lasciviousness, approachable lust, and a hint of sexual dominance, Juniper's eyes rested tenderly, almost chastely, on Guardian. She watched him as he listened to Thomas' song, and recognized that Guardian's mind was on someone else's eyes, whatever their color. With a sensuous shrug, she turned her focus back to the music.

Beside her, Lavender was oblivious to everything except Thomas. The music was beautiful; the song told a wonderful story she could well imagine. If she wondered whose Dangerous Blue Eyes he had encountered, she didn't wonder for long, because it didn't matter. All she could do was look at the man she loved and wanted, and wonder what it would be like to be the one he wrote songs about, the one he wanted, the one he couldn't live without.

> *She's midnight cold and fever hot*
> *When the full moon starts to rise*
> *She's far away and then she's not*
> *I find myself in her Dangerous Blue Eyes*

Someday he would write a song about her, wouldn't he?
Lavender promised herself she'd give him every reason to.

A little while later, the group sat in the grass together and drank the last of the water and wine from the picnic.

"I have an announcement!" Callie informed them. "I realize that it's been a very long time since we have played one of our favorite games. The heralds will carry the news throughout Elvenhome as soon as the details are set, but you will hear of it first. We are going to have a battle!"

"A what?" Thomas asked Guardian, who was sitting close enough to ask. "A battle?"

Pleased at the news, Guardian smiled, and nodded toward Callie, so Thomas looked at her instead.

The High Queen was beaming. The Folk around her looked very excited.

"Which battle will we be playing, Your Grace?" Zodiac asked eagerly.

"I'm still considering that," she said. "I decided against Agincourt...because it's never a surprise. But there are so many others that are such fun. I'll make the decision, and we'll have the battle next week."

Iris was doing a mental calculation. "We'd best begin preparations at once, then, Ladies."

"Can you not wait and consider preparations after breakfast tomorrow, my dear?" Zodiac winked at Iris. In response, Iris gave him a squeeze and a fast kiss.

"What did you mean about Agincourt?" Thomas asked Callie. "It's never a surprise, you said."

"It's not a surprise. It plays out the same way every time we do it, which always strikes me as funny somehow."

"No. I just don't understand about the battle thing," Thomas told her.

Callie thought for a second. "Oh. Sorry. We like to re-enact famous battles. We get all dressed up, we get exercise, we lose ourselves in the fun."

"You re-enact battles?" Thomas didn't understand.

"Yes, Thomas. Only we do it better than the original battle plan. Look at the way the strategy for the Battle of Bannockburn played out—"

He was getting more rather than less confused by the conversation. "Wait...what do you know about the strategy for the Battle of Bannockburn? That was in the early fifteenth century—"

"Fourteenth," Callie corrected.

"Whatever. How do you know about the way the strategy played out in a battle fought in fourteenth-century Scotland?"

"We had Folk watching, of course."

His brain was working hard to put the pieces together, but he couldn't quite do it. "Folk were *watching* the Battle of Bannockburn? They were watching *Robert the Bruce*?"

"Yes," Callie said proudly. "Watching, and taking notes."

"I've decided against The Battle of Hastings—it'll be Bannockburn. I love to imagine annihilating the English the way The Bruce did," Callie murmured dreamily from the warmth of Thomas' arms. They were in Callie's bed, snuggled together, watching as the dawn painted the first rose and peach colors across the picture of the new day.

Grunting, Thomas rolled over onto his back, and Callie shifted against him. "It's been a long time since we've had a battle. Everyone is quite excited."

Another grunt.

Callie smiled and leaned up on her elbow to look at him. "What's wrong?"

"I'm exhausted, Your Majesty. You've worn me out again. Can you plan your war quietly, so one of us can get some sleep?" He tried for a tone of annoyance, but he was smiling.

"Poor Thomas," Callie clucked at him, patting his arm. "I'll be quiet." Blessing him with a quick kiss, she slid out of bed and started for the door.

Thomas' head popped up. "Where are you going?"

"To begin the day," she told him. "I have a lot of things to do. The heralds need to announce my decision about the—"

"Don't you want to get a little sleep?" The sparkle in his dark eyes did not indicate that he had sleep on his mind.

She laughed, but pointed toward the closed door. "I should—"

"Callie," he said, "Come back to bed, please. Just for an hour or so."

She eyed him tartly. "I thought you wanted to sleep."

"I do," he replied, his smile warm and inviting. "But I'd like to do it with you. Come here, and let me hold you for a while."

He didn't have to ask her again.

Hours later, they ate lunch with everyone else in the Great Hall, Callie seated between Thomas and Guardian at the High Table. The Hall was full to overflowing with Folk, and everyone, it seemed, was talking about the coming Battle of Bannockburn: what they would wear, how their horses would be turned out, how they would choose sides, how they would dance at the Victory Feast.

On Thomas' right, an exasperated Zodiac was explaining to Rose that Bannockburn wasn't going to work for the game. "We would need the forest, naturally, but also the burn, and the carse if it we were going to do it right, and Her Grace has vetoed the additional landscape. The Scots had seven thousand men, the English had nearly three times that. It makes no sense to do it if we are not going to play it the way it happened."

Rose tilted her head and gave Zodiac an understanding smile. "We never do it quite right, do we? We always start out the way the original battles did. We get a bit carried away, though, after that."

"Then we shouldn't call it The Battle of Bannockburn! It's not The Battle of bloody Bannockburn if we don't do it right."

"Our Lord High Chamberlain is trying to manage the battle as effectively as he manages his many duties in the Castle," Iris' voice was gentle as it came over Zodiac's shoulder. She tugged his hair playfully as she stood behind him. "Why are you unsettled?"

"This will not be The Battle of Bannockburn. It is sacrilege to get it wrong," an irritable Zodiac mumbled, in as deep and heavy a Scottish accent as anyone had ever heard him use.

Iris considered this. "Ah. I understand, my dear. I will speak to Her Grace and tell her that, in order to best honor our history, we must play this game the way it was played in 1314. Shall I tell her that you wish to be Edward of England?"

Zodiac scoffed, then scowled at Iris, and took a long drink from his goblet. She playfully kissed the top of his head, and he chuckled in spite of himself, and winked at her.

"That is what I thought. Now calm yourself, and tell Rose all about the real battle," Iris said. "Then stand and proudly recite *Scots Wha Hae*. Do try to be a little less prickly, though, else you will frighten the Kitchen Hobs and they won't bring you any more wine." She winked at Rose as she turned to go back to her place at the High Table. "He is such a beast for historical details...at least the ones he likes. It's why I love him."

The Lord High Chamberlain harrumphed, regaining his dignity, then proceeded to tell Rose (who was thinking only about her new hat) far more about The Battle of Bannockburn than she was prepared to hear.

Thomas gave Rose a sympathetic smile, and turned his attention to the conversation on his left.

Beside him, Callie was making plans for the event with Guardian, her enthusiasm evident as she gestured with her fork. "Perhaps the best way to choose sides would be to go alphabetically and every-other by our new names. It will be fun to see who ends up on which side." She nibbled on a large slice of goldenfruit. "Traditional two days of battle, or one?"

Guardian thought this over. "One, I think. Too many of the foot-soldiers get bored and leave after the first few hours unless they're kept busy. Maybe we should let everyone have a second go this time, so the battle can be played longer."

"An excellent idea," Callie agreed. "Each side should have one half-day of practice, too."

As he spoke, Callie observed that Guardian was looking far better these days. There was still a quiet hint of sadness about him that seemed to shimmer beneath whatever activity had his attention at any particular moment, although he kept it under firm control. She wondered how he spent his time alone, but let the thought go as Guardian asked her, "You'll command one army, of course; who will command the other?"

"I think we will wait until both sides are determined, and let the Folk on the other side choose their own general." Her eyes sparkled with excitement.

That excitement was infectious; even Thomas, eating a sandwich very like an Upworld hamburger, with real Scottish ground beef and all of his favorite condiments on a wheat bun and served with crisps, found that he, too, was getting into the spirit of the thing. He definitely wanted to play.

He touched Callie's hand when she put her fork down.

She turned to him at once. "Yes, Thomas?"

He tapped his chest lightly with his hand, and raised an eyebrow, his wordless question easy to understand.

Callie smiled. "You want to participate in the battle?"

Thomas nodded, with increasing emphasis when Callie arched a delicate eyebrow. He darted a glance at Guardian, and nodded again.

"Oh, no, Thomas," Callie said. "You could get hurt."

He frowned at her, determination clear on his face.

Callie shook her head. "No. I mean it, Thomas. We Fair Folk take our play battles very seriously, and in the heat of it, someone might get careless, and you could be injured. I cannot allow it. I will not. No."

Thomas showed her an intensely frustrated face, partly because he had decided that he wanted to participate in the battle, and partly because he could not speak here in the Great Hall but felt the need to argue his point. He looked to Guardian for assistance.

Guardian nodded at him, and said to Callie, "But he can observe from the sidelines, can he not?"

Callie shook her head at her cousin. "That's not a good idea, either, and you know it well."

Thomas shot them both a confused look.

Guardian explained. "Callie's referring to an incident that happened long ago. A Court Singer who witnessed one of our battles got so excited that he forgot himself and started to speak, which of course he couldn't do, being obligated to silence." Guardian took a sip of his wine before he continued. "Fortunately, an elderly, somewhat lame Dwarf was standing nearby, also watching the battle, and he realized that the mortal was about to speak. He took care of the situation quite efficiently."

Thomas' eyebrow lifted. Callie began to chuckle.

"What happened?" Guardian asked, accurately translating Thomas' face. "The old Dwarf clubbed him neatly across the head with his walking stick, and knocked the Court Singer unconscious before the man could get half a word out. And it was a good thing, too..." Guardian pointed at Callie, and her chuckle burst into full-fledged laughter. "The poor man was in bed for a week, and, you know, he never looked right after that."

"The Dwarf had to do something," Callie forced the words out between giggles. "That Court Singer had turned out to be a positively insufferable man, everyone thought so. And if he'd actually spoken, he would have had to stay here with us to the end of his days, rather than for only that last—excruciatingly long—month of his year!" Callie and Guardian roared with helpless laughter at the memory.

Thomas pulled on Callie's sleeve to get her attention.

"What happened?" she read in his eyes. He nodded. "To whom? The mortal? He went back Upworld, and we all lived happily ever after." Guardian gasped for breath, banging his hand on the table. Everyone within earshot was laughing at the memory now.

Thomas shook his head: wrong question.

"Oh," Callie said, "You mean, what happened to the Dwarf? For nearly bludgeoning the life out of the man with his walking stick to keep him from speaking?"

Thomas nodded hard, frustrated beyond belief.

"I did the only thing I could do," she reported daintily as Guardian nearly fell out of his chair laughing. "I knighted him."

SHE STROLLED THE corridor toward The Court Singer's apartments, making easy chatter with the guards as she passed their posts.

The book in the pocket of her gown seemed heavy, although of course it wasn't; that was only her uneasiness talking, and she was not going to listen to it. She was doing a good thing for Thomas, and it would subtly make him aware that things were not as he believed them to be. Showing someone the truth (or something close to it) was always best, wasn't it?

Most importantly, being the one to point Thomas to the truth would show him how much she loved him. He would see that she was risking The High Queen's displeasure to help him. That had to count.

She turned the corner and moved gracefully toward Thomas' front door.

If he did not answer her knock on the door, should she leave the book somewhere in his rooms where he could easily find it? Or should she hide it and innocently discover it with him? She should have remembered to mark the story she wanted him to read. Perhaps—

"Hello, Child," Terena's kind voice came from somewhere near the door.

Caught by surprise, Lavender gasped. She recognized the voice, however, and bowed at once with genuine respect. "Lady," she said.

"He is not at home," said Terena. "I have been waiting for him to return. He and I talk about poetry on Tuesday afternoons."

"Ah, that sounds nice," Lavender admitted, with a touch of wistful envy.

Terena's soft chuckle made Lavender smile. "Shall I tell him you are looking for him?"

Lavender mustered up a passably confident shake of her head. "No, Lady Terena. It is not necessary. I thought to show him something—tell him a story—but it will wait."

"As you wish, my dear."

Lavender bowed again, then turned and walked back the way she'd come.

The book in her pocket seemed a little heavier.

CALLIE, ON CASSANE'S back, galloped past the walking horses that carried Thomas and Guardian. They smiled as she flew by, her happy laughter floating backward on the breeze.

"The battles are as close as we get to what you might consider 'high theatre.' The preparations before and after are fun, too," Guardian explained to Thomas. "Think of it as a major sporting event. Everyone gets a little crazed, everyone has a part to play. There are those who wring the life out of it," he chuckled. "There are always some injuries, of course, and sometimes worse, but it's always all right by the next morning, so we don't think about casualties too much. All in all, between the planning, the practice and the actual battle game, it's a fine way to spend a few days."

Holding to his obligation to silence, Thomas caught Guardian's eye and thumped himself on the chest.

"I know, and I agree with you. She should at least permit you to watch."

Thomas nodded.

Guardian continued. "I also agree with Callie. You should not participate. She was right about the possibility of you getting injured."

Thomas sniffed in disdain.

"You wouldn't want to hurt your hands, Thomas," Guardian advised.

Thomas rolled his eyes, but the expression on his face softened. Guardian was right, dammit. Still...

Making a helpless gesture with his hand, Thomas shot a look of frustration at Guardian.

"Don't worry," the Water Faerie assured him with a nod of promise, "I'll convince Her Stubborn Grace that you should watch the battle."

Guardian was as good as his word. Later that evening, as Callie and Thomas walked past the Library, they heard the royal Water Faerie's voice calling a hello to Callie from inside.

The High Queen and her Court Singer entered the Library, and went over to the table where Guardian sat among several large stacks of books. He ran a hand through his hair and smiled up at them as he closed the huge, hand-written book he held in his lap.

"I saw you walking by," Guardian said with a tired smile.

"Are you having any luck?" Callie asked, eyebrow raise in hope.

"Nothing yet," her cousin replied, frowning. "But I have several new stacks to look through, and Master Ocelot will have more ready for me when I finish with these."

Thomas shot a look at Guardian and Callie; he didn't know what they were talking about.

Callie put a hand on his arm. "Guardian is doing some research." She did not offer any further explanation. Instead, she moved a step or two closer to her cousin, and spoke with him very quietly.

This did not help Thomas to understand, but he got the message: it wasn't his concern. He let it go as his eyes feasted on the wonderful room. He liked coming here, and had several books in his apartment that Master Ocelot had suggested that he read. Considering this, he only looked back at Callie and Guardian when Guardian cleared his throat loudly.

Winking at Thomas, Guardian made his move. "Callie, the battle's going to be held when...? In four days' time?"

She nodded, pretending not to notice that her cousin was toying with her.

"And when will the final provisioning of the armies be decided?" he asked, his face a picture of innocence.

"Tomorrow afternoon," replied Callie. "You know that. We discussed it yesterday."

"So we did," Guardian agreed. "One thing we didn't discuss, though, was what Thomas would be doing while the battle is being enjoyed by everyone else in Elvenhome."

Callie looked at her cousin, her smile ingenuous. "A discussion was not necessary, Cousin. I decided that Thomas was not to watch the battle, lest he speak and thus break his silence before the entire assembled Court."

Thomas took a subtle step back as Guardian rose from his chair and met Callie's eyes. Despite his obvious amusement, Guardian kept his voice solemn. "I am not convinced that is the best answer, Your Grace," he began, bowing his head a little to keep Callie from seeing how hard he was working to keep a straight face. "It occurs to me that Thomas should see the battle himself—he may surely be inspired to write a song about it."

"Oh?" Callie sounded intrigued, as if she had not considered this before.

"Certainly, Your Grace. And what's more, there will be no need for concern over his silence if you grant him leave to speak for the duration of the battle. If you'd thought of that strategy long ago, that poor bludgeoned Court Singer might have been capable of a complete thought for the rest of his life."

Callie's eyes narrowed; Guardian was undaunted. He laughed and added, "You could post a guard to keep Thomas warded from any unwarranted approach...and that should cover everything."

Callie stopped and seemed to ponder this. Over her head, Thomas and Guardian exchanged grins of pending victory.

"Oh, please," Callie groaned, looking up at both of them. "You two are too much." She searched Thomas' face. "Do you feel that strongly about it?"

Thomas nodded.

"And you," she added to Guardian, "will arrange for him to be protected?"

Guardian nodded.

Callie laughed. "Very well. I will grant you leave to speak at the proper time. You may observe the battle, Thomas."

Thomas opened his mouth, as if to speak, startling both Callie and Guardian for a fraction of a second, then cheered silently instead.

Gasping, Callie glared at him. "I suppose you think you are terribly funny." She kissed Guardian on the cheek, and then glared at Thomas again. "You are not funny." She turned and walked toward the Library doors.

Shrugging, Thomas grinned his thanks to Guardian, who winked back at him. Thomas turned and followed Callie.

Once they were far enough down the corridor, Callie leaned against Thomas's arm and giggled. "Did you see him? This is the most cheerful he's been since he returned from Upworld!"

Thomas nodded, smiling. He had noticed it too.

"He is looking so well! He could have asked me for anything, I'd have given it to him, and gladly."

Smiling at her happiness, Thomas wondered if he should have had Guardian press harder to let him participate in the battle after all.

twenty

IN THE COMFORTABLE and informal living area of Callie's apartments a few evenings later, Thomas played his guitar in a corner, and half-listened to the conversations around him. Ten feet away, Callie, Zodiac and Guardian were seated close together at a large round table, planning battle strategies with enthusiasm. Orchid sat at a small table across the room, blending a fragrant potpourri of dried flowers and herbs in a sparkling silver bowl for the Queen's bedroom.

Nearly all of the Queen's Ladies were present in the large living area tonight, and the talk was merry. Iris and Carnation were sewing long, forest-green ribbons onto the gown the Queen would wear for the battle, while Dahlia sewed matching green ribbons onto the Queen's gloves. The three were talking about how exciting it was that Her Grace would of course be the general for the Green Ribbon army, and the other side, bearing white ribbons, would be commanded by the skillful Boston.

Across the room, Juniper was bent over a large tablet of paper, drawing gown designs with Violet hovering in the air over her shoulder. They were whispering and laughing together. Thomas thought he heard his name mentioned, and smiled to himself, but kept playing his guitar in an easy silence. Rose moved around the group, offering goblets of wine. Lavender was upstairs in Callie's bedroom, preparing the Royal Bedchamber.

Orchid got up from the table and carried the fragrant bowl filled with fresh potpourri up the stairs. She passed Lavender on the staircase, coming down, and they exchanged a few quiet words. Then Lavender moved to the table where Orchid had been working, and removed the small baskets of dried flowers and herbs, the garden tools, the scissors and the ribbons that Orchid had used for her potpourri. These Lavender took away, to another workroom.

When Orchid came back down the stairs a few minutes later, she walked over to Thomas, and asked, "Would you like some refreshment?"

Although he hadn't been speaking, Thomas was thirsty. He nodded his thanks to Orchid. "Water?" she offered. "Or wine?" At Thomas' brisk nod for the wine, Orchid smiled and went to get it. She was back in minutes, and handed him a filled goblet. "From the Queen's private kitchen," she told him. "Red wine, from Spain. Drink, Thomas, free from care."

Thomas nodded his thanks again, and took a sip. It was delicious. After a long drink, Thomas placed the goblet on a small table beside him. Orchid sat down on a hassock near Thomas' chair, and watched him as he played.

She beamed at him, her eyes wide with wonder and appreciation for the music. "That is so very beautiful, Thomas – but it's so sad! Is it one of yours?"

He gave her a wide smile, and nodded. She listened intently, caught up in the magic of his minstrelsy. The music caught the minstrel himself, too; closing his eyes, Thomas lost himself in the sounds he eased from the strings.

When he finished playing the sad melody, he opened his eyes, smiled to himself and then at Orchid, and began to play a different tune, this one with an undeniable sense of fun.

Mesmerized by the energy of his fingers on the guitar strings, Orchid questioned "May I speak to you while you play, or will that disturb you and stop the music?"

Thomas winked at her and kept playing. She listened, watching him, and then remarked: "It is said that you will be watching the battle. You will enjoy it. Her Grace is a wonderful general."

Thomas raised an eyebrow, and then looked over at Callie, open affection shining in his eyes. At the moment she was arguing somewhat heatedly with Guardian, telling him that he had to manage both the right flank and the rear guard. He was telling her that a rear guard would not be necessary, as it had not been at Bannockburn. Zodiac tried to point out that once the battle began, it was not going to look remotely like the strategy at Bannockburn for very long, but neither Callie nor Guardian were listening to him. Thomas chuckled to himself, and looked back at Orchid, who was laughing at them.

"The battle will take place where it always has," she told him. "We have not had one in quite a long time. There is a wide, open field several miles to the west of the castle. We have parties and picnics and Midsummer dances there. The carpenters have finished building the new gallery, from which the battle can be viewed. I would imagine that is where you shall be."

Fingers still caressing the guitar strings, Thomas pointed his chin at Orchid with a question in his eyes. She understood him easily enough. "Me? I may be there, it will depend upon the Queen's pleasure, and upon her need. Being a general is thirsty work, and if someone does not make certain that she gets refreshment, she will forget and will go without, and that will not do." Orchid glanced at Callie, her love for her Queen visible on her face, almost tangible. Her gaze flickered from the Queen when she realized that Thomas was looking at her with fondness. She blushed. "I carry on, sometimes." Clearing her throat, she asked, "Do you know the official Rules of Battle?"

Thomas nodded at her. He'd heard little else over the past two days, and he'd even had to listen to Callie talk about them when they were alone. He knew the Rules so thoroughly, repeated by countless Folk over and over again, that he thought he should be allowed to participate in the battle solely by virtue of the fact that he probably knew them now as well as everyone else did.

The Rules were these:

- Under no circumstances were horses to be attacked to get to a soldier. The horses were intended to give a formal solemnity to the transportation parade to and from the battle, for decorum and related posturing, and to lend the battle a decided air of dignity.
- Once a soldier was down, there could be no thwacking, hitting, kicking or stabbing.
- All downed soldiers were to leave or be moved off of the battlefield immediately. The battle would not stop in the likely event that someone—or many someones—got hurt,

but any of the Folk who left the battle to take wounded soldiers off the field could come back, and fight some more.

- If you found a shield, a sword, or any other useful instrument of battle in the field or on a downed body, you could take it, and it was henceforth your own, unless you yourself were downed and had to leave the field and someone else took it.
- Disobeying an order from a superior officer would get you turned at once into a Fachan (a possibly-extinct monopodal, single-handed, one-eyed, somewhat alarming-looking creature) for a full day. Thomas was not entirely clear on what a Fachan actually looked like but, predicated on the stunned expressions on the faces of the Fair Folk as they talked about this severe punishment for disobeying battle orders, they knew very well what a Fachan was, and evidently they did not wish to be one.
- If Master Ocelot, in his capacity as apothecary/battle surgeon, asked for assistance, all Folk in the area were to be available to help at once, and could return to the battle when assistance had been duly rendered to Master Ocelot's satisfaction.
- In order to participate in the battle, you had to be on the field, and in bounds. There was no fighting of any kind out of bounds, and everyone was very clear on the boundaries, which would be conspicuously marked with Green and White banners.
- Shape-shifting was not permitted during the battle on the field. If the soldier you were thwacking at the moment happened to be larger and stronger, or winged and faster, than you, you were not allowed to shift into something that gave you an immediate advantage. You could move out of bounds, off the field, and make a shape change, but you had to then engage someone else instead. Fair, after all, was fair.
- The battle was over when (a) there was only one army or (minimally) only one soldier left standing on the battlefield, or (b) one army surrendered to the other, or (c) both

generals and all senior officers were off the field and had agreed to a truce, or (d) when it was time for dinner.

The Victory Feast had been planned for the evening of the day following the battle, rather than on the same day as the battle, immediately following the victory. Thomas was not sure that he understood the thinking behind this, but he kept forgetting to ask about it. At any rate, all he cared about was that he was going to perform after the feast. Working on new songs, rewriting them and rehearsing had kept him as busy this week as Callie and his other friends had been with their battle plans.

He couldn't have said which event he was looking forward to the most: watching Callie play "Battle of Bannockburn" with the Fair Folk, or performing his growing collection of new work for a hungry and eager faerie audience.

He decided that he was enjoying his life in Faerie with Callie and his music and his new friends. He felt himself changing. The longer he was here, he was calmer, more settled, growing more and more at ease with himself—and with his surprising relationship with silence. The songwriting was better than it had ever been, and, for the first time in his career, he did not feel that the actual process of creation cost him more than he could afford to feel.

Stepping away from his stray thoughts, Thomas turned his head, and smiled again at Orchid, who had closed her eyes to better focus on the beautiful sounds coming from the guitar. He sighed to himself as he played. It was a wonderful night, he was at peace, and all was right with the world.

The next morning, he woke up cheerful but alone in Callie's bed, as he had known he would. Callie had gone out to the field at first light, there to have breakfast with her Green Ribbon army, which included Zodiac, Guardian, and half of the Fair Folk of Elvenhome who wished to participate. Battle practice was the order of the day for Callie's army. Boston, commanding the other side, was to have the use of the field later in the day. The actual full-scale battle event would take place the day following, at three o'clock in the afternoon, with Fair Folk on the field in full battle regalia. The event would be attended by Fair Ladies and

Gentlemen of all races, each dressed for festive fun. They would watch the proceedings from the new pavilion's two-level viewing gallery, cheering wildly or hissing their disapproval, whichever the moment might warrant.

Thomas spent the day in his own rooms, practicing and reworking songs for the performance at the Victory Feast. He ate lunch there with Zodiac, and was joined for a late dinner by a tired but happy Callie. They went to his bed early, and later slept.

THE MORNING OF the Faerie Battle of Bannockburn dawned bright and clear. Callie and Thomas lingered in his bed, but Thomas saw from the faraway sparkle in Callie's eyes that she was at least as focused on the day's events as she was on Thomas' early-morning attentions, so they laughed and got out of bed.

By the time Thomas emerged from the privy, she had already dressed and left. He shook his head in mock resignation and sighed as he read the note she'd hastily scribbled and left for him: *Meet me in front of the new viewing gallery at the field before the battle. One of my Ladies will come to you before three o'clock to escort you.*

Thomas spent the remainder of the morning eating breakfast and writing poetry. He toyed with a lyric he couldn't quite finish, and was fine with that, for now. He no longer worried about whether he could write or not; he knew he'd moved past the long months of his desperate dry spell. So, satisfied with the morning's work, he managed a short nap just after lunch.

When he woke, he bathed, and dressed for the upcoming battle event. Checking himself in the mirror in his bedroom, he knew Callie would like his sartorial choice: his favorite blue tunic, brown leggings, and darker brown soft boots.

He was drinking cool water and reading a hand-written, hand-bound book about Yeats and the Fair Folk when Juniper, dressed in a sheer, light-amber-shaded gown that actually covered nothing but her amusement, knocked on his door to escort him in silence to the battlefield.

As soon as he climbed down from his horse, handed her to a liveried groom, and walked with Juniper to the front of the two-level covered pavilion, Callie was already moving toward him. She was nothing short of breathtaking in a white silk gown, the long green ribbons from her shoulders sailing in the faint breeze. She wore long white gloves with shorter green ribbons streaming from wrists and elbows. Her dark brown hair was pulled back away from her face, tied with a chain of fresh daisies, which danced down her back almost as far as her hair did. Over her gown, Callie wore an elegant chain mail bodice. Thomas thought it must be very heavy for her to wear, but as she approached him and put her arms around him for a kiss, he touched the chain mail and was amazed by its lightness.

"It is feather-weight, mostly for show. We save true faerie metal for other things, of course," she pointed out as she nuzzled her head against his chest. "Pretty, isn't it?"

He nodded, took her chin in his hands, and kissed her again. She chuckled against his lips. "You might distract me from my battle! And I'd better take care of this, too…" She held both of his hands and, looking him in the eyes, said loudly "Watch and Ward, Thomas Lear! You have my leave to speak, wherever you are, to whomever you choose, from this moment until the sun goes down on this day."

Thomas noticed a faint shift in the air; was there a subtle tingling and buzzing around him? Perhaps it was simply the breeze that fluttered past as soon as she'd spoken. At any rate, he knew that he could speak freely now—until the battle was over, and then until sundown.

He was going to enjoy the hell out of this day.

The new pavilion's viewing gallery was draped with the same green and white banners that marked the battlefield's boundaries. These hung from the wide awning that protected the spectators on the top level from too much sun. Callie pointed to it. "You should go up now, we're going to start. Despite Boston's best efforts, which have always been considerable, I am going to win the day," she told him, confidence making her smile all the brighter. "Go, and watch me."

He turned obediently. She stopped him with a light touch on his arm. "Do you have a favor I can carry into battle, Thomas?"

He grinned; he was prepared. "You know, as it happens, I do have something for you." He flicked his wrist and removed his watch, which had a thick, woven leather band. "I stopped wearing this right after I got here, but I hoped that you might like to carry my favor with you into victory." She smiled at him, pleased. "Don't look so surprised, Callie. I know about carrying favors. I have a—"

"A Master's degree in Medieval Literature," she said along with him, and they both laughed. He fastened his watch around her left forearm, closer to wrist than elbow, gave her a final affectionate kiss, and smiled. "Have fun. I'll see you later," he told her, patting her gently on the shoulder. "Thanks for letting me watch the battle."

There was an odd, thoughtful look in her eyes now.

"What's the matter?" he asked.

She screwed her face up, trying to think. "I have a feeling I've forgotten something, but I can't remember what it is." She shook her head, moderately flustered.

"Don't worry about it. Let it go. You can tell me later."

"Very well," she said agreeably, and smiled at him. "Enjoy the game, Thomas."

The Battle of Bannockburn, as recreated by the Fair Folk of Elvenhome on a bright November day in 1975, was about to begin.

By the time Thomas had taken a seat next to the enticing, almost-dressed Juniper in the upper gallery, after climbing over two Spriggans who were standing on their seats, he could see that Zodiac and Guardian had already joined Callie, and the three were walking toward the center of the field. The two armies were assembling somewhat haphazardly until a sharp burst from a horn brought much of the movement to a halt.

Boston, accompanied, much to Thomas' surprise, by two of the Queen's Ladies—a sword-wielding Dahlia and a sky-dancing Violet—met up with Callie, Zodiac and Guardian. Boston bowed deeply to Callie, then kissed the High Queen's hand. Callie smiled, saluted her opponent, and turned to address the crowd. Her voice was soft and low, but she was heard by everyone on the field, in the pavilion, and on the sidelines.

"The time has come. Green-Ribbons, follow me. We go to the forest, to make our entrance on the battlefield." Thomas watched with interest as the Green-Ribbon army followed her lead, and headed for the west end of the field, dancing and shouting and laughing as they went. Boston's White-Ribbon army followed him to the east side of the field. He spoke quickly to Lady Violet, who hovered close to his face. When he had told her what she needed to know, she nodded, and sped through the air above the White-Ribbon soldiers. Violet carried her message to several Elves armed with bows and arrows. They nodded, indicated the White-Ribbon's left flank, and got into position, shouting orders and encouragement as they prepared for the battle.

Beside Thomas, Juniper was grinning. "This is going to be great fun to watch," she told him. "Once Her Grace leads the army out of the forest—"

"What forest?" Thomas had heard Callie's announcement, and had wondered what she had meant about the forest; there wasn't a tree for a half-mile in any direction. He could see Callie's army setting up, and grouping together, as though they couldn't be seen.

"Robert the Bruce's army came rushing out of the forest at the beginning of the battle," she told him. "It's not the Battle of Bannockburn if they don't come pouring out of the forest, Thomas. It's tradition."

Thomas looked at the Green-Ribbon army, standing without a sound in the open air, waiting for the order to charge, which came just as Thomas turned to Juniper and asked again: "*What* forest?"

Juniper pointed to Callie's soldiers. "*That* forest, Thomas." She looked at him strangely, as though there were something wrong with him.

There was no forest.

But Callie's foot soldiers seemed to think there was one, he realized. The Goblins and Pixies and Elves and Bogies on foot, male and female alike, all moved now as though they were breaking a formation to move through some kind of invisible obstruction, consistent with marching through the forest.

The sultry Glaistig on his right was staring at him. "You truly do not see the forest, Thomas?" she asked, eyebrows lifted in amazement.

Thomas looked from Juniper to the slowly-moving Green-Ribbon army and back to Juniper again. "I see the army, but I don't see trees," he frowned.

"He does not have the eyes to see the forest, my lady," a quavering voice murmured helpfully from behind them. "He is mortal, ain't he?" The owner of the voice, a very old male Pixie, pointed at Thomas and explained. "I know all about mortal seeing and not seeing. When I was a bairn, I knew a few mortals. He has eyes, he does, but his eyes are not Fey ones."

Juniper blessed the ancient Pixie with a provocative smile, and he blushed. "Thank you, Grandfather," she said. "I had not thought of that."

"Yeah," Thomas added. "Thanks...I think." He had no idea what to make of this, but he didn't have time to think about it. As the Green-Ribbon army cleared the "forest," Callie, riding Cassane, galloped out of the "trees" and led her troops onto the battlefield.

She was glorious in the afternoon sun, the light shining on the royal markings on her face and hands, her chain mail glittering. She was focused, fully engaged in the moment; watching her nearly left him breathless. She ordered her soldiers forward, and turned back to see Guardian and Zodiac, also on horseback, leading the left and right flanks respectively.

Boston, still holding back his foot soldiers, watched Callie approach for a moment. Then he smiled and gave the order for the White-Ribbon army to charge. Fair Folk of both genders and all races sprang into action at his command.

The battle began in earnest.

For a fraction of an instant, the Folk managed to fall into and hold their armies' historic, original strategic formations. When the instant passed, there was magic and mayhem everywhere, and Thomas found himself as caught up in the action as everyone else was. He laughed as a middle-aged Troll standing next to Master Ocelot's blue infirmary tent, twenty feet off the field and beside the pavilion, roared at her husband to remember to use both of his swords this time.

Exciting hand-to-hand encounters involving daggers, swords and shields peppered the field. Thomas watched arrows cutting through the air from both sides, horses and riders dashing around among the soldiers. He caught a glimpse of what could only have been Violet, darting above it all, relaying messages and orders as she ducked arrows.

This was better than the movies.

The thought of movies somehow took him to thoughts of movie sound tracks and music tracks. He'd recently been approached to write music for a film, and he had turned the offer down. It was then that his mind slipped into the lyric he'd been unable to finish earlier in the day.

The amusing chaos on the field, the nearly-real sounds of battle around him, and the sight of Callie riding Cassane everywhere at once, encouraging soldiers, issuing orders, and looking altogether regal, military, somehow tomboyish and irrepressibly sexy all at the same time came together in the moment, and gave him the hook he needed to make the lyric work. He was struck with the perfect phrasing for his unfinished song, and he closed his eyes to think about it. He wanted to hold this picture of Callie in his mind until he could get back to his apartment later and write it down. He memorized the imagery, and the words with which he painted it, and felt himself smiling.

Taking a deep, slow breath, Thomas ran the revised lyric through his head to hold on to it, and then turned his attention back to the field in front of him.

The afternoon light seemed brighter now. Suddenly he wished he had dark sunglasses, and binoculars, too, to more comfortably watch the doings on the field. He laughed out loud at the thought.

Juniper glanced at him, and he nodded his head at the battle. "This is so wild," he said.

"It always is," Juniper told him. "The victory feast is even wilder, you'll see." She smoothed the sleeve of her sheer amber gown with her long, alabaster fingers, and winked at him.

The first hour of the Faerie Battle of Bannockburn was over, announced by the sound of horns. It became clear that the Folk were taking a short break. Thomas watched in fascinated amusement as, right in front of the pavilion, a group of Goblins from both armies put down their weapons, leaned on their swords and mopped their faces, exchanging advice and critiques on their performance.

Far across the field, Thomas could just make out Callie and Cassane, momentarily out of bounds, attended by Lavender and her friend Buick. (Thomas cringed a little as he remembered the name he'd assigned to the handsome Elf.) Lavender was pouring something from a bottle into a goblet, which she then handed to a grateful Callie, who nodded and drank. Buick, whom Thomas had often seen around the castle, was wiping Cassane down with a bright blue towel, and giving him some water.

Five minutes later, the first horns sounded the end of the break, the participants resumed their places, and the battle revved up and continued where it had left off.

The second hour of the battle seemed much like the first, with much swordplay and arrows flying from bows, and a lot of noise. The difference was that a canon had been pulled onto the field by several armor-clad Bogies, and was being calmly loaded and aimed while the battle carried on around it.

Surrounded by Folk in the pavilion who cheered or booed depending on what they were watching, Thomas was fascinated by the spectacle, and looked around the field for people he knew. Zodiac was on horseback on the west side of the field, observing the soldiers he commanded on the High Queen's behalf and gesturing to his captains. Boston, standing on a large rock at the east end of the field, shouted an order that sent dozens of arrows sailing over the heads of the White-Ribbon army and into the mobilized left flank of the Greens.

Despite the activity around him, Thomas had the strange feeling that someone was watching him. He tried to shrug it off, but the feeling persisted. He looked around.

It took him several minutes to look toward the forest that wasn't there.

Dressed in brown trousers and a brown tunic under a rust-colored cloak, ScarF stood unmoving and alone, observing Thomas in the pavilion's upper gallery. There was no way to know how long the tall, once-handsome Elf had been watching him, or the battlefield. Thomas wondered why he hadn't participated in the day's event. He half-turned to point ScarF out to Juniper and ask her, but when he looked back toward the other man, ScarF was gone.

He didn't know whether to be concerned or not. Callie would know.

Where was Callie? Thomas scoured the field, and located her. She was engaging in rather impressive swordplay with an oversized, muscular Gnome. The Gnome, whom Thomas was sure he had never seen before, and whom he hadn't renamed, seemed to be taking his swordsmanship seriously, Thomas realized. Maybe too seriously? He was about to ask Juniper about that when he noticed Guardian galloping across the field directly in front of the pavilion. Momentarily forgetting Callie and the Gnome, Thomas watched his friend ride toward the canon.

It happened in a matter of disconnected seconds: Guardian's horse, frightened by the sound of a too-close clattering of swords, followed by the bellowing of the canon as it fired, reared violently backward. Prepared, Guardian slid himself forward to compensate for the horse's almost perfectly vertical stand. What Guardian didn't count on was that the horse would slip on the grass. In a blur of motion, horse and rider went down with a heavy thud.

On his feet now, Thomas strained to see his friend. He did, in a moment, when the horse struggled to his feet, and two Dwarfs ran onto the field from out of bounds and helped Guardian to rise. The Water Faerie was pale, and had had the wind knocked out of him, but seemed to be able to walk. Belatedly, and presuming it was a nasty trick of the light, Thomas noticed that Guardian's right shoulder seemed to be stuck in a strange and uncomfortable angle. The Dwarfs helped Guardian leave the field, and a Pixie with a tall purple hat walked Guardian's horse safely out of bounds in the opposite direction. As Thomas watched, the two Dwarfs gently handed Guardian off to Master Ocelot, who stood waiting to help.

Beside Thomas, Juniper had leaped to her feet, her wide, luminous Glaistig eyes nearly glowing with alarm. Focused entirely on Guardian, she told Thomas: "I must be certain that he is not badly hurt, Thomas. You will be safe, just stay here." She hurried through the seats, flew down the stairs, and rushed toward the blue infirmary tent.

Thomas scanned the battlefield for Callie and the Gnome. He couldn't find her right away. Instead he saw Zodiac rushing off on his horse toward the Green-Ribbon's right flank.

After a brush of uneasiness, he found her, sword slung across her lap, issuing orders from Cassane's back. The Gnome she'd been clanking steel with was nowhere to be seen. The sight of Callie made his heart beat hard in his chest; the sunlight shone on her hair, and sparkled off the chain mail on her torso. She was beautiful. It struck him again: she was indeed "Beauty in Motion", and he was quite proud of the title of his newest song. He closed his eyes and watched her dance in his mind.

Boston's White-Ribbon army suddenly charged, with the animal roar of one hundred fifty bellowing voices behind it. This jolted Thomas out of his reverie, and he opened his eyes just in time to see the two armies, weapons raised, colliding again in the middle of the field. Swords were clashing and clanging against each other, horses were prancing nervously. The frenzy of it reminded Thomas of a typical brawl at any European football match.

Everything on the field was in motion, and he couldn't track it all. Too much was happening all at once, and for reasons he couldn't calculate, something had changed; the battle before him seemed different somehow. Many of the Folk were being carried from the field. Too many were down, being stepped over by horses and soldiers alike as the battle continued. Thomas had to stop and listen hard. He could not make sense out of what he thought he was hearing. It couldn't be. He almost believed that he heard cries of pain, some of them very loud and convincing.

And then he looked more closely, and the color drained from his face as he grabbed the wooden banister in front of him for support. He saw blood—lots of it, on many of the soldiers on both sides. He shook his head to try to clear his vision, and then looked again.

A Brownie staggered weakly to a spot just barely off the field, blood pouring from a wound on her head. She fell forward, and did not get up. Thomas found that he could not breathe as the realization struck him hard in the chest: this battle was real. People were getting hurt. There was blood...

He whipped his head around to see how the other Folk around him in the pavilion were reacting, to see if they understood what was happening. The two Spriggans at the end of the front row, who he'd climbed over to get to his seat, were placing bets on the outcome of the battle, seemingly oblivious to the notion of the danger on the field.

"The battle's real!" Thomas shouted to the other onlookers in the gallery. "Do you see that? People are getting hurt!"

Everyone who heard him nodded gravely, and then, as something Thomas clearly missed happened on the field, they all began to cheer and applaud in wild approval. Thomas spun around and faced the fighting just in time to see Zodiac leap from his horse and take three

White-Ribbon Dwarf soldiers down. The three fell hard to the ground, and there was blood on Zodiac's sword.

Thomas felt sick. He also wondered, in some dark recess of his brain, if he had taken some nasty drugs by mistake or mischance today, and was tripping badly. This couldn't be happening. It just couldn't...

...but it was. Shaking, he watched the Folk in the gallery on either side of and behind him, and saw that they were fully focused on the battle, and did not seem to be overly perplexed. He looked at the action again, and saw that there were fewer soldiers standing than had been only moments before. There were only four horses on the field now, bunched together, and Callie's Cassane was one of them.

Had she not still been on the back of the extraordinary white and gray stallion, Thomas might never have found her. And when he did see her across the field, his heart stopped, and then banged painfully against his rib cage. She looked trapped, surrounded by three soldiers on horseback wearing White Ribbons, their swords waving at her.

Thomas didn't know if she was in genuine danger or not. There was no one for him to ask, and there was nothing he could do to help her or stop the battle. He could only gape at her, all the while glancing at the other pockets of the fighting moving closer to her.

On the field, Callie appeared to have decided to make a break for it. She dug her heels into Cassane. The great horse pulled back fractionally and then leaped high and long, clearing the heads of two of the other horses and their riders, and managing to knock the third rider neatly out of his seat. That rider, a hairy HobGoblin with back-facing feet, got up slowly from the ground, and limped his mount off the field.

The sounds of the battle were getting quieter. There were fewer soldiers fighting on the field. But the sounds of Folk crying out in pain on the sidelines and on the field grew increasingly louder, or so it seemed to Thomas. He was frozen on his feet, eyes glued to Cassane and the Queen.

He gasped as Cassane seemed to lose his footing and slip several times in wet, blood-smeared grass. From a panicked distance, he heard his own voice shouting "Take him off the field, Callie!" and was stunned when the Folk in the pavilion applauded him, nodding their appreciation of his spontaneously-proffered tactical advice.

He simply *had* to be tripping. This was too surreal, even for him. *And that was saying something*, he thought.

The battle had wound itself down to a handful of intense sword fights and some dangerous-looking hand-to-hand dagger contests. Desperation choking him, Thomas hoped that it would be over soon.

Out of the corner of his eye he could see Cassane carrying Callie across the field at a gallop, the two remaining White-Ribbon horsemen in hot pursuit, swords lifted in the air.

A hand touched Thomas' shoulder then, and he nearly leaped out of his skin.

"Easy, Thomas," Guardian said softly. "You're strung tight. Great battle, though, isn't it?"

Thomas whirled around to face his friend. Guardian was still pale, pain marking the corners of his eyes and mouth. His shoulder and arm looked normal enough now. He had a makeshift sling holding them in place.

"Dislocated shoulder and broken arm," Guardian informed him. "My horse fell on me," he grinned. "He's fine, of course, and only a little annoyed."

Thomas' eyes were wide with disbelief. "Guardian, what's going on? The battle's real, the blood is real, I think people are dying out there—and Callie..." he looked away from Guardian and back at the field, searching for her. "And Callie's—"

Guardian looked puzzled. "I told you. It's similar to a sporting event Upworld, Thomas, nothing more. People get hurt, but it's all right—"

"It's *'all right'???*" Thomas screamed. "This is the most *not* 'all right' I've ever seen! The Fair Folk are killing each other!"

Guardian was staring at Thomas now, trying to understand what his friend was thinking, when something occurred to him. "Do you think..." he began, looking for clues on Thomas' face, "that there could be danger or—"

He was interrupted by the sound of hooves barreling across the field toward the pavilion. The spectators cheered. The two White-Ribbon soldiers on horseback were closing in on Callie and Cassane. As the three horses reached the grass in front of the pavilion, they slowed to a trot.

Thomas could see Callie now. She had a long tear in the sleeve of her gown, leaving her right arm exposed. An ugly gash in her royally-marked bicep was seeping blood. She had a small cut on her face, and was very dirty, but looked well enough, despite the fact that she was breathing hard and looking a little tired.

One of the White-Ribbon soldiers taunted her. "Give over, Your Grace, and we may spare your royal life."

Callie barked over her shoulder with much dignity. "Queens do not surrender."

There was spontaneous applause. All eyes were on her, and Callie's smile was dazzling as she tilted her head in a tiny bow. Thomas was convinced that he was going to have a coronary any minute now, but could not look away.

After a series of movements almost too swift to see, Callie and Cassane were sandwiched between the two White-Ribbon horsemen. They were going to capture the Queen, and the battle would finally be over. Thomas wished they'd hurry up and get it over with. He couldn't stand much more.

Callie moved Cassane back as far as she could, and in a flash of inspiration, heaved herself off him, backwards, and slid down his rump.

No one had seen the four-foot-tall Bogie slip silently up to and behind Cassane, to watch the final moments of the battle. He was carrying a three-foot-long, very ugly ceremonial dagger, which he held in the air over his head so he wouldn't fall over it as he moved across the slippery field.

As Callie slid down Cassane's rump, she fell on to the Bogie and slammed into the dagger. It tore into her back, its tip poking through her chest, tight against the pretty but ineffective chain mail.

The spectators rose to their feet in a single movement, screaming and shouting in horrified surprise. Guardian's eyes went wild with disbelief. Already too close to overload, Thomas fought the urge to faint, even as his voice rang out above the crowd:

"Noooooo!"

As Thomas' foot left the last step of the pavilion, Squid, the guard who had been posted for his protection, reached out to stop Thomas from leaving. A quick shake of Guardian's head told Squid to let Thomas move unhindered.

Thomas Lear, Court Singer and Queen's Lover, took off like a shot, with Guardian right behind him. He ran to Callie, who was surrounded by the bruised and very worried Bogie, the two very shaken White-Ribbon soldiers, and other Folk who had run to help her or to move the horses. A tense and tight-lipped White-Ribbon soldier pulled the dagger carefully from her back.

"Callie! Callie!" Thomas called.

She lay helpless on the grass, breathing in liquid gasps.

He was unprepared for all of the blood, her blood. It was gushing, pumping from the gashes in her chest and back with every heartbeat. Thomas dropped himself on the ground beside her, and pressed his hands tightly against the flow from both wounds, knowing he couldn't stop it but pressing hard anyway. Guardian was at his right shoulder, struggling to breathe. Master Ocelot was hurrying toward them, his assistants running behind him with buckets of water and towels.

Her eyes were closed, and her face was as silky white as her gown had been earlier in the afternoon. "My God, Callie," Thomas croaked, his voice breaking as he pulled her into his arms, still trying to stop the bleeding.

She opened her eyes slowly, and it took several seconds for her to look up and focus on him. When she did, she gave him a tiny smile. "Oh, Thomas...now *that* was a surprise, wasn't it?"

"*Goddammit*, Callie," he barked, frightened out of his wits.

With an effort, Callie lifted her left hand slowly and brushed Thomas' beard with trembling fingers.

Thomas couldn't make sense of anything. "Callie," he stammered, "what can I do to help—"

With a groan of dismay, Callie suddenly realized what it was that she had tried to remember earlier, what she should have remembered days before. "Oh, Thomas, my dear Thomas, I forgot to..." A spasm of raw pain ripped through her, and she took a gulp of air before she could continue. Her eyes were wide with agony and wonder as she whispered "Thomas, I failed to tell you..."

And in half a heartbeat, she failed once again to tell him. With a final sharp intake of breath, Callie died in Thomas' arms, on the grass just inside the bounds on the battlefield.

The Folk assembled on and around the field collectively gasped in dismay, and then were as silent as they were numb. Dahlia and Violet raced toward them from the west, their faces registering shock and horror.

Unable to form words, Thomas looked at Guardian, his eyes spilling streams of tears. Master Ocelot examined Callie's body, and then motioned for the two Elves assisting him to bring a stretcher-like carrier over to the fallen Queen.

Master Ocelot looked at Thomas. "Thomas, you'll let me have her, please?" the apothecary requested quietly.

Thomas looked away from Guardian, down at Callie, and then dubiously at Master Ocelot. "What?"

"Let me take her, Thomas," Master Ocelot repeated.

The silent onlookers stepped back to make space for the carrier. Thomas stared at the carrier for a moment, trying to understand what it was for.

Guardian put a shaking hand on Thomas' shoulder. "Thomas," he said, breathing in little gasps, "let him have her."

"No," Thomas snapped, pulling Callie's blood-soaked body tighter against his own.

"Thomas," Guardian said again, his voice brittle with pain. "Thomas, let her go."

Master Ocelot positioned himself to be ready to take the Queen's body as soon as Thomas released her. "Thomas, let me tend to her, and then when she's ready, you can see her. You have my word."

Thomas stared at them all, his mind a blank. Together, Master Ocelot and Guardian maneuvered Thomas' hands and arms so that Master Ocelot could take Callie away from him as gently as possible. This accomplished, Callie's body was placed on the carrier, and was taken to the battle surgeon's tent, escorted by four of the Queen's personal guards, who wept as they walked.

Guardian looked around at the assembled Folk, the first lines of grief etched into his handsome face. Standing up, he steadied himself before he told them: "This has been a harsh day. Our most beloved Queen is lost to us. I will need a report of all battle-injured Folk and battle death. Within the hour, if you please, so that we will know who needs attention, and we can thus render aid. The Queen's Ladies should wait in her rooms until such time as she has been ministered to by Master Ocelot. They will then attend her and prepare her for...for the Royal Lying in State. Please find and send Zodiac to me; I will be with the Court Singer." Guardian's voice broke then, and he sobbed as he helped Thomas to his feet and half-walked, half-carried him to the area behind the now-empty pavilion where the horses waited to take them back to the castle.

Slowly, the stunned gathering of Fair Folk dispersed, some weeping, others talking in low, grief-stricken whispers.

To be continued in *Mischief and Menace   A Year and a Day: Part Two*

Mischief and Menace   A Year and a Day: Part Two
Coming soon

Mischief happens...and so does Menace.

Find more by Lisa Courtney
Web: http://www.courtneyink.com
twitter: @courtney_ink

Acknowledgements

It's my habit to write personal thank-you notes by hand (my grandmother insisted upon it, and I'm still a little neurotic about that).

That said, here is another thank-you note, sort of. Less personal than usual, and not by hand, but honest and heart-felt nevertheless.

Thank you, **Ellen Kushner**, for writing *Thomas the Rhymer*, and for the cover artwork by **Tom Canty**. The cover caught my eye at first glance, and The Rhymer took up residence in my head and never went on vacation. He simply waited for me to catch up with the magic.

Thank you, **Gordon Lightfoot**, for the lyrics and music that have been and continue to be part of the soundtrack that is my life. My love for your work fed my need to make Thomas Lear's songs worthy of you, and of me as well.

Quieter but sincere thanks to **Frey** and **Henley**, too, who taught me a little bit about composition and performance that I would never have grasped on my own.

Special thanks to **Paul Camelia**, my own Arrendel, for giving me plenty of room to do what I do.

Most of all, thank you, **Ladies of the Book**, who listened and read and watched me pace and fret, waited while I put the project down for a couple of years, and were the best emotional and creative support imaginable when I picked the thing back up and got serious about it again. And you **Ladies** who handled the production to get Thomas Lear and his friends (and, uh-oh, *me*) out there—there aren't words, not really. I love you all, and thank you so very much: especially **Stacey Eck, Jane Mackinnon, Kristie Lundberg, Sally Sloley, Brenda Potts, Nancy Monson, Shari Wetherby, Rebecca Stevenson**, and my beloved godmother **Betty** (even though she never took to Thomas, and suggested about two dozen times over the years that I kill him off because she did *not* like his attitude; I got even with her by giving her surname to Susannah, with the desired effect of annoying Betty ever so slightly, and potentially forever).

www.ingramcontent.com/pod-product-compliance
Lightning Source LLC
Chambersburg PA
CBHW070624260626
47161CB00007B/2580